Esther and the Genius

Esther and the Genius

Other Works by Mo H Saidi

Art in the City: A Book of Poetry
        Winner of the Edwin M. Eakin Memorial Book Publication Award,
        presented by the Poetry Society of Texas

Between A and Z: Poems

The Garden of Milk and Wine: A Collection of Short Stories

The Color of Faith

Female Sterilization: A Handbook for Women

The Marchers: A Novel

ISBN 978-0-692-84042-9

Cover: Illustration taken from Rembrandt van Rijn, *Ahasuerus and Haman at the Feast of Esther*, 1660. Adapted by Maria Oddo-Saidi.

Esther and the Genius

Mo H Saidi

Word Design Press
WDP
www.worddesignpress.com

Acknowledgments

The author wishes to thank Amelia Reyes and Jasmina Wellinghoff for their editorial prowess and enthusiasm for the novel.

He is also indebted to Dr. Abraham Verghese, professor and distinguished physician-writer, who provided valuable literary instruction during his Writers Workshop at the University of Texas Health Science Center at San Antonio.

Dedicated

To the late John Schmolesky, Professor of Criminal Law at St. Mary's University, for his legal advice and editorial suggestions;

To Brigitte, my deepest love, who read, edited, and supported the novel;

and to Sally Cooper, my centenarian book club partner, for her insight and critical comments regarding the book.

Esther and the Genius

CONTENTS

Esther and the Genius

PART ONE
The Genius Professor

It is an ordinary day for Dr. Jordan Hartman until he receives an urgent call from his wife, Esther, asking for help. "Please come home right away! Saul is in trouble," Esther pleads. Her voice is trembling; she is desperate, "I cannot deal with this on my own."

I
The Genius Professor

The medical students call Dr. Jordan Hartman the Genius; surgical residents, the Volcano; and the heads of other departments, the Grant Writer, envying his ability to attract an impressive team of researchers and obtain numerous grants for scientific research. His faculty members go out of their way to avoid confronting him because of his unpredictable temperament and sometimes sudden and uncontrollable bursts of fury. Dr. Hartman's son Saul is also afraid of him. Saul stays away from him as much as possible because he fears Dr. Hartman's aggressive and often unpredictable anger. Saul has occasionally mentioned to his friends that he would be even more worried if his father bought a gun and kept it in the house. However, his wife Esther loves him, for he has been a devoted husband and loyal partner.

Esther, an avid reader with a particular interest in the ancient Jewish Diaspora, has amassed a collection of related books in her library, including one about the ancient Persian Jews, and another, *Esther Queen of Persia*. Recognizing Esther's primary interest in the historical Esther, Dr. Hartman calls her "My Queen Esther." But Esther, who possesses the sensitivity of a poet and the imagination of a writer, believes that life is a talisman, a coin with two sides: one side represents happiness, the other misery—bad luck and good fortune. Although Dr. Hartman's primary devotion goes to the young medical school where he has been an iron rod and a boon for the school, in the short time that Dr. Hartman has been at the school, he has helped to elevate it to the list of the top fifty in the nation. However, in the opinion of Esther, he has neglected to pay adequate and meaningful attention to their only son, Saul.

At school, Dr. Hartman conducts crucial medical research in the field of stem cell applications in medicine, specifically in reproduction and infertility. He has published numerous significant medical articles reflecting his research and has written several textbooks, most of which are highly regarded by his peers and used as teaching materials in other medical school programs. Dr. Hartman has also attracted academically respected physicians from Europe and South America who have invented new surgical techniques and devised instruments to be used as a remedy for intractable medical problems. By employing these creative doctors and scientists to work in his department, Dr. Hartman allows them to expand their projects. But Dr. Hartman is most popular among the university's leaders for obtaining more grant money from the National Institutes of Health (NIH) and other funding sources than any other faculty member. The Dean of the medical school calls him his best grant writer, "A genius who like Benjamin Franklin can draw lightning from the sky."

At 55, Dr. Hartman is at the peak of his career, the envy of other professors and department chairs, until the day when an emergency call from his wife changes his life. The day has been predictable and smooth. Dr. Hartman is in the classroom lecturing fourth-year medical students, when his secretary interrupts the session, walks to him, and quietly says, "Sir, you have an urgent call from your wife."

He goes to the counter, picks up the phone, and hears his wife's voice. Distraught and sobbing, she says, "Saul is in real trouble! It's awful. I can't deal with the situation. You must come home right away."

Dr. Hartman is annoyed at hearing about another disturbance involving Saul. He remembers Saul's argument with a high school classmate who bullied him because he is Jewish, and his clash with Saul when Saul refused to practice the violin. When Dr. Hartman sought help from Esther to put pressure on Saul, her reply was, "Have you heard about the Suzuki method? Leave him alone."

Then, he remembers that his wife is still on the line waiting for his response. "I'm in the middle of my lecture," Dr. Hartman says. But Esther continues, "Saul is scuffling with a young man right outside our front door. Please come and stop this fight. I can't handle it!"

"Here we go again," Dr. Hartman says. His initial thought is to drop everything and hurry home, but he assumes that by the time he manages to get there, the fight will be over, and Saul will have left the house. However, regarding Saul's situation in general, Dr. Hartman reaches the gloomy conclusion that there is no hope for Saul's redemption unless a miracle changes his personality. Or perhaps somebody will become *the catcher in the rye* and save Saul from falling into an abyss. Dr. Hartman now firmly believes that that person cannot be his wife. "She is not strong enough to save Saul," he thinks.

———————

A few weeks before Esther's emergency call, Dr. Hartman is standing in front of a classroom filled with medical students when he suddenly feels a sharp pain originating from his right breast. It's radiating to his arm and causing a painful spasm in his right hand. Keeping the laser pointer in his right hand, he looks up at the screen where a big silvery, round mass glows. Dr. Hartman tries to raise his arm to point the beam at the image, but the twitching pain limits his motion, preventing him from fully extending his arm so that the laser beam can outline the border of the mass on the screen. He ignores the pain and continues with the lecture, "This innocuously appearing cyst with smooth walls shows no visible growths on its surface. It carries less than a one percent chance of being malignant."

The medical students are facing the screen: some are alert, a few sleepy, and one has his eyes completely closed. Meanwhile, the pain that bothers Dr. Hartman grows; it shoots outward from his right breast. Suddenly, the fear of breast cancer invades his thoughts. "No, that can't be it," he thinks. He considers that breast pain could be due to the onset of breast cancer, but he dismisses the possibility and murmurs, "Most likely, it's all due to playing tennis." On the other hand, he presses on his chest but feels no mass and notices

3

no tender spot. Then he mutters, "In men, the risk of breast cancer is negligible."

Only the students in the front row hear his words. They are utterly surprised by this unrelated remark from a professor who is known for his sharp focus on the subjects of his lectures. He notices their reaction but cannot disrupt his train of thought as facts tumble forward in a hushed voice, "Breast cancer occurs one hundred times less often in men than in women."

"Why is he changing the subject to breast cancer?" a student in the front row wonders *sotto voce*; then, he leans over to the student next to him and whispers, "It's the ovary, stupid!"

Dr. Hartman again presses his right breast with the left hand, but he feels nothing unusual. Relieved, he finally turns his attention back to the screen and continues, "Despite the gravity of ovarian cancer and the much higher incidence of breast cancer in women than in men, the male population has a shorter average lifespan. The masculine gender is the fragile one; men die earlier than women. Even though more male infants are born than female ones, at the end of the day, there are fewer men than women around. More men perish when young. More die in accidents and gun-related crimes. Of course, you know what happens in war; remember the battle of Somme, 24,000 young men slaughtered in one day.

Consequently, men live fewer years than women do. In the end, men lose the battle of the sexes. It is indeed possible that their shorter lifespan is due to weak genes and fragile bodies. We, I mean the male gender, die prematurely. We kill each other to equalize the scale. The majority of miscarriages are male embryos, and more of them fail to survive until birth. I conclude that this is all because of men's faulty genes. Man's an imperfect gender. This is nature's way of producing parity between the two. Unfortunately, the process goes too far; go to any nursing home and see for yourself. There are more widows than widowers in the world."

II
The Fatherhood Dream

Dr. Hartman's idea of having children is to have a son, as he tells his wife after consuming a few glasses of wine. So after several years of unsuccessful attempts, the couple decides to try in-vitro fertilization (IVF.) Ironically, Dr. Hartman is one of the pioneers of this technique, and his department is known for its remarkable rate of success with infertile couples. His grants for the NIH-sponsored research on the pathophysiology of fallopian tubes in women who experience infertility have produced many answers to this persistent problem. The addition of two innovative and energetic physicians to the faculty in Dr. Hartman's department recently resulted in a new technique that produces pregnancy. By injecting both a woman's egg and a man's sperm into the fallopian at the very moment that female organs are most receptive to host the sperm and facilitate fertilization has brought national attention to Dr. Hartman's scientific projects. The introduction of this new technique that is called GIFT (gamete inter-fallopian transfer) and the publication of related articles on the subject of "New Advances in Management of Infertility and Genetic Disorders," published in the prestigious *Journal of Clinical Surgery* and *Genetic Journal*, have made Dr. Hartman and his associates the most famous researchers in the field. To be able to conduct their research and meet teaching obligations, Dr. Hartman is often forced to decline many of the invitations he receives to give lectures at medical conferences nationally and internationally. Ironically, however, as reflected in the Persian proverb that a brick maker usually lives in a mud shack, his own family planning is problematic. Extensive clinical studies of him and his wife by other specialists have failed to pinpoint the cause of their infertility. After failed attempts at using the IVF and GIFT techniques on Esther, they give up all hope and decide to adopt a child, preferably a boy. They find a Jewish couple who already has three children and cannot afford to raise the fourth child. After meeting, the Jewish couple is delighted to give their infant son up to another Jewish family like the Hartmans.

The child is an infant when the Hartmans adopt him, and he quickly becomes the center of attention in the household. It does not take long before the joy of having their first child changes to heartbreak. When the boy is four years old, Esther takes him to the pediatrician for his annual check-up. During an examination of the boy's head and neck, the pediatrician notices a few bruises on his arms and a swollen lymph node in his neck. The doctor quickly orders a complete blood count, which shows too many white blood cells and not enough red blood cells and platelets. Adversely, most of the blood cells are of the immature type, which is usually only found in the bone marrow. The pediatrician suspects that the child has leukemia, and it is confirmed when he receives the results of the bone marrow biopsy. Unfortunately, the child does

5

not respond to advanced chemotherapy and dies at the age of five. Losing all hope, Esther and Dr. Hartman bury the issue of parenthood and look for other interests in life. He focuses on managing the department, teaching, and research; and Esther devotes her time reading and writing. Occasionally they travel to historic and scenic places together.

A year later, they take a luxury cruise around the Caribbean Islands, and Esther comes down with severe nausea and headaches.

"You must be suffering from motion sickness," Dr. Hartman opines. Esther starts taking Scopolamine patches. "But would it hurt the baby if I'm pregnant?" she wonders. "Nonsense, your symptoms are consistent with motion sickness," Dr. Hartman tells her. "I may end up sticking one behind my ear, too."

Her nausea does not go away, though. Esther's symptoms continue, even after they return home. A routine examination confirms Esther's suspicion: yes, she is miraculously pregnant and suffering from morning sickness. Although she worries about the effects of scope patches and liberal drinking during the trip, her pregnancy progresses well, but her labor is long, and the delivery requires the use of forceps. Even her epidural anesthesia wears off at the end.

Their son, Saul, is now in high school and has become a challenge to manage for his parents. He rarely studies and instead prefers to play video games. Often when Dr. Hartman is not around, loud metal music blares through the house. Dr. Hartman worries about Saul, but Esther argues that he will grow up soon.

"He's just showing the effects of hormones," she pleads. "Every teenager goes through this stage." When the housekeeper finds a pile of cigarettes, grass butts, and empty beer cans in their son's wastebasket, Esther instructs her to keep the matter quiet.

———————

Decades ago, as a student at Harvard University, Jordan Hartman was a serious and ambitious student. Coming from a middle-class Jewish family, he was raised to appreciate education, reading, and playing a musical instrument. However, he grows to dislike the long hours of practice needed to improve his piano playing. When his parents observe his attitude, they enroll him in tennis lessons at the Jewish Community Center instead. Physically strong and astute, Jordan excels in tennis and, in no time, starts winning matches and junior tournaments. He does best in singles matches and wins easily against opponents in his age group. His talent as a fierce competitor becomes an asset for him when he applies to Harvard University because he receives a scholarship for his tennis talent. After a few months, the university's tennis coach places him as a reserve on the Crimson team, the only freshman ever to play on the university's varsity team. He continues playing on the team into his senior year and wins a crucial match that brings his team to the National

Indoor Tennis Championships. It is here in the final game of the tournament against a Yale University tennis star that Jordan loses the game, causing his team to drop into second place. It is after this match Jordan loses his temper, breaks his tennis racquet, and refuses to come to the net to shake hands with the winner. And it is here where he meets Esther for the first time; Esther is a sophomore and has been following his matches throughout the season. Despite her regular attendance, Jordan has been so absorbed by focusing on his matches that he has never noticed Esther before.

After the championship match against the Yale team, Esther follows him and taps him on the shoulder. "You're excellent!" Esther says. "You should be proud of yourself for the way you played."

"This tennis match is my last one," he replies bitterly. "I'll never compete in any tennis tournament again."

"Come on! You almost beat their ace," says Esther, who only plays recreational tennis and avoids competitions. "Well, you can play with me anytime," she says. "I bet you will have much more fun."

Jordan, captivated by her beautiful smile, says, "Thanks. I'll consider it." Encouraged by his reaction, Esther says, "Let's go for a cup of coffee and talk."

Jordan nods and says, "Okay. Let's meet away from the tennis center." Esther calls him a few days later and says, "I would like to play tennis with you." Jordan replies, "I'm not sure that is a good idea."

"I have already reserved a court this afternoon. It will be fun."

Jordan is surprised by Esther's request, but when Esther insists, he says, "Okay, I'll be there."

At their first tennis rendezvous, they end up playing two sets. Jordan beats Esther easily in both sets. After that, they go to Mr. Bartley's Gourmet Hamburger, across the street from Harvard. They are more impressed with the exotic menu than the juicy hamburgers they have ordered. He gets a Harvard Double Burger with onion rings; Esther goes with a feta cheeseburger and French fries.

In subsequent weeks, they play tennis on midweek afternoons, and each time they go to a different place to have an early dinner. After several rounds of tennis, they grow to like each other and are soon best friends. That winter, Jordan receives acceptance letters from both Yale and Harvard Medical Schools. He tells Esther his choice is clear: Harvard so that he can stay close to her. After Esther finishes her bachelor's degree in English history and literature, she applies to the Master of Liberal Arts program at Harvard. "I like the Socratic ideal of the 'examined life' that liberal studies can provide," Esther explains when Jordan questions her choice. "I want to understand the world through the literature of different cultures," she continues. "There is so much to learn from ancient times."

"How far back will you go to study world literature?" Jordan jokes. "Are you going to analyze the epic poem of Gilgamesh?"

"Of course," Esther responds. "I'm going to gain knowledge about the ancient world through whatever has survived from those distant times. Yeah, even from the scrolls and clay tablets which have been recently discovered in a cave."

"Are you talking about the Torah?" Jordan asks. Esther says, "Indeed, the Book of Esther."

"Is it because it carries the same name as yours?" Jordan Hartman says, smirking.

"I love the story. It's magical," Esther says.

"Is it real? Was there ever a queen of Persia named Esther?" asks Jordan.

"Well, the Bible says there was," she says. And her assertive gaze closes the discussion in the best possible way.

———————

During his latest teaching tour, Dr. Hartman lectures on female infertility in general, and fallopian tubes disorders in particular. This time he travels with his popular associate, Dr. Carlos Bonilla, who has gained fame by introducing a new technique to produce pregnancy by injecting egg and sperm into the fallopian tube. Dr. Hartman gives lectures in Tokyo, Shanghai, and Beijing as a distinguished guest of the most prestigious local universities. He tours the three cities, delivers eight lectures, and attends dinners with department chairs, leaving some time for selected sightseeing tours. In the hotel, after dinner, he usually stays up, previews his lectures, and edits the slide presentations, while Dr. Bonilla has dinner at expensive restaurants and visits jazz bars with beautiful escorts.

Dr. Hartman often calls Esther and describes his visits to museums and other cultural sights as well as inquiring about local news and events at home. Every morning, the limousine comes for him and Dr. Bonilla at the hotel. It drives them to the university, where they enjoy coffee and local breakfast specialties with their hosts before going to the lecture hall.

After five weeks abroad, Dr. Hartman returns home to find Esther in a desperate state. She has developed nagging indigestion, rapid weight loss, and a puffy face. He puts his cold hand over Esther's warm abdomen and is surprised to notice a bulge. Her stomach has grown and now contains a mass as big as a three- or four-month pregnancy. He reckons that the last time they had made love was at least four months ago, maybe longer. He is sure that Esther's bulge cannot be a pregnancy, especially given their long-term inability to produce a pregnancy. Then he remembers his lecture in China regarding ovarian cancer, where he had shown many slides of large ovarian tumors.

While there, Dr. Hartman suffered from nostomania and wished he had brought Esther along. And now, here at home tonight, he is filled with desire.

He contemplates approaching Esther, but the possibility of a tumor in her abdomen causes him to be concerned. "It might disturb the mass or even rupture it," he surmises. Then, he becomes a medical professor again and whispers, "It cannot be pregnancy."

Esther hears his whisper and waves his observation off. "I'm too old to be pregnant."

"Do you remember when we last made love?"

"Oh dear, it was a long time ago," Esther responds. "Probably four or five months ago, perhaps even longer."

He thinks it could be more than five months since they last made love. Now, weary from the long flight, plus experiencing the effects of his welcome drink of a double shot of single malt whiskey on ice in a crystal tumbler, the unstoppable forces of jet lag make him drowsy. He abandons the idea of making love, and soon he falls asleep. For Esther, reading is more enjoyable, although she enjoys his presence, the warmth of his body, his energetic attitude. Esther is amused by thinking about sex. For her, when it comes to sex, even once a year is too much. She has waited for Dr. Hartman, her genius and caring husband, for a few weeks. Dr. Hartman trusts her and knows that she would remain loyal for much longer, even a year or more, if he were caught on the high seas. She is like Penelope, a steadfast wife. Now, in the quiet bedroom, Esther opens her book and resumes reading McCullough's *1776*.

III
Dr. Hartman Aims the Laser Beam

In the lecture hall, Dr. Hartman aims the laser beam at the large cystic mass on the screen. He describes it as a tumor with a low malignancy potential. He walks back to the podium and turns on the computer and clicks on the patient's information—her age, pictures of the ovarian mass, breast cyst, and ruddy nipple for the students. "Here, in this case, breast cancer is very likely. Look at that blood-stained ulcer on the nipple," Dr. Hartman reminds his audience. Again, he feels the intermittently piercing pain but continues with his lecture. "But how would you diagnose an ovarian mass?" He leaves the podium with the cordless microphone still attached to the lapel of his white coat next to three ballpoint pens, none of which has a logo from a drug manufacturer. He disdains cheap advertising. "Is this a benign ovarian cyst or is it malignant?" he asks a student named Debra, who is shifting her weight on the seat in the second row behind a sleepy male classmate.

"I think . . . it's benign," Debra offers hesitantly.

"This cyst could be malignant," the suddenly stirred male student interjects.

"So, what should we do now?" Dr. Hartman asks Debra, ignoring the other classmate.

Debra is thoughtful and hesitant to answer the question. Randy, who is in the first row, raises his hand. "Take her to the OR, sir."

"That's a very bold action, my son. Surgeons like to perform miracles with their knives." He shouts, "Surgical incisions are like trenches in war; they bring no progress; they prolong wars, cause massive damage, many casualties, and ultimately produce no peace. They only lengthen the patient's misery. Hasty surgical intervention could be harmful and could shatter the patient's defense mechanisms against disease, lessen the chance for a cure. My son, you must learn to think conservatively. When you ignore peace, you only face war."

"What about a biopsy, sir?" murmurs another student.

"How about removing the cyst first?" he challenges the students. "An excellent idea," several students mumble.

"We need to have some clues about the chance of cancer before we touch the cyst and perform surgery," he says. "We need a reliable marker to detect ovarian cancer in its earliest stage," Dr. Hartman continues. "Gilda Radner and Rosalind Franklin would have lived many more years if we had a test to detect their cancer at the onset. We could have seen Roseanne Roseannadanna on TV this Saturday night complaining about her neighbor, the obstetrician who frequently delivers babies in the wee hours of the morning, waking his elderly neighbors, most of them female."

"What about an x-ray of the pelvis?" a student suggests. "It can be done when we do the mammography of the breast, sir."

Dr. Hartman shows his displeasure when he hears the word "sir."

"Ridiculous!" Debra counters, "We already know the location of the breast lesion!"

Dr. Hartman is now bombarded by other student comments: "And the bleeding soreness,"; "The inverted nipple,"; "The large ovarian mass."

Now, Dr. Hartman barely hears the last comments. His mind wavers. Now, he recalls Esther's call. She sought his help. He knows she cannot handle Saul on her own. Esther is waiting. She wants him to come home and manage Saul. He remembers that more than once, Esther has told him about her dream that Saul will one day enter an Ivy League university and go on to Harvard Medical School like his father, fall in love with a Jewish classmate, and bring her home to meet with them. Someday, they will have a daughter-in-law, attend her son's graduations, and welcome one or two grandchildren. And when Dr. Hartman retires, the two of them will travel abroad. Go to Machu Picchu and Antarctica, go to Iran and visit the dome of Esther, the Queen of Persia, in Hamadan. But because Dr. Hartman disdains Iran and hates the mullahs, she will join one of the tours without him.

Dr. Hartman remembers the chilly early morning on the peak of the mountain on the island of Maui in Hawaii, which they visited for their honeymoon. The tour bus took them to the summit of Haleakala before sunrise. Some friends had recommended the tour, the impressive spectacle of the sunrise at Haleakala Summit, the veritable colors of the strips of clouds.

When the sun broke through the ribbons of cloud, Esther was mesmerized by the bright and glorious colors of the sunrise. Dr. Hartman was holding her because she was cold, shivering in the breeze on the edge of the dormant volcano. A few years later, looking at the photographs of the trip, she writes a poem about the sunrise at Haleakala Peak:

The eastern sky turns into a canvas
Of a mélange of colors: gray, blue, orange, and purple
The brilliant sun like a glowing bolt
Breaks through the ribbons of clouds.

Unopposed, it rises into perpetual space
The breeze brings the warm air
A salubrious vigor descends upon the couple at the peak
Golden light warms Esther's face.

In the lecture hall, Dr. Hartman wraps up his lecture. "Ovarian cancer kills two-thirds of its victims. Esther Tudor died at the age of 42. *Saturday Night Live*'s Gilda Radner died at the age of 42. There are more than 24 thousand

11

cases a year, 14 thousand deaths." Now his mind wanders again. He remembers Esther's age, "Well, my Esther is several years older than these victims." Then, he recalls that last night, he felt a bulge in Esther's abdomen. He succeeds in returning to the assigned lecture and says, "Many patients survive ovarian cancer by less than a year, some survive more than two years. A very few, five years. Somehow, the Australian Olympics Silver Medalist is still free of cancer."

He pushes the button, pulls up the screen, and walks to the blackboard. He places the X-rays on the bright display. "The mammography shows a scattered calcification within a well-confined area, which suggests the presence of a solid lump on the right side underneath the nipple. There is another lump on the left breast but away from the nipple, and without atypical calcification." He walks to the front row and asks the sleepy male student in front of him, "Would you biopsy these lumps?"

"I … I don't know," stutters the student.

"What! You don't know?" Dr. Hartman is incensed by the sheepish reaction; his face turns red. He cannot conceal his rage. The student's response reminds him of Saul's excuses. In the student's face, he sees the image of Saul. "Another stupid kid," he murmurs. He wants to throw a piece of chalk at the student, but he bites his lip, turns away, and flings it against the blackboard. The chalk bounces back, hits his chin, leaving a white mark. A few of the students cannot control their chuckles. He hears them and remembers there is a limit to his behavior and his impulsive interactions with the students. He must manage his temper; otherwise, they will complain to the Dean. "I hate to give the Dean another chance to preach to me about how to interact with the students," he thinks. After a pause, he regains his calm and continues, "Of course, we need tissue samples from these lumps to verify whether the lumps are malignant."

Right in the middle of the sentence, his mobile phone begins to vibrate. He looks at the phone and sees Esther's name and number. He stops the lecture and listens to her; she is again pleading for help.

After they settle in San Antonio, Esther becomes a well-liked member of the city's high society. They respect and like her because she is intelligent, educated, and productive. Esther uses the income from her successful college-recruiting business and freelance writing to advance several arts organizations in San Antonio. She currently acts as president-elect of the Junior League, sits on the board of directors of the San Antonio Symphony, and is a member of the city's Citizen Arts Advisory Board. Esther invites faculty members to arts performances and ensures financial support to these organizations from the university staff and faculty. Now, after living in town for over ten years, both she and her husband feel at home. However, in the confines of their private life, not everything is auspicious.

For Esther, Saul's misfortune is a constant worry. Dr. Hartman's drinking issues and his fiery temperament are other sources of concern for her. With Dr. Hartman collecting quality wine, both of them are drinking wine with dinner every night, usually one glass for her and two or more for him. Regularly, though, he finishes the bottle and often one or two shots of cognac before he goes to bed. There are sleepless nights for him and tired mornings for her. When Saul entered their life, it initially brought some excitement and kept her mind occupied. With her husband entirely consumed by his responsibilities of running the department and several research projects awarded to him by the NIH, she is the one who takes care of Saul and dedicates most of her time to his needs. With the help of a full-time housekeeper, Esther manages to oversee the physical care of Saul. Her husband, on the other hand, hardly spends any time with their son.

After the age of ten, Saul is enrolled at the Jewish Community Center in various cultural and sports programs. When he despises violin practice, Esther switches him to the piano. When he refuses swimming lessons, Esther convinces him to take tennis. From the age of three, she has made a habit of reading children's books to Saul at bedtime, hoping to instill intellectual interests in him. But as Saul grows older, he increasingly exhibits problematic behavior, so summer camps become a welcome break for Esther. They provide some sorely-needed quiet time for her so that she can catch up on reading the stack of historical books that she has purchased. Unfortunately, Saul becomes the source of a disturbance at summer camp, too. When he is ten years old, and at his second summer at the camp, Saul gets involved in repeated physical fights with the other campers. One late afternoon, Esther receives a call from the director of the camp, saying that they cannot keep Saul any longer. He is bullying two smaller campers and has frequently brawled with them. "We are facing a challenging situation with your son," the director says. "The parents of these two kids have pulled their children from camp."

When Esther fails to appease the angry director, convince him to give Saul another chance, she drops everything and drives to the camp without her husband's help to take Saul home earlier than expected. During the rest of that summer, Saul becomes a vicious troublemaker in the neighborhood. He bullies the smaller kids on the block and on a daily basis while instigates altercations and fistfights with his school classmates who live nearby.

"

IV
The Pressure in the Lower Abdomen

Esther feels no pain, just some pressure in her lower abdomen, a lack of appetite, and some heartburn. She lies on the hard, flat X-ray table with a small pillow under her neck. The X-ray tube moves toward her and stops above her pelvis, then below her navel. She hears a click. Then, two more clicks. There is a pause. Now, the X-ray tube is above her abdomen. The technician asks her to hold the breath. She hears the last click. Ten minutes later, she is in the lab, where a pre-med student working during the summer break punctures her vein and takes three tubes of blood. The student is embarrassed, "I'm sorry, ma'am."

"I'm fine, thank you," Esther says, hiding her discomfort.

The college student places a cotton ball and a Band-Aid on her puncture site to stop the bleeding. He is learning, gaining some experience. His first attempt had been two weeks ago. Esther looks at him with her teary eyes. He looks like Saul. The student notices Esther's glowing eyes. They resemble his mother's. His mother does not let anybody else draw her blood when her son is around. "Ma! I haven't punctured any flesh yet, only a manikin's," he says. But his mother insists. He creates a bloody scene that day, with his mother's blood running down and staining his new white coat. "It doesn't hurt at all," she claims.

After concluding a lecture in the main auditorium, Dr. Hartman walks to his office suite along a long corridor that passes by the dean's suite. Lately, Dr. Hartman does not get along with the dean. "The Dean is not qualified for the job," Dr. Hartman had boldly said a day earlier at a meeting of the department chairs. Now Dr. Hartman is unhappy about his lecture, about mixing up the history of the patient with a pelvic mass with the situation facing his wife, the woman he has loved and lived with for twenty-five years. Now he is worried about her condition. Dr. Hartman pulls a handkerchief out of his pocket, dries his sweat, and walks back toward his office ten doors down the corridor. He is in no mood to talk to anybody now. Anger is still rolling through his head. Even though he has a right to be unhappy, a lecturer should not throw things across the room. Such rules should not apply to him, he believes. Now he cannot get rid of his anger. He cannot leave the student's face behind in the lecture hall. "That stupid student," he murmurs.

He settles into his comfortable chair and calls Dr. Ralph Ross, his right-hand man in the department. He collects his thoughts and focuses on Esther's abdominal mass and the possibility of ovarian cancer. "Her age is the curse," he mumbles. Dr. Hartman is obsessed with the fact that she is in her forties. If she were 39 or 32, 50 or 60, he would not have worried as much. He laughs at

14

the idea that her age is a determining factor for everything. Suddenly the phone rings. "Yes, Ralph.... No, Ralph.... Yes, yes. I agree.... I can't wait until she undergoes the operation.... Yes, Thursday is fine. She'll be here in the ward tomorrow night.... Please, go ahead and see her this afternoon at the clinic.... No, wait a second. She might still be in the radiology department..... That's great.... Thanks."

Dr. Ross cannot find Esther's abdominal and pelvic X-rays. Because Esther has gone home, the idea of repeating the X-rays is irrelevant. The clerk frantically looks everywhere to find them. Dr. Ross leaves the department and calls Dr. Bahman Parsi, a surgical oncology fellow in the department who is a foreign medical graduate but has had his surgical residency education at Southwestern Medical Center in Dallas. Dr. Ross asks Dr. Parsi to go to the radiology department and try to find Esther's X-rays, but after a thorough search, Dr. Parsi is also unable to locate the X-rays. He assumes that the technician must have forgotten to attach an ID label to the corner of the X-ray box, or most likely, the label has fallen off, as this is not the first time that the X-ray label is missing. At the university hospital, it's not uncommon to lose or misplace test results. The labels do not stick well, and some films are left without the necessary ID. "It'll take a while to go through this thick stack." The technician is embarrassed. Dr. Parsi is annoyed but conceals his frustration. The secretary who prints the results is used to this kind of mishap. Dr. Parsi goes to the Vice-Chair's office to ask for help. Unfortunately, the Chair of Radiology is playing golf in a fund-raising tournament while the Vice-Chair is in Germany, giving a lecture at Charite Hospital in Berlin.

Disappointed but not surprised, because he had encountered the problem before, Dr. Parsi returns to the surgical ward empty-handed. He seeks refuge in the residents' conference room where Dr. Ross is giving a lecture. Dr. Ross looks at Roy, a third-year resident, and asks, "What are the X-ray markers of preclinical ovarian cancer?" Roy knows the answer to Dr. Ross's favorite question on every occasion. "They have done mammography, too," Dr. Ross adds. "What if the X-rays are lost?" Roy answers. There is loud laughter. "Or if there's no label on the film." Nobody is surprised.

In the late afternoon, Dr. Ross enters Dr. Hartman's office and finds him annotating the draft of a Small Business Innovation Research (SBIR) application. Dr. Ross tells him that Esther's X-rays are missing. They ponder the diagnosis of her abdominal mass. "There are no X-rays, no CA-125, no CBC results, and because she had fasted and couldn't pee, no urine sample either," Dr. Ross says.

"Look, Dr. Ross, it's all clinical," Dr. Hartman raises his voice, getting mad again. Furious about the missing X-ray ID tag, he says, "A good doctor must rely on clinical examination." He shows him the palm of his right hand and points at it with his left index and middle fingers. "It's all here. Esther has a growing mass. You know what I mean?" Dr. Ross nods. Dr. Hartman states with authority, "It's an ovarian tumor!"

In the darkness of their bedroom, Dr. Hartman stretches his hand and feels Esther's warm, sweaty abdomen. Esther puts her hand over his. Nothing moves. It is a silent night. They face each other, and without speaking, they seek each other's faces, then lips. A few weeks later, she writes about that night when they both discovered her enlarged abdomen:

> Two lovers, between them, an abdominal mass.
> The scent of sweaty skin
> And warm breath draws him closer
> Wow, the sense of smell is stronger than sight:
>
> His eyes are shut
> The salty tongues and lips unite.
> She loves his embrace.
> He loves her warm, swollen breasts.

V
Esther Arrives at the Hospital

When Esther arrives at the hospital, she is admitted directly to a semi-private room on the fifth floor. The room has two beds, one for Esther and one for another patient. But the floor supervisor has kept the latter one vacant in case Dr. Hartman decides to stay with Esther. Dr. Hartman comes to her room early in the evening. They have a short conversation; she looks calm and does not show any anxiety regarding the abdominal mass, but he is worried.

Dr. Hartman glances at the cover of the book in Esther's lap. "What are you reading?"

She replies, "*The Executioner's Song* by Norman Mailer."

After a pause, Dr. Hartman says, "Gilmore had a criminal mind and blind rage."

She does not respond, opens the book instead, and returns to the bookmarked page, while he focuses on perusing an application for an NIH grant. "Have you taken the sleeping pill yet?" he asks her. "I'll do that later after you leave, and before I turn the lights off," she promises.

He nods in approval and returns to his materials; she continues reading. He is there until Esther closes the book and stretches on the bed. He looks at her abdomen. The bulge is hidden under the washed-out hospital gown. Two buttons are missing as well—not the ones below the navel, but those above the abdomen. The right breast is exposed, the nipple, too, holding firm, slightly darker than usual. She still wears the perfume from last night. He recalls their previous trip, the night in the hotel room. There were watching X-rated DVDs, down pillows under their heads, and Giorgio perfume flowing in the air. He is aroused. He swallows his saliva. He feels a little bulge in his underwear. Esther arranges her hair. The scent flows into the room and anoints his face, enters his nostrils and gets into his blood, runs and reaches his brain, and finally jolts his mind. He remembers the night several months ago when they last made love.

Esther covers her breast when the nurse comes in to take a urine sample. "What's that for, Miss?" Dr. Hartman asks the nurse, uncouth as usual. Esther apologizes for her husband's brusque question. "It's for the pregnancy test, sir," the nurse answers. "What?" He is furious. "What a stupid idea."

"Dr. Parsi ordered it," the nurse says, shrugs off Dr. Hartman's frown and walks away with the yellow cup.

"That stupid oncology fellow. Why should we have these foreigners in our department?" He then pages Dr. Ross.

Dr. Ross answers the page quickly and explains that he doesn't mind the pregnancy test. "It's the routine urinalysis and pregnancy test." Dr. Ross tries to calm Dr. Hartman. "It's too late to cancel the order."

Dr. Hartman swallows his pride. "I don't want to see this fellow in Esther's room," he tells Dr. Ross.

"Your wife requested that Dr. Parsi obtain her H & P and answer her questions about the surgery and the tumor," Dr. Ross says. "Therefore, I have asked him to visit your wife and complete the chart and write the pre-op orders."

"Is he going to assist you with the surgery?"

"Of course. I need him there," Dr. Ross says. "He's the best assistant in the OR and has excellent surgical skills."

"I want the best team for Esther's surgery," Dr. Hartman insists. Dr. Ross says, "We will do our best."

"But, he can hardly speak English."

"You mean his accent?" Dr. Ross says, "Dr. Hartman, I don't have any problems understanding him; neither do the residents or the students."

When Esther left the house, Saul was still at school. "Have you heard from Saul?" Esther asks her husband.

"Not at all," Dr. Hartman says. "I'm sure he can take care of himself while you are here," Dr. Hartman says. "I'll check on him when I get home."

The couple talks about the challenges that teenagers, including Saul, are facing these days. "It is not just the flow of hormones in their body, but the peer pressure, too," Dr. Hartman says.

"Are we doing enough to help Saul?" Esther asks.

"What else can we do, my dear? We have arranged for him to see the school counselor every week," Dr. Hartman says.

"How about a family therapist for all of us?" Esther replies.

"I am sick of it," Dr. Hartman says. "I don't have time to visit a family therapist."

Now in a sour mood, Dr. Hartman changes the subject and begins to talk about Dr. Parsi. The man's accent reminds Dr. Hartman of a German accent. Dr. Hartman's mind drifts to the Second World War. The Holocaust. Auschwitz. Kristallnacht. Esther's father and her sister Ann. "I hate his accent, it reminds me of the extermination camps," Dr. Hartman says. Esther is annoyed. She says, "Honey, he's not German. He is from Iran. He's related to one of the Shah's aides."

"They're all related to somebody famous. Haven't you heard about the Russian expatriates after World War I?" Dr. Hartman says. "Hundreds of them were relatives of the Tsar."

"He's a good man, knows a lot about Jewish-Persian history."

"I'm certain they all hate Jews."

"Not at all. Dr. Parsi is not anti-Semitic," Esther says. "During the last departmental holiday party, he talked to me about the Jewish Diaspora in Iran. He also told me about the tale of Esther during ancient times in Persia."

18

"What does he think about the mullahs?" Dr. Hartman asks.

"Well, I don't know. Dr. Parsi always praises Jewish people: Jewish scientists, writers, and musicians." Esther says. "Also, being Persian, he reads and writes poetry. He talks about the Book of Esther in the Old Testament and the role of the Jewish Diaspora in managing the government during the Achaemenid Dynasty in Persia."

"Is that why you like him?" Dr. Hartman wonders.

"His vocabulary is excellent; it's better than that of your protégé, Dr. Ross. He reads a lot of medical journals and literature; I trust him completely," Esther says. "He makes a lot of sense to me. He reminds me of Saul. I wish Saul would become somebody like him."

"So he wastes his time reading and writing poetry," Dr. Hartman says.

"Yeah. Dr. Ross told me that he recites Khayyam's translated quatrains in the OR."

"What's his religion?" Dr. Hartman asks Esther.

"I don't know."

"Isn't he a Muslim?"

"I don't believe so," Esther says. "Dr. Ross says he doesn't practice any religion."

———

Moments later, when Dr. Hartman is gone, Dr. Parsi enters the room. While Dr. Parsi writes a medical report in Esther's hospital chart, he asks her a few questions about her menstrual periods and sexual activity. "Are you taking any precautions?"

"Sex is not on our agenda," Esther says. "We mostly hug and kiss. That's all."

"May I ask, why not?" Dr. Parsi says. "Of course, medically speaking, could it be because of pain, dyspareunia?"

"Not at all. Every evening when Jordan comes home, he is boiling over something. It's always one thing or the other, the Dean, this fellow or that resident. There is always the festering grudge about that colleague who is very popular among residents and students, the one who dares to disagree with him during the discussions after the lectures in the Grand Rounds," she says. Then she adds, "So, I don't think there is any need for contraception. I don't take any precautions for our few lovemaking occasions a year. Once every four or five months does not justify the risk of taking the pill. No, let's not even think about pregnancy."

"Still, it could happen," Dr. Parsi reminds her. Esther explains. "My husband is against taking the pill. He believes it is not worth the risk to take any cancer-causing pills."

"Well, between tumor and pregnancy, I'll bet on pregnancy," Dr. Parsi says. "But according to the gynecology textbooks, to verify the diagnosis, we must run the pregnancy test."

"Okay, if you think it's necessary to run a pregnancy test, go ahead."

"Thanks. I'll do that."

"But be ready, my husband will scold you if the test comes back negative," warns Esther.

"The X-rays would've clarified the issue earlier," Dr. Parsi says, "But we can't locate them."

Esther looks at Dr. Parsi and, after a sigh, says, "You look like my son, Saul. Your nose!" And she giggles.

"That's great. I'm honored."

"Your first name, Bahman, is different from other Iranian names I have known," Esther says. "What kind of name is it?"

"It's popular among Zoroastrians and Iranian intellectuals," Dr. Parsi says. "It's a modern form of an Old Persian name, which means 'sound mind.'"

"I like the sound of that," Esther says.

"Yes, it's also the name of a Zoroastrian God and the name of the eleventh month in the modern Iranian calendar."

"Wow, your name must be very dear in Iran," Esther says.

Dr. Parsi continues, "It's also mentioned in Ferdowsi's epic poem, *Shahnameh*."

Esther changes the subject and asks, "So what's your religion?"

"Well, to be honest about it, my religion is the same as that of Khayyam and Hafiz," Dr. Parsi says. "The same as Thomas Jefferson, the author of The Declaration of Independence."

"So, who is your God?" Esther asks.

Dr. Parsi laughs. He says, "The universe is my god, earth my saint, and rain my angel."

"Well, you are very poetic," Esther says. "What about the afterlife?"

"Okay, allow me to quote Omar Khayyam, who compared the mullahs' preaching to the rumble of distant drums."

Esther laughs. "Could you recite the full line?"

"Okay. Here it is:

Some for the glories of this world, and some
Sigh for the Prophet's Paradise to come,

Ah, take the cash, and let the promise go,
Nor heed the rumble of a distant drum!"

"That's quite a philosophy," Esther says.

"Well, I was born into an orthodox Zoroastrian family, but for me, nothing is settled."

"I don't know anything about Zoroastrianism," Esther says.

"I thought because of your namesake, you should know a lot about Zoroastrians," Dr. Parsi says.

"Not at all. My namesake came from the Tanakh. But tell me about your religion," Esther says.

"Should we say my family's religion, please?"

"Okay, tell me about your family's religion, please," Esther says.

After finishing the notes and writing the pre-op orders in Esther's chart, Dr. Parsi talks to Esther about his family's religion, Zoroastrianism. Although this religion is the smallest of the major religions of the world in the number of its believers, it is historically one of the most important. Its roots are in the proto-Indo-European spirituality that also produced the religions of India. Zoroastrianism was the first of the world's religions to be founded by an inspired prophetic reformer. It was also influential on Buddhism and especially on the Abrahamic religions of Judaism, Christianity, and Islam. Most likely, the prophet Zoroaster was born in the northeast of present-day Iran.

The fundamental doctrines of Zoroastrianism are reflected in the *12 Beliefs*. When Esther shows eagerness to hear the detail of these beliefs, Dr. Parsi says that the first and the most sacred one is the *Belief* in a Universal God called Ahura Mazda. He's omniscient and omnipotent. The second *Belief* is the duality of existence. The world is a battleground between good (Ahura Mazda) and evil (Ahriman). The third *Belief* is that at the end of the world, goodness will prevail. The fourth *Belief* is the existence of the soul. The fifth is the myth of creation in which Ahura Mazda is the Creator. He has created the entire universe, and six other divinities assist Ahura Mazda in managing the universe. The sixth describes the belief in human goodness and dignity. The seventh declares that Zoroaster is the first prophet. His birth initiated the current cycle of creation lasting 3000 years (that would make the world only about 6500 years old). The eighth *Belief* addresses the afterlife and a final judgment day on which God will resurrect the dead and, after thorough scrutiny, assign them either to Heaven or to a freezing place for eternity. The ninth *Belief* is the Three Commandments—good thoughts, kind words, and good deeds. The tenth *Belief* is sacrificial rituals to purify the world. The eleventh *Belief* is the duty to perform sacred chants. And finally, the twelfth *Belief* is the importance of righteousness and an obligation to remain on the side of goodness and assist Ahura Mazda in defeating Ahriman.

"How do you remember all these *Beliefs*?" Esther says in amazement.

"I memorized them when I was ten years old," Dr. Parsi shrugs.

"These *Beliefs* are quite similar to the commandments of other religions," Esther says.

"Probably subsequent religions have been influenced by these thoughts," Dr. Parsi says. Although she finds the topic fascinating, Esther resists succumbing to the sedative effect and boldly asks Dr. Parsi, "Do you believe in God?"

"Well, I haven't chosen one yet. Nothing is settled for me. When it comes to Zoroastrianism, the Prophet Zoroaster, and the Holy Book, I choose *Beliefs* that do not conflict with science and evolution," Dr. Parsi says. "When it comes to the creation of the universe and life, I discard Zoroastrianism's simple explanations. I have issues with several other *Beliefs*, too, like life after death, resurrection, and the continuous duel between Ahura Mazda and Ahriman."

Esther says, "The majority of us, I mean Jews, believe in evolution, though culturally, we are proud of our heritage."

"I wish it were the same for Zoroastrians," Dr. Parsi says. "For them, if you don't consider and practice the *Beliefs*, you are out. I understand it's the same for Muslims, too."

"Though we have so much in common with Islamic traditions," Esther says. "Too bad Jews and Muslims can't get along."

"Before the Khomeini era, Iranians of different faiths got along very well," mused Dr. Parsi. "Yes, most of my friends were either Muslims or Jews."

"You must be an exception."

"Not really. In Iran, during the last decades of the Pahlavi dynasty, the Jews enjoyed a very comfortable position in society. For example, when I was a student at Tehran Medical School, about ten percent of the students in my class were Jewish," Dr. Parsi says. "We often partied and traveled together. Muslims, Jews, Baha'is, and the few Zoroastrians that we had in our class ate and sat together. Educated Iranians are much more open-minded about other religions than the Arabs are," Dr. Parsi explains.

"Are you saying that the Arabs are more hostile towards the Jews than the Iranians are?" Esther asks.

"Of course. The animosity between Arabs and Jews goes back to ages."

Esther thinks about religious extremism. "Well, irrational passion morphs any religion into a dangerous doctrine," Esther says.

"Exactly! Radical Muslims and Jews are not the only adversaries. Look at the Sunnis and Shiites in Iraq, the Hindus, and Muslims in India, and the Catholics and Protestants in Europe." Dr. Parsi glances at Esther and finds her eager to hear more about the subject. "Even among the same religion, there are bloody clashes—yes, they go after each other savagely. I could lose my head in Iran if I say Allah is a human creation."

Esther is frustrated by discussing religion. She's more interested in conversing about Jewish history, so she asks Dr. Parsi, "Are many Iranians aware of the story of Esther in the Bible?"

"Of course. Most of us know the tale of Esther, the Queen of Persia," Dr. Parsi says. "So much so that the Jews of Iran are often called the Children of Esther."

"That's interesting. Esther is also referred to as a queen in the Book of Esther in the Bible." For an instant, Esther falls into a reverie. She imagines that she is the ancient Esther parading in front of the Persian king, Xerxes the Great, and drawing his attention.

She parts with the dream when Dr. Parsi says, "Well, when Cyrus the Great captured Babylon over two and half millennia ago and freed the enslaved Jews, many of them decided to settle in Susa, Ecbatana, Isfahan, and other large cities in the Persian Empire. Esther's family was part of that exodus. Jewish citizens grew to play essential roles in their new communities."

"My mother was an avid reader," Esther says. "She read a lot about the Jewish people in ancient Persia."

"Is it why your name is Esther?"

"I think so."

"Those centuries in Iran were the glory years in Iranian history," Dr. Parsi says. "The Achaemenid kings believed the gods had ordained them as emperors of the ancient world. When the empire expanded, after defeating and capturing other nations, those gods were respected and added to the other recognized gods. Although Zoroastrianism was the main religion of the empire, occupied countries could continue to practice their faiths, such as Judaism, Hinduism, and the Babylonian religion. In ancient Persia, most of the military and government positions were open to citizens of all faiths. During the reign of Xerxes the Great, Mordechai, a Jew and presumably Esther's uncle, became the grand vizier."

"So, what's Islam?" Esther asks. "Is it similar to Zoroastrianism?"

"Not at all," Dr. Parsi says. "In Zoroastrianism, the earth is nature's gift to man, sacred and invaluable; it's holy and must be protected. Zoroaster teaches people to seek happiness like the American Declaration of Independence that states that pursuing happiness is every person's inalienable right. However, an individual's behavior determines whether he may achieve enduring happiness. Ahriman continuously struggles to capture a man's mind, but Ahura Mazda is policing the situation and assists man in his struggle to resist Ahriman's temptations. The ultimate reward for conducting one's life according to the teachings of the Prophet Zoroaster in the holy book, the Avesta, is achieving complete peace and happiness."

"The Zoroastrians must keep their homes and cities free of pollution and poisons, live a happy life, drink wine, and celebrate holidays throughout the year. Fire is sacred, and Zoroastrians are instructed to safeguard the eternal flame, *Atashkadeh,* in their temples, and to conduct their prayers around that fire. The oldest fire temple is still burning its eternal flame in the Parsi section of Bombay, while the second oldest is in Kurdistan in Northwestern Iran. Zoroastrianism entered recorded history in the 5th century BC. Although Zoroastrianism wasn't the only recognized and practiced religion during the Persian Achaemenid Empire, it was the dominant religion for more than a thousand years, and it became the official state religion of the pre-Islamic Iranian Sassanid Empire until AD 640-50 when Islam forcefully suppressed all other religions."

Esther is fascinated by the information on Zoroastrianism, but she is more interested in another topic of Persian culture. "I understand poetry reigns supreme in Iran," Esther says. "Can you recite a poem by heart?"

"I can," Dr. Parsi replies. "Occasionally, I write poetry myself."

"So I hear. One of the nurses told me. I adore the verses of Omar Khayyam."

"So, you must have read his *Rubáiyát*? That is a collection of verses, and they all are in the form of classical Persian rhyming quatrains."

"Are all of his poems in that collection?"

"Well, several hundred quatrains are attributed to Khayyam," Dr. Parsi says. "But there are over a thousand other quatrains with some claim to his authorship. The English writer Edward FitzGerald spent a few decades researching, translating, and publishing five collections of Khayyam's poems."

Esther says, "I would love to hear one in Farsi." Now she can no longer resist the sleepiness. She whispers, "Let's talk more about Persian poetry later."

———

Like most Iranians, Dr. Parsi likes to recite Persian poetry by heart, especially verses in traditional forms with rhyme and rhythm. For him, the musical cadences of poetry provide a means to memorize a poem and enhance the pleasure of hearing lines of beautiful words that reflect man's most sacred feelings. Several days later, Dr. Parsi chooses a popular quatrain written by Khayyam in Farsi and recites it for Esther:

اسرار ازل را نه تو دانی و نه من
وین حل معما نه تو دانی و نه من

هست از پس پرده گفتگوی من و تو
چون پرده بر افتد نه تو مانی و نه من

"It sounds so beautiful, but I don't understand a word!" Esther says, "But what does the poem mean?"

From memory, Dr. Parsi speaks the translation of the quatrain:

The secrets of the universe neither you nor I know
The answers to the riddle neither you know nor I

Behind the curtain, there is much talk about us, why
When the curtain falls, neither you remain nor I.

Overwhelmed with the poem's premise, Esther changes her attention from Khayyam's verse to Dr. Parsi's poetry. "How about your poetry?"

As if Dr. Parsi has expected this question, he pulls a page of a notebook from his pocket and says, "I could leave this one with you so that you may read it later."

"Please do," Esther says.

"I wrote it a few days ago," he says. "Please remember, it's still an early draft. I need to work on it further."

"I will enjoy it, regardless."

Dr. Parsi says, "Thanks for your attention, but I will read it aloud at home and edit it."

VI
Dr. Parsi Lives near the University Hospital

Dr. Parsi lives in a modest one-bedroom apartment two miles away from the University Hospital. He usually gets up early, brews coffee, eats a light breakfast, and waters his small potted ficus tree near the window in the living room and the two rose plants outside the front door. Afterward, he reads a few poems from the internet, writes or revises one of his own, and leaves home for the hospital. Weather permitting, Dr. Parsi bikes to work and usually arrives at the hospital shortly after six-thirty. Today, Dr. Parsi is there at six, right on the dot. He goes to the lab, collects the tests, and walks up to the fifth floor. He reviews the lab results and enters a summary of them in the patients' charts. Pulling out Esther's chart, he searches for the blood and urine tests. The results of the blood and urinalysis are there, but he cannot find the result of the pregnancy test. He prepares the consent form for the surgery, goes to her room, and finds her awake in the bed. Dr. Parsi hands her the form and discusses the operation.

"Please take your time and read the form all the way through," Dr. Parsi advises Esther. "You and Dr. Ross have my permission to perform surgery," she says quickly, and without reading the text, she signs the form. "Dr. Parsi, did you get the result of the pregnancy test yet?"

"No. I'll check it out before we do the surgery." He goes to the Nurse's Station and asks the nurse for the test. Dr. Ross, who has just arrived, interrupts him. Dr. Ross asks Dr. Parsi, "Did she sign the form?"

"Yes, she did."

When the nurse tells Dr. Parsi that the lab does not have the result, he calls and finds out that the pregnancy test has not been done yet. He asks the lab to run the test quickly and call him with the result immediately. "Please call me on my mobile phone."

The surgery is scheduled for seven-thirty. Dr. Ross, Dr. Parsi, a third-year resident, and a senior medical student are the team. Dr. Ross calls the surgery floor the *war zone* and always emphasizes that Dr. Hartman has not been there for at least five years, because according to Dr. Hartman, "The operating room is a place for the young doctors to hone their surgical skills."

The lights above the operating table have been turned on. The OR is ready for the foursome who will perform the life-saving procedure. The IV poles with normal saline bags and a bottle of Ringer's solution are up and ready to be connected to the patient. The operating table is covered with green plastic sheets, which glow under the bright surgery lights suspended from the ceiling. The anesthesiologist checks the machine and secures the connections to the gas tanks. The OR Technician has scrubbed and is now counting the sterile instruments, the surgical pads, and gauzes on the tray. The count is even, and the surgical instruments are ready for Esther's surgery. Before they move Esther to the OR, Dr. Parsi goes to the nursing station, picks up the phone, calls the lab, and asks for the result of Esther's pregnancy test.

VII
In the Lecture Hall

In the lecture hall, Dr. Hartman is displaying the biopsy slides of the breast lump on the silver screen. He clicks the remote control and shows the first PowerPoint slide, and then the next. Another slide shows the mammography picture of a calcified mass, the other the oozing nipple, the third the needle biopsy kit, the fourth a microscopic view of the breast tissue with several groups of cells populated with clusters of ominous dark cells filled with large nuclei. The students are quiet. Dr. Hartman feels a twitch in his breast, an itch in his nipple. He moves his hand into his white coat and rubs the nipple, then continues with the presentation. The student who was apathetic in the previous session is sitting in the front row today, fully alert. Dr. Hartman approaches him and asks, "Do you see the tumor there?"

"Yes, Dr. Hartman," he says before Dr. Hartman's question is entirely uttered.

"Wow, I'm pleased. You are quite attentive today."

"Thank you, sir!" the student says.

Dr. Hartman does not like to be called "sir" by students. "Call me Dr. Hartman or by my first name, okay?"

"Yes, sir. No, no, no, Dr. Hartman!" The mesmerized student replies promptly.

"Why are you repeating 'sir' time and again?"

"I don't know!" he says, confused.

"Just shut up. Okay?"

Now Dr. Hartman is furious, but before he has a chance to continue harassing that student, his mobile phone goes off. Dr. Hartman knows it is from the OR. The male student gets a break this time. Dr. Hartman's sweaty face turns toward the screen. The amphitheater is quiet for a moment. The harassed student takes advantage of the pause when Dr. Hartman's head is turned away, quickly packs his papers, and gets up to leave the class. He does not want to face Dr. Hartman's fury again.

Dr. Hartman's lecture is interrupted by a call from the OR. He is surprised to receive the call so soon. It is only ten minutes after eight, and by his knowledge of the way the OR functions at the University Hospital, it should have been eight-thirty or nine before the team even begins Esther's surgery. Of course, he knows that Dr. Parsi is assigned to start the operation and make the initial incision because Dr. Ross relies on him in complicated cases. Dr. Hartman refuses to believe that Dr. Parsi is an excellent surgeon; nonetheless, he has agreed for Dr. Parsi to participate in his wife's surgery. He listens to the call. To his utter dismay, Dr. Parsi is calling him from the OR. Holding the phone tightly, Dr. Hartman says, "Hold on." As he walks to the hall, Dr. Hartman ponders, "Now he dares to call me regarding my wife's situation instead of Dr. Ross!" and mumbles to himself. "That stupid fellow who should not have been accepted into this program is calling me. Of course, if it weren't for Dr. Parsi's good scores and letters of recommendation, he would not have been here at all. Yes, I would have convinced Dr. Ross to pass on Dr. Parsi's selection."

Outside the lecture hall, Dr. Hartman yells into the phone, "Get me, Dr. Ross."

"Sir, Dr. Ross is in another OR helping a resident," Dr. Parsi responds matter-of-factly. His forehead is bubbling with pearls of sweat. Ignoring Dr. Hartman's rage, Dr. Parsi continues, "Dr. Ross is trying to stop massive bleeding in OR 11. He's not available now,"

"Talk! Tell me quickly. What's going on?" he yells at Dr. Parsi.

"Please listen… It is important. It's about your wife." Finally, Dr. Parsi has Dr. Hartman's attention.

"Is she okay?" Dr. Hartman asks anxiously.

"She is fine. But we have canceled the surgery."

"What? Why! Get me Dr. Ross, now!"

"Sir! We have canceled the surgery," says Dr. Parsi. "Your wife is pregnant. Fifteen weeks. The baby is a boy."

The bombshell hits Dr. Hartman hard. "What?" he shouts. A cold sweat appears on his forehead. There is a pause. "What happened to the tumor?"

"There never was a tumor, sir!"

Dr. Hartman is flabbergasted. For the second or third time, he has hit a wall dealing with Dr. Parsi. He would love to dismiss Dr. Parsi's call, but now he has grown curious about his wife's situation. "How is she doing?"

"She is shocked," Dr. Parsi says.

Dr. Hartman lets Dr. Parsi finish his report. Memories of his argument about the urine pregnancy test rush into his mind. Dr. Hartman says, "Well, good thing my wife took the urine test." And without saying goodbye, he ends the call and returns to the lecture hall.

He is quiet but looks dejected. Ambivalent about the situation with his wife, embarrassed about the dispute regarding the pregnancy test, he prepares himself to face Esther in the recovery holding area. He decides to complete his lecture as quickly as possible. The remainder of the lecture goes on without further confrontations. Dr. Hartman looks at the nervous student who has packed his knapsack and is about to leave the amphitheater. Afraid of Dr. Hartman's pestering and anticipating another furious outburst, the student is hurrying up the stairs aiming for the exit door on the top of the hall.

"Please stay in the class," Dr. Hartman tells the student. There is a sigh of relief as Dr. Hartman turns his face away from the class and moves on with the remainder of the slide presentation. The next slide shows an ovarian cyst deflated, flat on a green cloth in the OR. The following slide shows the histology view of the tissue: "This tumor is called serous cystadenoma," Dr. Hartman says. "It's a benign cyst." He goes on to explain the breast biopsy.

"The breast tumor is a non-invasive ductal carcinoma in-situ. The ovarian cyst is an incidental finding in this 42-year-old woman with stage zero breast cancer." He calmly continues, "Remember something imperative. When you're evaluating a pelvic mass in a woman in her early forties, always rule out pregnancy." The students are surprised. Some are writing notes, and others absorb Dr. Hartman's words. "This breast lump is not considered invasive cancer, but it's treated as such," Dr. Hartman says. "She will have radiation therapy to prevent local recurrence of the tumor. No chemotherapy. No more surgery. No sentinel lymph node dissection."

Dr. Hartman ends his lecture, picks up his laser pointer, and leaves the room. The students mutter to each other. "Is he all right?" one student murmurs. "What a change in his demeanor." Another student says, "He must have received some unexpected news about his wife's surgery."

"I just hope she's okay," the female student says.

———————————

In OR 13, Dr. Ross is supervising chief resident Linda Baldwin with the surgical staging of a patient with ovarian cancer. Dr. Parsi walks from the OR 3 through a wide U-shaped corridor, which is crowded with stretchers, anesthesia machines, and empty tray carts. They are lined up against the wall on the opposite side from the swinging OR doors. He joins the team in OR 13.

"Thanks for checking on us. You're on time, Dr. Parsi," Dr. Ross says. "Go ahead and scrub. I need to leave for a meeting."

Dr. Baldwin looks up and nods at Dr. Parsi. She is about to free the sizeable ovarian mass from its attachments to the intestines when Dr. Parsi joins her. They complete the dissection of the tumor without rupturing it. Dr. Baldwin places the tumor on the tray and returns to the surgical table. The specimen is handed over to the pathology resident, who sets the tumor in a bowl and takes it to his department. "Call us as soon as you can, please," Dr. Baldwin says.

They remove the other ovary, uterus, and most of the omentum. Dr. Baldwin carefully uses the laser beam and stops the bleeding from the dissected surfaces. Dr. Parsi is impressed with Dr. Baldwin's precision in employing the laser beam. "Great job, my friend," Dr. Parsi says.

"Thanks," Dr. Baldwin replies.

No transfusion is needed for this patient. Dr. Parsi pulls off his gloves and gown, taps Dr. Baldwin on the shoulder, and walks out of the OR. The double door of the OR swings open, and one of them hits his left shoulder, provoking a sharp pain in the shoulder he injured six months ago. Dr. Baldwin notices his wincing reaction, "Be careful, my dear. We need your hands." A third-year resident takes Dr. Parsi's position, and together with Dr. Baldwin, they complete the surgery.

As Dr. Parsi leaves OR 13, he says, "See y'all this afternoon at the grand-round."

"Thanks again for dropping by," Dr. Baldwin replies. "See you on Saturday for biking."

"I hope I'm ready by then."

The scenic bicycle ride on the gravel road along a broad valley outside Willow City northeast of San Antonio ends abruptly that day in a field of bluebonnets. In spring, the bluebonnets cover every inch of the valley. From the narrow gravel road, the whole valley appears blue like a sea. Dr. Parsi and Dr. Baldwin are riding on their bikes on the hilly road, enjoying the breeze and the view of the valley. They are mesmerized by the April wildflowers. Failing to see a rock on the narrow road, Dr. Parsi hits the rock and tumbles down the slope, his shoulder landing on a rocky flat covered by a patch of bluebonnets. Dr. Baldwin, who is following him, stops and helps him get up on his feet. Dr. Parsi brushes off his clothes. They sit next to each other on a flat rock. They catch their breath and assess the injury. Dr. Baldwin pulls off Dr. Parsi's blue-stained shirt and exposes his bruised shoulder. "It's a bruise, not bleeding," Dr. Baldwin says. "Can you move your arm?"

Dr. Parsi feels pain as he moves his arm. "Lucky me," Dr. Parsi says. "It's not serious."

Dr. Baldwin gently places her arm around Dr. Parsi's neck and touches the shoulder. "Is it broken?" she asks.

"I don't think so. It's only sore," Dr. Parsi replies.

"My God, you're bleeding from your forehead!" Dr. Baldwin says. "How did you get that cut on your forehead?" Dr. Baldwin asks.

"It's an old one. Happened last week when Dr. Hartman came to the OR to talk to Dr. Ross about his wife's canceled surgery."

"Did he hit you?" Dr. Baldwin says.

"He was furious about something and pushed me aside to reach his wife's stretcher. My head hit the corner of a locker," Dr. Parsi says.

"Why did you keep it secret?" Dr. Baldwin says. "You should have reported it to the Dean."

"It wasn't his fault. He didn't mean to hurt me," Dr. Parsi says. "He was pushing me aside to get to the OR nurse and talk to Dr. Ross and visit his wife."

"It was his fault. That guy is crazy," Dr. Baldwin says.

She takes her handkerchief and presses it on the oozing cut for a few minutes. When she takes it off and does not see any bleeding, she pulls a large Band-Aid from her backpack and places it over the cut.

Dr. Parsi looks at Dr. Baldwin's white face gleaming under the Texas sun, and touches her cheek and whispers, "Thanks."

"It all will work out okay," Dr. Baldwin says.

Dr. Parsi gently squeezes Dr. Baldwin's hand. Dr. Baldwin welcomes his touch and moves a bit closer to him. She gently pushes her arm against his and touches his neck and chin. Their eyes meet. The fragrant breeze has dried their sweaty faces. He turns his face toward Dr. Baldwin's and comes closer, and for the first time, touches her lips. Dr. Baldwin smiles. Dr. Parsi kisses Dr. Baldwin's lips, which taste and smell like wild petunias. He wants to say, "I love you, Linda," but doesn't muster the courage.

Dr. Baldwin nods as if she has read his mind. She whispers, "I always liked you, Bahman." She wants to say, "I'm crazy about you." But she only smiles. They both look elated, happy, and for the first time in their friendship, they love each other's closeness.

"You are beautiful, Linda," Dr. Parsi says. He has momentarily forgotten the forehead cut and the shoulder injury, but when he tries to embrace Dr. Baldwin, the sharp pain jolts him. He ignores the pain and says, "Linda, let's have dinner tonight."

"Are you going to be okay?"

"Of course. I'll take two tablets of Tylenol, a hot shower, and will be ready for a nice dinner with you." Dr. Parsi knows that the shoulder pain flashes when the slightest hint triggers it but subsides soon when he takes analgesics. And he is not worried about the forehead cut.

Dr. Parsi moves away from OR 13, passes the stretchers, and avoids hitting the anesthesia machine next to OR 5. The door is shut. The room is dark except for the panoramic lights hanging from the ceiling that brighten the operating table, a square area surrounded by four surgeons. They are quietly doing an advanced microsurgery procedure that a patient urgently needs. The lights in OR 3 are dim. The crew and technicians are cleaning the room and packing up the surgical instruments. They have created a pile of soiled disposable gowns, towels, drapes, and wrapping papers in the corner. They all wear masks, light blue surgical gowns, and beige gloves, and they will pack them into the red industrial bio-bags and cart them out before they wipe the floor. The bags will be added to the mountain of daily bio-waste on the loading platform at the rear of the central hospital building. By evening, there will be enough to fill two garbage trucks from Waste Management Company.

Today, in OR 7, Dr. Baldwin is leading a team doing an endoscopic Burch procedure for urinary stress incontinence. She is the most accomplished surgeon at the University Hospital for this procedure, and most residents and junior faculty have renamed the operation the "Baldwin procedure." Dr. Parsi, who is helping Dr. Baldwin, coughs incessantly and feels his groin bulging against the belt. He suppresses a sigh from the nagging pain of his hernia and moves on with the work. After the surgery, he walks to another room where a surgical team is doing an endoscopic hernia operation. Dr. Parsi peeks inside and greets the chief resident of surgery.

"How are you doing, Dr. Parsi?" the chief resident asks.

"I'm all right," Dr. Parsi says. "The bulge is only on one side and doesn't cause me any severe pain so far."

"Lucky you," the chief resident says. "You probably have two or three more years to go before needing our help."

"I have observed it for several years now; it hasn't changed any since last year. So, I'll wait," Dr. Parsi says.

"Don't delay it too long: it may rupture," the chief resident says.

Dr. Parsi has selected the same conservative approach for his shoulder injury after the accident along the narrow creek. That day, biking along with Dr. Baldwin, the gorge was covered with a layer of bluebonnets, like a mist covering a bay on a summer morning. He again remembers the first kiss, the sweetness of embracing Dr. Baldwin. Dr. Parsi recalls the poem he wrote about the gorge and whispers the first stanza:

Near Willow City lies a deep valley
Surrounded by spring-green hills
Rock and thick honey mesquites.
A sea of bluebonnets hides the rocky soil.
The fragrant breeze soothes your soul.

Dr. Parsi has read an article about balneology in *The Study and Popularity of Balneology in Europe,* and one about the value of bath therapy in conjunction with physical and massage manipulations for back and neck injuries. He is now advised by Dr. Brook, the chief of the Orthopedics Department at the University Hospital, to consider the same approach.

"How does it work?" Dr. Parsi asks.

"I don't know," Dr. Brook shrugs. "I'm an oenophile, not a balneologist. But it works." He laughs. He loves to use archaic words. "So does drinking a glass of wine after a session of hydrotherapy!"

"Would a glass of Shiraz wine help, too?" Dr. Parsi jokes. He remembers the vintage collection of red wine that his uncle kept in the basement when Dr. Parsi was living at his house while he studied at Tehran Medical School. His uncle would open a bottle for them when they played chess. The uncle was a good chess player. His favorite place to play chess was a small niche between the wine racks in the basement. Hearty red Persian wine from Shiraz, a game of chess, and cracking unsalted pistachios were his uncle's weekend entertainment on Friday afternoons.

For his chronic lower back and neck spasms, Dr. Parsi has used heat and physical therapy, and now he is doing the same for his shoulder injury. So far, he has avoided taking strong pain medications. Dr. Parsi always tells the residents that for most joint injuries, a combination of three modalities—physical therapy, warm baths, and non-narcotic anti-inflammatory drugs such as naproxen sodium—is better than draining a drought of opiates or undergoing hasty surgery.

33

VIII
In the Operating Room

A resident and an orderly are pushing the stretcher into OR 8. The ashen right leg of a patient lies above the sheet, but the rest of the body is covered, except for his face that anxiously looks at the resident as if he were pleading for reincarnation. He is alert despite a hefty dose of sedatives. He tries unsuccessfully to look down at his right leg. He knows he will not see the leg when he wakes up from the anesthesia. The stretcher is narrow for the patient's massive body, his face pale, his lips cracked. He is receiving insulin drips as he's taken for surgery. The stretcher enters the OR and leaves the corridor vacant.

Dr. Parsi is free to move on. Someone taps his injured shoulder. He twitches with shooting pain, but the pain dissipates quickly. "What's up, buddy?" a senior resident asks. Dr. Parsi knows he will question him about his encounter with Dr. Hartman. "I see you endured another rampage by Dr. Hartman."

"I'm safe. It was an easy one this time." Dr. Parsi has survived much rougher moments with Dr. Hartman.

"That's why I've been following you. I want to hear the whole story."

"Not now. I just finished one case with a third-year resident performing a hysterectomy and removal of the ovaries. Now I am going to talk to Dr. Ross."

"A drink, afterward? How about five, in the Piano Bar?"

"No, I'm meeting an acquaintance for dinner. Let's get together tomorrow after work," Dr. Parsi says.

"I'll be there."

"Let's have Dr. Baldwin there, too," Dr. Parsi says.

The senior resident enters OR 9. They are waiting for Dr. Parsi, who rushes into the scrub area and disappears behind the glass panel. In front of OR 10, Dr. Josh Childress, Dr. Parsi's co-author for their Small Business Innovation Research (SBIR) application to the NIH, stops Dr. Parsi and says, "What's the rush?"

"Sorry, bud. No news."

Dr. Parsi has received no response from the NIH. They mailed out the grant application over three months ago, and they were supposed to hear from the Grant Management Office after a few weeks. "In our case, no news is bad news," the friend says.

"I agree. I don't think we'll get it. You know, the study uses fetal tissue, and nowadays, the NIH people are very cautious about accepting any grant that involves fetal tissue. Dead or not." Dr. Parsi clears his throat and says, "I'll let you know as soon as I hear anything."

34

"That's a shame. My bonus depends on it."

"Mine, too. So, don't count on a bonus this quarter."

"What a bummer! That will disappoint my son and my wife, too," Dr. Childress says. "No bicycle for him, no trip to Europe for her this summer, and no new golf clubs for me."

"I'm sorry."

"You should have included Dr. Hartman as one of the co-investigators."

"He declined to get involved," Dr. Parsi says. "Dr. Hartman said his plate was quite full."

"That's too bad. Dr. Hartman is an excellent editor and knows how to write grants," Dr. Childress says.

"He wouldn't even look at it," Dr. Parsi says, shrugging.

Dr. Parsi enters OR 11, where Dr. Ross is repairing the transected right ureter, another accidental mishap by a second-year resident during a hysterectomy for endometriosis. "Come and look here. The chocolate-colored cyst had gone around the ureter at the rim of the pelvis," Dr. Ross says. "The cyst is out, and a stent has been placed through the bladder into the ureter up to the kidney."

The last few sutures approximate the edges of the transected ureter and conceal the stint completely. Dr. Ross turns to Dr. Parsi, "I had a conversation with Dr. Hartman this morning before he left for his lecture. He was complimenting your courage to order the pregnancy test."

"Wow, that's the first positive comment I have ever heard from him," Dr. Parsi says.

"But Dr. Hartman quickly reverted to his nature and patronized a colleague," Dr. Ross says. "He asked me whether that colleague will use Esther's initial misdiagnosis against him."

Dr. Parsi says, "I don't think so. That colleague is a gentleman. He wouldn't even discuss the matter."

Dr. Ross continues, "He advised me that when teaching about the evaluation of any pelvic mass in women of reproductive age, a cheap pregnancy test may shed some light on the issue." They both laughed.

"I'm pleased, Dr. Ross," Dr. Parsi says.

"Then, Dr. Hartman lectured me about the significance of clinical medicine. He said that surgeons are falsely over-confident; they believe they can cure everything with the knife. He also said that some ignorant surgeons are as dangerous as those fanatic mullahs in your country, or suicide bombers in the streets of Baghdad and Kabul. Terrorists kill to gain publicity or power, but surgeons harm people quietly, without remorse." Dr. Ross continues, "He has no respect for the hard work we are doing. How Dr. Hartman clings to his old views reminds me of those monkeys that hang by their tails from dead limbs." The residents who are present are quietly enjoying the conversation.

Dr. Ross continues, "Well, usually Dr. Hartman recovers from a setback and goes on ranting again. It's no use for us to argue with him."

"Come on," Dr. Parsi interrupts Dr. Ross. "He's a great scientist. He rarely gets rejected when he applies for medical grants."

"Let me tell you this, Dr. Parsi. This time he looks embarrassed. This one will strengthen your position in the department. Don't give him an excuse to come after you."

"I never do," Dr. Parsi says. "But I will continue to do my job as I'm supposed to."

"When you discuss medical issues at the ground rounds or conferences, or with him, be accurate but polite," Dr. Ross says to him. "Be sure you have reliable references to back up your statements."

IX
Esther Faces the Unexpected Pregnancy

Remembering the difficulties that she has overcome to become pregnant, Esther takes the news of her pregnancy with utter disbelief. She thinks about challenges dealing with Saul, especially the hard times they are experiencing in managing him, the tormenting therapy sessions with Saul that produce bitter feelings. Although Esther is relieved that she doesn't have ovarian cancer, she is now facing an unexpected dilemma. Her husband is also ambivalent about her pregnancy.

While Esther is in the hospital, absorbing the news of the pregnancy, she undergoes mammography, and this time the films are labeled accurately. They are read by the radiologist as normal without any suspicious calcifications.

The shock of an unexpected pregnancy, in addition to Saul's perpetual problems, worries both Dr. Hartman and Esther to the point that he arranges a therapy session shortly after she arrives home. Now in the session, they are sharing their frustration with the psychologist and each other, too.

"It's all because of his bad friends," Esther says. "The one with the red Camaro. He comes every evening and takes him for a ride," Esther says, "Otherwise, Saul is a good boy."

Dr. Hartman says, "I agree. When Saul leaves the house, he's okay, but when he returns home, he's different. Belligerent and filthy."

Esther repeats her thoughts, "Otherwise, Saul is okay." Her face shows her deep frustration, "Do you remember? He was such a lovely boy." Esther pulls out a handkerchief and wipes the tears.

"I'll stop that shadowy character who claims to be Saul's friend," Dr. Hartman vows.

"No, please. Don't. That boy is dangerous. Saul told me he keeps a handgun in the glove compartment of his car."

Saul has not said a word for almost the entire session. The therapist says, "Saul, maybe you should think about your friendship with this guy. Maybe he is not a good friend for you."

Both Dr. Harman and Esther nod in agreement.

The therapist says, "What's his name, Saul?"

"I don't know."

"What? You don't know?" Dr. Hartman yells.

Saul grudgingly says, "Marcel."

"Don't be involved with that boy anymore, my son," Esther begs. Saul does not respond.

"What's the problem?" Dr. Hartman asks Saul. "Why can't you simply avoid him?"

When the therapist presses the same suggestion, Saul jumps up and screams, "I don't know." Saul then abruptly leaves the session.

It is after office hours, and the staff has gone home already when Dr. Hartman stops at his office. He pulls out his keys and unlocks the door. He sees a large yellow envelope clipped to the pocket of his office door. As Dr. Hartman raises his arm, he feels a sharp twitching pain in his breast, radiating through his arm and hand, limiting his motion, preventing him from reaching high enough to pull out the envelope. He uses his left hand to pick up the large packet and goes into the office.

The urine test and the sonography films are in the packet, too. He looks at the films and sees the echoes of Esther's pregnancy, an innocent creature with male chromosomes, mute, flat like papyrus. His ambivalent feelings toward the pregnancy overwhelm any excitement the picture could have produced. Dr. Hartman ponders the fetus's genes. "Some are from Esther and some from me." He hopes that the fetus carries Esther's gentle demeanor, but also his scientific mind. Then he ruminates about Saul. He surmises that Saul's character is more like him than Esther. "Okay, the genes are important markers, but the upbringing is also relevant," he muses. "But with Saul, we have a clear case of peer pressure. All his worthless friends are influencing him. Otherwise, he would have been a star pupil at school. Yes, he would have been the smartest one like me, the envy of other students, most popular among the teachers. But what about this new creature?" He worries that it may have the worst of both worlds. Fewer of Esther's sweet genes, more of his restless soul. "Hell, he may carry nothing but defective genes!"

Occasionally, Dr. Hartman regrets his angry outbursts. "I hope he doesn't carry the anger gene," he murmurs. Dr. Hartman walks out of his office and down the long corridor. He sees Dr. Parsi walking, too, but in the opposite direction. Dr. Parsi nods and passes him without uttering a word. Looking at Dr. Parsi as he is walking away, Dr. Hartman contemplates, "Esther is right: he does walk like Saul." He notices that Dr. Parsi touches his aching right shoulder. "Just like Saul after the motorcycle accident when he tore his right rotator cuff," Dr. Hartman thinks. "Well, Saul did much worse. A low pain threshold. The surgery and the three months of physical therapy. And all those analgesics and narcotics. He was consuming Oxycodone every two hours. Could they have caused Saul's problems today?" Then he continues with his train of thoughts, "Could all of Saul's problems have happened because of that guy with the red Camaro? That no-good friend, Marcel. Yes, it is all due to peer pressure. Bad friend, bad neighborhood." He turns around and watches Dr. Parsi, who is now reaching the end of the corridor. "Yes, he does walk like Saul," he reflects again. He wants to call Dr. Parsi and ask him to come to his office for a talk, but about what? About the injury to the forehead, about ordering the pregnancy test, for considering the possibility of pregnancy? Instead, he turns and goes back to the office, to the stack of papers on his desk. There in the office, Dr. Hartman thinks about the pregnancy again. "It's a pleasant surprise," he mumbles, smiling. He hopes the fetus gets more genes from Esther. "Why am I so rough with Saul and with Dr. Parsi?" He finds no answer to the question. Then he whispers, "Poor Dr. Parsi! I never apologized to him for the accident in the OR."

Considering Saul's lack of progress at school, Esther asks her husband, "I hate to give up hope on Saul, but something tragic is bound to happen one of these days. Why don't we sell the house and move to a gated community?" Esther has mentioned this option several times before.

"Look, Saul will have that Marcel over to the new house in no time." Dr. Hartman waves off her suggestion. He continues, "Besides, we lose weeks, if not months, of our precious time with packing, unpacking and rearranging the house. And what about all the money we are going to lose: the real estate fees and capital gains taxes." Suddenly, an idea flashes in his mind. "If only Esther would agree to have a handgun in the house in case of an emergency. It will be useful to scare Marcel."

Esther is adamantly against having any gun in the house. "I don't want to have another worry," she says repeatedly. "What if Saul discovers the gun? It would be a shootout in front of our house between those kids."

Dr. Hartman tries to alleviate Esther's concerns. "I'll hide it somewhere. It'll be there only to scare Marcel. A warning. That's all. Maybe that will give Saul some confidence to resist that nasty Marcel and remove his ambiguity about the direction of his life. I'll hide it in the wine cellar with the bottles." Knowing that Esther likes only white wine, Dr. Hartman promises, "I'll hide it behind the row of red Napa wines." Then he remembers the collection of Shiraz wine. "The hell with those, I'll hide the handgun behind my favorite ones, the red Bordeaux wines from the Saint Emilion. They are now each worth more than $300."

The first encounter between Saul and Marcel happens on New Year's Eve when Marcel invites a group of classmates from the high school to a party at his house. His parents have taken a short vacation to celebrate the holidays with Marcel's paternal grandfather, who is struggling with terminal lung cancer. Marcel's father, a successful accountant and the local senior partner in a national accounting firm that manages the accounts of numerous large companies, rarely spends any time with his son. He travels around the country and abroad to audit the books of his clients, often accompanied by his wife. Their bizarre schedule frequently leaves Marcel alone in the house in the care of relatives or a housekeeper. To keep his son busy on weekends and as a present for his seventeenth birthday, Marcel's father buys him a used red Chevrolet Camaro, with only around 10,000 miles on it, with the proviso that Marcel pay for insurance and the maintenance expenses of the car. His father figures out that to cover his car expenses, Marcel will be forced to work every weekend and consequently avoid wasting his time with bad friends. However, Marcel finds out very quickly that even working every weekend at the nearby fast-food restaurant does not cover even half of his car expenses. But he loves his fancy car, and the way girls look at him when he cruises down the road. Soon he finds a way to maintain his expensive toy.

In Marcel's house, the party is in full swing. Several six-packs of beer, bowls of popcorn, and two large pizzas sit on the dining room table. More than a dozen high school boys and girls enjoy the loud rock music blaring throughout the house. Saul leans back in his lounge chair, sipping his beer and watching some classmates dance. Marcel circles the room, encouraging his guests to have fun, and finally turns to Saul and says, "Why are you so quiet? Come on, don't be chicken! Join the action!"

Saul waves him off. "Thanks, I'm okay." It is the first time the two have connected.

"Bud, I'm Marcel, this is my house," Marcel says. "Follow me, kid, you need something to cheer you up." Saul follows him to the kitchen where Marcel lights up a joint, inhales deeply and directly into his lungs, pauses, and exhales right into Saul's face. Saul inhales the air while observing Marcel and smiles. "Here, have some," Marcel says.

Saul does not hesitate. He takes the joint, inhales deeply, and holds his breath awhile.

"Wow, I'm impressed," Marcel says. "Now that you're in good shape, I'll leave you alone and join the crowd. But, you stay here and finish the joint."

Saul nods and smiles widely. He knows this is a place where he can relax.

––––––––––

When Marcel's parents return after a few days, all traces of the party have been thoroughly removed by the housekeeper. Two weekends later, Marcel's parents are off again. Saul visits Marcel and stays with him until after midnight. After a few beers and two joints, Marcel shows Saul a small packet of white powder. "This is great stuff. Do you want to try it?"

Saul, who already has a buzz from beer and weed, hesitates and says, "I'm fine right now."

He accepts two joints from Marcel and returns home. The next time Marcel's parents are away, Saul spends the night. This time he tries the powder and feels a sense of euphoria. "Wow, this is awesome." But in the morning, when Marcel tells him how much Saul owes him for the joints he smoked and cocaine he snorted, Saul is shocked. "Don't worry, do what I'm doing," Marcel tells Saul. "Join the club."

X
Dr. Parsi's Home

Dr. Parsi comes home from work shortly after six and drops his briefcase and his white jacket on the desk in the corner of the bedroom. The first thing he does is check his land-phone for messages. The first message is from Jasmine Sohrabi, a Persian-Jewish student who is scheduled to meet him for dinner at a nearby restaurant. She informs Dr. Parsi that she will be late. "Good, that means more time to get organized."

Dr. Parsi goes through the rest of the messages and, as usual, deletes most of them. He turns the radio on and removes his clothes to take a shower. He puts on a casual outfit, slips on sandals, and returns to the living room. If Dr. Parsi did not have an appointment at the restaurant, he would have gone biking in the park adjacent to the golf course. He usually rides on the paved trail for around ten miles. He bikes more on the weekends, 15 or 20 miles along the IH-10 access road, and the Scenic Loop, which is popular with cyclists because of the dedicated bicycle lanes. Some weekends there is a long chain of bicyclists in their tight and colorful outfits. He enjoys the long route into the Hill Country, through Fair Oaks Ranch, or on a calm day to Boerne.

He takes a sip of the cocktail and glances at the first page of the *Express-News*. The Spurs, the local NBA team, have won the final seventh game and are now preparing for the championship round. He glances at the headlines: "Gunman Murders Three People in Bar" — "Oil Prices Climbing to Record Levels" — "Texas Economy Surging because of High Oil Profits."

The student, Jasmine Sohrabi, who is meeting him at the restaurant soon, is a law school student at a local university. A recent immigrant from Iran, she shares a one-bedroom apartment near the university with another female student. Jasmine was practicing law in Tehran but decided to leave when the Revolutionary Guards kept harassing her with accusations that her law practice was focused on defending student activists. The Tehran Revolutionary Court had finally barred her from representing male clients and any student. During a visit with her brother in Vienna, Jasmine went to the U.S. Embassy, where she explained her situation and applied for a visa. Given the extensive media reports about the political situation in Iran and the harsh treatment she had received in Tehran, the U.S. Embassy issued her a visa to come to the United States.

Dr. Parsi has come across Jasmine a few times in the past several months at Persian holiday celebrations and found her story shocking and wanted to know more about it. When he arrives at the restaurant, Jasmine is already waiting. She wears a colorful silk scarf across her left shoulder. She accepts his offer of wine and chooses a glass of Shiraz.

"It feels good to be able to enjoy this simple pleasure. The mullahs always rail against the consumption of any alcoholic beverage, although Iranians have

41

a centuries-old tradition of enjoying beer, vodka, and red wine," Jasmine Sohrabi smiles. "Shiraz wine was always popular in Tehran."

The restaurant is owned by an Iranian expatriate and serves mostly Italian cuisine. "I like their lemon garlic shrimp pasta," Dr. Parsi says. "The food is fresh and the pasta, al dente."

She orders linguini with clam sauce and a small house salad.

Once they complete their meal, they talk about the news from Iran. Finding a willing audience, Jasmine talks incessantly. "The place has changed. Revolutionary Guard members are everywhere. The clergy exerts total control over the armed forces, the police, and the judicial system. But the real power lies within the Revolutionary Guard organization, which includes the hated Morality Police who enforce Sharia law and dress codes. Women must wear the government-prescribed hijab, a chador, a dark and long outfit to cover their hair, neck, knees, and legs, even in Tehran's hot summers."

They converse in English. Dr. Parsi mentions how often the first generation of immigrants to Western countries create animosity among locals when they seem not to want to assimilate because they try to preserve some of their old customs in their new home. Jasmine has visited the Persian community in Los Angeles, where almost half a million Iranian-American citizens live mostly in the conventional American way, except for some seasonal Persian celebrations. Their neighborhoods correspond to their socio-economic level, with a mix of Anglos and other well-to-do minorities. The women enjoy dressing California style, so women in strict hijab are a rare sight. Many Persian women also own businesses. At the same time, local shops, bookstores, TV channels, magazines, and Persian restaurants help them remember and celebrate their heritage.

Dr. Parsi is surprised by how fluent Jasmine's English is. "It was tough for me to acquire English proficiency," Dr. Parsi says. "When I was still in Iran, I took courses at the American-Iranian Cultural Center in Tehran to improve my English, and when I entered the US, I took more courses at local colleges."

The story of her learning English is similar except that Jasmine was raised in a Western-educated Jewish-Persian family in Tehran, all of whom were avid readers. "Yes, I'm Jewish-Iranian, and for us, education and speaking one or two foreign languages were essential."

"Will you ever return to Iran?" Jasmine asks Dr. Parsi.

"I'll visit my family, but I prefer to live here," Dr. Parsi says. "I don't want to live in a medieval society that the mullahs have created in Iran."

Jasmine says, "Don't you feel an obligation to return home and provide medical care for your people?"

Dr. Parsi laughs and says, "I'm not a Muslim actually, not religious either. I like this country very much. If I leave, I will miss reading *The New York Times* and listening to the Metropolitan Opera radio broadcasts."

"Well, Iran is not for me either," Jasmine says. "The mullahs have hijacked the 1979 Revolution and are having their fun with it."

She begins to tell Dr. Parsi what would happen when she travels to Iran. "As soon the plane crosses the Turkish-Iranian border and enters Iranian airspace, I must change my outfit, put on a dark scarf, and exchange my attire for a loose one that covers me from head to toe. And then remove all traces of lipstick and makeup, wash my face and hands to get rid of any perfume. It makes me feel like a medieval woman. The mullahs say all these requirements will free women from Western influence and transform them into real human beings rather than sex objects. However, I prefer the freedom of choice. I look better and feel better with some color on my face, especially in the morning when my puffy eyes, ruffled eyebrows, and disheveled hair look woefully ugly. I want to be in charge of these personal issues, in charge of my hair, lips, nails, and clothes."

After a while, Jasmine recalls her encounter with the Morality Police in Tehran: "Here I am, strolling on Pahlavi Street near Takht-e-Jamshid Boulevard in North Tehran when two armed Revolutionary Guards approach and order me to get into their jeep. Of course, I refuse. Who knows, they could be rapists who kidnap young girls and sexually assault them in their office. I remember the tale of a couple from my neighborhood who were arrested by the Revolutionary Guards in the same park where they were merely sitting on a bench, talking, and reading books. The young man was released a day later, but the body of the woman, a young doctor, was later delivered to her family. She had died in Evin prison after being tortured and raped."

"Naturally, I'm afraid I will suffer the same fate. They pull my arms back, grab my purse, and dump the contents on the sidewalk: a mirror, a lipstick and a small bottle of cologne, two photos of family members and one of my male law-school classmate, a small wallet with folded bills and some change, and my driver's license. With their unpolished boots, they stomp all over my stuff and yell, 'Get into the jeep, or we will drag you in!' I scream for help. Several bystanders are watching in fear, but one of them shouts, 'Leave her alone. Are you crazy or what?' More people surround us and holler. Two other Revolutionary Guards in an armored vehicle stop and join the melee. They roar at the bystanders, 'Be quiet, or all of you will be taken to the office.' One after another, the witnesses leave the scene."

"So, what happened then?" Dr. Parsi asks.

"After interrogation and a beating at the Revolutionary Guard Office, they let me go."

Jasmine is shaking now as she remembers the lashes, the insults as they were yelling at her, "You are a whore! Next time you will not be so lucky."

"Why then did they let you go?"

Jasmine replies, "I overheard one of them telling the others they had already reached their quota of arrests for the night."

"Lucky you," Dr. Parsi says.

"But I have horrible dreams almost every night," Jasmine says, her eyes full of tears.

"Would you consider therapy? I can arrange an appointment with one of the faculty members."

"Thanks. I'm already seeing a therapist at school. What about you and your relatives in Iran?" Jasmine asks. "Did the mullahs create any trouble for your family or fellow Zoroastrians?"

"Well, so far, the mullahs are avoiding us," Dr. Parsi says, "because we are popular among the Iranian intellectuals. The Zoroastrians in Iran confine their ritual and practices to the walled places to avoid any publicity. Instead of using the Tower of Silence for burial, they are now cremating their dead."

Dr. Parsi elaborates further, "Being at the crossroad of Asia and Europe, Persia has been besieged by various invaders. The most devastating conflict was the Arab invasion of Iran in the seventh century," Dr. Parsi says. "It was Islam against Zoroastrianism, fanatic Muslim fighters against Persian defenders." Now, motivated to tell the story of the fall of the Sassanid Empire," he continues.

"Against the valiant defensive struggle of Persian armies to guard their country against the repeated Arab invasions during several major battles from AD 633 to 642, the Persians eventually lost the critical battle of Nahavand in 642, which turned the outcome of the war in favor of the Arabs. Still, it took the invaders ten more years to completely squash the Persian resistance and conquer the entire country. By 651, most of the urban centers had come under the domination of the Arab troops. Many localities fought against the invaders; ultimately, none was successful. Although the Arabs had established hegemony over most of the country, many cities rose in rebellion by killing the Arab governors or attacking their garrisons. Eventually, military reinforcements defeated the insurgency and imposed strict Islamic control following years of costly resistance. Zoroastrian scriptures were burned, and many priests were executed, so tens of thousands of Zoroastrians fled Persia instead of converting to Islam and immigrated to India. The Persian Jews and Christians were also under duress.

"Historically, the Quran labels people who believe in single God *dhimmis*, the 'People of the Book,' e.g., Jews and Christians, as well as Sikhs, Zoroastrians, Hindus, and Buddhists. These people were nominally tolerated under Islamic law by a pact contracted between non-Muslims and authorities from their Muslim government, provided they paid tributes and taxes as Muslims did. Nevertheless, life became gradually unbearable for most of the non-Muslim people in the Islamic world.

"The Zoroastrians who were living in Persia during the Safavid Empire—which established Sharia law and officially became the first country to choose the denomination of Shia Islam—were given some rights, such as the right to practice their faith freely in private and to receive state protection. In turn, they had a legal responsibility to pay a special tax, the *jizya*. However, they were treated as second-class citizens and regularly faced discrimination and harassment by the religious authorities.

"The Quran details numerous tales of ancient prophets and categorizes them into major and minor categories. Mohammad, Ibrahim, Moses, and Jesus are the Major Prophets, delivering the holy books and considered the messengers of God. According to the Quran, there were over 120,000 Minor Prophets besides the primary four. Some of them are named in the text, like Daniel, who is buried in Susa, yet Adam, Noah, and many others who did not bring holy books have a special place in the court of God, according to the Quran."

At the end of his monologue, Dr. Parsi concludes, "Because of the harassment by newly designated Arab conquerors in Persia and their delegates, Zoroastrians fled and took refuge mostly in eastern India. These refugees were granted a haven in and around the city of Bombay under the condition that they did not marry outside their faith or proselytize Indians. In India, home to the majority of Zoroastrians, the community is declining by about 10% every ten years, according to a report released by UNESCO. Today, the declining Zoroastrian population in Iran remains tight-knit, forming secluded communities that strongly encourage marriage within the faith."

XI
A Message from the Dean

Upon arriving in the ward to start his early morning round, Dr. Parsi receives a message from the clerk. "It's from the Dean of the medical school," the clerk says. "I have had it since yesterday afternoon, but I couldn't find you earlier."

Eager to start the morning round, Dr. Parsi slips the message into his pocket and calls the nurse, three medical students, and the second-year resident to follow him to the surgical floor. Dr. Parsi leads the group into the first room and stops by the first bed. The patient is a thirty-three-year-old woman who had a miscarriage two days ago and was admitted to the hospital from the emergency room with sepsis. The senior medical student gives a short report, and the second-year resident reads her recent CBC and the Sed Rate, which is abnormally high. The IV line is running fluid containing a combination of antibiotics into the patient's blood system. The patient is alert and responds to their questions. She interrupts the senior medical student's report, looks at Dr. Parsi, and says, "Why am I not going home today? I haven't had any fever since yesterday. I'm eating and walking okay, too."

"We found an unexpected problem in your sonogram; there is a tumor in your right ovary," the second-year resident explains. "It's over four inches wide, so we need to examine it some more."

"I had no idea about this. Is it bad? Do I have cancer?" the patient asks.

The resident replies, "Well, most likely, it's a benign cyst, but we are not sure."

Dr. Parsi asks for her CA-125. "It's high," the resident says.

"Excuse me, what's CA-25?" the patient asks.

The student says, "It's CA-125, Miss."

Dr. Parsi explains to the patient that CA-125 is a tumor marker that goes up above the normal range when one develops a tumor or when one has an infection. "Considering you've just had an infected miscarriage, we cannot jump to any conclusion," Dr. Parsi says. "But because it's large, we need to rule out cancer."

"What's the chance that the cyst is cancer?" the patient asks. Dr. Parsi says, "It's probably not cancerous."

The second-year resident tells the patient that he will be back to talk to her about the options, "But first, the infection must be adequately treated."

The group moves to the next patient and then to the next. In the ward, three patients who had major surgery for benign tumors in the last several days are doing well. Two of them will go home that afternoon. A patient with cervical cancer who had radical surgery is losing blood from a drainage tube and struggling to maintain her kidney function. One patient with stage III endometrial cancer is ready for chemotherapy.

46

Esther's semi-private room is empty, though there will be two new admissions in that room later that day.

Dr. Parsi walks to the nursing desk to drop off a chart, but as soon as he sees the clerk, he remembers the message. He pulls out the slip of paper and reads, "Come to the Dean's office tomorrow morning before ten. He wants to talk to you for a few minutes."

Dr. Parsi remembers his morning schedule. After the round of patients, he has the pathology conference at eight for one hour. Then he needs to drive downtown to the university outpatient center there and see patients at the tumor clinic from ten o'clock on for the rest of the day.

He looks at his watch and decides to go to Dean's office after the pathology conference and before leaving for the clinic. He tells the senior resident who will also see patients at the tumor clinic to start without him. Dr. Parsi walks into his office, which is not far from Dr. Hartman's office, to pick up information regarding the patients that will be presented at the pathology conference. There is another note taped to the door. He collects the message. This one is from Dr. Hartman. He enters his office and turns on his computer. He does not want to guess why he has been called to Dr. Hartman's office. Could it be another ultimatum from Dr. Hartman that he could be fired soon? He brushes aside Dr. Hartman's issue and waits for the computer to boot and then turns on the virus protection program. He clicks on the Quick Clean and lets the firewall control and the spyware programs run their course. Then, he uses the Microsoft Disk Cleanup program to eliminate unnecessary files, and finally, he signs into the email server.

Dr. Parsi clicks on his inbox, looks at the incoming emails and sees there are more than eighty new messages. He sends eight of them into the spam folder, deletes thirty that have no subject line, forty without opening them, drags several into "Saved Mail," and begins to read the few that he believes are urgent. One is from the campus police regarding car thefts in the University parking lot number four, which is the least protected lot and located near the public bus station on the nearby road. There is one email from his brother in Vienna, two from his nieces in California, two forwarded emails from writer-friends regarding upcoming literary venues in town, and two from medical school classmates in Iran. He does not read any of them but looks at his watch. It is close to eight o'clock. He puts the computer into hibernate mode and leaves his office. He turns right and passes Dr. Hartman's office. A yellow announcement saying "Do Not Enter" is affixed to the door. He takes the elevator to the third floor and goes to the conference room in the Pathology Department. He is surprised to see who is not there; neither Dr. Hartman nor Dr. Ross is present.

Dr. Karam, a highly regarded Lebanese-American cytopathologist, asks him, "Where are your colleagues?"

Dr. Parsi doesn't have the slightest clue why they are not here. Dr. Ross had told him he'd be there to review two of the cancer patients. Dr. Hartman never misses this meeting unless he is out of town, giving a lecture.

"I don't know where they are." Dr. Parsi remembers Dr. Hartman's locked door and says, "Perhaps they are having a meeting right now."

The pathology conference goes on as planned. Two of the residents present the patients, and Dr. Karam shows the pathology slides. Dr. Parsi's presentation of the DCIS case mesmerizes Dr. Karam.

"This is a close call," he says. "If I didn't know anything about Esther's clinical history and the location of the lesion, I'd have asked for more samples."

Dr. Parsi continues with his mini-lecture about DCIS. "But it's not. It looks ominous, but it does not behave like invasive cancer. It has not metastasized anywhere, not even in the sentinel lymph nodes. For treatment, the literature suggests a lumpectomy, followed by limited local radiation therapy."

"I wish Dr. Hartman were here to argue with me as he regularly does. I hate to see him miss the meeting," Dr. Karam says. "Especially since he has such a keen interest in this kind of cancer."

Near the end of the meeting, Dr. Karam whispers in Dr. Parsi's ear, "I heard he gave you hell about his wife. Dr. Ross told me. He did not like the urine pregnancy test you ordered for Esther. Lucky you, you would have been crucified by now if the test had been negative."

"It's a routine test," Dr. Parsi says. "We do it for every patient of childbearing age with a pelvic mass."

After the conference, Dr. Karam inquires about Dr. Parsi's brother-in-law, Jamshid Hooshmand, "How is he doing in Tehran, the one with Multiple Myeloma?" he asks, "I enjoyed visiting him in your apartment when he stayed with you."

"Well, he's almost okay. His disease is in remission."

In reality, Dr. Parsi knows that his brother-in-law is not happy; candidly, he is miserable there. In Tehran, the smog and severe air pollution have caused poor health in many of his relatives. His mother is dying because of severe asthma, his older brother is also sick with multiple myeloma, and a classmate, now a pediatrician practicing in Tehran, suffers from deep depression and is contemplating suicide. His brother-in-law is glued to the BBC radio, hoping to hear a miracle, some news indicating the mullahs' downfall. He keeps drinking dubious quality whiskey and vodka, which he purchases on the black market sold by the neighborhood's Revolutionary Guards.

Dr. Parsi looks at Dr. Karam and says, "Honestly, he's not fine. Nothing is fine in Tehran these days."

XII
Esther's Urgent Call

In response to Esther's urgent call that morning, Dr. Hartman reluctantly drives home. There is a red Camaro with tinted windows parked on the road on the same side as his house farther down. Dr. Hartman parks his car in the garage and enters the living room. Esther is holding Saul's hand. Dr. Hartman looks at Saul's bruised face and asks his wife what is going on.

She says, "There is a guy out there chasing Saul."

Dr. Hartman turns to Saul and says, "Is it Marcel, who picks you up all the time?"

Saul does not respond.

"What does he want?" Dr. Hartman yells. Neither Esther nor Saul replies.

"For the family's sake, Saul, get rid of this boy!" Dr. Hartman shouts. He is getting angrier.

Esther begs Saul to listen to his father, "Please, Saul."

After a pause, Saul murmurs, "I can't."

"Look, I will go and talk to him," Dr. Hartman says. "No. Don't," Saul cries out. "Please, don't."

"What's going on, Saul?" Dr. Hartman says. Saul is struggling to open up and tell his parents why the boy is after him. Suddenly they hear the honking of the car outside. Dr. Hartman gets up and shouts, "Son, for God's sake, tell us what's going on!" When Saul keeps quiet, Dr. Hartman says, "Okay, I'll go out and get rid of Marcel."

Before Dr. Hartman can move out of the room, Saul pulls away from Esther, pushes Dr. Hartman aside, runs toward the front door, and hurriedly exits the house, leaving the front door agape. Dr. Hartman turns toward the door to follow him.

"Don't go out there, please," Esther begs Dr. Hartman. "Don't. It's dangerous!" Esther cries out. "There was a big commotion earlier in the driveway between those two guys."

"So why did you call me to come home?" Dr. Hartman says. The two parents stare at each other, bewildered.

"Please wait here," Esther begs. "Saul will handle him. He now knows we are here for him."

Through the open door, they can see the other boy leave his car, walk up the driveway, rush toward Saul, and grab his shirt. Esther and Dr. Hartman can barely see Saul's face. He is trying to free himself and only manages to screech, "Marcel, fuck off!"

Marcel pushes Saul against the garage wall and throws a few punches at him. Dr. Hartman rushes out of the house and stops a few paces short of the two teenagers. Looking at the intruder, Dr. Hartman shouts, "Hey, leave Saul alone. Get lost now!"

Marcel ignores Dr. Hartman, presses on Saul's neck, and yells, "You fucking bastard. You pay now, or you lose your fucking balls."

"What's going on, Saul?" Dr. Hartman asks.

Saul can hardly breathe. Dr. Hartman jumps into the brawl and pulls on Marcel's arm, trying to rescue Saul. Marcel, who is much stronger than his frame shows, kicks Dr. Hartman in the stomach. Dr. Hartman collapses to the ground. He looks up and sees that Marcel has put his hand in his pocket and is grasping an object, which to Dr. Hartman appears to be a handgun. Dr. Hartman is now afraid that Marcel will take out the gun to shoot and kill his son. Marcel screams, "Ten grand right now or you're dead meat!"

Dr. Hartman is shaken, but now livid, and he overcomes his fear with anger. Like a wounded creature, he gets up hurriedly, runs into the house, down to the basement, and retrieves his handgun from its hiding place in the cellar. He returns to the hall, holding the loaded handgun, and rushes toward the door. Esther is shocked at seeing the gun and tries unsuccessfully to stop him from going outside.

She begs her husband, "You're going to be killed. Please don't go out."

"He's killing Saul!" Dr. Hartman shouts. "I'm going to force him to leave."

Outside Marcel is shouting and hitting Saul in the chest. The pistol is still in his pocket. It's bulging, wobbling. Now, Marcel notices Dr. Hartman approaching him and waving a handgun at him. Marcel backs away a pace and shouts, "Your fucking son owes me ten grand. Pay me now, or your son is fuckin' dead meat."

"Leave now. Go away—otherwise, I'll call the cops," Dr. Hartman yells. "Do you hear? Get out!"

"I want the bags," Marcel shouts. "I want the money and the bags right now."

"What do you mean?" Dr. Hartman asks. "What is this all about? The money, the bags?"

Stunned, he stares at his son. Saul does not move a muscle in his face.

Marcel shouts angrily, "Don't you hear me? Get me the bags and the ten grand you owe me, now!" He now pulls out his handgun.

As Dr. Hartman rushes toward Marcel, Saul suddenly moves and grabs Marcel's hand. Marcel backs off quickly, aiming at Saul. When he sees Dr. Hartman raising his handgun, he quickly pivots, points the gun at Dr. Hartman's body, and fires. The bullet hits Dr. Hartman's leg. Dr. Hartman feels a sudden heat in his leg, and his body trembles, but he remains upright and aims his semi-automatic handgun towards Marcel's shoulder, pulls the trigger, and shoots once. When he sees Marcel has not fallen and is still brandishing his pistol, he pulls the trigger two more times. Marcel is hit, veers to the left, and falls. Saul is hit, too. Both Marcel and Saul are now on the ground. Dr. Hartman feels dizzy and cannot hold himself up, yet he keeps holding the handgun.

Esther, who has heard the shooting, rushes out and sees her husband on the ground, his leg covered in blood. The gun rests on the cement next to his right hand. Saul and the intruder are flat on the driveway near the garage door in pools of blood. She cries for help. The neighbor across the street who has heard the shots comes out and cautiously walks toward the scene, appraises the bloody sight, and dials 911 on his cell phone. Esther runs to Saul and sees blood oozing from Saul's right arm and his mouth. She is now screaming for help. Another neighbor walks up to the driveway and reaches Esther. After a few minutes, they hear the sirens of EMS ambulances from nearby fire stations approaching the house.

XIII
At the Dean's Office

Dr. Parsi arrives at the Dean's office oblivious to the impending catastrophe. He had left the Pathology Department, climbed to the fourth floor, and walked along the corridor to the Dean's office. Now he greets the secretary, "Here I am. Is he in?"

"Yes, he is expecting you," she says. "I'll buzz him and tell him you're here." He enters the office. "Good morning, sir."

"Sit down here, Dr. Parsi," the Dean says, "And please, call me Joe."

The Dean's amenable demeanor calms Dr. Parsi. "What can I do for you, Dean?" Dr. Parsi asks.

"I want to talk to you about your situation in the department. I am aware of Dr. Hartman's temperament and his prejudice against you, but he is the most valuable faculty member we have at this school. He carries a lot of weight around here, and you need to be careful of how you treat him. Just be polite and accurate in all your dealings with him." The Dean says, "You see, you have dealt a crushing blow to his pride, and I want you to be aware of that. Just avoid him for a few days unless he calls upon you directly to do something in the department."

Flustered, Dr. Parsi is taken aback. He says, "Okay. I'll do my best."

"As long as you do your work and get along with residents and students, I'll watch over you. But remember when it comes to taking sides between the two of you, I have no choice." The Dean shakes his head and murmurs, "It all boils down to the power of money, even at this university. This guy has brought over 30 million dollars of grants to the school."

"I'll do my best."

"He is our best grant writer, the busiest researcher. Don't forget, he's also our Deputy Dean."

At this moment, the secretary enters the office hurriedly. "Sir, there is an emergency, a call for you from Dr. Hartman's wife, Esther."

"Shall I leave the office?" Dr. Parsi asks the Dean. "No, stay, just sit quietly."

The Dean picks up the phone, and after saying "hello," he listens; his face becomes taut with concern and slowly turns red.

"My God. That is horrible." Then the Dean listens some more. "How is Dr. Hartman?" He turns his head towards the window and says, "Have they taken him to the University Hospital?" The Dean turns back and looks at Dr. Parsi. The Dean says, "Of course, we'll be in the emergency room. Okay, I'll call Surgery right now."

He ends the call and tells Dr. Parsi, "Let's go to the emergency room. There has been a shooting in front of Dr. Hartman's house. Three people, including Dr. Hartman and his son Saul, are severely wounded, though Esther says nobody was dead when the ambulances took them to the emergency room." He taps Dr. Parsi's shoulder. "Esther wants you to attend to Saul. Go! Leave Dr. Hartman's care to Dr. Ross and the other physicians." The Dean asks the secretary to alert the chiefs of emergency services and the surgery department and tell them Dr. Hartman is severely wounded. "Please page Dr. Ross and tell him to rush to the emergency room."

When the ambulances bring the three wounded men to the emergency room, Dr. Ross is waiting. The stretchers hurry the wounded to the triage area. The chiefs and several senior faculty members surround Dr. Hartman's prone body. Dr. Ross and the chair of the surgery department evaluate the wounds and notice a bloody gash in the right calf. The bullet has narrowly missed the tibia and the large vessels but has damaged the muscles and ruptured several small veins in the leg.

Dr. Ross pulls off Dr. Hartman's shirt, inserts an angio-catheter, and hooks up a liter of Ringer's Lactate solution. It is flowing in rapidly and maintaining Dr. Hartman's blood pressure. His leg wound is only oozing now. Dr. Ross quickly cleanses the wound and stops the bleeding by wrapping the calf with a pressure dressing. The situation is much gloomier for Saul, for he is unconscious and not responding to questions. He has been hit twice: One bullet has entered his chest, the other one hit and ran through his arm. He is bleeding from both wounds: one copiously in the chest, the other externally the arm. Dr. Parsi starts a central venous line and connects two more IVs with fluid running in from the IV stands. The doctors are calling the OR and ordering the operating room to be ready for emergency surgery. Dr. Parsi and a surgeon push Saul's stretcher to the elevator to take Saul to the OR. Marcel, the instigator of the shoot-out, has bullet wounds in his neck and chest. He is unconscious and seems paralyzed from the neck down. The emergency room physician detects no reflexes in any of the four limbs. Marcel is also bleeding internally. His blood pressure is hardly measurable, his rapid heartbeat weak. A surgery faculty member, his resident, and a neurosurgeon are taking him to the OR.

Meanwhile, Dr. Ross and the Emergency Department Chief are having an easier time with Dr. Hartman, who is in stable condition and conscious, but suffering from pain and restlessness. He receives injections of sedatives and pain medicine. There is now a drainage tube in the bullet wound under the dressing around his leg. The portable X-ray of his right leg shows neither fracture nor a bullet in the leg. It is now apparent that Dr. Hartman's wound is not life-threatening, and he will survive the shoot-out. He is even alert and promptly responding to questions from the Dean, "The guy was going to kill my son."

Meanwhile, Saul's situation remains critical. Dr. Parsi is in OR 7 to assist the surgeons in any way he can. They call for blood, any blood type will do, but they prefer AB positive. They have only two units of AB positive in the blood bank for Saul. They need more. Dr. Parsi volunteers to donate blood and runs to the laboratory for the required test to verify his type and cross-match. He then provides two units of his blood. The lab technician takes the blood units to OR 7 and comes back for more. Saul is still in a dire situation; he is in shock with very low blood pressure. They need more blood to keep Saul stable. They resort to giving Saul blood substitute solutions, while they place a call to the Red Cross Center for help. Despite the flow of fluids and ongoing blood transfusions, the surgeons have a difficult time raising Saul's blood pressure to take him out of shock. Suddenly, his blood pressure plunges to zero, and the monitor shows no heartbeat.

In the other OR, where the surgeons and residents are tending to Marcel, the situation is just as bad. Because of the excessive internal bleeding, Marcel suffers a cardiac arrest. Now the team is conducting resuscitation to keep Marcel alive.

The bleeding from Dr. Hartman's wound has stopped, and now the new dressing is clean. He is moving his toes and asking the Dean, "How's Saul?"

"Unfortunately, not so good," the Dean replies.

XIV
A Long Day for Dr. Parsi

After a long day, late in the evening before he leaves the department to go home, Dr. Parsi stops by his office and goes through his snail mail and the emails in his inbox. He deletes all the emails that are marked "Fwd" and drops those with "no subject" into the spam folder. He keeps several emails from his friends and relatives and reads an email from Jamshid, his closest friend during the long years in Tehran Medical School. He describes how he is keeping himself busy on weekends distilling vodka and beer and making wine from concentrated grape juice in the basement of his house. He writes that when they are short of grapes and other needed ingredients, they buy beer or whiskey at premium prices on the black market from the covert vendors who often appear on the streets late in the evening. Jamshid writes that he gets Heineken or Budweiser from one of his patients who happens to be a Revolutionary Guard. "The Revolutionary Guards carry on a sizeable clandestine business in trading forbidden beverages and share their proceeds with the local mullahs, who are supposed to be the eyes of the ayatollahs. Their goods are better than my vodka and beer, but because I can't always afford their prices, I still get concentrated grape juice to make my wine and vodka. I am not a bootlegger by any means, because I do not sell my stuff to anybody. Nobody would buy my alcoholic products because they are such low quality. As you may imagine, my beers are awful, bitter, and cloudy. But sometimes that's all I have to drink before I go to bed.

"I have a forbidden satellite dish, too, but it doesn't work anymore. Most of the channels are jammed, and the bribes to get a new satellite connection have become very costly. When the wi-fi is working, the internet is our only connection to the world. I love the BBC online news and always go right to the news clips in the Middle East section, hoping to find some positive news about my country. I like Wikipedia—it's free—and I enjoy the classical music pieces, even if the sound is full of static. Right now, they are letting us have an internet connection, but I don't know how long this will last.

"If you ever come here, which I'm totally against, definitely don't do it as long as the mullahs are still in power. Our streets are filled with the dark shapes of women covered in veils from head to toe or tented with large, dark scarves. The morality police keep checking women's compliance with all ordinances regarding proper *hijab*. But if you are brave enough to come here and survive the ordeal of immigration control, you still cannot go anywhere with any woman unless she is your wife or sister. Again, you need to carry verification documents. Women cannot go to any male sporting competitions, and neither are you permitted at any female sports events. The stadiums are only open to male customers. You can't play mixed doubles tennis. You cannot even go to the Caspian Sea beaches and swim with your sister because all beaches are now segregated by gender.

"I don't read newspapers anymore. They're only a venue for funeral and bankruptcy announcements. It's hard on all of us to bear the present living conditions in Iran. Sometimes I seriously consider ending my life, but when I remember what happened to our friend's children after he committed suicide and see the miserable life of his family, I change my mind.

"Another reason that I want to stay alive is to see the downfall of the mullahs. Don't laugh at me. I long to see that glorious day when the majority of this nation will finally regain their rights and freedom and rid our country of these imposters. Do I see the light at the end of the tunnel? No, not yet, but I'm a dreamer.

"Most of my Jewish relatives, colleagues, and friends have left Iran. I'm one of only a few Jewish physicians who still practice here. The main reason I'm staying here is that that I'm Iranian first, Jewish second, and I love my patients. There is a symbiotic relationship between them and me. Sometimes I question the wisdom of my ancestors who migrated to Western Iran when Cyrus the Great freed them from enslavement in Babylon. How could they prophesy the rise of Islamic militants in Iran! I understand some tests identify your ancestry through many generations. We don't have access to the service here, but if we did, I'd jump on it. Who knows, maybe I am related to Esther, the Queen of Persia. Perhaps I carry genes from both the Jewish queen and King Xerxes the Great.

"My friend, only these intoxicating images of a hopeful future are keeping me alive and making me tolerate today's poisonous smog in Tehran. I work, sleep, wake up the next day, check the news of the day on the web, and look for a sign that may indicate the coming of that day. I know you are amused by my reasons, but remember how many other societies have suffered similarly under forceful and tyrannical regimes for decades but finally saw their day of liberation. Yes, we are dreaming about seeing the light at the end of the tunnel. Yeah, we remember the fall of the Berlin Wall. The fall of the Soviet Union."

Amused, Dr. Parsi continues reading Jamshid's long letter, "Strange times like those in today's Iran are common throughout history. The Nazis, Stalinists, and Inquisitions in the Middle Ages wreaked similar havoc on their societies. Fanaticism and intolerance for other faiths and political aspirations have always produced disastrous social tragedies. Alas, Members of *Homo sapiens* are capable of committing the most horrific crimes against each other. In Florence in 1495, Savonarola, a mad fanatic monk, instructed his followers to go through the city and collect 'vanities' so that they could be burned. 'Vanities' included anything that the monk considered immoral, such as colorful clothing, books, musical instruments, and works of art. Similar to the mullahs' morality police in Iran, these 14th-century fanatics set fire to irreplaceable treasures. They repeated the 'Bonfire of the Vanities' every year until the pope intervened and officially excommunicated the mad monk and ordered people to stop. However, with the corrupt system, modern fanatics have succeeded in holding onto power and subjugating entire nations. Who knows when they are going to be dislodged from power?"

As images of bright Iranian women wrapped in hijabs and the bloody faces of protestors in the streets of Tehran are marching through Dr. Parsi's mind, his mobile phone rings. He looks at the caller ID and sees it is Esther who is calling. He clicks the call and hears Esther. She is sobbing. She mumbles, "Come and see me in the waiting room of the surgical floor."

XV
Dr. Hartman Survives the Shootout

There is only one survivor from the shooting on the driveway of Dr. Hartman's house. Despite the effort of the surgical team, resuscitation intervention, and flow of fluid and blood transfusions, Saul's condition deteriorates further in the OR. Resuscitation fails to bring his heart out of cardiac arrest. Saul's nemesis, Marcel, makes it to the surgical holding area but is declared dead just before he is to be transferred to the Surgical ICU. Dr. Hartman is stable and ready to be moved to the recovery room.

Esther is sitting in the surgical waiting room, still hoping for the best for her son, Saul. They take Dr. Hartman to the recovery room and invite Esther to join him. Dr. Hartman is alert, moving his eyes and looking at his wife. Esther touches his forehead and whispers, "I was so worried about you."

Dr. Hartman immediately asks, "How is Saul? Did he make it?"

"I don't know; he is still in the operating room." Esther wipes her tears and looks at Dr. Hartman's pale face. His eyes are now closed, and he breathes calmly. Esther is worried about Saul. Will he make it through the day? She wants to pray for him. She has not been to the synagogue in years, but she is wondering if a visit there and a contribution might help. She whispers, "God, please, save my Saul. I'll rejoin the synagogue. I'll donate."

She touches her abdomen and feels uneasy about the pregnancy, about the one who is growing inside her. She murmurs, "What will become of this one, another monster, or a healthy-minded son?" She remembers when Saul was growing up, how troublesome he was. From the onset, he would have wild mood swings. She could never manage him. He was always fighting with other children, would be late for school, bully other kids, and skip homework. He was often in trouble at home, always arguing. What will become of this one? Esther goes into deep thought. She contemplates a decision regarding the pregnancy, "At my age and with the dire situation we are in now, how could I carry this one to term and then take care of the new baby?"

After a while, and when Dr. Hartman is fully stable, the surgical team decides to transfer him to a regular room in the surgical ward. Esther follows Dr. Hartman's stretcher and waits in the hall until they move him to the hospital bed. Shortly thereafter, Dr. Parsi enters the hall and approaches Esther with a gloomy face. Esther is afraid to ask the question, but after a short pause, murmurs, "Is Saul okay?"

"I'm sorry, Esther," Dr. Parsi says. "I have no good news about Saul."

She mutters, "Don't tell me Saul is gone." After she hears the news of Saul's death, she weeps loudly. Still crying, Esther enters Dr. Hartman's room. Even though Dr. Hartman suspects that the shootout might have ended Saul's life, he asks Esther, "Why are you crying?"

As she weeps, Esther screams, "Saul is gone!"

Later that day in the hospital, sitting in a chair next to Dr. Hartman's bed, Esther touches her abdomen and feels disgusted with the pregnancy. "I can't go on with this," Esther tells Dr. Hartman, pointing to her bulging abdomen.

Dr. Hartman nods in agreement. "Well, it's your call," he says.

"I'll call Dr. Miller, okay?" Esther says. Dr. Paul Miller, the chief of the outpatient surgery, is a close friend.

"I support your decision," Dr. Hartman says. "It's a strange time in our life."

Shortly after that, Esther calls Dr. Miller and makes an appointment with him. She discusses the unexpected pregnancy and asks him to schedule a termination procedure as soon as possible.

The local newspapers get the information from the Daily Crime Report section on the Police Department website and send reporters to the scene of the accident and then to the University Hospital Emergency Room to cover the story. The next morning, the front page of the newspaper shows a large headline followed by the gory details: "Shooting Spree in Posh North Side Neighborhood." The second story is: "Dr. Hartman of University Hospital in Shootout with Drug Trafficker." The reports also shed some light on Saul's troubling days on the streets of San Antonio.

On the morning of the accident, Marcel, Saul's drug-dealing source, chases Saul with his red Camaro and stops him in front of the house. He wants to settle accounts with Saul, whom he accuses of selling packages of crack cocaine and holding back income from the sale. He hassles Saul for the money owed to him for nickel-rocks and dime-rocks he has sold at his usual street corner near the high school.

Dr. Hartman encounters the duo at the height of their argument when they are engaged in a fistfight. The three-way quarrel becomes physical and turns into a gun battle when Dr. Hartman brings a semi-automatic handgun out of his house to the scene of the brawl to intimidate Marcel. Dr. Hartman waves the pistol, and when Marcel doesn't take him seriously, he shoots at Marcel, resulting in a two-way shootout. The bullets hit all three individuals: Marcel and Saul fatally, and Dr. Hartman only in the leg. The doctor is in stable condition and the only survivor. The DA's office is trying to determine who shot whom and what bullet killed Saul. Did the bullet come from Marcel's or Dr. Hartman's gun?

XVI
Esther Terminates the Pregnancy

Esther sees Dr. Miller and discusses her decision to terminate the pregnancy. "It's almost a four-month pregnancy," Dr. Miller argues. "Are you sure you want to do this?"

Esther is adamant. "Dr. Miller, I can't go through this," she insists. "I'll take any poison to free myself of the burden."

"Why don't you wait a week?" Dr. Miller suggests.

Now Esther is sobbing. "I have thought about this since the shootout, ever since it was confirmed. It's as if there were still a tumor in my abdomen."

"You're shaken by the tragic events," Dr. Miller says. "Wait a few days. Let's have another talk."

"Dr. Miller, I'm sure. Please, schedule the termination." Esther says. "Esther, the fetus is a boy," Dr. Miller says.

Now, Esther cries hysterically. "I can't raise another Saul. If it is not done right away, I'll stab myself."

"Please, Esther. Calm down," Dr. Miller says, holding Esther's hand. "Okay, Esther. I'm sure you know that it's a bit risky to perform the procedure this late during pregnancy."

When Esther regains her composure, she says, "Dr. Miller, I want Dr. Parsi to do it. I trust him fully. He's an excellent surgeon."

Later that morning, Esther visits the Dean and thanks him for everything he did to save Saul's life. "I'm sorry about the whole episode," the Dean says. "Very sorry about losing Saul. My wife, Ruth, is trying to contact you. Please call her. She wants to be with you."

"It's not over for Jordan. We're going to face terrible times regarding this disaster," Esther says, referring to ongoing reports in the local media. "They are accusing my husband of instigating the shootout and blaming him for the death of Marcel."

The Dean comes and sits next to Esther and puts his hand on her shoulder. "We are standing by you two," the Dean says. "You two have suffered a great deal facing Saul's troubles," he says. "Did you know about his involvement with that drug dealer?"

"Not really. I had some inkling of what was going on, but never took my observations seriously," Esther says. "Jordan had no idea of Saul's issues, either."

"I'm sorry to tell you this, but you should have told Dr. Hartman about your suspicions."

"Stupid of me! I always thought Saul couldn't have gone that far into such a mess," Esther says. "That issue never surfaced during the endless therapy sessions involving Saul, either."

Esther shares her decision with the Dean about terminating her pregnancy. She says, "I'm going to care for my husband and worry about the consequences of the tragedy. I wouldn't be able to manage this unexpected pregnancy."

———————

Esther leaves the Dean's office and revisits Dr. Miller. Thoroughly convinced by Esther's determination, Dr. Miller promises to arrange the procedure promptly. He calls the OR, then locates Dr. Parsi and speaks with him while Esther is still in his office. "Dr. Parsi, Esther is here and wants to ask you a favor," Dr. Miller tells Dr. Parsi. "It is about her pregnancy."

"Okay, go ahead, please."

"Could you come here now?" Dr. Miller asks. "Esther is here, too."

When Dr. Parsi arrives at Miller's office, Esther looks at him and begins to sob. Dr. Miller is bewildered. Esther wipes her tears and stares out the window.

Dr. Miller tells Dr. Parsi of Esther's decision to terminate the pregnancy and mentions her request for him to do the procedure as soon as possible. Dr. Parsi is surprised and doesn't offer any comment. "Are you comfortable doing this?" Dr. Miller asks Dr. Parsi.

"I haven't done an abortion since my second year of residency," Dr. Parsi replies. "As you know, the residents always perform the procedures."

"We are all aware that it's an easy procedure," Dr. Miller says.

"Except for the 15 weeks pregnancy," Dr. Parsi says. "It carries some risks."

"Esther wants you to be the surgeon," Dr. Miller says. "She has complete trust in you."

Dr. Parsi pauses awhile. He looks at Esther and says, "You are facing a horrible tragedy. Are you sure about this?"

"I want to do it as soon as possible," Esther says firmly. "Today!"

Dr. Miller looks at Dr. Parsi and says, "I completely understand Esther's situation. She is the one who carries the burden."

"Well, it's a terrible moment in your life, Esther. I'm deeply sorry for you, my dear. You are making a crucial decision. Are you sure?" Dr. Parsi asks calmly.

"I am sure, Dr. Parsi," Esther says.

Dr. Miller tells Dr. Parsi that they have talked about the issue twice, and Esther's decision is final.

"In that case, okay. It's your choice, Esther, not mine or Dr. Miller's, or even your husband, Dr. Hartman's," Dr. Parsi says.

"Okay. Please, go ahead and schedule it," Esther says.

"Fine, I'll call you as soon as I schedule the procedure."

"Tomorrow morning is fine with me," Esther says. She rises and walks close to Dr. Parsi, and as tears flow from her eyes, she says, "May I hug you?"

She stretches her hand, catches Dr. Parsi's arm, and holds it gently. "Many thanks to you for doing this," Esther whispers.

XVII
The Night at the Hospital

Esther spends the night at University Hospital in Dr. Hartman's room. The next day in the early morning, she comes to the Emergency Room and undergoes a physical examination and another sonography by Dr. Parsi. She avoids looking at the sonography screen. The measurement of pregnancy shows that it's around 15 weeks gestation now. After the nurse gets the consent form signed by Esther, Dr. Parsi does a pelvic examination, inserts a speculum, wipes the cervix, applies a copious amount of anesthetic ointment to the cervix, and waits for more than ten minutes. Then he inserts a Laminaria into the cervical canal. Esther feels the manipulation of the speculum but no pain from the insertion of Laminaria. Dr. Parsi places tampons against the cervix to keep the Laminaria in place. After a while, she is helped by Ruth, the Dean's wife and her closest friend, to leave the examination table, and she goes back to the holding area of the outpatient surgery suite of the University Hospital. Ruth has been with her at every step, holding her hand, and assisting her in moving around.

After several hours, a nurse brings Esther to the procedure room. Ruth stays with her and holds her hand. Dr. Parsi starts an IV link in her right arm and injects a combination of sedative and analgesic through the IV tube. Esther is now well sedated, her eyes closed. She breaths smoothly. Ruth realizes that this is the first time after the tumultuous past week that Esther is relaxed and comfortable. Dr. Parsi sits on a stool, places a speculum in the vagina, and removes the Laminaria. He smoothly dilates the cervix to the number 15 Hegar dilator. He connects the flexible plastic tube coming from the suction machine to a sterile cannula and inserts it into the lower area of the uterine cavity. Using the vacuum, Dr. Parsi empties the contents of the uterine cavity, except for some pieces of the placenta that need to be removed by small clamps. The blood loss is minimal. Using a medium-sized blunt curette, he scrapes the last bits of tissues from the uterine cavity and concludes the procedure.

Esther is physically comfortable throughout the short process and does not feel any pain. After that, she remains in the recovery room for several hours. Leaving Esther in the nurse's care and Ruth's attendance, Dr. Parsi goes out and talks to Dr. Hartman in his hospital room. Surprised at how quickly the pregnancy was terminated, Dr. Hartman thanks Dr. Parsi for doing the procedure.

"Esther would have had a nervous breakdown if she had gone through with the pregnancy," Dr. Hartman says. "Thanks for doing this. Keep up your good work in the department, okay?"

Dr. Parsi is pleasantly surprised by Dr. Hartman's comment. He replies, "Of course. I'll do my best."

The next day Dr. Parsi gets a call from Dr. Karam, "I have a surprise for you. Come down, and I'll show it to you." Dr. Parsi walks down to the cytopathology section and finds Dr. Karam looking at the chromosome map of Esther's aborted fetus.

"Look at chromosome twenty-one. You see, there are three chromosomes here. The baby would have carried Down syndrome. I believe this finding should make you more comfortable about the abortion," Dr. Karam says.

"It doesn't," Dr. Parsi replies.

"Why not?" Dr. Karam asks.

"Because when I did it, I assumed the pregnancy was a normal one," Dr. Parsi says. "I did it to help Esther. Still, it was a difficult situation for me. And I'm sure it was as difficult or more for Esther, too."

"So it should make her comfortable," Dr. Karam says.

"I don't think so." Dr. Parsi says, "It would confirm her suspicion about what's wrong with her family. I'm positive this will make her feel terrible."

"I don't understand you," Dr. Karam says.

"Down syndrome would have been the least of her problems. Think about those few genes that you can identify and all the many millions that you cannot yet detect. The genes that bring paranoia, alcoholism, personality and bipolar disorders, and the tendency to fall for illicit drugs."

"You are talking like a geneticist. I'm only a cytopathologist," Dr. Karam says, "By the way, how is your brother-in-law, Dr. Parsi?"

"Please, don't change the subject."

"Okay, go on with your hypothesis," Dr. Karam says.

"We are all prisoners of our genes. We are mapped before we are born."

"Okay. Now can I ask how your brother-in-law is?" Dr. Karam asks.

"He sends his regards. He's coming to visit me in two months and with my sister."

"What for?"

"For a bone marrow transplant."

"Why?"

"As I have told you before, he has a bad case of multiple myeloma."

XVIII
Zoroastrians Consume Wine

"Zoroastrians drink good wine," Dr. Parsi says. One Zoroastrian, however, Mourad Hooshmand, Dr. Parsi's brother-in-law, who is visiting the U.S. for several weeks and loves to drink good Scotch whiskey, especially the kind he cannot find in Tehran's black market since the downfall of the Shah, says, "The mullahs should have studied the prohibition era in the United States." After another sip of Scotch whiskey, he says, "Okay, the Shah was a dictator, but at least we could sip excellent wine and even great single-malt whiskey, listen to good music, and go see real Western movies in the theaters with our women."

"But you didn't have freedom of the press and no democracy, only rigged elections," Dr. Parsi argues.

Hooshmand gets serious, "Come on, Bahman. These mullahs are worse than communists. At least in the Soviet Union, they had some great art, fantastic music, ballet, and good vodka. But with these mullahs, it's all glum, veiled women, dark beards of unkempt faces of Revolutionary Guards, and uncouth government employees." Hooshmand goes on and rants for a while. "The vodka from the black market is impure and contaminated with methyl alcohol. The whiskey is no better. The sellers somehow inject tea into the original bottles until it's half and half—half scotch and half tea. Ironically, the bootleggers who are selling these impure bottles for the price of the real thing are agents of the mullahs. They cheat everybody, even God. They lie to Him. Good wine is a rare commodity. I do not mess with what you can buy on the black market. My son claims he has an exquisite collection of homemade wine hidden in a concealed cellar, but I don't believe him. It's bound to be grape juice mixed with ethyl alcohol," Hooshmand says.

"Look, according to Zoroastrianism, consuming good wine is our religious duty. It facilitates happy feelings."

Hooshmand goes back to politics and berates the mullahs. "This year is one of the worst years for the intellectuals in Tehran since the revolution turned Islamic. Pick any year from 1979 until now; it does not matter which year, but this one is the bloodiest. We are in another season of mass killings in the streets of Tehran and executions in the prisons. Mobs of armed Hezbollah members roam the city streets by day and night, harassing women, secular gatherings, and independent newspapers. They break into the workplaces of the secular and liberal groups, disrupt their activities, and destroy their offices. Anytime a Hezbollah mob runs into trouble and is almost contained by protestors, they call the armed Revolutionary Guards to intervene on their behalf. Even the president of the country who claims to be a moderate is either powerless or one of their allies. He is not immune from the wrath of the hardline clergy. He has been accused of being too liberal and too lenient towards the enemies of

Islam. Every peaceful avenue for political dialogue between different political groups in Iran is forbidden. Violence and terror govern the political arena of Iran."

"How about other faiths, are they respected?" Dr. Parsi asks.

"They have persecuted over 300,000 Baha'is so far. Innocent people, they cannot serve in the military, be a government employee, or even practice law. Believers of other religions are also in serious trouble or fleeing Iran. Jews are going to Israel, and our fellow Zoroastrians are giving up too. The national parliament is filled with fanatic Revolutionary Guards. The libraries have been censured, and independent publications have been banned," Hooshmand says. "My nephew Babak was one of those anti-clergy activists. A member of the National Front, which was one of the pillars of the 1979 revolution, but now any government employee who is suspected of being a supporter of the National Front is fired. Babak wants to become a doctor, so he has turned his attention from politics to medicine and has become a hardworking and disciplined student. The Islamic government does not appreciate the disobedience of disenchanted students and is purging them from the universities and conducting nightly raids on their dormitories. Babak and hundreds of other liberals including writers, artists, and intellectuals, have either gone underground or fled the country.

"So far, the mullahs have spared our fellow Zoroastrians as long as we are compliant toward the regime, but many are leaving the country and settling elsewhere. In past centuries, India was a favorite destination because of the large community of Parsis in Bombay, but now Europe, Israel, and the United States have become the preferred destinations. For those who stay behind, like the remaining Persian Jews, life is burdensome. They must observe the Islamic government's rules."

Hooshmand continues with the monologue: "Amid frequent clashes between a few diehard anti-clergy groups, who still conduct quasi-military operations in Tehran and other major cities, minorities are well-advised to avoid being pulled into the melee. The mullahs will use anything to implicate the Jews and Zoroastrians in the uprising. During the political chaos, the mullahs harshly punish anybody who doesn't support them.

"A few years ago, one of these groups bombed one of the government buildings, while the officials and their aides were in session. They killed more than seventy high-ranking leaders of the Islamic Revolutionary government, including several ministers and a few Ayatollahs. The mullahs responded vehemently with ever more brutal force, looking for accomplices. They filled the prisons with members of opposition groups and killed a large number of them under torture. Some say over 800 in one week."

Hooshmand sips his Scotch whiskey, then says, "A mass execution usually follows a summary trial."

"What happened to Babak?" Dr. Parsi asks.

"It's been more than three months since we last saw or heard from Babak. He may still be hiding somewhere, but his parents believe he has been arrested and possibly executed in Evin prison."

"What can we do here to help his situation?" Dr. Parsi wonders.

"You can't do anything from here. Even if you were in Iran, you would be very ineffective. Even inquiring about prisoners can be life-threatening," says Hooshmand.

Disappointed, Dr. Parsi says, "What are you going to do, drink vodka?"

XIX
Tragic Loss of Lives in Schools

In his office, Dr. Parsi is reflecting on Saul, about gun violence in American cities, and Dr. Hartman's naive belief that a handgun would protect his family. Dr. Parsi has read about the tragic loss of lives in schools, churches, and in the streets. He is concerned about Esther, whose peace and tranquility have been shattered all at once in a flash of several bullets. He wonders why such an advanced country like the United States is so tolerant of gun violence. Dr. Parsi remembers frequently reading, almost every few weeks, in the local newspaper, the news of the gun violence in which sometimes five, ten, or even 26 schoolchildren lose their lives. He remembers reading the American Constitution before taking the Oath of Allegiance to the country to become a naturalized citizen and the judge's question regarding the Second Amendment, where Dr. Parsi had answered by quoting the entire amendment verbatim. His response to the Thirteenth Amendment was accurate, too. The judge had asked Dr. Parsi, "Who wrote the initial declaration of independence" Dr. Parsi remembers the judge's reaction to his answer, which was "Five of them, but Jefferson was the principal author."

"Did he possess any slaves?" the judge had asked.

Dr. Parsi promptly had responded, "Yes, Your Honor, as many as one hundred."

The judge nodded and smiled.

Regarding the Second Amendment, the other judge told Dr. Parsi that he believed the framers of the Constitution wanted, in the absence of a military organization and regular army during those precarious early years of the republic, to enable individuals to have the right to bear arms and have the freedom to acquire a gun to protect the country. However, the Supreme Court of the United States later ruled that the rights are not unlimited and do not prohibit some regulation of either firearms or similar devices by the government. The judge added, "We lose tens of thousands of lives annually in this country, many of them innocent children and bystanders." The judge opined that these regulations could keep guns out of the hands of criminals and insane people.

Now, thinking about Dr. Hartman's unpredictable behavior and his volatile fury, Dr. Parsi wonders why he wasn't prevented from acquiring a handgun. "Who and what law are there that could have stopped Dr. Hartman from buying a handgun at the gun store?" he asks himself. He remembers reading about a specific mass-shooter that before the massacre, the disturbed teenager's mother would encourage him to buy guns and ammunition, and they would practice shooting together at a range. Some weeks later, in a burst of frenzy, the teenager killed his mother first and then ambushed an elementary school and massacred 27 people: 16 six-years-olds, four seven-years-olds, and seven teachers. He also remembers the CNN documentary, which reported that annually, over 10,000 innocent children are wounded by guns, and many of them die needlessly.

———————

In the house recovering from the abortion, Esther is drowning in deep thoughts regarding Saul's situation. She blames herself for the tragedy. She believes it was her fault for not doing enough to keep Saul out of trouble with drugs and street crime, for not accepting Saul's shortcomings, and not convincing Dr. Hartman to visit a therapist to deal with his unpredictable temperament. The only thing Esther has magnified in her mind and always held dear in her heart has been Dr. Hartman's deep, lasting love for her. She has always been proud of him, loved him as much as Dr. Hartman loved her.

Now that Saul is gone, Esther's last glimmer of hope that someday she might get to raise a healthy child has vanished. Even had she kept the unexpected pregnancy, how could she have gained the strength to raise a child with an unknown genetic structure? She murmurs, "It would have been another Saul to deal with." Facing this complex and troubling circumstance by getting an abortion, she has selected a quick resolution.

Now, Esther contemplates a new issue in her mind and asks herself which one of them is genetically responsible for Saul's misfortune. She blames herself, not Dr. Hartman. She muses, "He's a genius, an almost perfect man with only one minuscule shortcoming, his explosive fury."

Esther now ponders the history of *Homo sapiens* and thinks about the major heroes and villains: Hitler and Stalin, Newton and Einstein. She thinks, "Yes, we are prisoners of our genes. We're incidentally mapped when we're conceived of two halves. Yes, only chance, a total accident decides who gets what. One sperm penetrates the ovum from among millions of sperm. It's a cosmic lottery."

———————

Dr. Parsi's thoughts are interrupted when Dr. Ross knocks on the door and comes in. "What a day. What a week. What a life." Dr. Ross lets out a deep sigh and looks at Dr. Parsi and says, "Cheer up, you'll be all right."

"What do you mean?" Dr. Parsi asks. "How can you tell what will happen tomorrow?"

They walk together to the ward to observe the residents at work, and then they continue down to the surgical ICU. "Dr. Hartman has been admitted to a regular room," the senior resident says.

"What about the two wounded teens?"

"They took them to the morgue straight from the OR."

———————

69

Dr. Hartman is recovering satisfactorily from his leg wound. He's not even taking any intravenous pain-killing medicine, only a capsule of oxycodone and an Ambien pill at night. Dr. Ross and Dr. Parsi walk into Dr. Hartman's room and find Esther, who has undergone her abortion a day earlier, sitting next to the bed. They find both Dr. Hartman and Esther in a somber mood. Dr. Ross is quiet; he contemplates that the couple must have talked about Saul and the abortion. Dr. Hartman ignores Dr. Parsi, which makes Dr. Ross wary of any interaction between Drs. Hartman and Parsi. Fortunately, the Dean of the Medical School arrives in the room where his charming demeanor defuses the tension in the room. Now Dr. Hartman smiles as he greets the Dean.

In the University, the Dean is called Grandpa, for he is the most helpful boss one might have the fortune to work for in academia. The Dean embraces Esther. He waves at Dr. Hartman. Looking at Esther and Dr. Hartman, the Dean says, "I'm sorry for both of you."

Two pillows have slightly elevated Dr. Hartman's right leg to prevent edema. The dressing is clean and dry, and a plastic catheter from the wound is empty. The bag has only a few drops of yellowish fluid that were collected last night. A surgical resident will be by shortly to remove the catheter and the urine bag.

Dr. Hartman breaks the silence, looks at Dr. Parsi, and whispers, "I understand you were attending to Saul's emergency care?"

"Yes." Dr. Parsi pauses and then says, "I'm sorry that we couldn't revive him."

"Well, I understand you donated a few pints of your blood to replace his lost blood," Dr. Hartman says.

"Altogether, he received eight units," Dr. Parsi explains. "I provided only two."

"I'm very grateful to you for your effort," Dr. Hartman says.

The Dean, who is pleased with Dr. Hartman's statement, looks at Dr. Parsi and nods. Dr. Hartman also thanks Dr. Parsi for doing the abortion. Esther gets up and embraces Dr. Parsi. "Thank you. It went so smoothly," Esther says. "I didn't feel a thing. As you see, I am here now and doing very well."

"Dr. Parsi, keep up your work," the Dean says.

Dr. Hartman seconds the Dean's statement, "Parsi, you remind me of myself when I was a fellow at Harvard. I was courageous and spoke my mind when I was confident that my comments were accurate. I read every medical journal related to my field and kept up with most of the ongoing research."

The Dean smiles. Dr. Parsi is surprised. He knows well that this is the first time during his entire Fellowship that he has received a positive comment from Dr. Hartman. Looking at Dr. Hartman, Dr. Ross says, "He's a good surgeon too."

"Well, that's okay, but one must maintain good medical judgment. To achieve that fundamental characteristic, one must be knowledgeable and up-to-date in medicine," Dr. Hartman says. "You must be fully aware of what is going on in your specialty in addition to being an excellent technician."

"He's a great doc," Esther says.

"Dear Esther, it's not for you to rate him. I'm talking about Dr. Parsi's primary medical education. As a foreign medical graduate, Dr. Parsi has got to work much harder to catch up to our good American graduates."

Dr. Ross, who has not spoken much, says, "Dr. Parsi has passed every board exam we have in this country, and with flying colors, too. What else can he do? It isn't his fault if he's born somewhere else."

"I'm talking about his primary medical education, his need to overcome the deficit of the past," Dr. Hartman insists.

"Dr. Parsi is doing fine. He's an excellent physician," Esther says.

Becoming annoyed by Dr. Hartman's comments, the Dean changes the topic and asks Esther whether she needs a ride home, and soon they all leave the room.

After the Dean drops Esther off at her house and drives away, she walks around and pulls the curtains in the living room and goes to the backyard. The fall leaves are scattered on the patio, covering the grass and floating in the fountain. She waters the plants for a while, goes inside, and turns on the classical music station. She gets a glass of water and listens to the music, trying to find her grounding after the harrowing events of the last few days.

A few hours later, the ringing of the doorbell disrupts her thoughts. She opens the door and is surprised to see the Dean and his wife, Ruth, at the door. "We brought you some delicious food and a bottle of wine," Ruth says.

"Well, that is so thoughtful of you. Thank you." Esther says. "How are you coping with the tragedy, Esther?" Ruth asks. "I've had better days," Esther says.

"I know what you mean," the Dean says. The Dean sits on a chair in the breakfast area while his wife boils water in the microwave oven and prepares tea for everyone.

"Esther, we have a new complication facing Dr. Hartman," the Dean says.

"I thought I was done with complications," Esther sighs. "What is it now?"

"Well, that's why we came by," the Dean says.

Ruth brings a tray with teacups, a dish of grapes, crackers, and cheese, and sits next to Esther. Esther is in no hurry, does not want to hear any more unexpected news, but she senses that it will be another blow.

"The media is regurgitating awful news 24/7," Ruth whispers.

Dean calmly reveals the problem. "The combination of CNN and local media searching for the next sensational story has focused on the events in your front yard. An old news adage has it that 'when it bleeds, it leads.' Shooting in the driveway in an affluent neighborhood involving a famous physician, his teenage son, and a drug dealer is incredibly attractive to them. That kind of story will improve their ratings. Now they are broadcasting the story of blood and gore in the neighborhood. Last week it was the gunfire downtown, and the week before, the shooting on the east side. What these reports all have in common is a loss of life and sensationalism. They are all about street brawls complicated by bloody clashes and guns."

Esther adds a teaspoon of sugar and pours in some milk, and the Dean does the same. His wife drinks her tea black without sugar. Esther lays her head on the Dean's shoulder, covers her face, and collapses into uncontrollable sobs.

"I had a premonition that having that handgun would bring tragedy to our house. I felt it in my bones that he would use it someday. I tried to find the handgun so I could get rid of it or else hide it, where he would never find it," Esther says. "But my genius professor had hidden it well. I searched the entire house, even under the wine racks in the basement, but to no avail." She paused for a moment and wiped her eyes. "Tell me, Dean, for how many years should I take on the wrath of his fury?"

"My dear, to err is human; only God is perfect," the Dean says.

"Dr. Hartman's shooting of Marcel is being described as a frantic action by your husband that had forced the shootout, resulting in the loss of the two lives," the Dean says. He adds that Marcel comes from an influential family. "His father is a workaholic and successful accountant who travels a lot and frequently takes his wife along, leaving Marcel alone in the care of a relative or a housekeeper."

"We didn't know that kid at all!" Esther cries out.

The Dean says, "I've heard that the prosecutor is preparing to issue an arrest warrant for Dr. Hartman on the charge of murder. He believes he can convince a grand jury that the shooting was unjustified and that Dr. Hartman's rage escalated the situation into a homicide. They're saying he provoked the incident."

Esther's reaction to the Dean's reports is mute at first. She hears the words but cannot grasp the consequences. Then the words resonate in her mind and echo in the chambers of her brain. She has loved her husband, but even more so, her son, Saul.

"If only I had avoided calling my husband on that rueful morning!" Esther profoundly regrets asking for his help in controlling the altercation in front of their house. "Why didn't I write the drug dealer a check for $10,000 and avoid all these troubles?" She is drawn to her painful thoughts. "I should not have relied on my husband to rescue Saul. He always worsens tense situations."

She now blames herself for the shootout. It should have been evident to her that her husband would lose control of the situation because of his unpredictable, furious reactions to family crises—immense waves of guilt wash over her soul. Indeed, by coming to the house, her husband complicated the situation and created a big, bloody mess.

Esther grasps Ruth's hand and sighs, "I didn't do enough for Saul." Esther is now crying. "He would have been a better person if I'd worked harder on him, and if I had loved him more."

72

"You did everything for him, Esther," Ruth says. "He was just impossible."

"I didn't do enough for Saul. He needed love," Esther sighs. Now the images of the many fistfights between Dr. Hartman and Saul march through her brain, on the canvas of the images of their family life. Now the frequent shouting matches late at night resonate in her mind. And all those tears, for nothing.

"We need a capable lawyer to defend Dr. Hartman," the Dean says. "We are standing by you and by him. He was defending Saul and himself against an attack on his home ground."

Ruth offers to stay with Esther during the next several nights until Dr. Hartman comes home. The Dean says, "Ruth can make calls and answer your phone and be your messenger. Ask either of us for anything, please, Esther."

Esther's recovery from the loss of her son is slow. She stays in the library most of the time, and at night she reads mystery books to keep her mind occupied. Writing notes daily in her journal has been somewhat helpful, too, but she still has insomnia and frequent nightmares. Esther's profound sense of grief does not dissipate but becomes more unbearable when Dr. Hartman returns home from the hospital. Ruth, who worries about Esther's condition, stays a few more days with the family. Eventually, Ruth convinces Esther to see a psychiatrist and get some help.

XX
Esther Awakened by a Nightmare

A nightmare awakens Esther in the middle of the night. She vaguely recalls the one part of the dream where an image of Saul with blood all over his face and chest was crawling in the driveway. She walks away from the bed and goes to the kitchen, gets a glass of tap water, and walks to the library. She does it quietly, so Ruth in the guest room is not disturbed. She sits still for a while and then looks at a row of books, and her gaze stops at *Esther the Queen*. She picks up the book and turns to the title page and the highlighted blurb on the next page and reads it. "She is a beautiful young Jewess, who is content in her life of anonymity." She sighs, wishes that she could be spared from the emerging publicity about the fatal shootout. She read the book some years ago, but now the tale of Esther has a new appeal for her. In the book, Esther is a beautiful young woman who has become the wife of the Persian king, the most powerful king in the world at the time. She remembers her last encounter with Dr. Parsi when she was leaving the outpatient surgery suite several hours after the abortion procedure, when he had told her, "Please call me if you have any problems or complications from the procedure." On another occasion, when they were conversing in the hall of the University Hospital waiting for Dr. Hartman to be brought to the regular floor from the Surgical ICU, Dr. Parsi again had said, "Call me if you want to talk about the events and Saul."

Esther now considers calling Dr. Parsi and asking him to come by the house for a visit. Dr. Parsi has given her his mobile phone number as well as his email address. She makes up her mind to call Dr. Parsi in the morning and start a conversation with him.

On his part, Dr. Parsi has also appreciated Esther's complimentary comments on the care he provided for her, the procedure, and him attending to Saul's emergency care, giving blood, and rendering the ultimately unsuccessful resuscitation in the OR, in the face of Saul's hopeless condition. Esther's comments, while Dr. Parsi and Dr. Ross were visiting Dr. Hartman in the hospital, have softened Dr. Hartman's attitude towards Dr. Parsi. When Dr. Parsi visits Dr. Hartman later in the hospital room, he even offers to meet with Dr. Parsi once he is back at work.

"Look, we can discuss the grant you are trying to obtain from the NIH," he tells Dr. Parsi. On that occasion, Dr. Hartman tells Dr. Parsi that one of the panel members of the NIH advisory committee called him before the shootout and referred to his application as a promising project that needs a few, but critical revisions to be approved.

"I know which sections need to be revised," Dr. Hartman says. Dr. Parsi credits Esther for Dr. Hartman's surprisingly collegial attitude toward him.

The next day, when Esther dials Dr. Parsi's number, she suddenly becomes anxious and quickly hangs up, for she is not sure how to start the conversation.

She does not have any complications after her procedure or even slight pain. As awkward as her call could be, Esther wants to speak with him. She remembers once during a visit after the abortion procedure, Dr. Parsi brought up the history of the Jewish Diaspora in ancient Persia and the tale of Esther. The story has always fascinated her, even though Dr. Parsi cautions her that the whole story might be just one of those mythical tales described in holy books.

Still, the story is a good excuse for her to call Dr. Parsi. Esther glances at the book by Jim Baumgardner, *Esther Queen of Persia*. She pulls out the book, takes it with her to the kitchen, and prepares a cup of tea. She returns to the library, opens the pages, and starts browsing. Esther read the book years ago and now finds the highlighted passages quite amusing. She dog-ears a few pages to discuss them later with Dr. Parsi in case he comes by to visit her soon. She is now resolved that she will call Dr. Parsi in a few days when Dr. Hartman is home to tell him how well she is doing after the procedure and bring up the issue of Jews in ancient Persia. More importantly, Esther feels a need to talk to someone about Saul's tragic end.

She looks at the stairs going up to the landing on the second floor and can see the locked door of Saul's room. She wipes her tearful eyes, goes upstairs, unlocks the door, and walks into the bedroom. The smell of dust has filled the air. The bed has been made by the maid with two blue pillows plumped against the headboard. The one on the top has a stain the size of a quarter.

Esther touches the pillow. It is oily and smells like Saul's hair. She picks it up and presses it against her face. Her tears pour out. She sits at the edge of the bed and sobs loudly.

Four days after the shootout, Dr. Hartman's condition is stable enough that with the help of a walker, he is moving around in the room and can walk down the hall to the nursing station. When his colleague Dr. Key visits him, removes the dressing, and inspects the wound, he decides to discharge Dr. Hartman from the hospital. "You don't need to be here anymore. There is no sign of infection in and around the wound," he tells Dr. Hartman. He cleanses the wound and places a light bandage dressing on it and says, "Change the dressing once daily and apply the triple antibiotic ointment on the wound. The sutures are absorbable, and they need not be removed."

"How about oral antibiotics," Dr. Hartman asks.

"Just for another week. Fortunately, I don't think the wound is infected. The initial swelling in the area of the gunshot wound is gone; there is only slight redness, which will disappear in a week or two. Please walk around and use a cane for a while."

After Dr. Ross brings Dr. Hartman home, he rests awhile in the bedroom and then slowly walks to the backyard and lies on a lounge chair enjoying San Antonio's mild fall weather, the clear skies, and the sun. He pulls out a medical journal and reads a few pages and then peruses the local newspapers, including their daily coverage of the tragic events in the city on previous days. He is keen to find newspaper coverage of fatal shootouts, which occur frequently. He reads in the local news section that the prosecutor has issued a warrant against him, and now the sheriff is waiting for him to be discharged from the hospital so he can come to the house and arrest him. He follows his case in the paper and reads that the prosecutor is reviewing new evidence collected by the Bexar County DA's office. On another page, he learns that the family of the young drug dealer has hired an experienced lawyer to represent them in civil court to sue Dr. Hartman shortly after the conclusion of the criminal trial.

The daily papers are not kind to Dr. Hartman. They are reporting that Dr. Hartman instigated the shootout. They interviewed the dead teenager's father, who is accusing Dr. Hartman of murdering his son in cold blood.

While Dr. Hartman is in the hospital, Esther follows the advice of the Dean. She contacts Francisco Barrera, a popular and successful lawyer in criminal cases, to become her husband's defense attorney. Barrera has served as County DA and as Secretary of State in the past. At the initial meeting, Barrera reviews both the police report and DA's statements and ponders whether the extensive coverage of the case in the local media, which has cast a dark shadow on the case, will influence the outcome. The lawyer asks Esther to allow him a few days to consider her request. What discourages Barrera is that it appears Dr. Hartman has done most of the shooting, seemingly out of control and in a state of frenzy. Luckily for Esther and her husband, they have some heavy hitters on their side. After receiving a call from the Dean and another one from the Chancellor of the University, who happens to be an acquaintance of Barrera's father, the lawyer takes the case. During his conversations with the Dean, Barrera learns that Dr. Hartman has an international reputation as a remarkable scientist and has enhanced the university's prestige as a successful grant writer and well-respected national leader in his specialty.

"My friend," the Dean tells Barrera, "unfortunately, Dr. Hartman has an issue, a temperament that has caused some problems for him in the past." When the lawyer asks for more specifics, the Dean explains that Dr. Hartman could have been the president of the professional college in his specialty had he not irritated so many of that organization's board members.

"Thank you for telling me right at the beginning. At least we can prepare and deal with that," the lawyer says thoughtfully. "Are there any adversaries in his department that the DA's office could call to testify against him?"

The Dean replies, "Of course, Dr. Hartman has some foes. But he usually makes up for his outbursts and rewards his subjects generously."

Barrera writes down the two names the Dean considers might harbor some resentment toward his client. He will deal with the issue later when the DA's office divulges its witness list. Meanwhile, he is most concerned about the details of the incident, the DA's report, and the text of the eventual indictment. Barrera is worried that the prosecutor will not consider the case as involuntary manslaughter based on either self-defense or accidental killing. Knowing the prosecutor, he is concerned that Dr. Hartman will be charged with committing murder, not criminally negligent homicide.

Barrera reviews a pile of newspaper clippings about the case. None of the reporters mentions "self-defense" or "accidental death" in the write-up. That worries him. A conviction on murder charges might put Dr. Hartman in prison for 20 years as well as destroy his career. In one article, the prosecutor states that based on the evidence he's seen so far, he plans to ask the grand jury to issue an indictment of Dr. Hartman for murder and issue a "true bill" to be considered for trial. Barrera hopes the grand jury will look at the circumstances of the case which are more favorable to his client and return either a "no bill," a vote not to indict Dr. Hartman at all, or indict him on some lesser type of homicide, like involuntary manslaughter.

On the afternoon of the day after Dr. Hartman's release from the hospital, Dr. Hartman takes a nap while Esther goes to the library room and dials Dr. Parsi's mobile phone number. This time she does not hang up, though she feels strange calling him. She is relieved when, instead of Dr. Parsi, a recorded voice invites the caller to leave a message. She hears a beep, begins slowly, and says, "Hello, Dr. Parsi. Everything is fine with my husband. I am doing fine, too. But I'd like to speak with you. Call me when you have a chance." She pauses, and when the voicemail asks her whether she has finished, or she wants to erase and re-record a message, she deletes the message and hangs up.

Two hours later, after Dr. Hartman has eaten an early dinner, taken the pain medicine, antibiotic capsules, and a sleeping pill with a sip of wine, and is settling down, Esther leaves him alone to watch the news. Knowing he will be asleep shortly, she goes to the library room to read. She picks up the book, *Esther Queen of Persia,* and picks a chapter randomly, but her mobile phone vibrates. She sees that Dr. Parsi is calling. She accepts the call and hears, "I noticed you have tried to call me. Are you alright?"

"Yes, I did. But I'm okay," Esther replies.

"Great," Dr. Parsi says. "How's your husband?"

"He's asleep. The wound is healing well. He hasn't complained of any pain. Now, he's more worried about the trial than his leg injury," Esther says.

"Well, hopefully, he'll be cleared from the accusations soon," Dr. Parsi says.

Esther is skeptical about the outcome of her husband's case. She says, "Well, I hope for the best." Then she says, "You're a good man. I'll tell my husband what you said."

"But how about you? How are you coping with these issues?"

"Well, not great. Physically, I have no complications: no fever, no bleeding," Esther says, "but I'm very concerned and confused."

"Please consider visiting a therapist," Dr. Parsi says.

"I am already doing that." Then, after a short pause, Esther says, "Dr. Parsi, you are welcome to come and visit us anytime." She pauses. She wishes to talk more about her misgivings regarding the tragedy, her husband's hasty action. Instead, she talks about the leg wound. "The leg wound has healed satisfactorily, and now, though limping, my husband walks around in the bedroom and the backyard without any support. There is only a light dressing around the wound. The incision is clean and has healed, just some mild swelling and red scarring around the incision." She says, "Noticing how well my husband is doing, Dr. Key said that he could have discharged him earlier. He told me that it would look better for the trial if my husband is hospitalized as long as possible." Esther realized that she is bloviating and wasting Dr. Parsi's time, so she abruptly completes the call and lets Dr. Parsi returns to work.

XXI
The Bullet That Killed Dr. Hartman's Son

Several days after Dr. Hartman has come home, when Esther has gone to the nearby supermarket to buy groceries, the doorbell rings unexpectedly. When Dr. Hartman gets up from the bed and slowly walks over to open the door, he finds a sheriff and an armed police officer standing on the front porch.

"We are looking for Jordan Hartman. Are you Jordan Hartman?" the sheriff asks.

"Yes," Dr. Hartman answers. "Yes. I'm Jordan Hartman."

"We have a warrant for your arrest in the killing of Marcel Oliver," the sheriff says. "And anything you say may be used in the court as evidence."

"I did not mean to kill that boy. I waved the handgun to scare him off," Dr. Hartman says. He becomes nervous and talkative. "Yes, I pulled the trigger. I did it when the drug dealer pulled the handgun from his pocket and pointed it at my son's face. I aimed at his shoulder and pulled the trigger, but I only did it to save my son's life. I didn't mean to kill anybody."

The sheriff says, "Sir, we are not here to argue your case. It's up to the court of law to decide on that. The court has issued an arrest warrant and orders us to execute it." The sheriff shows the first page of the warrant and repeats the statement in a firm voice. "We are also asking you to deliver the handgun to us. Somebody must have picked up your handgun from the crime scene and taken it into the house because police couldn't find it on the day of the shootout." The sheriff pauses and waits for Dr. Hartman's compliance. When Dr. Hartman doesn't move or respond, the sheriff says, "Sir, please give us the handgun."

Now Dr. Hartman nods and walks toward the bedroom. They follow Dr. Hartman as he enters the bedroom. The handgun is in his walk-in closet and is wrapped in a white towel. The sheriff takes the wrapped handgun and carefully places it into a plastic bag. "We will wait at the door for you to get ready," the sheriff says. "You have ten minutes."

As Dr. Hartman goes into the walk-in closet, pulls out a small suitcase, and collects the necessary materials to take with him, a car pulls up in front of the house. It is Dr. Parsi, who parks the car on the street. He has come to check on Dr. Hartman and, especially, Esther. Dr. Parsi is surprised to see a police car in the driveway. When he walks to the front door, he sees an armed sheriff and a police officer standing on the threshold. The sheriff is holding a plastic bag with a half-wrapped handgun. Dr. Parsi introduces himself and asks permission to enter the house.

"Please wait here in the hall," the sheriff says curtly.

A few minutes later, Dr. Hartman comes out of the bedroom, carrying a small suitcase and joins the group. Surprised and nervous, Dr. Parsi asks Dr. Hartman, "What is going on here?"

79

Dr. Hartman looks at the sheriff, who tells Dr. Parsi, "We are taking Jordan Hartman to police headquarters to be booked and then taken to court for arraignment."

Dr. Hartman looks at Dr. Parsi and says, "I'm glad you are here, Dr. Parsi. Please stay in the house until Esther comes home." His face red, eyes teary, Dr. Hartman pulls the suitcase and says, "Officers, I'm ready."

Watching the arresting officers handcuff Dr. Hartman, direct him to the police car, and push his head down into the vehicle like a defeated lion herded into a cage stuns Dr. Parsi. He is speechless. He has never imagined that the bullish Dr. Hartman would one day face this situation. In his heart, he feels sorry for Dr. Hartman, hopes he weathers this fraught situation. Now, though, he is more concerned about Esther, who has loved Dr. Hartman during many happy years of their life together and is presently facing a precarious situation.

The arrest of Dr. Hartman for murder after he is released from the University Hospital becomes breaking news in the media. The local newspapers cover the arrest on the first page. The TV correspondents rush to the neighborhood to provide eyewitness news of the event. They report that the doctor is charged with the killing of an 18-year-old boy during a shooting in front of his house earlier, as stated in the DA's warrant. The newspapers report, "According to the warrant issued by the DA's office, Dr. Hartman murdered his neighbor's son." *The Express-News* displays this headline at the top of the first page, "Doctor Faces Homicide Charge: San Antonio Physician Charged with Murder." The other daily paper, *The Light*, prints that three people were taken to University Hospital after the shooting: Dr. Jordan Hartman, his 17-year-old son, and an 18-year-old boy. Both teenagers died in the operating room that same night. Dr. Hartman sustains only a manageable gunshot wound to his leg and is in stable condition.

The next day, the two major San Antonio newspapers followed up the story and reported on their first page: "Doctor Arrested for Murder." One of the papers prints, "Professor Charge in Shooting Out on Bail." The article says that Dr. Hartman has been freed after an overnight stay in jail. The paper adds that the doctor's lawyer, Mr. Barrera, argued in front of the District Court for a writ of habeas corpus, stating that the charges lack merit because the shooting was self-defense. Furthermore, Barrera argued, Dr. Hartman is not likely to flee and should be released. At the hearing, the Chief DA counters that the crime was a killing arising out of Dr. Hartman's unpredictable fury, so he should not be released.

Esther, who is watching the proceedings with utter sadness, profoundly resents the Chief DA's arguments and wonders whether the prosecutor harbors some hidden personal vendetta against her husband. To her immense relief, the judge deliberates only briefly, then accepts the defense's argument and releases Dr. Hartman after he posts a bond of $250,000.

The local TV channel and the Cable Head-Line News also include stories about Dr. Hartman's arrest. HLN channel, which specializes in reporting sensational crime news, reports Dr. Hartman's story and mentions that at the time of the arrest, Dr. Hartman confessed to the crime and handed over his 9mm handgun to the authorities. However, what Dr. Hartman stated was quite different. He said to the judge at the time of arraignment that he did not intend to kill anybody. All he wanted to do was to scare the intruder and force him to leave. Still, the TV correspondent lauds the fact that the DA has stated that Dr. Hartman dangerously elevated the level of the disturbance between his son and the other boy by waving his handgun in the air. The newspaper quotes the DA official as saying that if Dr. Hartman had not brandished his gun, most probably nobody would have been shot or died. Next day *The Express-News* prints a follow-up of the story with a large, bold headline that states, "Still Unknown: Who Fired the Bullet That Killed Dr. Hartman's Son?"

The lawyer tells Esther that his defense strategy will involve trying to win an acquittal on the grounds of self-defense or, in the alternative, a conviction for a less serious offense such as involuntary manslaughter. His immediate priority, though, is to get her husband released from custody. A few hours later, he stands at the district judge's bench, asking the judge for an order to release his client on a writ of habeas corpus. Having argued the matter persuasively, he obtains the decree, walks to the police headquarters, posts a bond, and hurries his client from the jail into a car where his associate is idling at the curb.

Driving home from the court after the release of Dr. Hartman from overnight custody, Esther expresses her suspicion that the prosecutor must harbor a hostile attitude toward doctors. She looks at Barrera and says, "It seems to me that the prosecutor may have a vendetta against my husband."

Barrera says, "I believe the man was just doing his job, but I will investigate whether he has a hidden agenda."

Barrera, the defense attorney, is coming to their home, where he plans to discuss some points of the defense strategy with them. While he settles into the living room, Esther takes Dr. Hartman to the master bedroom and suggests that he take a warm shower.

"It'll make you feel better after your night in jail. Here is a set of fresh towels and underwear," she says.

Dr. Hartman stands for a long while under the warm shower. He treasures every drop of water rolling down from his head and over his shoulders, chest, abdomen, and down his legs. He ponders the shootout and recalls the scene when Marcel's hand had grasped Saul's neck and was choking him. Dr. Hartman shakes his head and tries to stop thinking about that moment without avail. He turns off the shower and wraps himself in a thick white housecoat, then joins Esther and Barrera in the library. Dr. Hartman hugs her, puts his head over her shoulder, and utters a loud sigh of relief. He whispers, "O my love, thanks for the support."

As if she might have read Dr. Hartman's thoughts, she says, "It wasn't your fault. You were trying to scare the guy and save Saul's life." She pats his back encouragingly. Then she goes down to the kitchen and prepares tea for the three of them.

"Okay, let's face it, you killed someone," Barrera says. "But not every killing is considered murder or manslaughter. We are going to argue strongly for justifiable homicide in self-defense and the defense of your son."

But only the word murder reverberates in Dr. Hartman's head. He tries to imagine what will happen to his life if he is convicted. The prospect of sharing a prison cell with another murderer makes him shudder. He remembers the case of the fugitive film director, Roman Polansky, who was arrested in Los Angeles and charged, among other offenses, with raping a 13- year-old teenager and then released after 42 days. Polansky fled the country when he heard that the judge at the sentencing hearing might not grant probation as promised in his plea-bargain. He settled in Paris, where he continued to produce films, many of which garnered prestigious awards at international film festivals. Dr. Hartman is now considering his options if he faces conviction. Should he flee the United States to avoid spending his precious time in jail? Later that day, he discusses the Polansky case with Esther and lays out the pros and cons of fleeing to Mexico in case the possibility of conviction for manslaughter becomes a real possibility.

"Why Mexico?" Esther wants to know.

"I have several close friends at the University of Mexico," he replies, "and I could continue my work on stem cell research there."

"I believe in the jury system," Esther insists. "They know you are not a murderer."

The next evening, the defense attorney shows up with shocking news. "The autopsy results indicate that one of your bullets hit the drug dealer. However, your handgun discharged three bullets, since there were three casings found at the scene, according to the preliminary police reports. Of course, in the heat of the argument and with Marcel's handgun about to go off, you were forced to act quickly. So where did the bullet that hit Saul in the chest come from?" the defense attorney asks. "Did it come from Marcel's handgun or yours?"

"What are you trying to say? The bullet that killed Saul came from Marcel's handgun!" Dr. Hartman yells.

"After you had been shot and Marcel had been hit, why did you keep shooting?"

Dr. Hartman's face turns livid with anger. "What are you implying? Marcel was going to kill us all!"

Esther joins the argument and explains emphatically, "My husband was concerned and had to act quickly. Yes, Marcel was going to kill my husband and Saul and me. All three of us." She begins to cry, "Don't you understand? Marcel murdered my son!"

Mr. Barrera feels uncomfortable for causing such havoc. He waits a few moments until Esther has regained her composure. After taking a sip of water, Barrera resumes. "Well, let's review the situation." Then he turns to Dr. Hartman. "Can you remember that very moment when you got the gun?" he asks. "Who were you trying to defend: your son, your wife, or yourself?"

Dr. Hartman recalls the instant when the assailant was punching Saul's face and pressing the muzzle of his handgun against Saul's neck. "He was about to kill Saul," Dr. Hartman exclaims.

"Were you trying to kill him when you pulled the trigger?"

"I aimed at his shoulder," Dr. Hartman insists. "I was close enough to target the right shoulder. He was holding the handgun with his right hand."

"You shot three times; one bullet hit his abdomen. The other two missed him."

"I aimed at his right shoulder," Dr. Hartman insists.

"The forensic evaluation of the gunshot wounds, as well as the examination of the handguns and the number of casings found so far, indicates that altogether five shots were fired. Two hit Saul—one hit his chest, and the other went through his right arm—one hit your leg, and one bullet hit the drug dealer. The last bullet didn't hit anyone and is missing."

"Have they determined who discharged these bullets?" Esther asks.

"Two came from the drug dealer's handgun, and three from Dr. Hartman's," Barrera says.

Esther is confused. "So, who killed Saul?" Esther asks. "Only one of the two bullets that hit Saul came from the drug dealer," the defense attorney says,

"Because he only fired two shots, and we know one of his bullets hit Dr. Hartman, the other either hit Saul's chest or arm. But the bullet that went right through Saul's right arm could have come from Dr. Hartman's handgun. Saul died of the bullet that hit his chest," the defense attorney explains. "I guess that bullet must have come from Marcel's handgun."

Dr. Hartman's handgun is a 9mm semi-automatic that he has fired only a few times at a nearby shooting range. Its magazine still contains five bullets.

"How many shots did you fire?" the defense attorney asks Dr. Hartman.

After thinking hard to find a correct answer, Dr. Hartman replied, "I don't remember."

"Do you usually fill the magazine after each practice?"

"Yes. I always do."

"So, you must have had eight bullets in the magazine, and you fired three times. As we thought, now we have a full count." Barrera has requested the ballistics results from the crime lab and the full police reports. "The DA is raising questions about the fatal shots that killed the two victims. The DA claims that, in anger, you aimed carelessly and fatally shot and killed not only Marcel but also your son. Marcel discharged only two bullets: one may have hit Saul's somewhere and the other, your leg. However, there were two bullet wounds in Saul's body. One of them must have come from your gun." Hearing the last comment shakes Esther, who begins to sob quietly.

Barrera continues, "Look, the prosecutor is going to draw a picture of you like a mad professor who is capable of killing even his son in the heat of his uncontrollable fury. I'm aware that you are a good, solid citizen, you took a course in gun safety, practiced at the shooting range several times, and registered your gun. Those gun shooting practices certainly enhance accuracy when you use the gun and shoot someone. This evidence will help me to argue against the prosecutor's accusations. But I need a written statement from your shooting instructor and your receipts from when you purchased the gun." Barrera pauses to drink water. Then, he continues, "On the other hand, Marcel's handgun is a used Taurus .38 caliber handgun, probably purchased on the black market for a pittance or swapped for a few packets of weed. His parents never knew that their son had a gun or was involved in drug dealing. They blame Saul for their son's troubles. And we are certain that he didn't take any lessons in the shooting range."

XXII
You Are Out of Control

"My friend, you're out of control," Dr. Key tells Dr. Hartman. "You have had so much anguish in the last few weeks that I'm afraid your mental foundation is shaken. You need a break. Do consider going to a good sunny place with white beaches and crystal blue waters."

Now that Dr. Hartman has recovered from the leg wound, his mind discovers the old issue of nipple irritation on the right breast. He has called Dr. Key, a professor in the surgery department, and has shared his concern regarding the nipple irritation with him. Dr. Key invites him to come to the surgical clinic building for an examination. Even before looking at Dr. Hartman's breast, Dr. Key says, "Stop worrying about cancer, okay?"

"But I have been irritated by this for weeks. The nipple stains my t-shirt with blood at night."

"Stop scratching the nipple," Dr. Key says. "Go and have a vacation."

"I'll talk to Esther about it. I can walk and drive and no longer need assistance. Let's remember that I'm lucky to be alive, Dr. Key," Dr. Hartman says. "But won't you evaluate my breast pain?"

"All right. What is going on here? Go ahead, Jordan, tell me the whole story," Dr. Key says. Dr. Hartman sits on the edge of the examination table and pulls up his shirt and t-shirt and shows his right breast. Dr. Key looks at the chest and touches the area around the nipple. After noticing some erythema around the nipple, Dr. Key gently presses on the tissue, but he doesn't feel any lump. He sees Dr. Hartman's frown and says, "It's sore, that's all. You've probably caused the tenderness by scratching it." He inspects the scratched nipple again and says, "Please leave your nipple alone."

Dr. Hartman says, "I can't. It itches and even wakes me at night."

"Use cortisone ointment for a few days," Dr. Key says. "If it doesn't go away in a week, please let me know."

"Could it be cancer?" Dr. Hartman says.

"I don't think so. Because you complained of chest pain after the surgery on your leg, I looked at your chest and saw only a little erythema around your nipple," Dr. Key says. "You mumbled that you had had some irritation there, but earlier, you had told me that you assumed the pain was from a tennis injury."

"It's not gone completely."

"So what! Go take some Aleve." Smirking, Dr. Key gets up, and as he leaves, asks Dr. Hartman to call him in a week if the problem has not disappeared. "I'll do a sonography and needle biopsy to check it out," Dr. Key says. "I'm sure it will not be there by then."

Dr. Hartman returns to work two weeks after his arrest and release from overnight police custody. Now, he can walk to the lab and observe the extraction of the zygotes in one area and the shelf of stem cell culture tubes in the other section, and he looks for a report regarding the NIH-sponsored project concerning fallopian tubes. In each chapter, the NIH co-director of the research program gives encouraging news. Also, the co-director adds a written statement for Dr. Hartman to review. Dr. Hartman's newest project is an SBIR grant identifying the unstable genes in the newly conceived zygote extracted from pigs' fallopian tubes 24 hours after fertilization. Two members of his research team—the chair of the genetics division and a faculty member from the pathology department—are scheduled to meet with him in the afternoon. Leaving the area, he takes the co-director's report and moves toward his office. He mumbles, "Wow, these people have done a great deal of work."

Research applications from Dr. Hartman's team usually find acceptance at funding institutions. Proper preparation, solid groundwork, distinguished collaborators, and precise descriptions of the proposed projects have been the hallmarks of his work. He carries significant influence at school as well as in the national medical arena. Dr. Hartman's accomplishments include several medical textbooks he has authored, many scientific articles he has published, speeches he has given, and numerous awards and prizes he has won in prestigious scientific contests. He is well known for his forceful rhetoric in scientific presentations at conferences. Since he is a top authority on stem cell treatments, female infertility, genetic disposition, and fallopian tube physiology, he has become a reviewer for the NIH scientific research applications for grants in these areas. Altogether, the team for the three research projects that he's directing or co-directing includes five more investigators from three departments, and five Ph.D.'s from Southwest Research Institute, where these investigators keep pigs, rabbits, and monkeys in a park-like secured section of the Institute.

Dr. Hartman has regained his sharp acumen for perusing and analyzing written reports submitted to him for critique. At school, and especially for the residents, his evaluations are unbeatable. The residents seldom engage him in a debate at the conferences. Even Dr. Parsi is still wary of Dr. Hartman. He, like others, has written down the Dean's advice on how to manage Dr. Hartman and affixed it above his computer: "Be accurate and polite whenever you discuss medical topics with Dr. Hartman."

Because Dr. Hartman takes the lectures for students seriously and provides a plethora of references, his classes are well attended, too. Even though he dismisses physicians in private practice with haughty disdain, his conferences for the regional medical societies are always well attended, and his many years of groundbreaking work have earned him respect and admiration in the local medical community.

Today, Dr. Hartman feels some pain in his right breast again. During the lecture in the classroom, the twitching sensation in his right arm is more irritating than it was last week. He can't raise his arm to a horizontal level, and the limited brachial movement is preventing him from completing the slide show. Only three months ago, he was able to raise his arm above shoulder level. Today, the spastic pain prevents him from lifting the laser pointer to the horizontal level and from achieving the extension needed to move the bright spot on the screen. Dr. Key, the surgery department's vice-chair, has told Dr. Hartman that he will biopsy the breast lesion if the spasm persists for a week. Dr. Hartman manages to conclude his lecture, leaves the classroom, and immediately heads for Dr. Key's office. There, he tells his colleague that he feels like the irritation is growing under his nipple.

"The cancer cells are moving to my arm and lymph nodes," Dr. Hartman says. "Let's find out what's going on."

Dr. Key disregards Dr. Hartman's statement and says, "It's all in your head, my friend, but let's walk to the radiology department and do something about it."

"You should at least do the needle biopsy," Dr. Hartman says.

Together, they walk to the radiology department. They look for Dr. Franklin. A junior faculty member who enters the hallway greets them. "May I help you?" he asks.

"We are looking for Dr. Franklin. Is he around?" Dr. Key says.

"Dr. Franklin is not here today. He is playing in a fund-raising golf tournament," the junior faculty member says.

"How about the vice-chair, is he here?"

"He's overseas lecturing somewhere. May I help you with anything?"

Dr. Key introduces Dr. Hartman and himself to the junior faculty member and describes the reason that they have come to look for Dr. Franklin.

"No problem, I'll postpone my next appointment to be at your service," the junior faculty member says. "Let me call the nurse to set up the lab for both sonography and directed needle biopsy."

"I agree with the Doc. Before any biopsy, one needs to have a sonogram," Dr. Key reminds Dr. Hartman.

In the mini surgical lab, the junior faculty looks at the nipple and says, "This is not a scratch; there's an ulcer in your right nipple."

"I've most likely irritated it," Dr. Hartman says. "But I hope it's not malignant. I'm afraid and feel that the cancer cells are now migrating all over my body."

"Please, don't jump to conclusions," Dr. Key insists. "Now, let the doctor arrange everything."

When the junior faculty member leaves the lab, Dr. Hartman airs his disappointment with Dr. Franklin's absence from the department and says, "He's okay, but I can't stand his wife. She is an annoying French socialist."

"Stop it. Leave the wife alone. How many times do you want to harass the poor woman?" Dr. Key says. "She's a bibliophile who recites Ulysses' Penelope chapter verbatim from memory."

"That doesn't mean she is not a socialist," Dr. Hartman insists. Dr. Key is pleased with the change of topic from Dr. Hartman's breast lesion to gossip about Dr. Franklin's wife. Dr. Hartman continues, "She is the one who always debates political issues at the department dinners and presses for a rebuttal."

"Okay, my friend. Let's get on with your medical problem," Dr. Key says while ignoring the comment. "Let's see the X-rays."

In the fluoroscopy lab, Dr. Hartman, Dr. Key, and the junior faculty are looking at the illuminated images. They all see a small patch of an irregular shadow full of scattered microcalcifications behind the right nipple.

"What's the size of the area with the calcification?" Dr. Key asks.

The junior faculty member measures the area and says, "It's about eight millimeters."

That's the area that needs to be biopsied," Dr. Key says.

Dr. Hartman says, "I'm ready."

A scrub nurse brings a wrapped biopsy kit and sets it up on the long metal table, so Dr. Key can perform the procedure.

"No need to do it in the OR," Dr. Key says. "I'll do it right here and now, in the fluoroscopy room." The presence of those calcifications under the nipple alarms Dr. Key. He asks the nurse to bring a larger size needle for a core biopsy. "I'll need it to get adequate samples."

Before the nurse sets up the surgery, Dr. Key, who does not need to explain the core needle biopsy of the breast to Dr. Hartman, gets an informed consent form out and asks Dr. Hartman to initial every page and then sign and date the last page.

Dr. Key calls one of the anesthesiologists to come and administer an injection of a sedative and analgesic, but Dr. Hartman refuses. "Local anesthesia will be more than enough," Dr. Hartman says. "I'm going back to my office because too much work has piled up on my desk."

"I'll have the anesthesiologist standing by in case you are uncomfortable," Dr. Key says. The nurse brings a new kit and sets up the instruments on a sterile green sheet, paints Dr. Hartman's breast with a Betadine solution, and then covers his chest with green towels. She then leaves an open area surrounding the nipple that includes the lesion, making it accessible for the core biopsy.

"Are you ready, Jordan?" Dr. Key asks.

"Yes, go ahead," Dr. Hartman says.

Dr. Key sprays the open area with an iodine solution and drapes the biopsy site with sterile green towels. He applies the same solution to the nipple and surrounding skin with an anesthetic solution, and, a few minutes later, with a fine needle, he injects Lidocaine into the nipple and the biopsy site to numb the area. Dr. Hartman is tense and whispers, "Get several samples. I don't want to be called back for more biopsies."

While Dr. Key is waiting for the anesthesia to kick in, he embarks on a conversation about San Antonio's weather and the recent long summer drought. Now, Dr. Key touches the biopsy area with the tip of a fine needle and notices no reaction from Dr. Hartman. He uses a hollow needle and inserts it several times into the skin and down into the breast tissue. Each time he extracts a long tube of pink tissue and drops it into the formalin bottle. In the end, he injects the hollow needle into the nipple three times and extracts more tissue samples, which cause Dr. Hartman to cringe. Dr. Hartman regrets his decision not to have any intravenous anesthesia and curses Dr. Key, but quickly regains his composure. Dr. Key adds the additional specimens to the solution, while the nurse cleanses the puncture points and applies pressure with several pads to stop the oozing of blood.

"It's all done, my friend," Dr. Key says.

"That was rough, guys," Dr. Hartman says.

"We should do permanent sections, not frozen," Dr. Key decides. Dr. Hartman nods in agreement. Dr. Key sends the small bottle containing the breast tissue samples down to the pathology department.

XXIII
Insomnia from Drinking Black Tea

Esther has been tossing and turning for a while. That last cup of black tea after dinner is keeping her awake. She hears Dr. Hartman's snores, so she gets up quietly and goes to the library.

She picks up *Blind Assassin,* this month's assignment in her book club, and forces herself to read a few pages. Her tired mind cannot absorb the words. She returns to bed again, but when she still cannot fall asleep, she goes to the dressing room and takes a tablet of Ambien. The bed is now more attractive, and Dr. Hartman's snoring is not as annoying as it was earlier.

After a few hours of sleep, she wakes up and finds that Dr. Hartman has left the house. Although it is Saturday, she believes that Dr. Hartman has gone to his office at the University. She dials his direct line. Dr. Hartman picks up the phone promptly and says hello.

"Are you coming home soon?" Esther asks.

"I'm reviewing a bulky package of legal papers related to the shootout," Dr. Hartman says. "Go ahead and have your breakfast, please."

There are three thick stacks of envelopes on Dr. Hartman's desk. The bulkiest one is from his defense attorney, Mr. Barrera, who is representing him in the case that has arisen from the shootout. That parcel contains complete copies of the recent depositions he has given to the prosecutors. The second includes copies of the incident report and coroner's findings, and the third a set of clippings of published articles covering the tragic aftermath of the shootout in the local press. Then there are several notes from colleagues expressing their support, and one from a CNN correspondent requesting an interview.

It has been more than a month since Dr. Hartman's arrest after the shootout. The newspapers in San Antonio, Austin, and other Texas cities have reported that a medical school professor has been arrested and charged with manslaughter in the slaying of a teenager in front of his house. One paper printed Dr. Hartman's mug shot with the case number affixed to his shirt. Another newspaper had graphic photos of Marcel on a stretcher being pushed into the University Hospital's emergency room. Another photograph shows Dr. Parsi and two other medical staffers pulling Saul's stretcher from the ambulance. They reported that the shootout was instigated by the professor when he threatened the teenaged Marcel with his handgun. They published police reports showing Saul's multiple misdemeanors arising from altercations with neighbors. They also reported that both Marcel and Saul were in critical condition and had died during or shortly after emergency surgeries. Now, the DA's office is investigating the causes of their deaths, as well as the question of whose bullets killed the two teenagers. The papers noted, though, that the professor is the only one who escaped serious injury and survived.

Since Dr. Hartman's arrest and release from police headquarters, life has not been easy for Esther. Dr. Hartman's academic troubles are mounting as well. With a possible indictment for murder hanging over his head and adverse publicity in the media, his position at the university is in jeopardy. On the personal front, there is news that the result of his breast biopsy revealed that the breast lesion is a non-invasive inflammatory tissue reaction. The good news regarding his breast lesion comes personally from Dr. Key, who walks to Dr. Hartman's office immediately after receiving the result of the biopsy and says, "I told you, it is all in your head."

"I wish all my troubles were in my head," Dr. Hartman replies.

"My friend, why don't you go and see a therapist?" Then he reads, "The biopsy has revealed inflammation around the nipple with minimal atypical cells and no invasive cancer."

Dr. Hartman is relieved. "I thought I had an infiltrating ductal carcinoma or DCIS, or possibly Paget's disease," Dr. Hartman tells Dr. Key. Dr. Hartman insists that more tests must be done to rule out any doubt about the diagnosis, so Dr. Key reluctantly orders a series of tests to search for the presence of metastases in other organs. Fortunately, the MRI and CT-scan reveal no spread of cancer to the lungs, liver, or brain. Now Dr. Key offers Dr. Hartman some sedatives and recommends that no further breast biopsy should be performed.

"Please see a therapist," Dr. Key tells Dr. Hartman.

In response to Dr. Hartman's initial insistence that the biopsy had missed cancer, Dr. Key gives him a lecture. "There are only 1,500 cases of invasive breast cancers diagnosed every year in men in the US, and annually, only 500 of these cases result in patient deaths. Even if it had been Paget's disease, no one dies of stage 0 Paget's disease of the nipple even with atypical cells like yours. My friend, this rash will not kill you." Looking at Dr. Hartman, Dr. Key says, "Considering your resilient body, you are going to live a long life free of cancer. Look, you have survived the shootout in front of your house, the wound in your leg, and I'm confident you will survive this nipple irritation as well."

––––––––––––

The date for the trial is set for after Labor Day. Because of the local publicity of the case, the selection of the twelve members of the jury could present a challenge for both the prosecutor and the defense lawyer, Mr. Barrera. Esther, who had witnessed the shootout, firmly believes that Dr. Hartman's action was in self-defense and that he had no choice but to save Saul and himself from Marcel's attack by using the handgun. However, she wishes Dr. Hartman had not brought out the pistol and threatened the drug dealer with it. Without the gun, the altercation might have ended differently. They might have discovered the basis of the dispute between their son and the drug dealer and settled the matter with a check. She is now convinced that the combination of her husband's easily provoked anger and his possession of the handgun was responsible for the tragic outcome.

In his office, in the quiet of a Saturday when the staff is away, Dr. Hartman completes perusing the documents related to the shootout. For the first time since the incident, he is seriously worried about the outcome of the case and Esther's handling of the situation, her welfare. Now, Dr. Hartman has become overwhelmed about his life-long endeavors at school—the work he has done for the department expanding his research into new medical fields, especially the relevance of using stem-cells in the treatment of cancer—making the department one of the top units in the school, if not in all of Texas. In a conversation with the Dean, he shares these concerns and seeks some guidance and support. Initially, the legal team is less concerned about the outcome of the case than the venue of the trial. The Dean agrees with the defense team's position, primarily because the adverse publicity generated by a local jury trial would be detrimental for the medical school's reputation. Considering Dr. Hartman's persistent suspicion that he may have breast cancer after all, and may need additional surgery and possibly radiation treatment, he hopes that the judge will order moving the trial to Houston so that he can take advantage of the location of the trial and visit the M.D. Anderson Cancer Institute and seek a second opinion.

Eventually, the issue of requesting a change of venue for the trial to another community because of local publicity is set aside, because the follow-up articles regarding the case in local newspapers, as well as papers in Austin, Bryan, and Laredo are not as adverse for Dr. Hartman as earlier articles. The defense counsel concludes that Dr. Hartman will not become a sacrificial lamb and an outcast in the community but could benefit from his positive medical image in town. He contemplates, "After all, he does carry a good reputation among the patients he had helped." At last, after weighing the pros and cons of the situation, Barrera decides to withdraw the request to move the venue to another city.

XXIV
Saul's Bedsheets

Esther goes to the laundry room and picks up Saul's bedsheets from the dirty laundry basket. She climbs the stairs, unlocks Saul's room, and places the sheets on the bed. The photo of Saul on the wall, his innocent face looking straight at her, causes her to tremble. She sits on the edge of the bed between the sheets and Saul's underwear and inhales the scent of her son's unwashed blazer. She feels bereaved, sad, and predicts more trouble to come her way. She is in a state of delirium and hopelessness.

Feeling blank and overwhelmed by the recent tragic events, Esther wonders about her past, the troubling time she had with Saul, and Dr. Hartman's ignorance of Saul's depraved life. The gloomy thoughts grow in her mind. She is afraid of what life has in store for them. She squeezes Saul's blazer as if she were embracing him. A profound sense of guilt fills her head. She wipes the tears from her eyes and walks down to the medicine cabinet, searching for something to dispel her gloom. The bottles of Ativan and Zoloft and Ambien draw her attention. How would it feel to take a handful of these tablets together and all at once? Does she still possess a small glimpse of hope for the future? Will the trial shatter their peace of mind so deeply that she will be pushed to the edge of insanity? Now she looks at herself in the mirror. She sees a troubled woman with disheveled hair and puffy eyes. She wishes the time machine would roll back 2500 years to when Esther was the Queen of Persia. She fantasizes that she is that Esther, living in the king's palace and being indulgently tended by several young maidens.

During the two days that Dr. Hartman is recovering from the breast core biopsy, his office receives a package from the NIH indicating that his recent grant application has been approved. They will fund up to 10 million dollars paid in several stages as the research project progresses and is implemented. At the same time, Dr. Parsi also receives a letter from NIH requesting further clarification of a handful of issues regarding his grant application. Dr. Parsi is pleased that this letter indicates something other than an outright rejection of his proposal. He gives plenty of credit to Dr. Hartman for reviewing the application and almost rewriting some sections. However, Dr. Parsi knows that without Esther's support, Dr. Hartman would not have supported his research.

Pleased with the NIH letter, Dr. Parsi calls Dr. Hartman to express his gratitude and obtain some guidance about how best to proceed.

"You must comply with their inquiry verbatim," Dr. Hartman advises Dr. Parsi. "These reviewers are highly qualified experts in the field of your research area. Comply with the NIH request fully and thoroughly revise those questioned sections. I know the director in charge of this application. He has given your package high marks," Dr. Hartman tells Dr. Parsi. "I am confident that you will be approved and get the grant money, but only after quite a bit of extra work on the proposal. Respond correctly to their questions. Investigate other similar programs. They will give you more clues for your research. When you're done, bring a copy of the final version to me before you send it back to NIH."

———————

As Dr. Hartman's trial date moves closer, his attention is divided between teaching and leading the research projects, and preparation for the case against him. After the Dean convinces Dr. Hartman to take a break from his work, he stays home and prepares for the trial. He gradually begins to take his legal situation seriously, and he worries about its consequences if he is convicted.

Esther and the Dean are Dr. Hartman's two most steadfast supporters, encouraging him to stay calm and remain confident. Quietly, though, Esther is worried that Dr. Hartman might be convicted of involuntary manslaughter and go to prison for years.

Whereas Dr. Hartman's public image has not been so positive in the press, Esther's standing in the community has seen an impressive spike as there are genuine expressions of support from friends and acquaintances coming her way who voice their empathy for her situation. Quite understandably, under the stress of the upcoming trial, Dr. Hartman has become an introverted and quiet person, somewhat depressed. Occasionally, he speaks of the possibility of a jail term. And for the time being, the bursts of fury for which he is so well known for have subsided. Even Dr. Parsi, who in the past has frequently been the subject of harassment, now receives the occasional positive comment from Dr. Hartman. Dr. Parsi, in return, manages to show respect and express gratitude to Dr. Hartman.

In a rare gesture, Dr. Hartman has invited Dr. Parsi to bring the final version of his SBIR grant application to the house. Believing Dr. Hartman to be at home, Dr. Parsi calls their home phone and, after four rings, leaves a message that he's coming over to visit and present the grant application to Dr. Hartman for his review. Esther is unaware of the arrangement between her husband and Dr. Parsi. When she comes down from Saul's room and opens the front door, she is surprised to see Dr. Parsi standing outside. She gently says, "Well, what a surprise."

"I called earlier and left a message that I'd come by and visit Dr. Hartman and you," Dr. Parsi says.

"That's all right. Come on in."

On the one hand, he is carrying a backpack; on the other, a bouquet of fresh flowers.

XXV
The First Date at the Piano Bar

It is a mild afternoon in San Antonio. The recent rain has rejuvenated the flora, and the grass in the front yards is green again. The trio of Dr. Childress, Dr. Baldwin, and Dr. Parsi plan to meet at the Piano Bar after six PM. Dr. Baldwin gets a ride from Dr. Childress, and they join Dr. Parsi, who has waited there for several minutes. She orders a glass of Becker Chardonnay and nibbles on roasted peanuts. Dr. Parsi gets a California Pinot Noir, and Dr. Childress, Bud Light.

"I'm on call tonight," Dr. Childress explains.

"Is that why you're drinking non-alcoholic beer?" Dr. Baldwin jokes. "You might as well gulp lemonade."

"It tastes better and is less filling," Dr. Childress says.

"So, what's happening in our department?" Dr. Childress asks Dr. Parsi.

"Dr. Hartman has been hiding in his office," Dr. Baldwin says. "I miss seeing him at the Thursday morning Grand Rounds."

"It just doesn't feel the same when he's not around."

"He's not hiding anywhere," Dr. Parsi says. "The weight of the adversities and accusation of manslaughter is pulling him down."

"How did you ever dare cancel Esther's surgery?" Dr. Baldwin asks Dr. Parsi. "Initially, I had no suspicion that she was pregnant," Dr. Parsi says. "But when she said that she is not using any protection when having sex, I felt a simple pregnancy test was necessary. After all, it's a regular part of any pelvic mass evaluation, especially in a sexually active woman who uses no contraceptives."

"What would have happened if the test had been negative?" Dr. Childress asks

"We would have gone ahead with the surgery," Dr. Parsi says.

"And what would have happened to you?" Dr. Baldwin asks Dr. Parsi.

Dr. Childress interrupts, "Dr. Hartman would have thrown you out of the department."

"I'm not sure," Dr. Parsi says. "He's not as nasty as you think."

"You are too nice of a guy," Dr. Baldwin says. "He would have fired you the next day."

"I believe the test was necessary, and Dr. Hartman knows that. It is clearly stated in the gynecology textbooks," Dr. Baldwin says. "But he still would have fired you as he did with our popular vice-chair, as he did with one of the residents."

Dr. Childress pays and gets up to respond to a call from the hospital. After he leaves, Dr. Parsi asks Dr. Baldwin, "What are you doing for dinner tonight?"

"I have no plans," Dr. Baldwin smiles at Dr. Parsi. Dr. Parsi says. "So, do you like Mexican food?"

"Yes, especially cheese enchiladas."

"How about we go to La Fogata?"

"I like their menu, especially their spicy green enchiladas, but I'm afraid that the cacophony of the noisy Mariachis could destroy my appetite."

"Okay. Let's go to the Mexican restaurant on the River Walk, the one that is quiet and has the delicious green enchiladas."

It is calm and cool outside, and Dr. Parsi and Dr. Baldwin have to wait thirty minutes before they are seated in a booth near the fireplace. Dr. Baldwin orders a house margarita and a dish of cheese enchiladas; Dr. Parsi chooses spicy green enchiladas and a prickly pear margarita. As they are sipping their salted frozen margaritas, they look around and admire the colorful Mexican art piece hanging above the large fireplace. Dr. Baldwin downs her drink and asks for another one.

"I better slow down," Dr. Parsi smiles at her. "I'll be the designated driver."

Dr. Baldwin giggles and holds Dr. Parsi's hand.

It is not their first date, but Dr. Parsi feels delighted to be sitting next to Dr. Baldwin in the booth as her face is reflecting the flames of the fireplace, her white cheeks glowing, and her smile indicating her happiness.

"I think I have had enough of this delicious drink," Dr. Baldwin says. After adding a teaspoonful of green tomatillo sauce to her dish, she takes several bites and then stops eating. The waiter offers to pack up the rest of her meal for her to take home. Dr. Parsi eats his entire plate and asks for the ticket. "I'll pay my share," Dr. Baldwin says.

"Not tonight. You may pay the next time we go out," Dr. Parsi says. He gives Dr. Baldwin a ride to her apartment. "We can pick up your car tomorrow morning," Dr. Parsi suggests. Dr. Baldwin explains that Dr. Childress had given her a ride to the Piano Bar. "You can take me directly to my apartment," says Dr. Baldwin.

Dr. Parsi accompanies her to the apartment. When they arrive, Dr. Baldwin takes off her shoes and promptly takes a seat. She is too sluggish for any conversation. "I think you need to go to bed, Linda," Dr. Parsi says.

Before Dr. Parsi pulls the door open to leave, Dr. Baldwin gets up and embraces him and says, "Thanks for dinner." Her face is warm.

Dr. Parsi touches her lips and says, "Sleep well, my love." He takes her to the bedroom and watches her fall on the bed. He gently moves her legs to the bed, watches her closed eyes as she breathes calmly. He turns the lights off and leaves the bedroom.

PART TWO
Esther and the King of Persia

Esther turns the pages of the book, *Esther Queen of Persia*; and in a reverie, she imagines herself as a young woman garbed in exotic dress among a group of beautiful virgins coming from all over the Persian Empire, seeking Xerxes the Great's attention. She envisions the king's face as if it were Dr. Parsi's with a thick black beard.

I
A House of Prayer for All Faiths

Dr. Parsi loves to tell his audience, whether it's Esther, Dr. Baldwin, Dr. Ross, or the residents all about Persian history. Among his audience, Dr. Baldwin is most interested and eager to gain knowledge about Dr. Parsi's background. "So how did the Persians get along with other religions: Zoroastrians, Hindus, and Jews?" Dr. Baldwin asks.

Dr. Parsi promptly replies, "Well, the majority of Persians in ancient times were Zoroastrians. But to build an empire and then expand and maintain it, the Persian kings needed capable bodies and industrious people. They also were sincere to please various nations under their sphere by respecting their faiths and heritage."

Dr. Baldwin says, "That's interesting. It must have been a great time to be Persian."

"Yes, it was. The Achaemenid kings like Cyrus the Great symbolized this approach. After capturing Babylon in 539 BC and freeing the Jews from enslavement, he declared, 'My house shall be called a house of prayer for all faiths.' Among freed Jews, there were many warriors, artisans, and learned people who filled the military and administrative ranks of the Babylonian Empire as slaves with no citizenship privileges. Upon conquering Babylon, Cyrus the Great encouraged the Jews to return to their original habitat in Jerusalem, where he appointed a Jewish satrap to represent the Persian Empire. A significant number of formerly captive Jews elected to migrate instead to the principal capitals of the Persian Empire: Susa, Ecbatana, Pasargadae, and Persepolis.

"Despite what's happening in Iran today and the hostile conduct of the mullahs against other religions, Persians have coexisted peacefully with Jews for millennia. Persian Jews are among the oldest continuous inhabitants of that region. The origin of the Jewish Diaspora in Persia came about through the shifting political powers in the ancient Near East in the area known as the Fertile Crescent. The first wave of Jews was deported to Persia in the eighth century BC when Media (Western Iran) was part of the Assyrian Empire. Historical documents from both Assyrian and Elamite empires indicate that after the conquest of ancient Israel by the Assyrian invaders, around 27,000 Jews were deported and forced to settle in Ecbatana (Hamadan) and Susa in Southwest Persia. They are considered part of the Ten Lost Tribes of Israel."

Dr. Baldwin asks for a pause. She picks a glass of water and offers it to Dr. Parsi. She says, "This side of Persian history is completely new to me. Please go on."

So, Dr. Parsi continues, "The next wave of Jewish settlers arrived in Persia to escape persecution from a Babylonian king, Nebuchadnezzar II. A large Jewish Diaspora settled in Isfahan around 580 BC. And the third influx of Jews to Persia was after the conquest of Babylon by Cyrus the Great, the founder of the Achaemenid Empire. Because Jerusalem was frequently ravaged by neighboring states, the Assyrians, Egyptians, and Babylonians, the freed Jews went to Persia to avoid the hardships of reconstructing Jerusalem and enjoy the safety and comfort of life in flourishing Persian cities. That's how the largest Diaspora of Jews freed by Cyrus settled in Susa, where a few generations later, a beautiful female child was given the name of Esther."

The resilience of the Jewish people, who wandered around the ancient world and survived by migrating from region to region, impresses Dr. Baldwin. "Why didn't Zoroastrians take the same approach as the Jewish tribes?" Dr. Baldwin asks Dr. Parsi.

"We didn't need to because we were doing fine until the Arab invasion of Iran in the seventh century AD when Zoroastrianism was the official religion of the Sassanid Empire, and its priests carried a substantial influence at court. After the collapse of the Sassanid Empire, the Arab conquerors forced Iranians to convert to Islam from Zoroastrianism. They did not annihilate us but applied political pressure. As long as we converted to Islam, we could keep our positions, assets, and businesses. Soon, the number of Iranian Zoroastrians who held onto their old faith had dwindled to several thousand. Ironically, the major assault on our existence came when the Iranians gained independence from the Arab rulers by uniting under the Safavid kings and forming a strong government. The new Iranian empire chose a modified version of Islam, the Shia brand, as the official religion of the empire. Ultimately, the Empire ruled a large expanse of Asia covering the Near East, eastern India, the Arab Peninsula, Armenia, Cyprus, and Caucasia. The Shia mullahs became influential at court and convinced the rulers to oppress all other religions, especially Zoroastrians and Jews. Many of us migrated to India, while the families who couldn't afford to leave concentrated in the city of Yazd."

"But what happened to the Jews?" Dr. Baldwin asks.

"They gradually chose to extricate themselves from hostile Shia neighborhoods and moved to separate districts, where they lived quietly in relative isolation. Because they played significant roles in running trade and banking, they were permitted to continue living inside the walled cities and to maintain their businesses."

Dr. Parsi believes Iranians will be much better off if they return to their glorious past, convert to a modern version of Zoroastrianism, and abandon Islam. Even though the Safavid kings created one of the greatest Iranian empires, they also established one of the most fanatic religious ideologies in Iranian history. They inflicted an impractical and inferior way of life onto Iranian society when they let the mullahs demean the glorious Persian past and establish the Twelve Imams School of Shia Islam as the official religion of the empire. He says, "Another unfortunate turning point that left Iranian society in the lurch happened when the mullahs in the Safavid Empire issued a series of fatwas banning production and consumption of alcoholic beverages including the popular Shiraz wine, all singing by women in public, drinking and eating during the month of Ramadan, and celebrating any Persian national holidays. Modern-day mullahs in Iran once again enforce these fatwahs, making life unbearable for millions of people in Iran."

"Considering how modernism entered the Middle East, Iran should be celebrated as the country that implemented the first bicameral parliamentary system in the region. The major change was brought about by Persian intellectuals who had traveled to and became educated in modern political traditions. Iranians revolted against the despotic regime in 1905 and established a constitutional monarchy in Iran. They formed two houses of representatives elected directly by the people. Because the bazaar merchants and the mullahs played a major role in supporting the revolution, a significant number of representatives either were from the clergy or were their supporters. The success of the revolution drove the evolution of the country towards modernism. When in 1925, a nationalist officer by the name of Reza Shah took over the government, the process of modernism in Iran accelerated. Because Reza Shah was secular, the mullahs lost their power, and the Zoroastrians, and to a lesser degree the Iranian Jews, regained equality and respect in society."

"So, what happened after that?" Dr. Baldwin says.

"Well, the Anti-Shah Revolution of 1979 brought the mullahs to power, and that changed everything for Jews and Zoroastrians, as well as for secular people and intellectuals in Iran."

II
Dr. Baldwin's Mother Is Startled

Dr. Baldwin's mother, Barbara, is startled when she hears Dr. Parsi's name. "How long have you been seeing him?" she asks.

"Well, I have worked with him for eight months," Dr. Baldwin says. "But it's been only during the past several weeks that we have become close friends." Dr. Baldwin explains to her Jewish mother that even though Dr. Parsi is from Iran, he is not a Muslim.

"So, what is his religion?"

"He is from a Zoroastrian family," Dr. Baldwin says.

"What?" Barbara shouts.

"But he's not a Zoroastrian either."

Dr. Baldwin knows that her mother would wish dearly to hear that she is dating a wealthy Jewish doctor, though Dr. Baldwin's mother herself married a doctor who is not a Jew. The only reason she accepted the doctor's marriage proposal, as she frequently mentions, was that he agreed to raise their children in the Jewish tradition.

"Well, I loved your father very much, even though he's not Jewish," the mother says. "But it wasn't easy to convince my parents to accept him."

"Mom, we're just friends, okay?" Dr. Baldwin says. "We don't even know what is going to happen to us in four months after I complete my residency, and he finishes his fellowship. For now, we are just good friends."

"Good. Keep it that way," Barbara says. "But what's this [*Zoroastin]* religion?"

"It's an ancient religion, even older than Judaism. Go and google it, Mom!" Dr. Baldwin says.

"How do you spell it?" Mom says.

"It's Z for Zebra, O for olive, R as in radio, O for olive, A for Adam, S as in Sam, T for Tom, R for radio, I for India, A for Adam, N for the navy, I for India, S for Sam, and M for mom. I'll email you his photo," Dr. Baldwin says. "He's a nice guy."

Since Dr. Baldwin and Dr. Parsi's intimate friendship is young, Dr. Baldwin does not think it is relevant to elaborate further on the issue, especially not with her inquisitive mother. Later, when Dr. Baldwin is researching interfaith marriages, she is surprised to learn that a recent survey conducted in the United States by the Pew Research Center's Religion & Public Life Project found the interfaith marriage rate to be 58% among all Jews and over 70% among non-orthodox Jews. She also researches interfaith marriages among Zoroastrians and finds that the rate is significantly lower. Zoroastrians are forbidden to marry people of other faiths. Therefore, interfaith marriage is not an option for strict practitioners of Zoroastrianism. "But he doesn't practice Zoroastrianism," Dr. Baldwin whispers.

Dr. Baldwin considers herself ethnically rather than religiously Jewish. She does not believe in the Genesis tale as written in the Old Testament, or the story of Adam and Eve, or heaven and hell. She believes in evolution and doubts her spirit will continue after she dies. But what about her feelings toward Dr. Parsi? She realizes that she is becoming more interested in him than she had understood. She then continues to research information for her mother's sake to provide her with information about ancient Persia. During the research, she reads about the story of Esther, as mentioned in the Holy Book, and the passages where the Persian king marries an orphan Jew and appoints her the Queen of Persia. She chooses these pages in addition to an introduction to Zoroastrianism and sends them to her mother as an attachment to an email.

A few days later, her mother's reaction arrives in an email that included this question, "Was that Persian king a Muslim, a Zoroastrian, or a Jew?" She shakes her head and wonders whether her mother had read the information thoroughly. If her mother had read the information, she would have known that Esther's story took place over a millennium before the rise of Islam. As Dr. Baldwin delves more into Persian history, she discovers Zoroastrianism was only one of three major contemporary religions recognized by the Persian kings at the time of Esther's rise. She writes to her mother that these three religions were Hinduism, Judaism, and Zoroastrianism, and not Islam. Dr. Baldwin's mother is pleased that the Persian king who married Esther was not a Muslim.

Dr. Baldwin writes, "Mother, Islam was not even around yet!"

III
The Jewish People Arrive in Susa from Babylon

So, the arrival of thousands of Jewish people from Babylon breathes new life into the city of Susa, the administrative capital of the Persian Empire and a city almost as crucial as the ceremonial capital, Persepolis, or the other two capitals, Ecbatana and Pasargadae that are the centers for political and military affairs. The Empire's offices at Susa employ a significant number of Jews who are experienced, educated, craftspeople to manage accounting, personnel, construction, and communications across the empire.

During Susa's mild winter months, when Xerxes the Great resides there, dignitaries from the empire's many nations stretching from India to Egypt come to the palace for an audience with the king in the King's Hall. Before they are admitted to the hall, they assemble in the Apadana, an enormous reception hall with 120 tall marble columns supporting its high ceiling and large capitals with two heads of wild bulls holding the massive beams. It has been claimed that Susa's Apadana could have held up to 10,000 people. These dignitaries enter the King's Hall one by one, bow, pay homage to the Persian king, submit the annual tributes, and deliver the gifts of precious stones, gold, and silver.

Although the rise of Jewish influence in the Persian government benefits the empire in many ways, it also instigates angry reactions from the Zoroastrian Magi, who were competing with Jewish officials for influence at the court. Gradually, this conflict between Jewish and Zoroastrian officials grows and sometime later results in a plot orchestrated by Haman, the Grand Vizier to King Xerxes the Great, to eliminate all Jews at court and in the major cities of Susa and Persepolis.

After many years of a temperate climate and adequate rain, the weather changes, and the summer in Susa becomes brutal. In the middle of the day, one can hardly see a soul in the streets and alleys. The Karkheh River has gone down to a level not seen in generations. Now, one can even see the very base of the Prophet Daniel's tomb at the embankment of the river, and the thick layers of sandstone holding the tomb are now as dry as a bone. The city's population has dwindled to less than half of what it was during the pleasant winter months. It is after the second hot summer when the Mordechai family, including Esther, moves to Ecbatana and settles on a charming property with a spacious adobe house surrounded by a large farm.

Several years after the Mordechai family settled in Ecbatana, a large crowd celebrates Persia's recent military victories in Egypt and Cyprus and awaits the arrival of the king. The dignitaries include a group of satraps from Jerusalem, Babylon, and Egypt, where Mordechai's brother is the governor. Other notables include the Zoroastrian, Jewish, and Hindu grand priests. Two of the king's three wives are attending, but the queen's throne is vacant. Xerxes the Great has spent all day conferring with his military commanders about the new military campaign toward the western stretches of the empire to Sardis. The final stage of the plan includes a massive military expedition to Greece.

Earlier in the day, Esther's uncle assigns several maids to attend her. She is bathed in rose water and groomed in the newest styles as she is about to parade in front of the king. Esther's beauty impresses friends and foes alike.

The Great Victory celebration at the King's Hall begins with an evening ceremony, where Esther walks among the young maidens of the city. It is there that she draws Xerxes the Great's attention. Soon after that, her uncle Mordechai gives her the great news that she is chosen to meet the king. She sobs in elation, not knowing that she will climb the ladder of heavenly fortune and sit next to Xerxes the Great on the queen's throne in the King's Hall. Her new title brings power and prosperity to her but also a better position for her uncle Mordechai at court. Xerxes the Great promotes Mordechai to Grand Vizier in charge of the administration at the palace in Ecbatana.

IV
The Allegory of Esther, the Queen of Persia

Dr. Parsi analyzes the story of Esther and says, "Like the tale of *One Thousand and One Nights,* the allegory of Esther is told in several versions in the different sources. There are discrepancies between these versions, especially regarding the main characters of the story. For example, Esther's presumed uncle Mordechai was also mentioned in ancient tablets discovered in Babylon. Using the date of the tablet referencing Mordechai, which is long before the regime of Xerxes the Great, and following the events chronologically, Mordechai would have been at least an improbable 150 years old when Xerxes the Great became the king of Persia and over 160 when Esther became the Queen of Persia. Likewise, there is no mention of Esther in the ancient Persian tablets discovered in various Achaemenid palaces.

"However, Esther's tomb in the Iranian city of Hamadan—ancient Ecbatana—is considered by Iranian Jews as physical evidence of her historical existence. In this tomb, Esther is presumably buried next to her uncle, Mordechai. The place is a popular destination for Jewish-Iranian visitors who believe the version written in the Book of Esther in the Old Testament as a historical fact." Dr. Parsi adds that the tomb was renovated in 1971 as one of many projects in preparation for the Shah of Iran's 2500 years of the Persian Empire anniversary celebration. Even in the today's Islamic Republic of Iran, the tomb is well maintained by the Jewish-Iranian community and has become a popular tourist attraction in the city of Hamadan.

Dr. Parsi goes on and narrates the story of Esther as he knows it from Persian-Jewish sources and includes some passages about Persian history around Esther's time. He says the story about Esther began when she was an orphan living in Susa with her uncle, who had adopted her. At the time of Xerxes the Great, Susa was one of the four major capitals of the Persian Empire. It has been estimated that at that time, several thousand Jewish-Persian citizens were living in the city of over forty thousand people. Today Susa is a much smaller town, and apart from the remains of the Achaemenid palace on a mound overlooking the city and the tomb of Prophet Daniel at the embankment of the Karkheh River, there are not many exciting places to visit. Nowadays, there are hardly any Jewish residents in Susa.

"Nevertheless, at that historical juncture around the year 486 BC, when Xerxes the Great becomes the king of Persia, a prosperous and influential Jewish Diaspora lives in Susa. There, Esther's uncle, Mordechai, raises her as a member of his family. A few years later, though, Mordechai leaves the brutal summers of Susa behind and moves his entire family, including Esther, to the city of Ecbatana. Here, Esther, beautiful and smart, learns to read and write. She becomes a good dancer, recites songs, and plays chess—a favorite game at the court. While Esther grows to become a beautiful and bright young woman, her uncle Mordechai gains vast knowledge and experience in governmental affairs during his years of service in the court. Eventually, he exerts a significant influence on court affairs and decisions. Ultimately, he is elevated to become an aide to one of the king's viziers.

"When Xerxes the Great arrives in Ecbatana to spend a few weeks at the summer palace, Mordechai's grooming of Esther is rewarded. She joins the parade of beautiful young women in front of the king. The night becomes a magical occasion for Esther, for she draws the king's attention and is chosen to join the palace and live among the king's concubines. Through the influence of her uncle, who was now an aide in the administration of Xerxes the Great, she soon becomes a fixture in the palace."

Dr. Parsi says that Esther becomes popular among the king's staff as an incredibly talented and beautiful young woman. He continues, "While Xerxes the Great is at Persepolis for the summer to escape the unbearably hot climate of the other capital, Susa, where one can cook an egg on a flat stone in the mid-day sun, the Royal Victory Celebration moves to Persepolis. Susa remains one of the two winter capitals of the Empire; the other one is Babylon.

"Xerxes the Great's father, Darius the Great, is mentioned in the Book of Daniel as the great king of the Medes and Persians. He expanded his empire eastward to include parts of India and China and then threw his military might beyond the western regions of the empire. Darius the Great retook Egypt after a brief revolt by the local satrap. He then triumphantly returned to Persepolis to create the world's first multicultural state in which a diversity of ideas took precedence over dictatorial oppression. By implementing this liberal approach to governing his vast empire, Darius managed to pacify most conquered communities. Following the tradition set by Cyrus the Great regarding human rights, Darius the Great established respect for diverse ethnicities, heritages, religions, and cultures. In several ancient tablets from the Achaemenid era, Darius declares that he will not tolerate the idea that weak and defenseless people suffer injustices brought upon them by the powerful groups. He calls upon his subjects to respect the faiths practiced by other nations. He authorizes local rulers to manage their affairs, provided they submit an annual financial tribute to the empire, in addition to delivering soldiers, arms, and raw and manufactured materials. Darius is known as one of the great builders of antiquity. To expand Persepolis, he called upon architects and artisans from every corner of his vast empire, from northern Africa to India and China, from the Caucasus Mountains to the Persian Gulf, to work together with Persian architects to create a new and uniquely Persian cityscape. When Xerxes the Great ascends to the throne, he follows the Persian tradition regarding human rights and respecting other faiths.

"Bearing the crown of the largest empire the western world has known at the time, Xerxes the Great spends most of his time in Persepolis. As is the empire's custom, his building projects sprout up all over the empire. He expands Susa, another Persian Empire capital, and now with his eyes set on building a significant addition to Persepolis, he is selecting architects from all over the empire to work with Persian experts. The first project is a new Apadana at Persepolis much larger than the ones in Susa and Athens. The new Apadana has a stone floor of over 1000 square meters, an enormous roof supported by 72 columns, each 24 meters tall, and made up of marble imported from Anatolia, thus completing a project that Darius the Great had started to build. The Hall of the Kings, where Xerxes the Great receives foreign dignitaries and appoints satraps, lies adjacent to the Apadana and impresses all visitors with its tall, 20-meter-high marble columns with huge capitals with bull's or lion's heads in each corner. Here, the great king accepts tributes from all the nations in the Achaemenid Empire and gives presents in return. Here, the king is entertained at night, drinks exquisite wine, and observes performances by musicians, dancers, and singers from near and far. Here, the king sees Esther in her diaphanous robe gracefully walking in the line of young women selected for their outstanding beauty.

"Departing from the Ecbatana palace with a royal entourage, Esther enters the Apadana at Persepolis, the magnificent spiritual center of the Achaemenid Empire, which was a great world power. The third Achaemenid king, Darius the Great, had expanded Persepolis significantly and established it as the official summer capital. Now, his mighty son, King Xerxes the Great, is celebrating the Persian success of crushing an uprising in Babylon and has ordered Esther to dance among the young maidens at the court. It is earlier on this day that Esther enters the palace, escorted by her entourage, with Mordechai following at a distance. Climbing the monumentally wide stairway leading to the entrance on the palace's east side and surrounded by tall marble walls decorated with reliefs depicting delegates of the 23 subject nations of the Persian Empire paying tribute to Xerxes the Great, Esther is overwhelmed by the power of the Empire. She stares at these kings who receive honorable reception at the court as long as they remain submissive and peaceable and pay their levies regularly. The central section of the relief shows Darius the Great seated on his throne with two trusted aides in military uniforms holding a golden umbrella above his head."

Dr. Parsi continues, "What happens next accelerates Esther's ascent. It occurs on the seventh day of the national celebrations of the victory of Xerxes the Great, the fourth king of the Achaemenid Empire defeating another Babylonian revolt. At the end of the day-long entertainment, a parade of beautiful virgins in celebratory dresses ensues. Esther, who is among these beautiful young women, captivates the king's heart. When Esther spends a night with the king, she reveals that she also sings, plays music, and knows the game of chess. Being a great chess player himself, Xerxes the Great has Haman, his Grand Vizier, bring a magnificent chess set made of ivory and gold and orders Haman to challenge Esther. When Haman loses the game to Esther, the king is surprised and considers playing against Esther. The king dismisses Haman, so the result of his game will be kept confidential in case Esther wins.

He asks Esther to play white against him. During the match, Esther offers Xerxes the Great a serious challenge, but finally, she errs when she misses a chance to checkmate the black king and loses the game. Xerxes the Great is pleased with the win and orders Esther to become one of his nightly companions.

"Xerxes the Great is so enchanted by her beauty that he chooses her immediately as one of his concubines and soon after, as his fourth wife. (Persian kings during the Achaemenid Dynasty usually had, at any period, a queen, several wives, and numerous concubines.)

"Shaken by the rise of Mordechai and the Jewish influence at the court, the Zoroastrian officials and priests react with intimidation and a sinister campaign to protect themselves. Concerned about his position, Haman, a Zoroastrian and the Grand Vizier of the Persian Empire, develops a plan to blame Mordechai and several of his supporters at the royal court and in the capital in planning to assassinate Xerxes the Great and take over the Empire. On the other hand, when Queen Amestris—the one that Esther will replace—witnesses the promotion of Mordechai to one of the king's viziers and as an adviser to Esther, she takes Haman's side, joins him to eliminate Mordechai and the Jewish people. With the help of Queen Amestris, they seek the aid of one of the king's sons, who is also not happy with the situation.

"Haman convinces the king that a Jewish group has hatched a plot to assassinate him. Knowing that more than half of all Achaemenid kings were killed by relatives or insiders, and not realizing that his favorite wife Esther is a Jew, Xerxes the Great believes the claims of Grand Vizier Haman and Queen Amestris and has Mordechai arrested. The king orders that if the accusation can be proven, Haman should prepare a decree to detain and eliminate all Jewish leaders and people in Susa and Ecbatana and elsewhere in the Persian Empire.

"Ironically, there is some truth to the Grand Vizier's claim, but it is not the Jews who are plotting to murder the king; rather, it is the king's oldest son and three of his concubines who have hatched a plot to assassinate the king. The real conspiracy is discovered by one of the other concubines and reported to Mordechai right before his arrest. Mordechai discloses the actual plot to Esther and delivers to her a scroll including the names of the plotters, begging her to inform the king immediately to save the king's life and the lives of the Jewish people."

Dr. Parsi continues telling the story and explains to Esther that Xerxes the Great and his military advisors are preoccupied with the preparations for the next major military campaign to reinforce and expand the empire's might in the western regions and neutralize Greek pressure against allies such as Cyprus and Sparta. Meanwhile, Haman goes to work to find a way to eradicate Mordechai and the Jewish staff at the court. At the same time, the king's oldest son hopes to go further and eliminate his father and capture the throne. The planners are hoping that the king does not have either the time or the attention to discover their plan. Just in time, though, Esther succeeds in arranging a private audience with the king.

In the privacy of the king's chambers, Esther lays out the details of the actual murder plot. "Your Majesty, I'm genuinely worried about your life," Esther says. "The danger is coming from your flesh and blood."

"Be careful, Esther. Are you accusing my son of involvement in a murder plot?" Xerxes the Great asks. "Are you trying to save Mordechai's life by fabricating this story?"

Esther implores the king to give her a chance to explain the seriousness of the matter. "Your Majesty, please allow me to disclose that besides being my guardian, Mordechai is also my uncle. He is a Jew, so am I. Our ancestors were freed from Babylon, migrated to your vast empire, and settled in Susa many decades ago."

The king, who loves Esther above all his other wives and concubines, is bewildered. "So she is a Jew. Is she trying to save her own life, as well as the other Jews?" The king contemplates this turn of events. "Please!" Esther is bowing, and she is on her knees. "Please, look at this scroll. Here are the names of the conspirators. It is not only your son but your closest aide and these concubines who are plotting to assassinate you."

The king takes the scroll and reads the names. He is shaken when he sees the name of Haman and weighs the accusations. After a short moment, he decides to investigate the matter promptly and thoroughly. "Go to your quarters now!" the king roars. "You will pay with your life if the accusations are false."

The king calls the chief of the royal security guard and shares the information with him. The commander reads the scroll and is utterly shocked. "Your Majesty, it appears that we may have two simultaneous plots against you. First was the plot by Mordechai and his Jewish group, the second, by Haman, Queen Amestris, and your oldest son to oust and eliminate Mordechai and the Jewish people and to harm your Excellency." Now, the commander is worried about the king's safety. "Your Majesty, do I have your permission to arrest any or all of these accusers?"

"You must do whatever you deem necessary to find the truth and discover who the plotters are!" the king roars. The king summons Haman and orders the arrest of his son and the three concubines. "I want the matter to be investigated as soon as possible," he tells the commander. "Go now and waste no time."

The commander begins his investigation in the privacy of the King's Hall. Without much fanfare, the guards bring the three concubines as if they were called to entertain the king. Under threat of torture, the concubines confess to the plot and reveal the involvement of both the king's oldest son and Haman. The commander has Haman and the other co-conspirators arrested and brought to the King's Hall. The fate of the queen is uncertain because Haman has not yet revealed her involvement, but her absence from the court re-enforces the king's suspicions.

When the full truth of the plot is finally revealed, the king decrees that the Jewish personnel in the court and the capital must experience no harm. Instead, he orders the commander of the royal security guards to execute the three concubines and his oldest son. He also calls for Mordechai and Haman to be brought to the King's Hall for interrogation by the commander in her presence.

Although Dr. Parsi's description of the tale of Esther, the queen of Persia, differs in detail from the Book of Esther in the Jewish Bible, Esther likes Dr. Parsi's version much better.

Esther says, "It makes the events much more plausible. But what happened to Esther herself?"

Dr. Parsi replies, "Since there is no historical evidence of her existence in the Achaemenid accounts and in the material that has so far been discovered in the ancient ruins of the Persian empires, I refer to the Book of Esther for the rest of the story. Many Persian-Jewish scholars referring to her tomb in the present-day city of Hamadan (the ancient Ecbatana) believe that Esther might have become one of the Persian king's wives. It's plausible that after the assassination of Xerxes the Great several years later—ironically by the commander of the Royal Security Forces—she was given private quarters in the palace in Ecbatana."

"I would love to visit Esther's tomb," Esther says.

"I believe that after her death, she received a royal funeral and is appropriately buried in the Jewish tradition. Subsequently, a large tomb was constructed for her and Mordechai, who is buried next to her crypt. There is another alleged burial place of Esther in a village in northern Israel. Some Israeli scholars argue that this place is the real burial place of Queen Esther.

"Another story told by Jewish Persians is that after the assassination of Xerxes the Great by a commander of the royal security guard some years later with the help of one of Xerxes' sons, Esther is moved in 465 BC to a private palace in Ecbatana with several servants. With an adequate pension, she lives like a retired queen in a palatial abode. After her death of old age, the Persian-Jewish community buries her next to the grave of her uncle Mordechai by enlarging the original vault, which was a modest structure, and adding a blue roof. The burial site of Esther and Mordechai gains much significance several decades later when the site is expanded to include an additional courtyard and a large fountain surrounded by open chambers for Jewish visitors."

"So, this is it!" Esther says. "This explains the connection between these events and the Jewish holiday of Purim."

Dr. Parsi says, "Of course, the anniversary of the three-day fast observed by Esther when she becomes the wife of Xerxes the Great and Queen of Persia, has come to signify another episode among the myriads of challenges and tribulations that faced Jewish people throughout their history. In this historical event in ancient Persia, the Jewish holiday of Purim commemorates the saving of the Jewish people from a massacre by Haman, who was planning to kill the Jews in all four of the capitals of Persia. Given the significant historical link between Jewish-Persians and the story of Esther, current Persian Jews are called 'Esther's Children' even though the Jewish Diaspora was established in Persia centuries before the birth of Esther."

"But how did Esther become the Queen of Persia, and what happened to Queen Amestris?" Esther says.

"The part of the story that addresses the rise of Esther to the throne is very fanciful," Dr. Parsi says. "I believe the fall of Queen Amestris is related to the plot by Haman and the king's oldest son to kill Xerxes the Great. When Xerxes the Great dismisses Queen Amestris, because she was involved in the plot, she left the queen's throne vacant. Now Esther, who had become Xerxes the Great's most beloved wife, is the primary candidate for that position."

Amused by the story, Esther asks Dr. Parsi, "What about you? Do you believe in the story of Esther?"

Dr. Parsi scratches his head, and after a pause, says, "No matter which version of the narrative we accept, the tale of Esther is a great story like the story of Cinderella. It is so appealing that it has inspired poets, musicians, painters, and opera composers to create many masterpieces for it. Yes, I love the story even if it hasn't been verified by any historical documents or tablets found in Ecbatana, Persepolis, or Susa."

"But the Torah has dedicated a whole book to the woman," Esther says.

"Of course, if you believe the Bible verbatim, or for that matter, any other holy book, then yes, Esther's story is true," Dr. Parsi says.

Bewildered by the myths of the Holy Book, Esther likes the story, agrees with Dr. Parsi, and says, "I guess this story is as factual as the seven-day creation of the universe." Then she changes the subject and asks Dr. Parsi, "I meant to ask you, so what's your religion? Who's your God?" While Dr. Parsi is trying to compose an answer that will summarize his faith, Esther adds another question, "And where are you from, Yazd or Tehran?"

V
The Most Important Zoroastrian Center

"I was born in Yazd," Dr. Parsi says proudly. "The city of Yazd is the most important Zoroastrian Center in Iran and shelters the oldest Fire Temple in the country. To reach the city, one must first travel to the historic city of Isfahan, which is more than two hundred miles south of Tehran. Far removed from Tehran's skyscrapers and its divided highways, the city of Isfahan lies on the northern hillsides of the Zagros mountain range. During the Middle Ages, it was one of the largest cities in the world, flourishing from AD 1050 to 1722. In the 16th and 17th centuries, the Safavid Dynasty named it the capital of Persia. The *Naghsh-e Jahan* Square in Isfahan is one of the largest city squares in the world and an outstanding example of Iranian Islamic architecture, with beautiful ceramic art covering its ancient mosques and awe-inspiring domes and minarets. Another outstanding feature is the forty columns of the *Chehel-Sotoon* Palace. UNESCO has designated the square and its surrounding historical structures a World Heritage Site. Today, Isfahan's City Center Market is the fifth largest covered bazaar or shopping mall in the world." Esther has read a short introduction about the Safavid Empire, whose capital was Isfahan, but is eager to learn more. She says, "Please, go on."

"For centuries, Isfahan had been a crossroads of different nations and faith systems that respected each other. Its Jewish community settled there some 2,700 years ago; its Zoroastrian society tolerated the influx of new religions over the millennia. Ultimately, these two communities became the largest concentrations of minority religions in Persia. When the Safavid Dynasty adopted Shia Islam as the official religion of Persia, Jews, Sunnis, and even Zoroastrians were deprived of many ordinary privileges that they had had in the past. They were forced to live in certain quarters in Isfahan. The mullahs called Jews *nejes*, meaning impure, the Zoroastrians, nonbelievers. Gradually, many Jewish families began to leave Isfahan and move to Ecbatana—present-day Hamadan, while the Zoroastrians relocated to Yazd. Ecbatana became the most significant Jewish business center in the Persian Empire, a hub for commerce and productive farming, and the city of Yazd became a haven for Zoroastrians." During that era, Dr. Parsi proudly tells Esther, his forebears moved to Yazd from Isfahan and succeeded in establishing silk and handicraft businesses.

"The city of Yazd is surrounded by *Kavir-e-Loot*—the salt desert—one of the two vast salt deserts in east-central Iran. Because many generations had to live with the *kavir* and its unrelenting and ethereal hot and dry breezes, Yazd developed a unique native Persian architecture characterized by the ancient Persian wind catchers. As a result, Yazd gained the nickname, City of *Bad-be-geerah*—wind catchers. It is also well-known for its Zoroastrian heritage, fire temples, and a few still standing but no longer functioning funerary towers or

112

towers of silence, a neologism coined by Robert Murphy, a translator of the British Colonial government in India.

"Yazd has a history of over 5,000 years, but its present name is derived from Yazdegerd I, a king of the Sassanid Empire. It was during the reign of his grandson, Yazdegerd III, that the Arabs invaded Persia, and after twelve years of bloody warfare toppled the Sassanid Empire. To escape the brutal treatment of the new Islamic regime and to find a haven, many Zoroastrians migrated to Yazd from neighboring provinces. By paying tribute, Yazd was allowed to remain Zoroastrian even after the Arab conquest, although Islam gradually became the dominant religion in the city. Its remote desert location and its inaccessibility protected the city and left it largely immune to destruction and pillage by invaders like the Mongols in the mid-thirteenth century. In 1272, Marco Polo visited the city and remarked on the fine silk-weaving industry. In his book, *The Travels of Marco Polo*, he described Yazd as a 'good and noble city with a significant amount of trade, yet quite isolated. When you leave this city, you ride for seven days before you reach another habitation.'"

"Now let me say something about the basic elements of the Zoroastrian religion and explain that death is the work of Ahriman, who is the embodiment of all that is evil, whereas the earth and all that is beautiful is the work of Ahura Mazda, the Great God. Man must not pollute the earth with his remains after death. Because the open burial in the Tower of Silence is no longer practical, most pragmatic Zoroastrians are choosing cremation." Dr. Parsi adds, "Zoroastrians believe they should practice good deeds."

With a saddened expression, Dr. Parsi says, "Yet even with its 3,000-year history of open burials, these days there are not enough proponents of the open burials in Yazd to keep even one center open. Instead, today's Zoroastrians who want to observe traditional burial practices must have their bodies sent to a forested suburb of Mumbai, India, where the last Tower of Silence still operates." Dr. Parsi says, "There are vultures all around the center as if they had a vulture farm."

Esther laughs. She says, "I recently read that there is a steep decline in vulture population in the area because of the cattle farmers' use of poisonous chemicals."

Dr. Parsi nods and continues, "Although nowadays Zoroastrians are small in numbers, historically speaking, their faith has influenced Judaism, Christianity, and Islam with its teachings of a single deity, a dualistic universe of good versus evil, and a final day of reckoning. As I mentioned before, Zoroastrians believe that humankind is designed to evolve toward perfection, but that path is complicated by evil forces such as greed, lust, and hatred. These evil forces must be challenged proactively by embracing a life of good thoughts, good words, and good deeds. Indeed, a triumvirate of goodness."

"So, do you observe a daily ritual like the Muslims?" Esther wonders.

"I, for one, do not practice suggested Zoroastrian rituals like chanting Avesta hymns or reading its verses daily," Dr. Parsi says, "but I do have a volume of Avesta in English and Farsi in my library."

"Do the mullahs harass the Zoroastrian in Iran?" Esther asks.

"Yes, they do," Dr. Parsi says. When he notes that Esther is eager to know more, he adds that despite their shrinking population, Zoroastrians remain fiercely divided over whether to recognize interfaith families, let alone accept Zoroastrian reformists.

"When tens of thousands of Iranian Zoroastrians fled Persia during the initial Islamic incursions in the 7th century, they were granted refuge in India under the condition they would not marry outside their faith or proselytize among the Hindu majority," Dr. Parsi says. "We don't seek neophytes. That's why our population is declining. For example, in India, home to the majority of Zoroastrians today, the community is dwindling by about ten percent every decade or two."

"We have the same issue in Judaism," Esther says. "More and more Jews have either become agnostic or have married people of other faiths."

Dr. Parsi says, "With all the adversities against the Jewish people, I'm surprised that you still have around 14 million Jews in the world. That by itself is a miracle."

"What's the population of Zoroastrians in the world?" Esther asks.

Dr. Parsi replies, "It's a dying religion. Unfortunately for us, we have less than 200,000 Zoroastrians left worldwide."

A call interrupts Dr. Parsi and Esther's conversation. When Esther takes the call, she recognizes Barrera's voice, who says, "I have some important news regarding your husband's case. Is he awake?" When Esther gets up and peeks into the bedroom, she finds Dr. Hartman's eyes closed and an open medical journal lying on his blanket. She returns to the library and describes the situation to the defense attorney.

"May I stop by this evening?"

"Sure, how about 6:30?" Esther suggests. Barrera accepts the appointment and hangs up. Because Barrera served three years as Chief Prosecutor for the Texas State Attorney's office and as the Texas Secretary of State for two years, he knows more about the nuts and bolts of legal procedure and especially criminal law than anybody else in town. It is for that reason, and because more than sixty percent of the city's residents are Hispanic, that Esther and Dr. Hartman have hired him, hoping he would win a "not guilty" verdict.

Barrera has an additional advantage at a time when most local lawyers practice solo; he took a novel approach to conduct his legal practice by forming a group practice. Taking advantage of his smooth demeanor and his administrative prowess as a county and state prosecutor, Barrera launches the first group law practice in town after convincing a highly popular Anglo criminal defense attorney who graduated with him from the same law school to join him. To overcome this Anglo friend's initial reluctance to join him, Barrera offers to place his name first in their business's title, provided he, Barrera, could select the location of their practice. They added their family savings together, bought a vacant lot across from the old courthouse near the San Antonio Riverwalk, and hired a Mexican-American architect to draw up the blueprints of their building, a large two-story edifice in the Spanish-Mexican design decorated with colorful murals from Mexican artists. It takes them a few years to establish their business. The key to their success which overshadows all other, mostly white, law practices is a well-publicized case of an innocent man on death row that goes all the way to the Supreme Court of the United States and results in a decision by the high court to scrap the conviction and order a new trial. That case puts their practice on the map of Who's Who in Law. A year later, Barrera becomes the first Mexican-American President of the Texas Trial Lawyers Association, and a few years later, the president of the State Bar of Texas. His critical success in court has been in choosing as many Mexican-American jurors on his juries as possible. Now in the case of Dr. Hartman, he will try to include one or two Jewish jurors.

———————

That evening Dr. Hartman waits for Barrera with some misgivings, afraid to hear more negative news about his case. But when Barrera arrives at Dr. Hartman's house, Barrera's face shows only determination to win. With his usual positive demeanor, he greets both Dr. Hartman and Esther.

"The final ballistics report on the three recovered bullets from the case has been submitted to the court. It shows as I thought, that a shot from your handgun killed Marcel and that a bullet from Marcel's pistol hit your leg. The bullet that killed Saul passed through his body and smashed against the wall of your house, destroying the striations that could have identified which handgun fired it. Since the weight of 9mm and .38 caliber handgun ammunition are almost identical, there is no way to tell its origin. We have no accounts of two bullets: one that passed through Saul's arm and the fifth bullet fired from either your handgun or Marcel's. If someone were to recover the missing bullets and determine which gun they came from, we would have a better idea of what exactly transpired that afternoon in your driveway. If both of the missing bullets were recovered and determined to be from your handgun, we would know that Marcel's gun killed Saul since all three of your bullets would be accounted for. If only a single bullet is recovered and proved that it was fired from your handgun, it would mean that the chance that your gun fired the fatal shot that killed Saul is only 50%. Assuming that is the case, it should be more than enough to produce reasonable doubt in the minds of the jurors. It might even inspire the judge to issue a directed verdict in our favor. As it stands, I will argue that there is a great deal of reasonable doubt concerning who fired each of the two missing bullets.

"There is one slight wrinkle, however, to this story. The DA is claiming that you fired the first shot, starting the melee. Now, it's up to the DA to prove that you killed that boy recklessly and not out of fear for your son's life or in your self-defense."

Dr. Hartman becomes impatient and cries out, "I told the police that I waved the handgun to scare him off, to force him to leave Saul alone. Then that drug dealer began to shoot first at me and then at Saul."

"But the DA's office claims you were the one who pulled the trigger first," Barrera says. Dr. Hartman is now furious, "How can they possibly say who shot first? He was going to kill me. First, he kicked me in the abdomen, and then he shot me in the leg. So I just pulled the trigger to stop that son of a bitch. It was his bullet that killed Saul, not mine."

"I was there watching the whole disaster," Esther says. "My husband is telling the truth."

"Well, the DA's office claims that you overreacted because you were angry. They claim you were totally out of control," Barrera says. He suggests lining up a few witnesses, including Esther, to testify during the trial. "The DA is subpoenaing the victim's father and also one of Dr. Hartman's junior faculty members."

"Who is that faculty member?" Dr. Hartman asks.

"The DA's office hasn't released the list to me yet. Have you shown any personal animosity toward anyone on your staff?" Barrera asks. "The prosecutor claims you frequently harass certain students, a fellow in your department, and two junior faculty members. He is trying to draw a horrible picture of you for the jurors."

Dr. Hartman immediately presumes Dr. Parsi will be one who testifies at the trial. He asks the defense attorney, "When will you find out who is on the subpoena list of the DA?"

"I'll let you know as soon as I receive the names, maybe by tomorrow."

———————

That evening, Esther and Dr. Hartman avoid talking about the trial. They eat a light dinner and dessert, Esther goes to the library and immerses herself in a book, while Dr. Hartman picks up a few medical journals and retreats to the sitting area of the bedroom. Esther is not surprised that the DA's office is trying to magnify Dr. Hartman's weaknesses—his fiery temper and violent encounters with residents and colleagues. For a while, she contemplates discussing the issue with Dr. Parsi but then decides to leave the matter in the hands of Barrera. She thinks about Dr. Parsi and hopes that he will not hurt Dr. Hartman's position in the case when he's called to the bench by the DA to testify. Ensconced in her comfortable reading chair, she returns to one of the old-fashioned detective stories that she always finds comforting in a crisis. Although they are in separate rooms, for some reason, they both recall the last year of Saul's life and search for clues of his downfall, his involvement with illicit drugs, and his turbulent relationship with Marcel.

VI
Why Are You Standing There?

"Dr. Parsi, why are you standing there? Come on in!" Esther gestures for Dr. Parsi to enter the house. "My husband is taking a nap. Let's sit in the library for a while."

Dr. Parsi enters the house and follows Esther to the library. While they chat about Dr. Hartman's health and affairs at the University, Dr. Parsi's eyes rove across the stacks of medical textbooks on one side of the room and the literary books on the other. Then he notices the book *Esther Queen of Persia,* among the volumes in the fiction section. "May I look at it?" Dr. Parsi asks Esther.

"Of course," Esther says. "But I thought you already read the book, haven't you?"

"No, not this book," Dr. Parsi says.

"Knowing you have read a lot about the history of ancient Persia," Esther says. "I'd like to hear more about what you know of the role Esther played in the Persian Empire."

Dr. Parsi is pleased to continue telling his account of Queen Esther's tale. "The Achaemenid kings, like their contemporaries around the ancient world, collected beautiful young concubines. They were maidens, and each carried some light duty during the day. The kings had several wives, of whom the most popular and beautiful one would eventually become the queen. The same scenario applied to Xerxes the Great, the Persian king some 2600 years ago," he says. "The wives' job was to provide children, especially boys, so the king would have heirs as well as trusted sons, to command his military expeditions."

"How many sons did they need?" Esther wonders.

"As you may know, the infant mortality rate was very high in those times. They would lose most of their children during infancy. Xerxes the Great was fortunate in one way because from his six wives, he had more than twelve legitimate sons, of which six survived to adolescence. He was eventually murdered by one of his sons."

"How about the concubines' offspring?" Esther asks, "Weren't they counted?"

"Their children were not considered legitimate sons and daughters of the king, so they could not become kings and queens." Dr. Parsi says.

"How many slaves did the king keep at court?" Esther asks.

"Well, in general, mass slavery as a whole was never practiced by Persians, and in many cases, the situation and lives of drudges and prisoners of war were somewhat similar to those of the laborers."

"But slavery was a norm then, wasn't it?" Esther says. "Didn't they usually enslave their prisoners of wars?"

"The POWs were semi-slaves. Provided they would work as laborers or low ranked soldiers, they would live among the low class and poor population. Though slavery was an existing institution in Egypt and Babylon before they were conquered by Cyrus the Great, I don't believe the Achaemenid government promoted or practiced slavery." Dr. Parsi asks a rhetorical question, "How could they promote slavery when Cyrus the Great freed the enslaved Jews when he captured Babylon?"

"That's interesting but hard to believe," Esther says.

"Cyrus the Great offered the freed Jews two choices: either migrate to Persia or go to Jerusalem. He even financed the construction of the second Jewish Temple in Jerusalem."

Returning to her favorite character, Esther, the Queen of Persia, and amused by the various tales surrounding her mysterious life, Esther asks, "So what happened to Esther? Was she the first, second, third, or fourth wife?"

"I'm afraid to tell you, dear Esther, that what I know perhaps only half-truth," Dr. Parsi says. "According to Iranian Jewish tradition, Esther was so beautiful and talented that on her very first parade at court, Xerxes the Great became enchanted with her and ordered that she be kept in the palace to perform music and dance for him in the evenings. When she became the fourth wife of the king, she convinced the king to promote her uncle Mordechai as her aide."

"You Persians love good stories," Esther says. "It sounds like the tale of the *One Thousand and One Nights*."

"But there is more truth to my story than Shahrazad," Dr. Parsi smiles. "After all, it's written in the Holy Book."

It is a mild, sunny day in San Antonio. The spring weather has brought beneficial rain, which has saturated the Edwards Aquifer, enhanced the growth of grass and plants, and created islands of colorful wildflowers all over the Hill Country, especially along the farm roads and in the medians of the highways. The popular Scenic Loop Road north of the city has become a place for cyclists to bike for miles to as far north as the town of Boerne. If they are in good shape, they continue toward Luckenbach, where the traditional dance hall used to host Willie Nelson's Annual Fourth of July Concert and Celebration.

On the south side of the city, a newly constructed hike-and-bike trail connects all five historical missions from the Alamo and the city center to Mission Espada, 10 miles south of downtown. Along the beautifully landscaped trail, there are shaded rest areas with limestone benches, water fountains, thickets of live-oak, and redbud trees to provide bikers and walkers alike places to stop and rest. From spring to fall, patches of morning flowers, daffodils, and wild roses grow alongside the banks of the San Antonio River and display a picturesque panorama to visitors of the trail.

On a beautiful and sunny day in early spring, Dr. Parsi and Dr. Baldwin park the car at the Blue Star Arts Center, pull their bikes from the rack and begin to pedal on the Mission Trail. The trail goes for over ten miles along the San Antonio River, passing the shadows of Mission Concepción, Mission San José, Mission San Juan, and Mission Espada, with the river flowing below.

After biking for several miles, Dr. Parsi and Dr. Baldwin stop at Mission San José, which initially was called Mission San José y San Miguel de Aguayo. The large mission edifice, which was built from 1758 to 1782, is still in good shape. Once it was called the most beautiful church along the entire frontier of New Spain, locally it is known as the Queen of the Missions. *La Ventana de Rosa,* or the Rose Window, considered one of the finest examples of baroque architecture in North America, is set into the south wall of the church sacristy. They visit the church, read the historical notices around the building, and take in the short movie about the history of the mission. Having biked for a while, they decide it is time for lunch in the lush green yard, which is surrounded by limestone walls. Dr. Parsi pulls two wrapped sandwiches from his knapsack and offers one to Dr. Baldwin. "Go ahead, unwrap it."

Inside, on top of the white bread, Dr. Baldwin finds a small plastic bag. She is surprised.

"What is this?"

Dr. Parsi smiles, "Please, just open the bag."

Dr. Baldwin carefully opens the small bag, and inside finds a note and a white gold ring with a square sapphire. "What's the meaning of this, Dr. Parsi?"

"Please read the note," Dr. Parsi says.

Dr. Baldwin unfolds the small note and reads it out loud, "Happy Birthday, Linda,"

Dr. Parsi says, "Isn't tomorrow your birthday?"

"Yeah, it is." She tries the ring on and holds the stone up against the sun. It glows in the bright light. "Oh, I love it. It's beautiful, my favorite color."

Dr. Baldwin snuggles close to Dr. Parsi and looks at him and meets his eyes, "I love this."

They hold hands. Dr. Baldwin reaches up and touches Dr. Parsi's face.

Dr. Parsi whispers, "Happy birthday, my dearest." They kiss passionately and then quietly eat their sandwiches.

VII
Dr. Hartman Reviews Dr. Parsi's NIH Application

Dr. Hartman peruses Dr. Parsi's application for the NIH research grant. He uses a red highlighter, marks two sections, and then he calls Dr. Parsi into his office.

"You have done an excellent job revising the application." Dr. Hartman says, and adds, "The NIH director has no excuse to reject it. The only crucial point in the package that needs to be strengthened is the detailed steps to conduct the first stage of your research. I believe it will help your position if you add another investigator who has already achieved some success in one of the areas of your project. You need a faculty member from the pediatrics department. Go and talk to Dr. Mike Hoffman. He's very eager to be associated with us in one of our research protocols," Dr. Hartman says. "By the way, why don't you add another junior faculty member to the list?"

Dr. Parsi replies, "Dr. Baldwin has shown some interest in getting involved, but she is leaving the department at the end of her residency."

"Well, this is confidential, but I'm considering offering her a faculty position if she scores sufficiently high on the board examination." Dr. Hartman says.

"That's great. I'll keep that under wraps," Dr. Parsi promises.

"She's a great resident," Dr. Hartman says, "but she tends to become anxious if I put too much pressure on her."

Dr. Parsi is utterly surprised by Dr. Hartman's statement. He knows the pressure on his staff is the hallmark of his approach to running the department. Dr. Hartman interrupts Dr. Parsi's train of thoughts and asks him to leave the revised draft of the grant application on his desk, "I will read it one more time, perhaps write a few comments, and if necessary, I'll pencil in some suggestions. You can come to my home tomorrow and pick it up."

It is one of the rare occasions that Dr. Hartman is complimenting Dr. Parsi's work. Since the shootout, Dr. Hartman has morphed into a reasonable person when he deals with Dr. Parsi.

"I must admit, without your help, the application would have been rejected. You have assisted me a lot in advancing this process. Thank you," Dr. Parsi says. "I appreciate your suggestion about adding Dr. Baldwin as an associate researcher on the project."

"Good luck with your attempt to acquire her commitment."

———

Glancing at the pages of the book, *Esther Queen of Persia*, Esther imagines herself at a young age of sixteen, garbed in an exotic transparent dress, joining the group of the most beautiful virgins from all over the Persian Empire seeking King Xerxes' attention, the king who could eliminate the entire

Persian Jewish diaspora including her family with a wave of his hand. Attending the large celebration of the recent Persian military victories in Egypt and Cyprus, Mordechai, whose brother is now the governor of Egypt, observes the group of satraps, including those from Jerusalem and Babylon, and the Zoroastrian, Jewish, and Hindu Grand Priests. Two of the king's three wives are in attendance, but the queen's throne next to the king's stands vacant. Xerxes has not yet arrived because he has been busy all day conferring with his military commanders regarding a new campaign toward the Western stretches of the Empire to recapture Sardis, and perhaps contemplating an expedition to Greece.

The trumpeters and drummers begin to play as Xerxes the Great finally arrives and strides to his throne. He addresses the audience members who have risen and are bowing deeply, asking them to take their seats. A queue of servers brings trays of fruit, grilled and poached meat, fish, fowl, loaves of bread, and jugs of red wine from nearby vineyards. After the first serving of wine in a silver goblet, a golden one is offered to the king by Haman, the Grand Vizier. The king looks at the empty throne of the queen with displeasure and whispers a few words to Haman. Then he turns away and raises his goblet. The audience does the same, and cries of "Long live the King of Kings" fill the air. The music begins, and a line of beautiful young girls enters the Hall of Kings from the portal to the Apadana.

Since she arrived at the palace, Esther has paraded several times around the Hall of Kings, but that was when the king was away at other palaces or on a military campaign. Tonight is the first time she is brought in when the king is presiding on his throne. Haman notices that the king pays extra attention to Esther. While the rest of the young women stay in the hall to entertain the guests, Esther and two other girls are asked to be seated next to the king's wives. The king indicates to his Grand Vizier that he wants to know more about Esther. At this point, Haman calls upon Mordechai to come forward and present the information to the king.

———————

While Esther is rooted in her reverie, Dr. Parsi picks up another book, *Esther's Children,* written by a contemporary Jewish-Persian author, and starts flipping through the pages. One of the illustrations shows a Jewish-Persian architect proudly standing in the courtyard of the tomb of Esther in Hamadan. Dr. Parsi points out the picture to Esther and explains that the entire structure was renovated entirely by the last Shah of the Pahlavi Dynasty of Iran in 1974.

When Dr. Parsi is about to leave, Esther peeks into the bedroom and sees that Dr. Hartman is hard at work, perusing Dr. Parsi's grant application. "Please ask Dr. Parsi to come in and pick up the binder," Dr. Hartman says. "I just finished reading the application and added only a few comments."

After Dr. Parsi comes in and sits on a chair near the bed, Dr. Hartman pauses for a moment until Esther has returned to the library, looks at Dr. Parsi apologetically and says, "There is something I'm obliged to disclose to you before I tell you more about the upcoming trial." Dr. Hartman speaks in measured syllables. "Do you remember a note? Well, I mean a message that you received from the Dean?"

"Yes, I do," Dr. Parsi says.

"It was sent to you after I had a meeting with the Dean. He was going to tell you something that you wouldn't have liked to hear," Dr. Hartman says. "Also, do you remember the meeting I had with Dr. Ross while you were in the pathology conference?"

"I do remember that you and Dr. Ross didn't come to the conference," Dr. Parsi says.

"Yes. It was one of the few pathology conferences that I have ever missed." Dr. Hartman says, "Those two meetings were related to the issue of terminating your fellowship in the department."

"I am not surprised. But why didn't you fire me?" Dr. Parsi says.

"Because you taught me a lesson," Dr. Hartman says. "Listen, even for an old professor, it is never too late to acquire a new pearl. I was wrong, but I was so certain that Esther had an ovarian tumor that your insistence on the pregnancy test infuriated me to the point that I made up my mind to fire you."

Visibly shaken, Dr. Parsi says. "I had no idea you would go that far in response to an academic argument about a routine urine test!"

"I even convinced the Dean to go along with my decision," Dr. Hartman admits. "Esther was the only person who was supporting you. She tried to persuade me to change my mind."

"How about Dr. Ross? Did he agree with you?" Dr. Parsi wants to know.

"By the time I was going to inform Dr. Ross of my decision, you had already called me and told me that the pregnancy test was positive, and there wasn't a tumor at all," Dr. Hartman says. "I'm sure what I've told you now enrages you. I completely understand. But I feel you needed to know this before I proceed to my second point."

"What else do you have in mind?" Dr. Parsi says curtly. "Please say it quickly, for I need to leave and go to a quiet place to absorb all of what you have said so far." Dr. Parsi is filled with disgust and clenches his fists.

"Please don't rush to any quick conclusion. What you did with Esther's presumed abdominal mass was a big lesson for me. I want to apologize to you most sincerely for arguing with you and wanting to fire you. Even if the pregnancy test had been negative, and Esther was harboring an ovarian tumor, I should still have respected your call. As you said, it's written in every medical textbook that one must run that test in women with a pelvic mass during childbearing age, even if they take contraception, even when they have infrequent sexual activity."

Both Dr. Hartman and Dr. Parsi are now quiet. A few tears roll down from Dr. Hartman's eyes over his cheeks. For Dr. Parsi, the revelation is devastating. How close he had come to being dismissed in the middle of the fellowship! That would have been disastrous for his career. Dr. Hartman breaks the silence. "Please accept my sincere apology. I'm not seeking your help and do not wish to influence your testimony in court. That will be at your sole discretion, but I'm apologizing to you because you were right, and I was wrong."

"I don't believe you," Dr. Parsi says. "You are saying this because of the trial."

"I don't blame you, Dr. Parsi," Dr. Hartman says. "However, my apology is sincere."

Before Dr. Parsi leaves the room, Dr. Hartman hands him the grant folder and says, "Congratulations. You have done a great job with this application. It is good to go. I am confident you will do a great job of conducting the proposed research. You will be the first fellow to obtain a five-million-dollar grant at the University."

Dr. Parsi takes the folder, rises, and walks toward the door, but before he reaches it, Esther opens the door and enters the room. Esther sees the flushed face of Dr. Parsi and says, "Dr. Parsi, please accept his apology. He truly means it."

When Dr. Parsi does not respond, Esther says, "My husband wants you to stay in the department and carry on your research."

Several days later, Dr. Parsi returns to Dr. Hartman's home. Dr. Hartman's confession regarding his initial plan to fire Dr. Parsi, and then his apology, has left the desired impression on him. He looks at Dr. Hartman with an air of sympathy and suddenly sees him as a finicky and wounded soldier who needs help to survive.

"Are you able to walk?" Dr. Parsi asks.

"The leg feels heavy. It's still a bit painful when I stand on it for any length of time," Dr. Hartman says.

"Well, I'm sure you're doing physical therapy," Dr. Parsi says. "That should help."

"I am," Dr. Hartman agrees. Becoming quiet, he begins to ruminate about his legal challenges. The uncertainties of the jury trial cast a shadow on everything he says or does. After a deep sigh, Dr. Hartman whispers, "Dr. Parsi, my defense attorney says that the DA is about to request that you attend an interview, and he also plans to call you as a witness during the trial."

"What do you want me to do?" Dr. Parsi asks Dr. Hartman.

"I cannot tell you how you should conduct yourself during the deposition or the trial," Dr. Hartman says. "But it could help you if you talk to the Dean. He has told me they have a legal expert to guide you through the process."

The conversation is interrupted when Esther enters the room. She brings a tray of tea with a plate of almond cookies. Esther looks at the stack of paper on the bed and asks, "May I put these papers together?" Esther says.

"Thanks. I'll do that when we are done here with the project," Dr. Hartman says. "I'll put the binder here on the bureau."

Esther sits on a chair next to the bed and looks at scattered papers and folders. Pointing to the package, Esther asks, "How does it look?"

"Dr. Parsi has done a solid job. It's good to go," Dr. Hartman says. "But, I'll do another review to be sure that every single one of the grant director's questions is satisfactorily answered."

After a while, Esther and Dr. Parsi leave the room and walk to the library, while Dr. Hartman goes over the application and begins to organize and read through it once more.

VIII
Esther Becomes the Queen of Persia

According to the Persian-Jewish folk tales, against all the odds, Esther, an orphaned Jew, eventually becomes the Queen of Persia. The unexpected absence of Queen Amestris at the royal banquet in the *Tukta* or Hall of Kings to celebrate Xerxes the Great's recent military victories leaves the throne of the queen vacant. The sight of the empty seat right next to his own enrages Xerxes, whose roving eyes settle on one of the young dancers. Esther's appearance in the hall leaves an impulsive romantic impression on the king. When he asks Amestris to explain her absence, she speaks with an extreme disdain against Esther. She reminds him that Esther comes from an unknown family, cannot be trusted, does not deserve to be in court, and certainly should not have too many private audiences with the king. Queen Amestris' scheming against Esther produces the opposite effect. She has given the king grounds to consider dethroning her.

The misfortunes of Queen Amestris start when the king spends more time with Esther than with her. Meanwhile, the queen's confidant, Haman, feels threatened by Mordechai's promotion to the vizier. Knowing that Mordechai is a Jew from Susa, Esther's hometown, he invents the story of a Jewish conspiracy at court and shares it with Queen Amestris. Together, Haman and the queen spread the rumor that the Jewish guards, under the direction of Mordechai, are plotting to murder the king before he departs for the upcoming military expedition against Greece. Eventually, the tale reaches the ears of the king.

The Greek historian Herodotus, who had exaggerated the number of Persian fighters at the battle of Marathon by ten times, thereby giving that military encounter a momentous significance in Greek and Western history, also reports on several plots to murder Xerxes the Great, one of them orchestrated by two sons of Xerxes the Great from a senior wife. The Greek historian indicates that the plot to assassinate the king arose from a family feud, unrelated to the rise of Jewish influence in the court or Esther's training to become a new queen. Similarly, the evidence discovered at Persian sites disagrees with another historical report, which says that the murder plot against Xerxes the Great was due to the king's foul play with one of his sisters-in-law. On the other hand, Jewish-Persian tradition holds that the alleged scheme to murder Xerxes the Great was much more serious than a mere family feud.

When the rumors come to Xerxes the Great's attention, he calls upon his grand vizier, Haman, a Zoroastrian, to investigate. Haman, who was longing for such an opportunity to get rid of Mordechai, echoes the rumors and warns the king that all Jewish personnel at the palace and their supporters in town are behind the plot. The outraged king orders the arrest of all Jews at court, including especially Mordechai, and promises harsh punishment for all Jews if a thorough investigation proves the allegations. Just before Haman's men come to arrest him, Mordechai reaches Esther with the disturbing news.

"We are facing a serious problem, niece," Mordechai tells Esther. "Haman and the queen are accusing the entire Jewish community of concocting a plot to murder the king."

Esther does not understand the gravity of her situation, and naively replies, "But the king doesn't know I'm a Jew."

"Beware! Haman is going to tell the king that you are a Jew," Mordechai warns. "You are going to lose everything, perhaps even your life."

"So, what should I do?" Esther asks.

"The situation is dire for all of us and for the king too, because he is truly in danger of being assassinated. While Haman is spreading the rumor that we, the Jews, are about to murder the king, there is a real plot in the making to kill the king. The actual plot has been orchestrated by the king's son and his second wife as well as a few concubines," Mordechai tells Esther.

"How sure are you about this plot?" Esther asks.

"I have received the information from two concubines who are trustworthy. They have requested that their names be protected and only be revealed to the king." Mordechai pulls out a rolled parchment and gives it to Esther, "Here are the names of the real plotters. Present it only to His Majesty."

Esther looks at the list and tells Mordechai, "But the king is busy planning his expedition to Greece. He has not called upon me to visit him tonight."

"The decrees to arrest all Jews who reside in the palace and to eliminate all Jews in the capital have been prepared by Haman and will be signed in a day," Mordechai says. "Haman wants to destroy us. Look, time is crucial here. The lives of all Jews in Persia may be at stake!" Mordechai is desperate.

Ultimately, good fortune smiles on the Jewish side. Exhausted by the preparations for war against Greece, the king seeks a break and calls for Esther to visit him in the royal suite that evening. Esther carefully chooses her gown, perfume that the king likes most, and follows her two escorts to the king's private chamber. She is cleared by the guards at the entrance and enters the chamber alone, aware that the fate of her entire tribe depends on her. The king is pleased to see her and invites her to rest on a lounge chair next to his. A jug of wine, a bowl of fruit, a chess set, and two golden goblets are on the table. After two cups of red wine and some foreplay, the king asks Esther why she is so sad. Here, Esther takes advantage of the opportunity to reveal the information about the real plot against the king. She asks the king for permission to bring a grave matter to His Majesty's attention. The king, who is not in the mood for any stern news at first, denies Esther's request, but when he observes how concerned and unhappy Esther is, he gives her permission to place the scroll in front of him.

"Your Majesty, I'm worried about your safety," Esther says. "I have crucial information about a plot, God forbid, to seriously harm you."

The king, who already has Haman's information, says, "I value your concern, but we already know who the plotters are, and tomorrow early in the morning, they will all be eliminated."

"Your Majesty, there is indeed a plot, but the Jews are not the ones conspiring against you!" Esther pulls out the parchment roll, which she carried in her silk robe, with the names of the real plotter and adds, "Your Majesty, here are the names of the actual plotters. I beg you to believe me. Haman is the leader of the plot." Esther drops to the king's feet, "I beg you to look at the names and seriously consider the information included herein."

The king pulls Esther up, points to the lounge chair, and tells her, "Go. Sit there." He wants to change the subject of conversation. He looks at the chess set. The unfinished earlier second game from the night before is intact; he was playing white. The white king was in a precarious position, soon to be checkmated. The king tells Esther, "Let's finish the game." They both occupy their chairs. Xerxes cannot find a safe move for the king to avoid checkmate. The king looks at Esther and says, "Esther, let's switch our positions. I'll take the black piece; you, the white." Esther obeys the king's command and plays white. "Can you propose a move in which the white king gets out of the trap?" the king says.

Esther concentrates on the game, and after several minutes, she finds a way to save the white king. After three moves and after she brings the knight forward and sacrifices a bishop, Esther saves the king. She says, "Here it is, your majesty. The king is safe now."

Esther settles again at the king's feet. She pleads, "I beg you to read the information. Your Majesty's safety is in jeopardy, the actual plotters are closing in, and you, our great king, may perish if nothing is done right away."

The king, who is impressed by Esther's maneuver to save the white king, softens his position and says, "Okay, I'll read the document while you try to rescue the white king."

"So what happens to poor Mordechai," Esther says, "Did he survive the wounds from the torture?"

"There is a good ending for both Mordechai and Esther," Dr. Parsi says. "The king rescinds his order to arrest and eliminate the Jews in the palace and capital. Mordechai's position is not only restored, but he replaces Haman as Grand Vizier, and Esther ascends to the throne and is named Queen of Persia."

"How long did she serve as the queen?" Esther asks.

"Not for long. Eventually, Esther became a sacrificial lamb, a pawn in the brutal competition for power between the Jewish and the Zoroastrians groups, between the king's sons and Mordechai," Dr. Parsi says.

"You should be pleased about the rise of Zoroastrians in the Persian Empire. Right?" Esther inquires.

"Not at all. The cooperative relationship between the Jews and Zoroastrians was beneficial for both parties. However, the Zoroastrians paid dearly for those fleeting decades of power in the government," Dr. Parsi says.

"How so?"

"The peak of Zoroastrian domination in Persia wasn't during the Achaemenid Empire, for during those centuries the empire had a liberal policy towards all faiths, whether it was Zoroastrianism, Judaism, or Hinduism. The kings would accept other deities, especially when their cults supported the empire. Recognizing and believing in the power of the major Babylonian god, another Achaemenid king, Darius the Great, after putting down a revolt and re-conquering Babylon, called himself a direct representative of Marduk."

"It was only during the Sassanid Empire when Zoroastrianism became the empire's only recognized religion. Those centuries were a Golden Era for Zoroastrians, whereas it is during those centuries that, for the first time, Jewish-Persians, Hindu-Persians, and *Zuhacs* were bitterly oppressed. When the Arabs invaded Persia, toppled the Sassanid Empire, and imposed Islam, all other religions, including Zoroastrianism, were outlawed, and their followers were persecuted."

"So, the history of Persian Jews is somewhat similar to Jewish history elsewhere," Esther concludes. "But why didn't Zoroastrians survive the adversities as well as the Jews and remain a viable religion?" she asks.

"That is an unfathomable puzzle for me, since all Iranians are proud of their heritage, and Zoroastrianism is part of their ancient history," Dr. Parsi says. "I'll blame this tragedy on the takeover of Persia by Islam in the seventh century in general and the mullahs in today's Iran in particular."

"But the mullahs are persecuting the Jews, too."

"Well, yes, the mullahs are against any group that does not conform to their radical Islamic doctrine. In ancient Persia, it was different: Jews were an important part of the community. They comprised up to 20 percent of the population during Xerxes the Great's regime and played a crucial role in the affairs of the government," Dr. Parsi says. "So much so that a beautiful and intelligent Jewish woman became Queen of Persia."

IX
Dr. Parsi Is Appalled

Dr. Hartman's admission that he was about to fire Dr. Parsi until Esther's positive pregnancy test saved the day infuriates Dr. Parsi. The fact that Dr. Hartman had even obtained the support of the Dean also wounds his feelings gravely. The realization that a simple urine test, which is standard for evaluating a pelvic mass in a woman of reproductive age, could trigger Dr. Hartman's rage with potentially adverse consequences for his life and career keeps Dr. Parsi awake several nights.

After leaving Dr. Hartman's home, he brings the grant application to his office and drops it on his desk. He no longer cares about the grant and has lost all desire to open the binder and read Dr. Hartman's annotations. When his co-investigator asks him about the grant after the grand-round, he sidesteps the question with, "I'm still working on it." And when the co-investigator finds him uncharacteristically preoccupied and unfocused at the pathology conference, he asks, "Are you alright?"

Dr. Parsi's says, "I'll be okay."

A few days later, Dr. Parsi gets a call from the Dean, "Come and visit me at my office after work at 5:30 PM."

When Dr. Parsi enters the Dean's office, the Dean introduces him to Mr. Barrera, an experienced attorney in town. After an initial greeting and handshake, Barrera tells Dr. Parsi, "You are going to be subpoenaed by the DA's office to testify at the trial, and they would like to interview you first."

Dr. Parsi says, "That's fine with me."

"They have tentatively set a date for next Wednesday morning. As you know, we have a serious challenge on hand. They are going to highlight Dr. Hartman's occasional anger during the trial." Barrera goes on to elaborate that they may question Dr. Parsi about instances when Dr. Hartman treated him harshly, and probably about other cases when Dr. Hartman treated other students and residents badly as well.

The Dean says, "As we all know, Dr. Hartman is an excellent educator and demands the best from everybody. Please be sure to arrive at Mr. Barrera's office, where the deposition will take place an hour before the DA's team arrives."

The Dean notices how quiet Dr. Parsi remains during the discussion. Not knowing how deeply Dr. Hartman has hurt Dr. Parsi's feelings, the Dean continues with the lecture, telling Dr. Parsi to be pragmatic with his testimony. The Dean hopes the briefing will prepare Dr. Parsi to be helpful to Dr. Hartman.

Barrera continues the discussion and tells Dr. Parsi, "Please be as brief as possible. Do not elaborate. There is nothing wrong with saying, 'I do not know,' or 'I'm not sure.' The prosecutor will try to manipulate and force you to say something that may help his case against Dr. Hartman." Barrera reads several hypothetical questions that the prosecutor may ask Dr. Parsi, like "Did he ever insult you?" or "Did he ever belittle you because you are from Iran or because you are Muslim."

The Dean interrupts Barrera and says, "Mr. Barrera, Dr. Parsi is not a Muslim."

"Excuse my ignorance, Doc. So, what's your religion?"

"I was born into a family of Zoroastrians."

———————

On the way to his office, Dr. Parsi comes across Dr. Ross in the hall and asks him about a patient who will undergo a radical hysterectomy for cervical cancer the next day. "I have postponed the surgery until Thursday."

"Why did you do that?" Dr. Parsi asks.

"Because of your appointment at Barrera's office," Dr. Ross says. "By the way, I understand your grant is completed and ready to be re-submitted" Dr. Ross slaps him on the back.

Dr. Parsi shakes his head, "It is still on my desk."

"What's the problem? Why don't you send it out?"

"I'm having second thoughts about submitting the grant request."

"What is going on with you? Did you have another argument with Dr. Hartman?" Neither of them is willing to entertain gossip about Dr. Hartman, not at this uncertain time. "Give the man a break," Dr. Ross says. "Granted, he has a short temper, but when he gets to like you, he is very supportive."

"But if he doesn't like you, then he can fire you at a moment's notice, ruin your career, and leave you with no recourse," Dr. Parsi says.

"Look, when he's furious at something or someone, the best thing to do is to avoid him for a day. In the first two years of my assignment here, he did not have much respect for me. He was always looking for excuses to harass me. Do you know that he fired me not once but eight times, only to retract his threat a day later?"

"So, I'm not alone. But I'm confident that I would have been fired if Esther's pregnancy the test had been negative."

"Look, you did the right thing regardless of the result of the test," Dr. Ross says. "I'd have done the same thing. After all, you have an admirer in his place who would not have let him fire you."

"Who is that?" Dr. Parsi asks.

"Duh, you don't know?" Dr. Ross says.

"Really. No idea."

"The Dean," Dr. Ross says.

Dr. Parsi keeps quiet and does not discuss the matter any further with Dr. Ross.

———————

The trial of Dr. Hartman for manslaughter is fast approaching. The DA's office has completed pretrial examinations of witnesses except for Dr. Parsi, who has agreed to be interviewed by the prosecutor. The prosecutor hopes that Dr. Parsi might be helpful to his side in the case against Dr. Hartman. Barrera has encouraged Dr. Parsi to agree to the interview in the hope of convincing the prosecutor that Dr. Parsi would not help the state against Dr. Hartman. On a Wednesday morning, Dr. Parsi arrives at Barrera's office at eight for a preparatory meeting. He is ready to be prepped by Barrera for the subpoena, which was ordered by the DA, but now the legal assistant informs the defense attorney that the DA's team has encountered a conflict in his schedule and has asked to postpone the meeting for a few days. Dr. Parsi is disappointed and asks Barrera's associate why they did not inform him earlier.

"It's completely out of our control. They just called us ten minutes ago. Unfortunately, this situation occurs quite frequently," Barrera's associate says. "Let's hope it will not happen again."

Later that day, a few hours after Dr. Parsi returns to the department, he receives a message from the Dean to come to his office after work. A quick call to the Dean's secretary confirms that the Dean wanted to know how the deposition went. The meeting is called off when Dr. Parsi informs him that the interview with the DA has been postponed.

Meanwhile, Dr. Hartman, who is fully recovered from his leg injury, has resumed his daily early morning workout, returned to work full-time, and is keeping up with his multiple responsibilities. At lunchtime, he is in his office, calling his defense attorney to hear a report about Dr. Parsi's encounter with the DA's team. Dr. Hartman does not hide his disappointment when he hears that the interview has been delayed. He is eager to know what Dr. Parsi will say at the deposition. Then he calls the Dean and wishes him a great trip during his upcoming vacation to Italy.

Later that day, Esther, who is working on the first draft of a collection of short stories in her office at home, decides to include a fantastic short story about Esther, the Queen of Persia and a young Jewish man who is in love with Esther but loses her when she becomes a concubine in the court of Xerxes the Great. Esther fancies that the heartbroken male character who lost Esther could have been somewhat physically like Dr. Parsi. She decides to revise the short story and develop the young Jewish man accordingly. She reads the first paragraph:

"Once upon of time, in the city of Ecbatana, there lived a young Jewish fellow who fell in love with a Jewish teenager named Esther. After losing his beloved Esther to Xerxes the Great, he began a perilous journey on foot, crossing the dangerous lands of the Western Persian Empire to reach Jerusalem."

A few days later, when the short story is completed, Esther calls Dr. Parsi and asks him whether he is interested in perusing and commenting on it. Esther tells him, "The young Jewish character in the story is almost your doppelganger."

The phone rings, and when Esther picks up the call, she recognizes the JCC's director, who is soliciting her participation in San Antonio's Tricentennial preparation.

"The Mayor wants the Jewish community to play a role in the events," the director says.

"I have a lot on my plate," Esther says. "I'll contact you when the situation in my life is more suitable."

The oldest and once the most significant city in Texas, San Antonio has fallen behind Houston and Dallas in growth and population. However, for the people who have chosen San Antonio as their home, the city is a great place to live and raise a family. Although three essential elements —the Alamo, military bases, and the Riverwalk—have kept the economy afloat, the lack of high-paying jobs from major corporations has slowed the growth of the city and kept the prices of homes and living expenses low. The city attracts thousands of tourists annually because of the Alamo, "the Cradle of Texas Liberty,"and its mild climate during the fall, winter, and spring. The low cost of living makes the city an attractive place for retirees to move to. The city's healthcare industry, notably the University Health System, along with other nearby hospitals and several bioengineering companies, has become another steady source of growth and tax revenue for the city. The city, with its expanding universities and medical centers, has become a destination for well-educated researchers and educators, many of them Jewish, to fill the university and college positions in the medical school and other institutions. Subsequently, there is a large Jewish community with several synagogues in the city.

Esther, though not affiliated with any of the city's synagogues, is a member of the Jewish Community Center, which supports Jewish artists and stages music, theater, and literary events. As an educated woman and writer, she is a member of two book clubs and runs a monthly workshop at the Jewish Community Center. During the last several months, Esther has given lectures regarding the Jewish Diaspora in the Middle East, China, and Africa. Since she has become fond of Dr. Parsi, the history of the Persian Diaspora in Iran has attracted her attention, too. At the last workshop meeting, Esther volunteers that during the next session, she will present information about the history of Jews in Iran. When the participants react positively, she asks whether there are individuals in the audience who have come from Iran. Two members raise their hands. One is a Jewish-American psychiatrist who immigrated to the United States some forty years ago and was born in the city of Hamadan, which was called Ecbatana, who knows a lot about the Persian-Jewish version of the tale of Esther and has visited her tomb in that city frequently. The other member is from Tehran, but his family was originally from Shiraz, which is only 30 miles south of Persepolis.

Esther welcomes these two individuals' participation in the conversation and says, "Could we make the review of the history of Jewish-Persians an interactive one, please?"

X
The Jewish-Persian Diaspora

Dr. Habib, the Persian-Jewish-American psychiatrist, gives a lecture at the workshop at the Jewish Community Center regarding the precarious situation surrounding the Jewish people in today's Iran. "The tale of the Jewish-Persian Diaspora is the history of ancient Persia, but Jewish intellectuals, thinkers, and talented poets were involved in major events during modern-day Iran, too. The Persian-Jewish Diaspora in Iran mirrors the struggle of Jewish people throughout human history. The anthropology of the Jewish people, *anthro-Judea*, as a whole depicts the significant impact of the Jewish people on human progress and its advances. Therefore, I would like to postulate that observing the hostilities of the mullahs in Iran toward the Jewish state of Israel, there is a deep-rooted historical animosity challenging Jews in the Middle East, dating back to the Assyrian Empire and beyond, and continuing into the present era."

The workshop members are delighted to hear eyewitness accounts of the contemporary Persian-Jews in Iran provided by Dr. Habib and his wife, who lived in Iran until the downfall of the Shah of Iran in 1979. During the ensuing sessions, the group reviews the formation of the earliest documented Jewish Diaspora in ancient Persia at the time of the Assyrian Empire to the liberation of Jews from Babylon. But the group is more interested in the Jewish-Persian situation in Iran in the twentieth century and the present time. In response to the members' request, the psychiatrist prepares a twenty-minute slide presentation to cover contemporary Jewish-Persian history. So Esther dedicates the next session to the slide presentation by Dr. Habib.

In an animated show, and after introducing his credentials, Dr. Habib begins with an introduction to the history of Jewish-Persian communities in Iran from 1925 to 2015, and says, "The story of my life is strongly linked to the course of Iranian history during those many decades. I was born in the city of Hamadan, which, over 2500 years ago, was called Ecbatana. I have frequently visited the Tomb of Esther in Hamadan. In that ancient city, the Persians enjoyed a prosperous life. The city was one of the capitals of the Persian Empire at the zenith of its power over two and a half millennia ago. The most famous building in the city is the Palace of the Kings, or *Qasr Shah* in Farsi, which was mentioned in Ferdowsi's epic poem *Shahnameh*. Most of it was built by Xerxes the Great, who was called *Shahanshah*, or King of Kings in Farsi.

"The city was a major trading center in that era. The Jewish and non-Jewish merchants, shop-owners, artisans, builders, and construction workers populated the neighborhoods within walking distance from the city's bazaar. Wool and silk rugs, fabrics from Isfahan, exquisite wine from Persepolis, gems from the northeastern regions of the empire, fruit and vegetables from local farms, spices from India, and household implements from Mesopotamia were traded in the busy bazaar from sunrise to sunset. The coins issued by the empire's treasury were used for local purchases, but the bartering of products was also permissible and very common. After the arrival of a vast number of Jewish families from Babylon via Susa, the Jewish population in Ecbatana increased significantly. At the zenith of the Persian Empire, Jews comprised as much as 20% of the population of the capital."

Dr. Habib next describes the situation of the Persian-Jewish people in Iran during the twentieth century. "It was after the rise of the Pahlavi dynasty in 1925 that Reza Shah, the first Pahlavi king, implemented modernizing reforms, established new high schools and universities, and allowed Jews and Zoroastrians to expand their educational institutions. The king weakened the influence of the mullahs to the point that all Islamic schools or madrassas were required to obtain permission from the government to stay open. He outlawed the Islamic hijab and encouraged coeducational schools. Reza Shah's western-style reforms increased the literacy rate among Iranians from a mere 30% to above 50% by the time he abdicated the crown in 1941. The literacy rate among the Jewish minority was always significantly higher than that of the Muslim population, and in 1945, about 80 percent of the Jewish population were literate."

Dr. Habib goes on to explain that the life of Persian Jews became perilous again after the rise of Nazism in Germany, when Reza Shah, influenced by Iranian nationalism and the concept that Iranians are Arians, shifted his strategy toward supporting Hitler and his anti-Semitic policies. Anti-Jewish sentiments accelerated with the arrival of German political, financial, and military advisors in 1936 when the head of the Reichsbank and the financial masterminds of Nazi Germany traveled to Tehran and signed relevant commercial and industrial agreements between the two countries. In 1939, Nazi Germany sent thousands of books and pamphlets to Iran, many with anti-Jewish bias, advocating for greater collaboration between Aryan Persians and Germans. Nazi Germany designated Iranians as pure Aryans and considered Iran as a unique country when it came to trade and educational relations between the two nations. The Berlin Radio Farsi broadcasts became very popular among Iranian intellectuals and those who could afford to have a radio in their home.

"Thus, many Persian Jews welcomed the British troops and other Allied Forces, when they attacked Iran in 1942, forced the pro-German King Reza Shah, to abdicate, and installed his oldest son, Mohammad Reza Shah—only 21 years old, inexperienced and naïve—as the new king. The pro-democracy parties, as well as the Persian Jews, celebrated the change as an acceptable alternative to being taken over by Germans. During the reign of this king, who became the last king of the Pahlavi Dynasty, Persian Jews faced alternating periods of anti-Semitism and harassment from the clergy and episodes of peace and tranquility. The years between 1953 and 1979, when the Shah was firmly in control of the country and was expanding ties with Israel and curtailing the power of the mullahs, were the best years in recent history for Iranian Jews. But everything changed for them as well as for other secular and intellectual Iranians when the 1979 Islamic Revolution with Ayatollah Khomeini at its helm came to power.

"The decline in the Jewish population in Iran accelerated at the time of the establishment of the State of Israel in 1948 when approximately 150,000 Jews lived in Iran, but about 40% had since immigrated to Israel alone, with immigration hastening after the 1979 Islamic Revolution, when the Jewish population dropped from 100,000 to about 9,000 today. The majority of recent Persian-Jewish émigrés settled in Israel, although many others have come to the United States and Western Europe."

At the end of the presentation by Dr. Habib and during the question-and-answer part, one of the participants asks, "Is there another story related to the tomb of Esther in Hamadan?"

As if he were expecting the question, Dr. Habib says, "As a matter of fact there is. Some years ago, when electricity was new to the city of Hamadan, a wealthy Jewish merchant by the name of Nader Habib bought a subscription to the power company and provided free electric service to the Tomb of Esther. He dug a well in his orchard and installed an electric pump for extracting water on his large orchard. He trained his teenage son, Alvand, to maintain and service the electric pump. On a midsummer day, the son was repairing the disabled pump to resume watering the orchard when his father, who was hunting pheasant a short distance from the son, accidentally shot and killed him. The loss of the son was devastating for the family and deeply saddened the Jewish community. To memorialize the teenager and honor the family, the Jewish community dedicated a burial site for the teenager in the yard of the Tomb of Esther." In response to a question regarding the fate of the father, the psychiatrist says, "The father never recovered from the tragedy and ended up in an asylum, where he killed himself."

XI
Dr. Parsi Attends the Deposition

Sometime before the shootout and after Dr. Hartman successfully obtained a significant grant to research stem cell projects, one of which focuses on the use of stem cells for enhancing the immune response of patients with advanced cancers, he's hardly ever at home. He leaves early in the morning and returns late in the evening only to have dinner with Esther and then again disappears into his haven, the master bedroom, to read medical articles and review his projects. Late in the afternoon, when Saul is at school, and Dr. Hartman is in the lab at the hospital, the housekeeper is vacuuming the second floor and encounters the distinct smell of marijuana in Saul's bathroom. She looks around and finds a few half-smoked joints of marijuana in one of the drawers. She immediately takes them to Esther.

The unsuspecting mother does not want to believe her son ever smokes marijuana and asks the housekeeper to avoid bringing the matter to Dr. Hartman's attention. She whispers, "After all, they are selling weed in stores in many other states. Please don't disturb my husband with such a trivial matter. He is so busy with his work at the medical school that he does not have any energy to deal with this."

During Dr. Hartman's academic trip to Chicago to present a recently completed scientific study, Saul does not come home until way past midnight. Esther stays up and reads several chapters from *A Little Life* when she hears a loud exchange outside the front door. She opens the door cautiously. Saul and another teenage boy are arguing loudly about money.

The boy pushes Saul against the wall and shouts, "You dummy! You better bring me the dough in the morning, okay?" Saul tears himself away and turns toward the house, not responding to the taunts. The other boy can be heard screaming, "Look, man, this time your life is on the line. Okay?"

Saul enters the house, pushes past his mother without greeting her. She remains standing mute and bewildered in the hall. Saul stomps up the stairs to his room and bangs the door shut behind him. Esther follows him with tears in her eyes and hopes that he, their only son, will eventually find his way. Although she does not believe in supplication, she is so desperate that she resolves to send a contribution to Temple Beth El. Esther hopes Saul somehow will come to his senses and avoid further trouble. She murmurs, "O, Almighty, please save my son. Make him a saint. I promise to give $1,000 to your temple."

––––––––––––

A day before attending the deposition by an associate DA, Dr. Parsi receives a call from Esther. She does not bring up her husband's case but instead talks about her desire to travel to Iran and visit Esther's tomb in Hamadan. "I hope once my husband's case is concluded in his favor, he and I can tour the Middle East and visit some historical places," Esther says. She asks Dr. Parsi about available tours to that part of the world. "How difficult is it to arrange a trip to Susa and Ecbatana in Iran?"

It is quite painful for Dr. Parsi to describe the current situation in the small town of Susa, especially compared to its glorious distant past during the Achaemenid Empire. He says, "To reach Susa, one needs to travel first to Ahwaz, which is located in the oil-rich state of Khuzestan, and then drive about 60 miles north-northwest on a busy and sometimes dangerous two-lane road. There is the historically important Trans-Iranian Railroad that starts near the Iranian shore of the Persian Gulf and crosses fertile plains before it climbs up and meanders through the Zagros Mountains reaching Tehran. It continues farther, through the northwest region, to the Russian border—this is the same railroad that was essential to supply arms and war material to the Russian army who were battling German military forces during World War II and helped turn the tide during the critical battle of Stalingrad. It is a sad fact that although this railroad passes within a few miles of Susa, it is not possible to travel to Susa by train. There is no station or road to Susa from the railroad.

"Unfortunately, there is no comfortable overnight lodging of any kind in Susa nowadays," Dr. Parsi tells Esther. "Susa does not even have a decent restaurant compared with the many options in Isfahan or Shiraz. Therefore, very few Western tourists come to visit the tomb of the Prophet Daniel and the ruins of the Achaemenid palaces in Susa. The prospects for visiting Ecbatana, Isfahan, and Persepolis are entirely different. Those places offer world-class accommodations and many guided tours of their historical sites."

Dr. Parsi is quite surprised by Esther's conversation. "With the looming trial of your husband, don't you think any plans for such an elaborate voyage should be put on hold for the time being?"

"Yes. Yes, you are quite right. I'm just trying to divert my attention away from the troubles of our present situation by projecting into the future."

PART THREE
The Trial

Esther approaches Ruth and whispers, "No. I cannot face the man who might have killed my son." She remembers a bottle full of opiate painkillers in her house and murmurs, "I'm afraid somebody will put those pills to improper use."

I
Remembering the Abuses by Dr. Hartman

Remembering the abuses by Dr. Hartman, Dr. Parsi struggles with his impending testimony at Dr. Hartman's trial. When he sees Dr. Ross in his office, he knocks on the door and asks whether he may enter. "Of course, Come in," Dr. Ross says.

"I want to talk to you about Dr. Hartman's trial," he says. "About my testimony."

"Go ahead," Dr. Ross says.

"What am I going to say if the prosecutor asks me whether Dr. Hartman has ever threatened to fire me for no good reason during one of his angry outbursts?"

"Well, I understand what you are saying. But do not prevaricate," Dr. Ross says. "My friend, tell the truth. Stay the course, and never change your story."

"It's funny, that is exactly what Dean told me to do too," Dr. Parsi says.

Dr. Ross says, "Look, what I do when I see Dr. Hartman upset, I find an excuse and leave the scene. About your negative experience regarding the pregnancy test, you shouldn't take it personally. That reaction was coming from his medical opinion."

Dr. Parsi says, "I'm sure you know that he has almost fired me several times for no reason."

"Yes, we all know what he can do when he is furious," Dr. Ross says. "Didn't he threaten to fire that third-year resident a while ago? He almost fired two faculty members when they were late for surgeries. But they are all here and happy with their positions."

"Yes. I know about those occasions." Dr. Parsi says.

"So he tells you what's going on in the department," muses Dr. Parsi.

"He trusts me because I am straightforward with him," Dr. Ross says. "But how many of those who were threatened with dismissal were ever fired? In this strange way, Dr. Hartman wields his authority."

"C'mon, man! Dr. Hartman forces the staff to quit. Remember the resident who changed his specialty because he could not stand Dr. Hartman's insults? Or the senior faculty member who left and moved to the family practice department?" Dr. Parsi says. "He always keeps us on edge. I never know whether he is serious and would go through with the threat and fire us."

In the afternoon, Dr. Parsi receives a call from Esther. She mentions his upcoming testimony at the trial and tells Dr. Parsi, "You are not under any pressure to change your testimony, but I believe he has always respected you, Dr. Parsi," Esther says. "He, like other geniuses, demands a lot from you and everybody else, but also himself. Since we lost Saul, we look at you as if you were our son."

Dr. Parsi remembers what Dr. Ross has told him about Dr. Hartman's tough talk and a soft heart.

"He has made the department very successful. In the matching program where the medical school graduates choose a residency program, our department is ranked as one of the best in Texas."

Dr. Parsi doesn't mention to Esther the tense situation in the department. However, he knows the condition and the politics of the other divisions are entirely different from Dr. Hartman's department. There is a general sense of anxiety among the faculty, for there is always a possibility that at any time, any one of them might be called to Dr. Hartman's office for an evaluation. They dread those encounters that could put their position in jeopardy. Dr. Parsi has been through a few of those evaluation meetings himself and has survived them all. Still, he knows if he makes a mistake in patient management or encounters serious complications during or after surgery, he will be in a grave position.

The next day, Dr. Parsi gets a call from the Dean, who tells him that Barrera is in his office and wants to visit with him. At the Dean's office, the Dean tells Dr. Parsi that academic arguments should not be considered personal criticism or insult. "In dealing with you and other members of the department, Dr. Hartman has, as far as I'm aware of, always been appropriate."

Barrera follows the Dean and tells Dr. Parsi, "Remember that we all have a responsibility to differentiate people who are tainted with prejudice from those who have a strict leadership style. The DA's office will try to manipulate the witnesses, including you, to convince the jurors that Dr. Hartman is a dangerous individual. To have a bias against Dr. Hartman when you testify as a witness, especially as someone who works in the department, will weaken my position. The DA's office will press you and other witnesses to testify at the trial that Dr. Hartman often explodes with anger with unpredictable results. You must take a stand and support your department."

In the end, Dr. Parsi promises the Dean that he will take a neutral stance in Dr. Hartman's case. "This is the best I can do."

That same night Dr. Parsi receives another call from Esther who wants to talk about her visit with Barrera when she was deposed by the prosecutor at the law firm's office.

"So how was your conference before the deposition session with Barrera?" Dr. Parsi asks.

"Barrera treats me as if I were a teenager," Esther says. "He thinks I know nothing about the case."

"What did he say?"

"Barrera explained the procedure and discussed whether he might call on me to testify at the trial on behalf of my husband."

"How did you respond?" Dr. Parsi asks.

"I told him I have no hesitation to testify," Esther says.

"So, what happened later?" Dr. Parsi says.

"Of course, I went to Barrera's office."

"Are you anxious about appearing as a witness at the trial?" Dr. Parsi asks.

"Yes. I am frightened, but I want to do it. What else can I do?" Esther says. "Maybe I should have called the police in the first place, instead of making the urgent call to my husband."

Barrera had already explained to Esther that calling the police before any serious offense occurs is a waste of time. They would not have taken the quarrel between the two teenagers seriously.

Now, she reminisces about the shootout, "I should have paid the drug dealer the money. I could have saved two lives." Her voice is full of sadness. Now, Esther recalls a few of the prosecutor's questions. "The prosecutor even dared to ask me whether my husband has ever threatened to kill me. Then he went on with: 'Did Dr. Hartman ever threaten to kill Saul?'"

After Esther mentions Saul, there is a moment of silence on the line, and then Dr. Parsi hears Esther's sobbing. Puzzled, Dr. Parsi does not know how to respond to Esther's predicament. Feeling sincere sympathy for Esther and concern about her state of mind, Dr. Parsi says, "I'm so sorry to hear your pain. How can I help you?"

"I'll be alright. Thanks for listening to me," Esther says. She tells him goodbye and ends the call.

For the first time during Dr. Hartman's ordeal, Dr. Parsi witnesses Esther's emotional frailty. The hasty termination of the pregnancy, the loss of their son, now the heavy burden of the trial of her husband for murder, has deeply shaken Esther's peace of mind. Around the time of the aborted surgery for Esther's presumed abdominal mass and when Dr. Hartman directed his fury at him, Dr. Parsi recalls that Esther had tried to calm the roiling waters. She supported him on several occasions when dealing with Dr. Hartman. Those instances were all before the shootout. Now, Dr. Parsi concludes that Esther is sincere in dealing with him. In some mysterious way, Dr. Parsi welcomes Esther's calls and attention. Esther reminds him of his mother. His eyes well with tears, as he remembers his mother, whom he hasn't seen for years.

Eventually, Dr. Parsi softens his position toward Dr. Hartman's case and decides to throw in his lot with the defense team. He does it because Dr. Hartman has apologized to him for almost firing him after ordering the pregnancy test. Surprisingly, Dr. Hartman has helped him rewrite the NIH grant, most likely because of Esther. Dr. Hartman would not want to disappoint her and has lately even shown some respect for Dr. Parsi's work in the department. Dr. Parsi now believes that Esther's support of him in the past few months has been genuine and has nothing to do with appeasing him or enticing him to testify on behalf of her husband.

In the next call, Barrera tells Dr. Parsi, "Regarding your testimony, and in responding to the prosecutor's questions, I suggest that you be brief in your answers. There is nothing wrong to say, as far as I recall, Dr. Hartman played his role as an effective chairman. He was strict and professional. Do not elaborate further. That way, you will never contradict yourself during the trial. Just be honest and consistent."

Dr. Parsi knows that as a fellow in the department, he can be compelled by the prosecutor to testify in Dr. Hartman's case. Once, during a telephone conversation, Esther told him that any refusal to testify would be counterproductive.

"The DA will claim you are hiding damaging evidence against my husband." She adds, "Being truthful during the trial will be much more beneficial to my husband's position than your absence."

In the fateful days before the trial, Dr. Parsi recognizes that the Dean, Barrera, and Esther are expecting him to stand by Dr. Hartman at this critical turn of events.

During a visit to the library in their home, while Dr. Hartman is reviewing a pile of medical articles in the sitting area of the master bedroom, Esther calls Dr. Parsi and tells him that regardless of the outcome of the trial, she will always feel her husband is innocent. "My husband never wanted to hurt anybody," she tells Dr. Parsi. Then, she recalls an incident where Dr. Hartman had threatened to expel one of the residents from the residency program because the resident was moonlighting every weekend instead of devoting his time to study his specialty. Esther quotes Dr. Hartman, who told the resident that if he does another weekend of moonlighting in emergency rooms around town, he would be fired at once. Esther tells Dr. Parsi that the resident had done very poorly on the pre-board examination because of inadequate study. Dr. Hartman's ultimatum worked, and the resident quit moonlighting and studied his material so hard that his next in-house pre-board examination turned out to be above average. That resident has since shown his gratitude in many ways and has become a successful specialist practicing in town.

II
Dr. Parsi Testifies on Behalf of Dr. Hartman

A day before Dr. Parsi's appointment for the interview by the prosecutor, Dr. Parsi gets another set of lectures by the Dean and Barrera at the Dean's office. "It's imperative for everyone involved in the case to recognize that Dr. Hartman acted in self-defense to protect his family and himself," Barrera stresses. The Dean is still worried that the adverse publicity from the case may hurt the university's image in the city. Barrera adds, "I believe at the end of the day, people will understand Dr. Hartman's position. Okay, so the guy has a bad temper, but who doesn't get furious when some rogue teen comes around and threatens to kill your son?"

Both the Dean and Barrera remind Dr. Parsi to be mindful and wary of the DA's manipulations. "He will try to corner you, forcing you to say Dr. Hartman is dangerous and may kill other innocent persons," Barrera warns Dr. Parsi.

The Dean reinforces Barrera's recommendation and tells Dr. Parsi, "It is important for you to differentiate Dr. Hartman's academic encounters with his staff from a situation where a dangerous verbal or physical threat could jeopardize one's safety."

The defense attorney follows up on the issue of whether Dr. Hartman has ever threatened physical harm to anybody, and asks Dr. Parsi, "Did he ever threaten to throw you out or raise his voice while confronting you during a medical argument?"

Before Dr. Parsi gets a chance to answer that question, the Dean presses the issue. He amplifies the defense attorney's supposition, "Has Dr. Hartman ever been inappropriately and physically aggressive with you?"

Dr. Parsi's answers to these questions satisfy both the Dean and Barrera. The Dean's involvement in the case to the extent of directing the witness, in this case, Dr. Parsi, surprises Barrera. He hopes these machinations will not be revealed during the trial and hurt his defense strategy. However, he presses on and asks Dr. Parsi to establish a firm stand in the case and to be consistent. The Dean asks Dr. Parsi whether he has any questions for either of them.

"Okay, my reservation to fully support Dr. Hartman is that no one can deny his harsh treatment of several of us. At times, he has been more than unreasonable with me. What happens if the prosecutor asks me whether Dr. Hartman has ever threatened to fire me for a trivial reason?"

The defense attorney replies that Dr. Parsi should be as truthful as possible. "Yes, you must say he would have fired you if you had erred in caring for a patient."

The Dean adds to the defense attorney's comment. "Dr. Parsi, when one follows the truth at all times, then one will always repeat the same narrative. Just be accurate in your statements, whatever they are."

146

It is not winning or losing the case that concerns the Dean, but the potential loss of public support for the university. "Dr. Parsi, this gentleman has made the university a recognized center for the advancement of medicine. He could be at the threshold of achieving a breakthrough in the application of stem cells for the treatment of incurable illnesses. But let's face it, he is not an angel. To err is human; only God is infallible," the Dean concludes.

At the end of the meeting, the defense attorney thanks Dr. Parsi for listening to their advice and says, "I truly believe my client didn't intend to kill Marcel. All he wanted to do was to scare him off and force him to leave his son alone."

III
At the Pretrial Hearing

It has been many months since the grand jury reviewed the situation when they opined that the present evidence was sufficient for the prosecutor to proceed to trial and submit the case to a jury. Now, Dr. Jordan Hartman appears at the pretrial hearing accompanied by his defense attorney. Knowing a defendant does not have to prove his innocence, he declares in front of the judge and the other lawyers that he is not guilty.

The judge advises Dr. Hartman of the charges filed and asks whether Dr. Hartman knows that over ninety percent of defendants in criminal cases plead guilty rather than go to trial.

"Your chance of receiving a lenient sentence is high if you plead guilty now compared to your chances after an excruciating trial if the jury finds you guilty. Do you understand that?" the judge asks Dr. Hartman.

"I do, Your Honor," Dr. Hartman replies, "but I'm certain that I did not intend to kill anybody."

After Dr. Hartman pleads Not Guilty, the judge permits the defendant to return to his home under supervision, the same arrangement as before. "Because you have not previously violated the terms of your bail, I will not order any electronic monitoring, but your attorney must report every week on your compliance with the court's requirement that you stay in town until the trial. Furthermore, you are not permitted to leave Bexar County at this time."

During the drive home, Esther cannot conceal her trepidations regarding the upcoming trial. They are both quiet for a long time and worried mainly about the outcome of the forthcoming trial.

Dr. Hartman finally breaks the silence, "Tell me, Esther, what you think would have happened if I had not come home to face Saul's situation that fateful day?"

Esther is stunned by the question and wonders, "Is he trying to put all the blame on me?" A sob overtakes her. "Dear, what would have happened if you, yes, you had not bought a handgun in the first place?" she mutters. "That guy only wanted money. We could have brought them both inside the house to discuss things, and then we would have discovered our son's troubled life."

"You liberals always blame guns for everything. Believe me, Esther, that gun saved your life," Dr. Hartman insists.

Esther is dismayed. "What are you talking about? Don't you realize that bringing your handgun to the scene had the tragic end of killing both teenagers?" Esther says while sobbing. They did not talk anymore for the rest of the ride home.

A solemn group of people, the twelve members of the jury, are sitting in the jury's bench on one side of the courtroom intently watching the opening statement by the prosecutor: six of them are women, four are men sporting loose shirts hanging over their lumpy torsos, and the other two men are very obese. Earlier that morning during the *voir dire*, from a jury pool of over sixty adult women and men in the waiting room of the courthouse, thirty-five individuals were called in for questioning by the judge, the prosecutor, and Barrera to be either chosen or rejected for the criminal trial of Dr. Hartman. Adhering to standard procedure, the prosecutor and Barrera alternately question the candidates. Any one of them who has met Dr. Hartman before the shooting or has formed an opinion regarding the case or lacks the stamina to withstand a potentially lengthy trial is sent home.

As if they were racing against time to reach the final mile and get to the moment when the trial of Dr. Hartman for manslaughter finally begins, the parties quickly strike out jury candidates who have a racial bias against minorities, especially Jews, or who believe that the Second Amendment to the United States Constitution does not guarantee the right to purchase and possess a gun under any circumstance. Dr. Hartman is surprised when he observes that no peremptory strike is used against a jury candidate who stated that he believes people should have the right to carry a concealed gun in schools, churches, or synagogues. Although the prosecution's attempt to strike a potential jury member for the cause is rejected merely because he is a doctor who had read several of Dr. Hartman's scientific papers, the prosecutor uses one of its peremptory challenges to eliminate him from the jury.

At break time, Barrera justifies his inaction against the pro-gun individual as a necessary decision. "We need people on the jury who understand your tenuous position, accept your decision to bring the handgun out to defend your family."

In reaction to Barrera's statement, Esther shakes her head and says, "I never thought I'd see the day when everybody can carry a gun on the street."

"Well, that's the way it has been for some years now," Barrera says calmly.

They return to the court where the lawyers complete the selection of the jury. Each member of the jury signs a document declaring that they carry no bias and are free of preconceived opinions about the case, and then they swear the oath. At the end of the session, the twelve-member jury includes no African-American members, no one with a doctorate or a master's degree, and no nurse or doctor. This is the first time Dr. Hartman and Esther have seen the process of jury selection in action.

"Do you know why we have millions of people incarcerated in the U.S. prisons?" Dr. Hartman asks Barrera while they walk to the nearby parking lot.

Barrera answers, "Our system is not perfect, but it works because we have no better alternative."

"I'm afraid the prosecutor can easily manipulate the jury," Dr. Hartman says.

149

"Not to worry, the makeup of this jury is in your favor," Barrera says. "At least one of them is pro-gun and may support you. He may like how you waved your gun to scare off the intruder before shooting him."

"That's sad. I despised that jury member's comments," Esther says.

"All we need is one person who believes you are not guilty to prevent a conviction in the trial," the defense attorney says. "And he may be the one.

———————

Dr. Hartman has driven to the courthouse in a separate car, for he had first gone to Barrera's office to be briefed on the jury selection procedures. When he arrives home, he finds an empty house. Esther's car is not in the garage, and there is no note on the message board behind the front door. His call to her smartphone goes to voicemail. He walks to their living room bar and pours himself a double shot of Baby Blue Single Malt Whiskey and drops two ice cubes in it. Then, he aimlessly paces around the living room. After a few sips of whiskey, he picks a CD and inserts it into the player. It is Beethoven's Emperor Piano Concerto. He calls Esther again but refrains from leaving a message on her voicemail. Wandering around the ground floor, he notices the warming drawer in the kitchen is holding a dinner dish, his favorite, shrimp with rice and asparagus. Esther has set a place for him to have dinner in the breakfast nook. Next to the empty water glass is a note from Esther: "My darling, I hope you like the way the jury selection went. Your dinner is in the warmer. I will be home soon, but first, I have to visit Dr. Parsi at University Hospital. He had a bicycle accident after leaving work."

Dr. Hartman is stunned that Esther has not responded to his calls. He is now getting worried whether Dr. Parsi will be in a supportive mood and good spirits to testify at the trial. He goes upstairs to his walk-in closet, changes to a lighter outfit, and redials Esther's number. He hears the mobile phone ringing at low volume and follows the sound. To his surprise, Esther's mobile phone lies on a shelf in her walk-in closet next to a pair of slippers. He turns it off, goes back to the kitchen, and finds a dish of salad in the fridge. He pours a glass of Becker Chardonnay and sits down to eat his dinner. Exhaustion from the long day at the courthouse washes over him. Now, after the whiskey, dinner, and two glasses of wine, he can hardly keep his eyes open. He goes to the bedroom and collapses on the bed.

IV
Tragic Homicide, Accidental Filicide

Esther is now solemnly watching as the sheriff who arrested Dr. Hartman walks to the witness stand and answers the prosecutors' questions. In response to a question by the prosecutor to describe Dr. Hartman's arrest, the sheriff says, "He was surprisingly calm as if nothing serious had happened at the time of the shootout. Then, when I asked him, 'Did you shoot the victim?' he replied in a measured tone, 'Yes, officer, I am the person who accidentally shot the victim.'"

"Did he say anything else?" The prosecutor asks.

"Yes. Dr. Hartman described what happened when he arrived at the scene," the sheriff says.

"What did he say?" The prosecutor says impatiently.

"He said, 'As soon as I came home, I tried to stop the fight between the intruder and my son, but when I concluded that I could not calm the brawl, I went inside and brought out the handgun.'"

"Did he say why he fired several shots?" The prosecutor asks the sheriff.

At this time, Barrera rises and objects to the prosecutor's question, "Your Honor, the prosecutor is manipulating the witness instead of questioning him. As we know, it is established as the fact that Dr. Hartman never intended to kill anybody."

The judge sustains the objection and asks the prosecutor to rephrase the question.

"What else did the defendant say?" the prosecutor asks.

"He stated that he waved the handgun at the intruder, who was threatening to kill his son."

"Did he say why he killed the intruder?" The prosecutor asks the sheriff.

Here again, Barrera rises and objects to the prosecutor's use of the word "killed." Barrera pleads, "Your Honor, the court has not yet determined the nature of the incident."

The judge sustains the objection and asks the prosecutor to avoid using the word "killed." The prosecutor rephrases his question, "Did the doctor say why he shot the intruder?"

The sheriff replies, "The doctor said he was waving the handgun toward the intruder to force the intruder to leave the property."

"Did he confirm that his bullet hit the intruder?" the prosecutor asks.

"Yes, the doctor admitted that his bullet hit the intruder."

At this point, the prosecutor submits a certified copy of the police statement describing the arrest of Dr. Hartman to the court as exhibit one and places it on the judge's bench. He also presents a box containing the handgun to the court and asks the sheriff, "Is this the handgun that was used by the doctor when he shot the victim?"

The sheriff replies, "This is the gun that the defendant delivered to us at the time of his arrest."

In another smaller box, the prosecutor presents a bullet and says, "In this box, exhibit three, there is the bullet that was obtained from Marcel's body." The prosecutor presents another box and says, "Your Honor, exhibit four contains the bullet that hit the doctor's leg." After submitting the exhibits, the prosecutor announces that he has no further questions for the sheriff, and goes to his bench and sits down.

Now Barrera walks toward the witness and asks, "When you faced the doctor, how was his state of mind?"

"He was calm and cordial. When I asked him to bring the handgun that he had used, he promptly led one of my officers inside, showed him where the handgun was, and the officer brought it outside and handed the handgun to me."

"Please describe the physical appearance of the handgun," Barrera says.

"The handgun was wrapped in a white towel. It seemed to the police officer who was standing next to me that whoever had removed the handgun from the scene of the shooting handled it very carefully," the sheriff says.

"Do you know who had taken the handgun inside the house?"

"Dr. Hartman said that his wife had brought a towel and wrapped the handgun in it and took it inside," the sheriff says.

At this point, Barrera asks the sheriff to describe the model and specifications of the handgun. "The handgun was a Smith & Wesson 9mm semi-automatic."

The prosecutor now presents exhibit six, a box containing the bullet that smashed into the house. "Can you identify this bullet, Sheriff?" asks the prosecutor.

"Yes, that's the bullet that the forensics analysis says killed the victim, Saul."

"Can you determine which handgun fired it?"

"Unfortunately, no. After passing through the victim's chest—particles of the victim's tissue, his aorta, were found on the bullet—the bullet impacted the brick wall of the defendant's house and was crushed, mutilated beyond identification. Additionally, 9mm and .38 caliber handgun ammunition weigh about the same, and all our lab could determine was that the bullet could have been fired from either of the two handguns involved in the shootout."

"So, the bullet could have come from Marcel's handgun," the prosecutor says, then pauses, "and it's equally possible that it came from the defendant's Smith & Wesson 9mm semi-automatic weapon."

"Yes, that's correct," the sheriff replies.

———————

This interpretation of the evidence shocks Dr. Hartman, Esther, and the jurors as well. Esther begins to wonder whether she is living with the man who has killed their son. That possibility shatters her mind.

She begins to pray, "God, please, don't do this to me. I cannot live in the same house if the test verifies…." She cannot finish her prayer, buries her face in her hands, and sobs as a heart-wrenching image of Saul demoralizes her.

Shaken by the sheriff's testimony that her husband's bullet may have killed Saul, Esther turns to her cellphone and searches for information about the cases of parents killing their offspring or vice-versa. First, she researches the word filicide. She reads on the mobile phone, "In Ancient Greece, justifiable filicide was permitted." She then reads about patricide in the play, *Oedipus the King*, when Oedipus kills his father, Laius, whom he does not recognize, at a crossroads. When the facts are known, Jocasta, Oedipus' mother now married to Oedipus, commits suicide, and Oedipus the king gouges his eyes out and flees to Thebes.

Esther, who is sitting next to the Dean's wife, Ruth, shows the mobile phone text to Ruth and sighs. Ruth, who is also a bibliophile, notes Esther's misunderstanding and whispers in her ear, "My dear, here we are facing a case of filicide, not patricide. Google Agamemnon, who sacrifices his daughter before the Trojan War."

"My husband didn't sacrifice Saul, he just went berserk and killed a teenager, and our son as well," Esther whispers. "It was a horrific act—in a blind fury."

The word "filicide" resonates in her mind repeatedly. She still compares herself to Jocasta and remembers the stage where Jocasta, upon discovering the truth about Oedipus' identity, rushes out and hangs herself in the bedroom. She approaches Ruth and whispers, "No. I cannot face the man who may have killed my son." She remembers a bottle full of opiate painkillers in her house and murmurs, "I'm afraid somebody will put those pills to improper use."

Later that night, after she returns from the emergency room where she had visited Dr. Parsi, who had only sustained a minor injury from his bicycle accident, Esther goes to their library and drops flat on a sofa. She is exhausted and shaken by the prosecutor's claim. After a while, and when she does not hear any noise in the house, she gets up and walks to the master bedroom, where she finds that Dr. Hartman has succumbed to a stupor in his hideout. He had eaten only a small portion of his dinner, and now, in bed, is listening to a *Crime and Punishment* audiobook. Consumed by the thought of her husband, who may have killed their son, Esther returns to the library and googles the history of filicide. In one of the references, she reads that filicide has existed since the dawn of humankind. In ancient Greco-Roman times, a father was allowed to kill his child—daughter or son—for a cause, without legal repercussions. Despite the rise of Christianity and its greater respect for life, and the implementation of severe punishment for the crime, filicides continued and were perpetrated equally by either parent.

The question of "Did my husband kill Saul by carelessly shooting at the intruder and accidentally hitting our son?" keeps Esther awake for most of the night. She spends the night in the library until daylight breaks.

V
Marcel Wouldn't Have Killed Saul

"I knew Marcel. He wouldn't have killed Saul," the neighbor who lives across the street from Dr. Hartman's house testifies in court. He is the prosecutor's second witness. "They were buddies."

"I object, Your Honor," Barrera asserts loudly. "This is pure speculation."

The judge nods and asks the clerk to delete the witness's statement. However, under questioning from the prosecutor, when the neighbor asked whether he had ever argued with Dr. Hartman, he responds, "I hardly know the doctor. He keeps to himself. We have never spoken to each other."

Dr. Hartman's defense attorney cross-examines the witness. "Have you had any interactions with the doctor's son or his wife?"

"I have always found his wife to be a friendly and courteous neighbor."

Barrera continues, "Have you had any interactions with the defendant's son, Saul?"

"Not much, only when Saul was arguing with the other teenagers on the block."

"Could you elaborate, please?"

"In the weeks before the shootout, I could see Saul and Marcel together, actually more than a few times. I could hear them carry on a loud argument in the street. A day before the shootout, they were pushing and shoving each other near Marcel's car."

"Did you know the nature of their argument?"

"I was not privy to their dispute, but there were plenty of rumors running around the neighborhood," the man says.

"We don't want to ask you for hearsay, but do you know for a fact the nature of their arguments?"

"I guess it was about money."

"Are you sure?"

"No, sir."

The Leon Creek Trail—suitable for running, walking, and bicycling—is part of over 100 miles of well-paved and landscaped bicycle and walking paths around the city of San Antonio. These trails have been built during the last decade. Pro-environment and pragmatic mayors from Henry Cisneros to Phil Hardberger and Julián Castro have pushed for the development of a vast green belt using numerous flood zones and dry creek-beds to expand San Antonio's urban spaces with recreational and safe trails and parks. The Leon Creek Trail, which begins in the northwest of San Antonio, goes for 17 miles. After the Mission Trail on the southern side of San Antonio with its 20 miles of the paved path along the San Antonio River and wildflowers and plants on both sides, the Leon Creek Trail is the most popular in the city. It is a favorite bike path for Dr. Parsi and Dr. Baldwin, who are exploring the city together on their weekly bike outings. The trail is conveniently close to the Medical Center area, as it runs from the northwest corner of the town near the UTSA campus southwestward toward Ingram Park.

It is here at the sharp turn of the trail under UTSA Boulevard that Dr. Parsi's bike hits a rock, and he tumbles into the creek and injures his knee. Dr. Parsi is so worried about Esther and Dr. Hartman that he keeps talking about the case rather than paying enough attention to the trail. Fortunately, Dr. Baldwin is there to help him get up and climb back to the road. In the car, Dr. Baldwin calls Esther and tells her that Dr. Parsi has been injured, and they are on their way to the University Hospital emergency room, so they cannot visit her that evening to be updated about the trial.

Later that day at the trial, before the next witness makes his appearance, Barrera asks for a break and walks to the judge's bench to discuss the issue of the next witness. He informs the judge that the next witness, Dr. Parsi, a junior faculty member at the medical school, was injured in a bicycle accident and cannot testify today. After the judge receives the emergency physician's report, and since both prosecution and the defense agree on the postponement, he grants the motion to delay Dr. Parsi's appearance for one day. "Go ahead then and call your next witness," the judge instructs the prosecutor.

The next witness is a female classmate of Marcel, an eighteen-year-old high school senior who was dating Marcel.

After the preliminary questions regarding her name, age, and school, the prosecutor gets to the essential point. "Did you witness the shooting?"

"No, sir."

"Did you know the victims?" The teenage girl covers her eyes, sobs, and struggles to regain her composure. After a deep breath, she answers, "Yes, I knew both of them."

"How did Marcel usually behave?"

"Marcel was always polite and appropriate. He was a cool guy." Now she weeps.

"Do you think he was the kind of person who could ever kill another human being?"

"Absolutely not."

At this point, Barrera stands up and objects to the witness' statement, "Your Honor, this is total speculation." The judge promptly sustains the objection.

The disappointed prosecutor continues questioning the witness.

"Did you know Marcel was selling illicit drugs?'

"They both did."

"What do you mean, they both did? Please explain."

"Well, both Marcel and Saul were selling bud—marijuana. They were friends and helped each other in whatever they were doing."

"Did you know Marcel had a handgun in his car?"

"Yes."

"Did he tell you why he was carrying a handgun in his car?"

"No. But Marcel was not the only kid who carries a handgun. I know several other students who usually have a handgun in their car."

"To your knowledge, did Marcel ever threaten anybody with his handgun?"

"I never even saw him pull his handgun from the glove compartment. He just kept it there."

The prosecutor turns to the judge and says, "Your Honor, I have no further questions."

Barrera promptly rises, walks towards the witness, and asks several routine questions. Then, he continues, "Did you ever buy marijuana from Marcel?"

"I never paid Marcel for bud."

"So, did he give you marijuana for free?"

Immediately, the prosecutor rises and objects to the question as irrelevant to the case. The judge asks Barrera to re-phrase the question.

"Did you ever see Marcel selling illicit drugs like coke or crack?"

"No, sir."

"Did you know Marcel was carrying cocaine in his car?"

The witness looks bemused. She starts to mumble a word but hesitates to say it out loud.

"Was he selling cocaine to students?"

"I never saw him selling cocaine or any hard drug to anybody. He just sold bud."

"Did you know he was using cocaine?"

The witness pauses for a while, perhaps hoping for an objection from the DA. After a minute, the judge breaks the silence and reminds the witness to reply to the question. She asks to hear the question again.

Barrera walks closer to the witness stand and asks her, "Were you aware that Marcel was using cocaine?"

She mumbles reluctantly, "Yes."

"Where was he using that drug?"

"Everywhere. In his car. In his house."

"With you?"

"Yes, once, in his house."

"Was there anybody else present at the time?"

"No. It was just Marcel and me. His parents were out of town."

"Was he selling cocaine to other students?"

"No. For sure, not around the school."

"How about away from school?"

"I don't know."

"Did you ever see him sniffing cocaine in his car?"

The girl looks down at her hands, which are trembling. After a long pause, she speaks. "Yes."

Barrera turns around, looks at the jury, and loudly announces, "Your Honor, I have no further questions."

The prosecutor calls the next witness, the chief resident, who is on record stating during pretrial questioning that Dr. Hartman is an angry man with an unpredictable temperament, and he was always afraid Dr. Hartman could have punched him or fired him at any moment. The prosecutor does not manage to get any more specific damaging testimony from the resident, just a few unproven claims.

At the end of the questioning, though, the resident volunteers this statement, "We were all afraid of Dr. Hartman. Sometimes when he was in a gloomy mood, he would look for one of us to unleash his frustration on."

Immediately, Barrera gets up and says, "Objection, Your Honor. The statement by the witness is hearsay. The witness cannot speak for another resident who is not present to verify the account."

After the judge rules for the defense, the prosecutor ends the questioning, and Barrera takes over.

"Did Dr. Hartman ever attack you physically?" Barrera asks.

"No, sir."

"Did he ever threaten to fire you?"

"No, sir."

"Did he ever insult you for personal reasons?" Barrera continues.

"No, sir."

Barrera announces, "Your Honor, I have no further questions," and sits down.

The next witness is a third-year medical student who criticized Dr. Hartman's lecture hall behavior in his subpoenaed statement. Under oath, the student had stated that Dr. Hartman threw pieces of chalk at students on several occasions and called some students "idiot." And on one occasion, Dr. Hartman kicked a student and pushed him out of the classroom.

However, on the witness stand, seeing Dr. Hartman next to his lawyer, he is less critical. In answer to the prosecutor's question regarding Dr. Hartman's angry fits against students, he responds, "Dr. Hartman would become agitated when our answers were wrong. On one occasion, when I did not understand his question, he became mad, raised his voice, and in a burst of anger, threw a piece of chalk at me."

"Do you think Dr. Hartman would have physically harmed you if you were standing near him?"

Another objection by Barrera, but the judge overrules it and instructs the student to answer the prosecutor's question.

The student pauses and fails to respond. When the prosecutor repeats the question, the student says, "I'm not sure he would have physically attacked me."

When Barrera takes over, his first question is to ask the student to clarify what he meant by "kicked."

The student quickly changes the wording to "kicked him out of the class," and explains, "Dr. Hartman dismissed my classmate and told him to go to the library and study the topic, which had been discussed during the lecture."

A moment later, Barrera rephrases the same question the prosecutor had asked. "Were you ever afraid that Dr. Hartman might physically harm you?"

"I never thought he would attack me physically." Barrera is pleased, turns to jurors and smiles after the student answers,

Barrera continues. "Is it true that Dr. Hartman was furious because you were taking a nap during the lecture?"

The student looks embarrassed. He stutters, "I don't remember."

"Isn't it true that Dr. Hartman was irritated because he expects all his students to listen to his lecture attentively and know the answers to related questions?"

"He would become furious when our answers were wrong."

"When he caught you unaware and surprised you with his specific question, did you think Dr. Hartman would attack you physically at the very moment when you couldn't answer his question?"

"No. I don't think so."

Barrera turns to the judge and says, "Your Honor, I have no further questions."

During the lunch break at a Bill Miller BBQ place nearby, Barrera analyzes the medical student's testimony and tells Dr. Hartman, "You can't make everybody in this world happy. There are always people who may not like you no matter what you do."

Esther, who is nibbling on a small salad, remains skeptical. "That student's testimony may damage my husband's standing with the jury."

Dr. Hartman remains quiet. He remembers how he would pressure his students to pay attention to his lectures. He clearly remembers that day and how furious he was at the student for napping right there in front of him.

"Honestly, that student deserved to be kicked out of medical school. But, of course, we are coddling our students these days."

"Are you going to express this sentiment on the witness stand, too?" Barrera asks Dr. Hartman.

"I probably will express my opinion in a somewhat milder tone. I'll say that the student was ignorant and exhibited little interest in studying the subject before the lecture. If he continues like that, he is going to become a lousy doctor."

Barrera admonishes him. "I'm sure you are perfectly correct in your assumption, but please do not go that far. Just say he was unprepared and had not paid attention to your lecture."

VI
The Case of Roman Polanski

The case of Roman Polanski is coming to Dr. Hartman's mind. During the week before the trial, when Dr. Hartman is genuinely afraid of losing the case, he fears he may end up having to serve time in prison after being declared guilty by the jury, and he contemplates his options. He recalls the case of Roman Polanski, who fled the United States for Paris the night before sentencing by a hostile judge in Los Angeles in 1977. Polanski had several charges against him, including the rape of a 13-year-old Samantha Geimer. Now, Dr. Hartman considers bolting to Mexico in case the impending verdict of the jury is against him. When he mentions this to Esther, she calls her husband's plan to flee the country before the testimony given by the director of the forensics laboratory during the trial or the jury's decision a grave mistake. In Esther's opinion, although there is no similarity between Polanski's case and Dr. Hartman's, the fact that they both are considered geniuses in their professional fields is remarkable. Polanski is a gifted international movie director and producer with numerous award-winning movies. At the same time, her husband is called a genius by his colleagues and has achieved remarkable medical breakthroughs in the field of replication of fetal tissue. He is also a pioneer in the application of stem cells for the treatment of incurable diseases.

A survivor of Krakow's Jewish Ghetto during the Nazi German occupation of Poland, Roman Polanski had managed to hide in an old building moments before his parents were taken to a concentration camp. He was rescued later by a Catholic family. Polanski's mother was killed in Auschwitz, but his father survived and then reunited with him after the end of World War II. After making *Chinatown* and other great movies in Hollywood that brought him to the apex of his movie-producing career, Polanski was arrested at Jack Nicholson's home for the sexual assault of a 13-year-old girl, who had been modeling for Polanski during a Vogue magazine photoshoot around the pool. Polanski was indicted on six counts of criminal behavior, including rape. At his arraignment, he pleaded not guilty to all charges. His attorney arranged a plea bargain in which five of the six charges would be dismissed, and Polanski would undergo 90 days of psychiatric evaluation and treatment. When the judge abruptly denied the plea bargain agreement and rumors spread that Polanski would be sentenced to 50 years in prison, he quietly packed his belongings and fled the United States for Europe. He has lived in several European countries since then but mostly resides in Switzerland.

Even though Esther and Barrera are optimistic about the outcome of the trial, the prospect for a guilty verdict looms as a possibility when the trial is nearing the final stage of arguments. Without dropping any hint to Barrera, Dr. Hartman ponders his chances of fleeing the country across the porous Texas-

Mexico border and driving to Mexico City. Esther believes that appealing a guilty verdict is a far better approach than fleeing the country.

At the end of the second day of the trial and without telling Barrera or Esther about his final decision to flee to Mexico, Dr. Hartman calls Dr. Ross, his lackey in the department, to arrange the impending trip.

Emotionally drained after a long day at the trial, Esther goes to the kitchen and prepares two cups of green tea. She brings one to the reading corner in the master bedroom for Dr. Hartman and carries the other one with her as she goes to settles down in the library. Meanwhile, her husband, having changed into comfortable clothes, sits in his reading chair, and succumbs to disturbing thoughts. The trial has shaken his confidence. He clearly remembers the moment when he entered the front yard holding the gun but cannot recall the instant when he pulled the trigger, and when the actual shooting occurred.

The next scene he remembers is when he was wheeled into the ambulance and taken to the University Hospital. Frustrated, Dr. Hartman gives up trying to squeeze his exhausted mind and instead looks at the cup of tea and begins to drink it.

In the library, Esther finds her usual haven, the fantastic world of Esther, the Queen of Persia, and submits herself to her recurrent reverie. She imagines she is in Ecbatana preparing to parade in front of Xerxes the Great in the Hall of Kings. "I would have paced the hall like a ballerina," she murmurs, but her imagination is confined to the inside of the palace. She wishes she would be able to tour the city, which is nowadays called Hamadan. To visit the Jewish neighborhood, their bakeries, kitchens, dining rooms, and taste their fragrant and colorful rice and stews. She goes to her desktop computer and googles Ecbatana.

She glances at the historical references. Then, she clicks on information about the modern city of Hamadan. According to the encyclopedia, Hamadan is the oldest Iranian city and one of the oldest in the world. During the era of the Medes, at the dawn of Persian history over three millennia ago, the city was called Hegmataneh. In Greek documents, the city was named Ecbatana. The valley around the city contains abundant relics of many eras: the Medes, Achaemenids, Sassanids, and Muslims have all left their traces there. Many relics have been unearthed. Some are in major museums in Europe, while others are on display in the Iranian museums.

Esther scans reports of various historical monuments, and her eyes stop at a photograph of Esther's tomb with its blue dome. She smiles, "I love the color of the dome." She reads about the *Stone Lion*, which is almost two-and-a-half millennia old and dates back to 324 BC when Alexander the Great conquered the city. The statue, which has survived, is now the symbol of the city, which was the center of Iranian medicine, poetry, and science during the post-Arab dominance of Iran, and produced famous physicians and philosophers, among them the physician Avicenna, the chemist Jami who discovered and produced alcohol, and many Persian poets. Another note catches her eyes. It's a gravestone note of a young Jewish son who was killed accidentally by his father in a hunting outing in the courtyard of the Tomb of Esther in Hamadan. She reads the inscription on the gravestone:

The Eternal Resting Place of Arvand
Who at the Age of 16 Was Accidentally
Killed on a Hunting Trip by His Father

Esther recalls the story that the Persian-Jewish-American psychiatrist had told to the attendees at the Jewish Community Center a few weeks earlier.

Later, Esther reads about the city of Hamadan in the foothills of mountains whose highest peak, the snowcapped summit of Alvand Mountain at 12,000 feet, looms over the city. She dreams of traveling to the area, visiting Esther's dome, pausing at the teenager's grave, and climbing up to the mountaintop. She is now more determined than ever to escape her current gloomy situation.

"Oh, if I could escape the torture of spending long hours at my husband's trial," she sighs and falls into a reverie, imagining herself boarding a plane to the Middle East and visiting Israel and Iran. She contemplates, "Yes, I could tour the Jewish sites in Jerusalem and then travel to Iran. Yes, travel to Hamadan and visit the tomb of Esther, and climb that fearsome Alvand Mountain."

Descriptions of the many amazing caves in the Alvand mountain range fascinate her. One is forty miles long and contains two large lakes on which one can sail on a well-lit guide boat. A pleasing sense of calm engulfs her at the prospect of going to the Middle East, going to Susa, Persepolis, and Isfahan, and for a moment, the troubling thoughts of the trial are buried under the pleasant feelings.

It is dinner time for Esther and her husband. They have not talked to each other since they returned home after their exhausting day at the courthouse. She asks what she should prepare for dinner. "I am not hungry," Dr. Hartman says.

"How about a slice of vegetarian pizza?" Esther asks Dr. Hartman.

"That would be fine."

Esther calls Rome's Pizza and orders a large pizza, though she knows they cannot eat even half of it. "We can save the rest for tomorrow night," she mumbles.

When the doorbell rings later, she opens the door expecting the pizza delivery but finds Dr. Ross instead. "I have come with some information for your husband," Dr. Ross says.

"Sure. Come on in," Esther says. "He is in his reading corner." They find Dr. Hartman listening to an audiobook.

"Sit down, Ralph," Dr. Hartman says.

"I have some information for you about the border," Dr. Ross says.

Esther is about to leave the master bedroom. "Please, don't leave," Dr. Hartman asks Esther. "How about we all go to the breakfast room. Then, we can also eat when the pizza is delivered."

The three of them move to the breakfast room. Dr. Hartman pours a glass of water for Dr. Ross and a glass of red wine for himself, while Esther brews a pot of chamomile tea for herself. They settle around the table.

"Do you all remember that fellow who left the department and became Director of the Stem Cell Project at UCLA?" Dr. Ross asks.

"Are you talking about Dr. Carlos Bonilla?" Dr. Hartman says.

"Yes, that's the one. Dr. Bonilla is now in Mexico City chairing the Advanced Medical Technology Department at the University of Mexico."

VII
Fifty Stolen Fertilized Eggs

Dr. Carlos Bonilla produced more than fifty pregnancies in his infertile patients using stolen fertilized eggs without the knowledge of either donors or recipients. Dr. Hartman recalls the debacle surrounding Dr. Bonilla's scandalous behavior in California. He remembers every detail of Dr. Bonilla's colorful career and life in San Antonio. Dr. Hartman had been the one who had recruited Dr. Bonilla onto his departmental research team to work on their fetal stem cell replication project. At the time, Dr. Bonilla was a young and promising investigator from a distinguished Mexican family with brilliant credentials from a major medical school in the United States. Dr. Bonilla succeeded in culturing healthy stem cells and injecting them into the blood of fetuses, which had been diagnosed with Down syndrome. For that, he received a national award and international recognition.

When Dr. Bonilla was able to alter the genetic format of a fetus with Down syndrome and do it in utero when the pregnancy was only at fourteen weeks, he became a medical sensation. Shortly after that breakthrough, he served as the keynote speaker at a national symposium at UCLA. Subsequently, he was offered a lucrative employment contract from UCLA that included a professorship and an invitation to open a private center dedicated to fetal stem cell treatment of children with genetic disorders. Dr. Bonilla rapidly climbed the ladder of fame and success and accumulated sizeable personal wealth. His Achilles' heel was his insatiable thirst for luxury, for an extravagant lifestyle, for driving ultra-expensive Maseratis and Lamborghinis, and for flying first-class to international luxury vacation spots. He bought an expensive house in Beverly Hills and a beautiful villa near the Pacific Ocean in Big Sur.

Within a few years, Dr. Bonilla's UCLA-affiliated center employed around forty highly qualified doctors and Ph.D.'s specializing in embryonic treatments. The addition of a fertility program for women who failed to conceive with available techniques and who would spend any sum for new and effective remedies added an abundant source of revenue for the university. On a few occasions, the center had set aside hundreds of fertilized frozen embryos. The temptation to produce a pregnancy for desperate women willing to pay enormous amounts of money became very difficult for Dr. Bonilla to resist. In one case, when he failed to produce a pregnancy with the patient's egg in his newly invented GIFT (Gamete Intra-Fallopian Transfer) technique, he gave in to temptation. He implanted another patient's fertilized embryo from storage into the new patient's fallopian tube, where it successfully matured into a pregnancy. Over time, according to the later testimony of people who sued him for stealing their eggs, Dr. Bonilla produced over fifty pregnancies in patients with the stolen fertilized embryos of other women.

When it all came out, these families were devastated. Meanwhile, other parents were unsuccessfully trying to find their own stored eggs through legal action. After genetic tests and a thorough review of patients' files had validated the charges, UCLA suspended Dr. Bonilla and fired his three principal associates. Faced with seemingly insurmountable legal troubles, Dr. Bonilla and his right-hand associate, Placido Allende, quietly sold their homes and luxury cars and fled the country.

"Dr. Bonilla is inviting you to join him in Mexico City," Dr. Ross tells Dr. Hartman. "He promises he will name you honorary chairman of the Fetal Stem Cell program."

Dr. Ross explains to Dr. Hartman that the drive from San Antonio to Laredo takes about three hours. "Crossing the Mexican border is easy. Hundreds of tourists and local commuters do it every day. Americans need no visa to enter Mexico. Your best option is to drive across the International Bridge into Nuevo Laredo, Mexico," he advises Dr. Hartman. "Yes, some *coyotes* will help you ford through the Rio Grande in the middle of the night, but why would you want that? Behave like any ordinary tourist, cross the border, show your passport to the Mexican border agents, and ride on into the dusty Mexican border city. Then, you drive to the Hilton Garden Inn in Nuevo Laredo and check-in and wait for news of the jury's verdict. I sincerely hope that you will not need to continue to Mexico City."

"I feel a gloomy premonition about the jury's verdict," Dr. Hartman says.

"I'm confident you will be cleared of all charges." Esther does not like the option of fleeing to Mexico. "You must trust your instinct," she insists. "If you are confident that you didn't mean to kill anybody and the bullets were only discharged to stop the drug dealer, then you need not fear the jury. Yes! Trust the jury system and face the consequences. After all, we can always go to appeal in the case of a guilty verdict." Esther now has her husband's full attention. "Carlos's story is different," Esther pleads. "He was indicted in absentia while a fugitive in Mexico City. Your situation will be more like Polanski. He fled when he was certain the judge would ignore their plea bargain and sentence him to fifty years in prison."

"Well, this is what happened to Dr. Carlos Bonilla: he got indicted on six counts of tax evasion, for stealing patients' embryos, and fleeing justice," Dr. Ross explains. "In Mexico, he opens the most advanced genetic center in the country and convenes an international symposium in the field of New Medical Technologies to eradicate genetic disorders. The Mexican government ignores California's request for extradition to the United States. Two of his associates who were also sought by the authorities in California have joined him in Mexico City."

The thought of her husband fleeing the country like Dr. Carlos Bonilla and Roman Polanski disgusts Esther. However, Dr. Hartman makes his decision.

He says, "Carlos is doing well in Mexico, as is Polanski in Europe. Carlos' use of eggs and embryos without the consent of patients has ultimately bolstered his medical and financial success. As for Polanski, he has produced a large number of award-winning masterpieces since he fled the United States."

Saddened by the prospect of her husband fleeing the country, Esther says, "If you are found guilty, your legal problems will far exceed Dr. Bonilla's medical misconduct. Despite all of his awards and recognition for his medical success, Dr. Bonilla's tarnished reputation from his actions at UCLA mars an otherwise impressive career. It is important to differentiate between the loss of lives and the ethical and legal consequences arising from genetic and stem-cell treatments. The only thing that can save you is to be declared 'Not Guilty.' If you are not cleared, you must fight the verdict all the way to the Supreme Court of the United States. Let us testify sincerely and explain your real emotional state at the time of the shooting, and hope for the best. Let us remember that under no circumstances were you planning to shoot and kill anybody that horrible day."

Now Esther is sobbing. "Please, tell the court that we are left without our son. Tell them you feared for your life when you waved the handgun in self-defense. Inform the jury that you feared for the life of your wife and that of your son, too, when you pulled out the handgun."

In a telephone conversation later that night, Dr. Bonilla assures Dr. Hartman that he is welcome to join him at Mexico City University.

"Quite a few of our fellow faculty members have studied with you and remember you well." With the cynical sense of humor for which he is well-known, Dr. Bonilla adds, "I understand your mishap happened when you tried to defend your son. My innovative actions were to create sons and daughters for families who were childless and desperate. I hope you feel as comfortable about the events as I do."

VIII
Dr. Parsi's Employment

On several occasions, Dr. Hartman had put Dr. Parsi on notice that his job could be terminated at any time. Since Dr. Parsi is well aware that Dr. Hartman had once forced out a tenured professor from the department, Dr. Parsi's apprehension about his employment is quite understandable. He remembers more than one occasion when Dr. Hartman had questioned his management of patients. He also recalls Dr. Hartman's statement that one may have a tenured position but can still lose a well-deserved assignment in the department and instead be assigned to menial work in one of the affiliated clinics. In the case of Esther's abdominal procedure, Dr. Parsi believes that he would have been fired if her pregnancy test had come back negative. The Dean's advice to be truthful and consistent also resonates and rings through Dr. Parsi's mind. Therefore, when he steps into the witness box, Dr. Parsi resolves to answer the prosecutor's questions, as required by law, as honestly and candidly as he possibly can.

The prosecutor wastes no time and gets straight to the point. "Did Dr. Hartman ever threaten to fire you and leave you jobless in the middle of the academic year?"

"Well, he would have fired me if I had committed a major clinical misjudgment." Barrera crosses his arms and nervously frowns at the witness. Both Dr. Hartman and his wife worry whether Dr. Parsi is about to fall into the prosecutor's trap.

"Let us be clear, did he ever threaten to fire you in a burst of anger?" the prosecutor asks.

Dr. Parsi promptly replies, "I don't recall such a situation."

"Did Dr. Hartman ever use invectives against you or insult you when you disagreed with him?"

"Dr. Hartman is always emphatic and forceful when voicing his medical arguments, but he has never personally insulted me," Dr. Parsi answers calmly.

Esther, who is anxiously listening to the interaction between the prosecutor and Dr. Parsi, is thrilled. The prosecutor continues trying to put the screws on Dr. Parsi and press the issue from different directions. Still, Dr. Parsi, tranquil like a funambulist and without hesitation, answers every question honestly and truthfully and denies the prosecutor any opening.

Hoping for a misstep on the part of Dr. Parsi, the frustrated prosecutor asks him, "Did Dr. Hartman ever insult or belittle you in front of other medical staff?"

"I do not recall any such occasion."

The prosecutor goes on and presses Dr. Parsi, trying to get him to paint a nasty picture of Dr. Hartman. "Has Dr. Hartman ever insulted you privately?"

Without hesitation, Dr. Parsi answers, "No, sir."

"Did he ever discuss academic issues with you?"

"Yes, of course, he did," Dr. Parsi says.

"Was he cordial or angry with you when you disagreed with him on academic issues?"

"He was deliberate and forceful in emphasizing his point of view."

"Has he ever been unfair to you or treated you worse than the other doctors in the department?"

"He treats me no better or worse than other staff members."

The prosecutor is getting discouraged. He hoped Dr. Parsi would be a star witness for his case against Dr. Hartman, based on information received from one of the residents that Dr. Hartman bears a prejudice against foreign medical graduates, in particular against staff members from Muslim countries. It is becoming apparent that further questioning of Dr. Parsi will be futile.

Before he gives up his effort, the prosecutor asks Dr. Parsi, "Did he ever insult you during a conference?"

"No, he did not."

"I understand he has a very low impression of you. Is that because you are from a Muslim country?"

"He has never expressed that sentiment to me."

"Aren't you a Muslim?"

"No, I am not."

"Can you tell us what your religion is?"

"I was born into a Zoroastrian family," Dr. Parsi says.

Confused because he does not know anything about Zoroastrianism, the prosecutor counters, "Isn't that religion a branch of Islam?"

"Not at all. These two religions are quite different from each other. Zoroastrianism precedes Islam by over 1,500 years," Dr. Parsi explains in a level voice.

Embarrassed by his ignorance, and disappointed with Dr. Parsi's conduct as a witness, the prosecutor ends his questioning.

Now, it is Barrera's turn to clarify a few points for the jury. He asks Dr. Parsi, "Do you consume wine?"

"Yes, but in moderation."

"What country are you from?"

"I am from Iran. I was born in Yazd," Dr. Parsi answers promptly.

Barrera continues, "For the sake of the jury, please explain, in a few sentences, the difference between your religion and Islam."

At this point, the prosecutor rises and objects to the question, "Your Honor, the description of these two religions is irrelevant to the case. Furthermore, it will needlessly consume the court's time."

After the judge rules in favor of the prosecutor, Barrera says, "Your Honor, I have no further questions."

Knowing the mood of the public has turned against Muslims and all immigrants from the Middle East in reaction to the series of horrific terrorist attacks in this country and abroad, Barrera and Esther have anticipated more problems with the issue of religion. Now, they are pleased that it is on record that Dr. Parsi is not a Muslim and that Dr. Parsi has gained some measure of credibility with the jury during the exchanges between the prosecutor and the judge.

IX
My Son Was Not a Drug Dealer

At the end of the second day of trial, Marcel's father is the last witness of the day. After the oath, the prosecutor asks Marcel's father to introduce himself, describe his profession, and tell the jury in a few words about his son's life and habits. After he has responded to the first set of the prosecutor's questions, Marcel's father admits, "Yes, I do know he possessed a handgun. He told me some kids in the neighborhood were harassing him. That's why he went and purchased a handgun."

Marcel's father tells the court that he has never seen Saul, the defendant's son, in his house. "I'm sorry to say that the only time I saw my son and Saul together was the night before the shooting when they were sitting in my son's car in front of our house arguing about something."

The prosecutor asks Marcel's father, "Did you know they were in the business of selling marijuana and cocaine on the street?"

"I know, my son. He would have never done anything like that." Now, with an agitated voice, he cries out, "My son was not a drug dealer!"

"Had you seen him use any illicit drug?" the prosecutor says.

Marcel's father says, "I assume, like many teenagers, he did occasionally smoke marijuana, but that's all."

When Barrera takes over the questioning of Marcel's father, he shows exhibit seven, a large color photograph, to the jury and then approaches Marcel's father.

"According to the examination by the forensics lab, the green bags in this picture contain marijuana, and the ziplock bag is filled with packets of high-quality cocaine." Barrera brings the photograph to the jury bench and lets them hand it round. He returns to the witness stand and asks, "Do you know, sir, where this photograph was taken?"

Marcel's father looks bemused and shakes his head. "No, sir. I have no idea."

Barrera turns to the jury box and says with a loud voice, "These illicit drugs were located in the glove compartment of Marcel's car." Then he approaches the witness and asks, "Do you know what the market value of these drugs is?"

"No, sir."

Barrera pulls out a page with a formal statement that shows the value of the drugs obtained from Marcel's car. Barrera looks at Marcel's father and says, "Sir! According to the police report, the street value of these drugs exceeds five thousand dollars. Do you agree with me that a person carrying this amount of drugs could be in the business of selling at least a portion of them to other people?"

Marcel's father is overcome with rage and shouts, "I told you, my son was not a drug dealer!"

After a pause, Barrera turns his attention again to the father and asks him, "Sir, do you know how your son purchased the handgun?"

The father says, "I do not know."

"Do you know that because of his age, your son could not legally purchase a handgun?" Barrera asks the father. At this moment, the prosecutor rises and objects to the question. The judge overrules the objection and instructs the witness to answer the question.

Then, the witness says, "No, I did not know that."

"Is it plausible that your son purchased the handgun illegally on the black market?" Barrera asks. Once more, against the prosecutor's objection, the judge instructs the witness to answer the question. The witness says, "I do not know."

Barrera looks at the jury, then turns around and tells the judge, "Your Honor, I have no further questions."

"Do you have any more witnesses?" the judge asks the prosecutor.

"Not at this time, Your Honor. The prosecution rests."

"The court is adjourned for today. We will start with the defense presentation tomorrow," says the judge, and Barrera nods his head in agreement.

X
Remembering How Esther Saved the Persian Jews

Remembering how the Jewish people were saved from extinction in ancient Persia by Queen Esther, Dr. Hartman's wife is resolved to keep her husband from going to prison by showing how loving and caring he is, lest his furious outbreaks damage his case.

On the third day of the trial, Esther is the first witness to testify on behalf of the defense. So far, the proceedings have been void of earth-shaking breakthroughs. Most members of the jury wonder whether the prosecutor is following a clear strategy during the first two days of the trial. The foreman speculates, "Maybe he has additional evidence that he's presenting at the last minute."

After taking the oath, Esther sits down cautiously and is led through the events of the tragic day by Barrera.

"So, you were an eyewitness to the shooting?" asks Barrera.

"Yes, I was."

"And you're confident that Marcel fired first?"

"Yes, absolutely!" replies Esther, with tears in her eyes. "My husband was trying to protect Saul and me. Yes, Saul …" she says while her voice trails off.

After allowing Esther to regain her composure, Barrera continues. "Did Dr. Hartman ever become physically violent with Saul?"

"No, never. Saul frustrated both of us, and we struggled to deal with him, but he was a good boy. My husband would never have intentionally harmed our son."

After Barrera finishes his questions, Esther faces the prosecutor, anxiously awaiting his questions. She confirms that she is indeed the defendant's wife of more than 20 years and the mother of Saul, one of the two fatally shot teenagers.

In response to the cross-examination by the prosecutor, who asks, "Speaking of your late son, Saul, do you believe your husband was a caring father?" Esther hesitates a while and then says, "With all of his professional duties, my husband has always tried very hard to dedicate quality time to his involvement in our son's upbringing." Regaining her confidence, she adds, "When it comes to family matters, Dr. Hartman is a loving but traditional husband who supported me one hundred percent in how I managed Saul's affairs."

"Allow me to repeat the question," the prosecutor comes closer to Esther. "Do you believe your husband was a caring father?"

"Yes. My husband is a devoted husband and was a caring father."

"What would your reaction be if it turned out that your husband, in his blind fury, shot not only Marcel but also shot and killed your son Saul?"

The question unsettles Esther. Her face turns pale, tears overflow her eyes, and she has to hold on to the railing of the witness box. The notion of her husband committing filicide makes her dizzy, speechless. Before she can rally her thoughts and construct an answer, Barrera stands up and objects to the question, "Your Honor, the prosecutor's question is purely speculative and therefore, without merit. It is based on a false assumption."

Esther is relieved when the judge sustains Barrera's objection and asks the clerk to delete the question. However, the mere possibility of filicide as the result of her husband's impulsive act, in the heat of the crisis, rattles the foundation of her blind faith in her husband's innocence.

The prosecutor continues his cross-examination, turning his attention to Saul's illicit drug use. "Were you aware that your son owed Marcel more than ten thousand dollars?"

"I had no idea."

"Did you know that Saul not only smoked marijuana and used cocaine, but that he was helping Marcel sell these drugs to other high school students?" the prosecutor asks Esther.

Saul's parents had eventually realized that their son smoked weed, but they only found out about his involvement with using and selling cocaine after the shootout. Esther replies that she did not know the extent of Saul's involvement with illicit drugs before the shooting. The prosecutor again suggests in passing that Dr. Hartman may have killed Saul, and the mention of her husband's possible involvement in Saul's tragic death makes Esther shudder. She looks at Barrera but avoids making eye contact with her husband. With horror, Esther remembers the plot of the well-known Greek tragedy where the father sacrifices his offspring. She also recalls true crime stories on cable channels and in supermarket tabloids reporting on how a father much older than Dr. Hartman killed his son because the son had been addicted to multiple illicit drugs and had been institutionalized off and on for years. That father had intentionally killed his son to save their family the burden of taking care of a troubled family member. The flow of disturbing thoughts makes Esther shudder.

Could her husband commit such a crime? She now recalls another recent report where Los Angeles County prosecutors charged a highly educated man with premeditated murder for shooting and killing his son because that son was gay. That murder was committed because of the son's sexual orientation. She wonders, in the case of Saul, whether her husband could have been so disgusted with their son's sorry situation that he carelessly shot and killed both the drug dealer and their son. Faced with another question from the prosecutor concerning her husband's lack of concern about Saul, or even disdain for Saul, Esther clears her thoughts. She focuses her attention back on her testimony. She says, "Let me assure you that my husband never wanted to harm a soul."

"Could you explain the scene in front of your house at the moment when your husband aimed his handgun at the two teenagers as they were entangled in a physical scuffle?" the prosecutor asks.

With a sad face, Esther replies, "The whole thing was just like something out of a horror movie, like a modern version of a Greek tragedy."

"What do you mean by 'modern version of a Greek tragedy'?"

"Well, in several Greek tragedies a father's action knowingly or unwittingly results in the loss of his son's life. But at that moment, my husband was trying to save rather than harm Saul. He wanted to protect us from a shooter. As I know for a fact, he brought the handgun to convince the intruder to leave us alone. What happened next was a total accident, just bad luck for everybody involved."

Barrera is not happy with the exchange between the prosecutor and Esther. Dr. Hartman shakes his head and mumbles, "I should have been more attentive to Saul's struggles." Barrera, who is sitting next to Dr. Hartman, asks him, "What are you saying?"

"I'm not sure whether Esther helped or hurt my case," Dr. Hartman says.

Barrera jots down a note on his scratch pad and quietly tells Dr. Hartman, "She did her best to draw a realistic picture of your encounter in the front yard. She was honest, and the jury believed her."

XI
The Defendant Agrees to Testify

The trial reaches its climax in the late morning of the third day when Barrera calls Dr. Hartman to the witness stand. The decision by Barrera to present Dr. Hartman as his final witness for the defense astonishes the judge and the prosecutor, who knows that the defendant rarely appears as a witness in criminal trials. Barrera has scheduled the defendant to testify during the last hour of the trial, hoping Dr. Hartman's experience as a powerful orator will convince the jury that he acted in self-defense against an intruder on his property and that the shooting of the victim was unintentional and purely accidental. Moreover, he has one more trick up his sleeve.

Barrera begins questioning Dr. Hartman. His questions permit the accused to present his credentials as a dedicated physician and an innovative researcher who has saved many lives by practicing and teaching high-quality medicine. Then, he asks Dr. Hartman, "Did you know that your son was using cocaine?"

"No, I did not know."

With the next few questions, he reminds the jury that Dr. Hartman is indeed a considerate person. "Your wife testified earlier that you are a caring husband," the Barrera says. "Have you ever physically assaulted your son or your wife?"

The answer is a resounding negative.

Then he asks, "As a renowned lecturer, don't you expect your students and residents to study and understand the topics of your lectures?"

Surprised by the vague question, Dr. Hartman says, "Yes, of course, that is my expectation."

Barrera adds, "Would it be reasonable to expect that your students should thoroughly study and comprehend the medical subjects you are teaching them?" Dr. Hartman's quick answer is affirmative.

With the next several questions, Barrera highlights Dr. Hartman's strong commitment to the medical school, other departments, his patients, and the students. Then he asks, "At the time of your arrest, didn't you surrender the handgun to the patrolman?"

"Yes, I did," Dr. Hartman says. "I voluntarily surrendered the handgun and myself to the arresting officer."

"Did you make any statement?"

"Yes, sir. I stated that I waved the handgun to scare the intruder and to force him to leave my son, my wife, and me alone," Dr. Hartman says.

"Do you remember shooting the intruder?"

"I remember seeing fire bursting from the intruder's handgun. I remember hearing a boom and feeling a hot blow to my leg," Dr. Hartman says.

"What else do you remember?"

"I remember the handgun in my hand, waving it at the intruder."

"What do you remember next?"

"The next thing I remember is being in the ambulance on the way to the emergency room of University Hospital."

The defense asks several more questions regarding Dr. Hartman's research on the application of stem cells for combating incurable diseases.

Then, Barrera turns to face the jury and says, "Dear members of the jury, this physician, Dr. Hartman, has set a very high standard for teaching at the medical school, and it's obvious that he expects a proper response from his students, residents, and faculty members. He has successfully obtained large grants from the National Institutes of Health and other agencies to conduct significant research." Barrera adds, "He intended not to harm anyone. Only to help patients."

Being confident that Barrera is totally off the course in bringing Dr. Hartman's medical research to the fore, the prosecutor rises and objects to Barrera's statement and asks the judge to order the deletion of Barrera's account from the record. The judge sustains the objection and instructs the court to delete the account. Barrera, who is happy that, at a minimum, he has aired the statement, decides to present Dr. Hartman's valuable medical research during the closing argument.

Barrera's last questions produce the most desirable reaction from the jury, especially when he asked Dr. Hartman, "Dr. Hartman, were you aware that Marcel had a handgun in his pocket?"

"Yes. Marcel was pressing on an object, in his pocket, which I correctly believed was a handgun," Dr. Hartman says.

"Did you believe he would pull the handgun and shoot you or Saul?" Barrera asks.

Dr. Hartman says, "Yes. He was shouting and saying he would kill Saul unless he got ten grand."

"Is that why you went inside the house and got your handgun?" Barrera asks.

"Yes. After the drug dealer kicked me, I got up and went into the house to bring the handgun and wave it at him so that he would vacate the driveway," Dr. Hartman says.

Barrera announces that he has no further questions for Dr. Hartman.

Now, the prosecutor rises, walks around, looks at the jury, turns toward Dr. Hartman, and loudly asks the most unpleasant question for any parent, "Did you know that your son was using and selling cocaine to his high school classmates?"

Humiliated, Dr. Hartman answers, "I did not know that." His reply to the question about Saul smoking and selling marijuana is similar. "I'm embarrassed to say, no, I did not know my son was smoking or selling grass."

A few of the jury members try to conceal their sympathy for Dr. Hartman, for they know how hard it is to control teenagers nowadays. A few of them have had similar problems with their children. The prosecutor recognizes his misjudgment in following that line of questioning and quickly changes his strategy—the calmness of Dr. Hartman and his measured answers to the prosecutor delight Barrera.

In response to the prosecutor's question regarding the shooting, Dr. Hartman says, "I threatened the intruder to force him to leave my property."

The prosecutor presses Dr. Hartman to admit that he pulled the trigger, knowing the action would result in the loss of one or maybe two lives. "I was threatening the drug dealer so that he would leave the driveway so that my son and my wife would be saved."

"So, who killed Marcel?" the prosecutor asks Dr. Hartman.

"I believe that it was bad luck. Marcel brought his dreadful fate with him. It was the handgun, which was there in his pocket, in plain sight. I believed he was about to pull it out and point it at me, so I waved my gun at him, hoping he would turn around and run away."

A moment of silence prevails in the court. Neither the prosecutor nor the jury or the judge blinks an eye. The prosecutor breaks the silence and asks Dr. Hartman, "Do you remember what happened next?"

"No, I was frantic. I was shaken. I was fearful. I don't remember what happened next," Dr. Hartman says.

The prosecutor asks again, "Do you remember when you aimed at Marcel and pulled the trigger?"

"I heard a boom, then I felt a sudden burst of fire in my leg," Dr. Hartman says.

"Then what happened? Who did you aim at when you pulled the trigger?"

"The next thing I remember was when I was in the ambulance."

"Were you trying to kill Marcel?"

"No! I just waved the handgun to force him to flee the scene. Instead, he pulled out a gun from his pocket and shot at me."

"Do you remember the moment when Marcel collapsed on the ground?"

"No. The last thing I remember was a boom, then a burst of fire in my leg."

At the lunch break, Barrera, Esther, and Dr. Hartman walk to the Bill Miller BBQ across the street from the courthouse. They have no appetite and order only the salads with iced tea. Esther adds a slice of pecan pie to the tray. Barrera was amused by Dr. Hartman's use of the phrase *bad luck*.

Encouraged by Barrera's reaction, Dr. Hartman says, "Indeed, it was *bad luck* for all of us involved in the tragedy: Marcel, Saul, Esther, and me."

Esther picks up the issue and says, "Nobody would have been killed if Saul didn't use illicit drugs, or if Marcel didn't drive the expensive sports car which forced him to buy and sell illicit drugs to pay for its maintenance. My husband would not have rushed to the cellar and taken the handgun to scare the drug dealer."

Barrera is mesmerized by Esther's argument and murmurs, "She must have read *The Stranger* recently."

Esther continues with her testimony and says, "Yes, it's a combination of drugs, handguns, and *bad luck* that produced that fatal storm on the driveway and engulfed all of us that day."

The phrase "bad luck' makes so much sense to Barrera that he quickly jots down Esther's comments and underlines the phrase "bad luck."

Barrera is pleased with the morning session and considers that Dr. Hartman's testimony has impressed the jury. He looks at Dr. Hartman and says, "I observed that your words and your calm demeanor impressed the jury."

When the court continues that afternoon, the prosecutor resumes the cross-examination of the defendant. "Did you realize that by bringing the handgun to the scene of the brawl, you were escalating a scuffle into a shootout?"

"I did not," Dr. Hartman says.

"Were you aware that brandishing the gun against Marcel might force him to react and pull his gun?" The prosecutor asks Dr. Hartman.

"I was trying to scare him off so that he would leave our property, to save my family's life," Dr. Hartman says.

"Dr. Hartman, as we know now, your action resulted in the loss of two lives instead of saving your son?"

Barrera jumps up, raises his hand, and yells, "Your Honor, objection. The prosecutor assumes that Dr. Hartman intended to act carelessly, which is far from the truth. Dr. Hartman was waving his handgun, threatening the assailant, aiming only to persuade the intruder to leave his property and save the lives of his family."

To the utter disappointment of the prosecutor, the judge ruled for the defense. "Objection sustained."

Frustrated, the prosecutor asks a few irrelevant questions and then ends the questioning.

"Both sides have presented their cases," the judge says. "We will adjourn for the evening and resume tomorrow morning with rebuttal witnesses." All rise as the judge leaves the courtroom. Despite the gloom he senses from Dr. Hartman and Esther, Barrera is pleased with the way the trial has gone. He is confident they will get a 'not guilty' verdict.

The prosecutor, on the other hand, leaves the courtroom disappointed in the day's events. "If only the bullet that killed Saul had not been so severely damaged, or if we could have found the missing bullets. Then my case would have been much stronger," he thinks.

After a few warm and sunny days, the gardening crew digs out the wilted pansies to replace them with yellow lantanas, roses, daylilies, and black-eyed Susans. The house they are working on is located straight across the street from the Hartman home. The crew has brought fresh topsoil and trays of plants and other mainly yellow flowers to prepare the garden for San Antonio's summer heat and brazen sun. The neighbor loves gardening and always starts rejuvenating the courtyard before any of the other neighbors. He chooses yellow pansies for the winter and predominantly yellow lantana and other native flowers for the summer. These native Texas plants are not only beautiful outside, but they are also ideal for clipping their blooms and bringing them indoors for decoration. The black-eyed Susans get their name from their prominent dark centers. The petals are most often golden yellow and attract butterflies.

The crew pulls up the dead pansies and brings a yard of fresh topsoil to replace the old, crusty dirt. While digging through the old soil, one of the workers hits a bullet with his shovel as he is removing the dirt. He calls out to the boss, "Hey, look, I found a bullet down here."

The boss takes the muddy bullet, wraps it in scrap paper, and pushes it in his pocket. He mumbles, "I wonder who shot this bullet?"

The leader of the gardening crew washes his hands under an outdoor tap, and then knocks on the front door and asks for the owner. "Look, sir, guess what we have found in your garden?" He pulls out the scrap paper, opens it, and displays the bullet. "We found this in your front yard."

The neighbor who dislikes Dr. Hartman and is aware of the trial takes the muddy package and asks, "Did anybody clean the bullet?"

"No, sir."

He thanks the gardener and carefully rewraps the bullet. "This may be a useful piece of evidence."

———————

Early the next morning, the prosecutor appears in front of the judge requesting permission to include new evidence in the case against Dr. Hartman. In the presence of the Barrera, he says, "Your Honor, the neighbor across the street from the Hartman house has found a stray bullet, which is presently being investigated by the forensic laboratory of the DA's office. We suspect this is one of the missing bullets from this case, and we need to determine who discharged the bullet and whether it is the one that went through Saul's arm or the one that hit no one." He further emphasizes that this bullet is one of two unaccounted bullets that they have searched for since they obtained and examined Dr. Hartman's handgun. He further says, "The study of tissue and DNA, if any, will reveal whether the bullet hit Saul or not. I request a continuance until this new evidence can be examined."

In response to Barrera's objection, the prosecutor emphasizes that this new evidence is vital in determining who fatally shot Saul. Against the vehement objection of Barrera, the judge issues an order permitting the inclusion of this new evidence at the trial, granting a continuance until tests have been completed.

Two days later, the lawyers appear before the judge, in the absence of the jury. The prosecutor hands a copy of the ballistic and forensics reports to both the judge and Barrera. "The bullet has been examined, and there is now no doubt that the bullet that killed Saul came from the defendant's handgun," says the prosecutor.

"Your Honor, I renew my objection to the presentation of new evidence this late in the trial. The prosecutor has already rested his case," says Barrera. "It's too late in presenting new evidence."

"Your Honor, as you know, this evidence just came to our attention two days ago. I will present it as part of the state's rebuttal evidence," the prosecutor says.

The judge glances at the report and reads through the findings and says, "You may present this evidence." Then he tells Barrera, "I will grant you a day to consider this new evidence and to devise a strategy for dealing with it."

XII
Dr. Baldwin and Dr. Parsi Plan to Travel to Cancun

Dr. Baldwin and Dr. Parsi plan to travel to Cancun together. They discuss their plan for dinner at their favorite Mexican restaurant, Paloma Blanca, after the third day of Dr. Hartman's trial. Looking around at the colorful decor, Dr. Parsi says: "We can experience Mexico without leaving San Antonio."

Dr. Baldwin is an excellent swimmer who is practicing scuba diving at a nearby public pool and likes the prospect of diving in the clear Caribbean waters near Cancun. She says, "But really, when are we going?"

"First, we have to wait for the elephant to leave the room," Dr. Parsi says, referring to the upheaval generated at the medical school by the trial.

"Let's take a break a few weeks after the trial," Dr. Baldwin replies. She remembers a conversation she had with Dr. Hartman two weeks earlier. She tells Dr. Parsi that the main topic of the discussion was that Dr. Hartman would decide what to do with their positions in the department after the trial was over.

Dr. Parsi wonders, "What happens with our research if he's convicted and sentenced to spend many years in prison? Who will be in charge of the department?"

"Okay, in that case, we will just get away for a week and look for other possibilities when we return."

As if they were caught on an island in the aftermath of a storm, they avoid further speculation about Dr. Hartman's trial. However, both are aware of the connection between the outcome of the trial and their positions in the department. They had hoped to separate their professional futures from the outcome of the trial. They finish dinner and postpone a decision about scheduling their trip to Cancun until after things have settled.

"I sure love the prospect of snorkeling in Cancun and seeing the beautiful, colorful fish swarming around us," Dr. Baldwin sighs wistfully.

Looking at Dr. Baldwin's glittering birthday ring and contemplating something more romantic about their relationship, Dr. Parsi says, "I hope we can take off soon and float around holding hands and looking at exotic fish."

"So, let's go," Dr. Baldwin smiles at him. "We have another hurdle to overcome: our position in the department."

"No. Let's not put all our eggs in one basket," Dr. Parsi says.

Dr. Baldwin says, "You are such a wise man."

"Thanks. So, as soon as we know about our positions for the next year in either the department or somewhere else in town in a private group practice, we should take a vacation," Dr. Parsi says. "And then, we will fly away to a nice place, and dive in the crystal blue waters."

Dr. Baldwin objects. "Why should we connect our trip to Dr. Hartman's trial?"

Dr. Parsi worries whether the new chief of surgery, whoever that might be, would be in a position to offer them both employment contracts for the next year. And if Dr. Hartman does not go to jail, will he resume his prejudice against him? Will they both remain in the same town after their present employment contract?

"No matter who takes the helm of the department, our positions have already been discussed and decided," Dr. Baldwin says. "I know that for a fact." Then, she explains that the department's vice-chair has alluded to that possibility.

"I have an appointment to meet either Dr. Hartman or the vice-chair after the trial."

"Nobody has given me a clue whether they are offering me a job next year," Dr. Parsi says. "I have applied to several places in case I don't get an offer at the school."

"I know you will be given a contract. Let's pray our embattled chairman survives the trial."

"What happens if he's found guilty and sentenced to several years in prison?" Dr. Parsi asks.

"Then, we are in limbo."

"I don't think so." Dr. Parsi changes the subject. "Linda, my dearest, I'd like to share something with you. I prefer to look for other options here in San Antonio because I like the city. Our poet laureate calls it the 'lazy city,' as it offers comfortable living and is a great city to raise a family."

Now, Dr. Baldwin giggles and says, "Whose family are you talking about?"

Dr. Parsi holds Dr. Baldwin's hand, looks at her blue eyes, and says, "Linda, may I say our family?"

Dr. Baldwin smiles widely and squeezes Dr. Parsi's hand and murmurs, "Are you serious?"

"Linda, will you marry me?" Dr. Parsi says and waits for her response.

"Are you serious?"

Dr. Parsi, bending his knee and holding Dr. Baldwin's hand, says, "Linda, I love you. You are the one I'll do everything for. I was going to propose to you in Cancun, but I can't wait. Linda, will you marry me?"

Dr. Baldwin's face glows with happiness. She says, "Yes. Yes. Yes!"

"I have written a poem for you for this moment. I'll print it and give it to you the next time we drink champagne and celebrate our commitment."

"Read the first line to me now," Dr. Baldwin says.

Dr. Parsi murmurs the first four lines:

In the bright daylight,
You are radiant and bright.

So splendid it is
When I glance at your eyes.

———————

Dr. Parsi talks about the prospect of living in San Antonio as a couple, about the pleasant weather year-round, biking trails, tasty Tex-Mex restaurants, museums, and the performing arts centers.

"How about riding our bikes to work?" Dr. Baldwin says.

"I am for it," Dr. Parsi says. "It will be the best thing to do. You and I are biking together to work."

"I'm ready, too."

"Well, regarding Dr. Hartman, I understand he wants you to stay in the department. But regardless of the possibility of an offer for me to stay on as a junior faculty member next year, I'd like to look around and find another option."

"Are you looking for a position outside Texas?" Dr. Baldwin asks. "It sure would be nice if we both could stay here in San Antonio."

Dr. Parsi holds Dr. Baldwin's hand and says, "Of course. We will stay here, but there are other options for me to practice in San Antonio." He gently squeezes Dr. Baldwin's hand and says, "The other day, I had lunch with this fellow. He's the head of a large private surgical group in northeast San Antonio. They are looking for a surgical oncologist. He was the chief resident when you were a medical student and remembers you very well, even raved about you. He discussed the possibility of hiring me, and if you will, both of us as new members of the group. They will pay us an annual salary plus quarterly bonuses, and if it works out for both sides, we could become partners in the group after two years."

After Dr. Parsi gives the doctor's name, Dr. Baldwin recalls a rotation she had during her senior year of medical school and suddenly remembers the doctor's face. She smiles, "He was impressive. I learned a lot from him during the rounds and in the operating room."

Dr. Parsi says, "Great. He also commented favorably about you and told me you were the most promising student in that group. I have a follow-up meeting with that doctor two weeks from today. Do you want to join me?"

"Yes. Yes, I am serious," Dr. Baldwin says.

"That possibility would separate our lives from Dr. Hartman's affairs," Dr. Parsi says.

Dr. Baldwin whispers, "I have heard he may flee the country if the closing arguments indicate that he may lose the case."

———————

On the second evening after the announcement that one of the stray bullets has been recovered, Esther brings two trays with warmed-up leftover dishes for dinner for both of them to the master bedroom. Dr. Hartman waves her off and says, "I'm not hungry."

Esther urges him to eat at least a small portion. He becomes reticent in an attempt to hide his concerns about the trial. "I hope the forensics report doesn't create a major setback," Esther says. "Yet, I'm worried." She looks at her husband and can read his mind; his face displays hopelessness and despair. Dr. Hartman is consumed with a deep fear that the forensics report may deliver a last-minute bombshell like the recent October bombshell that changed the course of the presidential election.

"What if it reveals that I fired the fatal bullet into my son's chest?" He ponders in silent anguish. Then, he murmurs, "That would be the last nail in my coffin."

As if Esther hears a voice that says, "The father has killed his son," she closes her eyes and shouts, "Please, stop it. I don't want to hear another word about Saul's death."

The couple becomes eerily silent for a while. Then, they quietly consume a small portion of their dinner and gulp down white wine without noticing its high-quality bouquet, as if they both had dysgeusia. Esther takes the trays to the kitchen and then goes to the library, leaving her husband playing with his Kindle Fire, listening to an audiobook, once more to *The Stranger*.

"This is the third time he has listened to that book," she murmurs. "I wonder why. Is he anticipating the same tragic ending for himself?" She sits for a while and tries to meditate, but fails to free her mind from flashing images of the prosecutor walking deliberately around the courtroom, imploring the jury to declare Dr. Hartman guilty as charged, shouting, "The defendant escalated the tension by pulling out the handgun and carelessly aiming at two innocent teenagers."

The only topic that can divert her attention from the trial is her favorite subject, the tale of Esther, the Queen of Persia. Now, she dreams she is fleeing San Antonio, boarding a plane, and flying to the Middle East. And when she gets there, she will hire a local guide who speaks English and drive to Hamadan. Visiting the tomb of Esther has become an obsession for her, though she has no clue of the difficulty of such a trip to Iran in these troubling times when the war in Iraq, in Syria, and Yemen has put the whole region on a disastrous course. She remembers how one of her close friends left town after discovering her husband's infidelity and traveled to Kolkata to join Mother Theresa's group for a while. And how another friend, an immigration lawyer, went to Iran for two weeks and returned safely after completely ignoring the news about the arrest of two Americans who had accidentally crossed the Iraq-Iran border and were charged for spying. She remembers their comments, "We had no problem whatsoever. The Iranian people are great."

She prepares a cup of green tea, comes back to the library, and resumes her thoughts. "I'll leave the day after the jury enters its judgment." She has traveled to the Middle East before and thoroughly enjoyed the experience.

"Yes, I will travel to Iran immediately and become a volunteer at Esther's Tomb in Hamadan." She knows from previous experience arranging and traveling to Israel that the voyage is not complicated at all. So, she will extend the flight and smoothly land in Tehran. "I'll pack my luggage, travel to Israel, and then to Iran," she murmurs. "I'll become a volunteer. Yeah, Esther, the Queen of Persia did it 2,700 years ago on foot, so why shouldn't I visit Ecbatana in these modern times?"

Esther is ignorant of the limitations and challenges that she will face traveling to Iran at a time when the Iranian government's position is so hostile toward Israel that no one who goes to Israel can ever set foot on Iranian soil. After a while, she googles the issue of traveling to Iran and finds links to several travel agencies with information and opportunities for group tours to Iran. She saves the links in her Favorites folder and decides to revisit the issue the next night or after the completion of the trial.

It is late in the evening, and Dr. Hartman sits in the dark bedroom, listening to an audiobook of *The Great Gatsby* when the phone rings. Barrera is on the phone. "Bad news Doc," he says. "The forensics representative is going to appear as a witness when the trial resumes the day after tomorrow."

"What is he going to say, Barrera?" Dr. Hartman says.

"I'm not sure. I'll have more information when we meet with the judge in the morning." They both turn silent. Barrera says, "Okay, I'll see you in the morning, Doc."

The ominous warning by the U.S. Department of State for American citizens who are considering travel to Iran makes Esther realize that visiting Esther's Tomb in Hamadan, Iran, is not as simple as she thought. The U.S. Department of State has a red warning symbol at the top of the page with the large bolded heading, "Iran Travel Warning." Esther peruses the warning and copies and pastes several passages on a page in her computer for future reference. She reads, "U.S. citizens traveling to Iran should very carefully weigh the risks of travel and consider postponing their travel. Iranian authorities continue to unjustly detain and imprison U.S. citizens on trumped-up charges, including espionage or posing a threat to Iranian national security. Iranian authorities have also prevented the departure, in some cases for months, of some American citizens who traveled to Iran for personal or professional reasons. The US government does not have diplomatic or consular relations with the Islamic Republic of Iran; therefore, it cannot provide protection or routine consular services to U.S. citizens in Iran."

Esther further reads, "The Iranian government continues to repress some minority religious and ethnic groups, including Christians, Baha'is, and Zoroastrians, among others. Consequently, visiting some areas of the country where these minorities reside, including the Kurdish northwest of the country, Hamadan, and Kermanshah, remains extremely unsafe."

When she looks at the map of Iran, she sees that the city of Hamadan with Esther's Tomb is located at the periphery of the Kurdish Northwest region of Iran, an area that has seen frequent uprisings and unrest. This information adds to her already shaken plans of traveling to Iran. However, when she opens a few more websites, she finds some encouraging notes. On the Iran Luxury Tours website, she sees no discouraging comments, but rather exciting information.

For example, one Iranian tour site writes, "Many Americans mistakenly assume a trip to Iran requires special permission from the U.S. Government, much like a trip to Cuba. This is not the case. While for a long while, the relationship between Iran and the U.S. has been strained, American citizens can travel to Iran freely, as long as they comply with government rules. However, they can only visit Iran as part of a group tour or with a private guide. Their guide must be specially licensed to guide American citizens and be aware of current Iranian government regulations." She reads that even though the itinerary of any group tour must be pre-approved by the Tourism Department of the Iranian Islamic government, this does not mean all individuals are required to adhere to the structured schedule fully. So Esther realizes that there is an opportunity to leave the group with a private guide, wander around cities and sites of interest, and visit Hamadan in case it's not included in the tour. She is amused when she reads the dress code when visiting Iran, which emphasizes that female adult visitors need to wear a headdress at all times in public, and should stick to loose-fitting clothes with a long shirt over trousers. Men have fewer restrictions, although they should avoid shorts and wear long-sleeved shirts when appearing in public.

When Esther visits the site of Vantage Adventure Tours and sees their itinerary to Iran, she quickly clicks on a short video about the Zoroastrian Heritage of the City of Yazd, the city where Dr. Parsi was born. She enjoys the scenery and historical information and saves the link to revisit it later. She goes on and emails the link to Dr. Parsi.

It is after two in the morning when she finally turns off the lights and retires. Not being able to fall asleep, thinking about the evidence that has recently been recovered, she contemplates that tonight could be one of the last nights she sees her husband at home if he is taken directly to prison if the jury declares him guilty as charged.

She picks up the Kindle, turns on the Bluetooth connection, clicks on the audiobook app, and plays the Teaching Company's lectures of *The Persian Empire* by John W. I. Lee from The Great Courses. She turns to Xerxes the Great and listens to the king's adventure, hoping to hear about Esther, the Queen of Persia.

XIII
Escaping to Mexico

Knowing the story of the embattled Dr. Carlos Bonilla, who successfully fled to Mexico, Dr. Hartman makes his decision to leave the U.S. as soon as possible. He recalls how Dr. Bonilla convinced his family to stay behind and live quietly in Los Angeles until he was settled in Mexico. Before he escapes to Mexico, Dr. Bonilla quickly sells his properties in California, transfers the ownership of his infertility center to a trusted friend, and leases a condominium for his wife and children. He then takes plenty of cash, packs his most valuable personal belongings, and under cover of night drives south and crosses the Mexican border. The move takes by surprise the large group of individuals who are involved with protracted legal actions related to the stolen human embryos: the women who had received the embryos and became pregnant, carried the babies to term, and delivered them; the families who were the actual owners of the embryos; UCLA who is fighting numerous lawsuits related to these stolen embryos; and the group of lawyers who are connected to these cases.

Because Dr. Bonilla is well-known and highly popular in the medical communities of Mexico, South America, and Europe, he is not worried about his future. As soon as he crosses the border, he contacts his colleagues at the University of Mexico and asks for advice. He avoids crossing the Mexican-California border at Tijuana because of the publicity of the stolen embryos in the state, instead driving all night through Phoenix, Arizona, and then on to El Paso, Texas, where he stops for breakfast and fills up the gas tank. It takes him most of the morning hours to follow the queues of bumper-to-bumper cars and enter the inspection gate of the Mexican Border Agency. Knowing how to communicate with the agents, he quietly passes fifty-dollar bills to whomever he deals with at the station and succeeds in crossing the border with his belongings with ease.

Driving into Ciudad Juarez, Mexico, gives Dr. Bonilla mixed feelings. He stops in a paid parking lot, looks at the map of the city, and googles the Trip Advisor's list of safe hotels. He chooses Hampton Inn by Hilton, downloads the directions onto his mobile phone, and follows the GPS and the busy road toward the hotel. The hotel receptionist asks for his passport at the registration desk, and per his request, he assigns Dr. Bonilla a luxury suite.

Now safely ensconced in a luxury suite, Dr. Bonilla sighs in deep relief, takes off his sweaty clothes, and takes a warm shower. He asks for coffee and orange juice, sits on a comfortable sofa, and begins to make calls. His first call is to his wife, where he reports the successful crossing of the border.

"I'm in a very comfortable suite in a good hotel," he tells her. He then calls his friends in Buenos Aires, Madrid, and London. He discusses his departure from the U.S with a colleague at the University of Mexico and explains to him the anticipated salvo of legal challenges, including a possible extradition request from the United States. Upon the Mexican friend's advice, he tentatively chooses to settle in Mexico City for a while and set up his practice there. Knowing the corruption of the legal system in Mexico and the strong support he anticipates from the university community, he mutters, "Yes, I agree. After all, it's very difficult, almost impossible, to have me extradited from Mexico."

―――――――――

Perusing the article in the *Medical Encyclopedia* about Dr. Carlos Bonilla, Dr. Hartman solidifies his decision to flee the country if the jury delivers a verdict of guilty as charged. Dr. Hartman reads that after escaping from Los Angeles, Dr. Bonilla continued his reproductive research, held a full professorship, and became the Chair of the Department of Human Reproduction at the University of Mexico. When Dr. Bonilla was still in Los Angeles, he told Dr. Hartman not too long ago, "I am indebted to you for my scientific achievements." When Dr. Bonilla settles in Mexico City, he calls Dr. Hartman to deliver an invitation, "Come here and lead our department." A fugitive genius is telling another genius that no matter where you land, the people in science and medicine will greet you with open arms. Dr. Bonilla boasts about his situation in Mexico and assures Dr. Hartman, "Actually, I receive more invitations now to lecture and teach at medical schools around the world than during my time in California. Plus, I have a lot more money now than when I was in Los Angeles."

Dr. Bonilla, who loves the high society lifestyle, says, "Look! I have my private jet with a full-time pilot, which enables me to fly anywhere in the world and perform procedures, give lectures, and in return, I receive substantial payments. My second favorite place to give lectures is Milan. Last May, when I was there for five days, on the second day after I had performed five procedures, I took off and had dinner with the director of the *Teatro alla Scala di Milano*. It was a fabulous dinner, a gift from the director to me for performing a GIFT procedure on his wife. The best part was sitting in the VIP box and seeing *La Traviata*. To my utter surprise, on the night after my departure, that opera house was performing *Porgy and Bess*."

Dr. Bonilla keeps bloviating, "But my favorite medical school to visit is the *Università Degli Studi* in Padua, Italy, founded in 1222. Although it is now ranked low among European medical schools, during the Italian Renaissance, it was the most important place in the Western world to study astrology, medicine, and anatomy. Just imagine, geniuses like Copernicus and Galileo Galilei studied at that university. I had an opportunity to visit the oldest surviving anatomical theater, which is amazing and has been used since 1595."

Dr. Bonilla is ready to go on at length with more hyperbolic assertions about life after fleeing the US. Dr. Hartman, who is familiar with the rhetorical style of his friend, asks only one question that all of a sudden stops the gushing

189

verbiage, "Where are your wife and children—are, they with you in Mexico City?"

After a pause, Dr. Bonilla says, "They did not like living with me in Mexico City. Presently, they are studying in American universities, at UCLA and Brown University. However, they visit me here at every opportunity. My wife, who now mostly lives in Los Angeles, spends long weekends with me here, and also travels with me when I fly to Europe when I visit universities and give lectures. She meets me at whatever European airport I land."

"I'm glad you are happy there in Mexico," Dr. Hartman says. "I hope I don't need to go through that transition. But if it happens, I may use your help." Then he remembers that there is an extradition treaty between Mexico and the United States. He asks Dr. Bonilla, "How did you manage to escape extradition?"

"Because Mexico needs my expertise, the Mexican judge denied the California Attorney General's request," Dr. Bonilla says. "Besides, here, money speaks louder than any treaty."

The night before the new evidence is presented is the hardest time in Dr. Hartman's life. The stories of Roman Polanski and Dr. Carlos Bonilla keep churning through his mind and keep him wondering for hours on end. He contemplates, "Could I become another wondering genius fleeing the US?"

Because he anticipates the next day to be critical, he turns off the reading light and seeks to fall asleep. When at two AM, he still feels quite restless, he changes the alarm clock to seven and takes a tablet of Ativan. Ironically, Esther has done the same a short time earlier. Neither Esther, who spends the night in the library, nor Dr. Hartman can find any tangible rest. Dr. Hartman twists and turns for a long time like an infant suffering from abdominal cramps, and Esther only manages a short nap and is quite awake when the alarm clock goes off. In an exhausted state of mind, they leave the house and drive to Barrera's office for a final briefing before they all walk across the square to the courthouse.

"There is a last-minute bombshell waiting for us," Barrera tells the couple. "As far as I know, the forensics laboratory has completed the work of analyzing the findings, and the director has prepared their final report. The prosecutor, judge, and I are going to have a quick meeting concerning that report before the trial resumes."

"Why shouldn't you know about the forensics report before the trial convenes?" Dr. Hartman cries out, his face burning with anger. "Didn't you read the report when it was presented as new evidence to the judge?"

Barrera is annoyed by the fiery reaction of his client and contemplates the implications of Dr. Hartman bursting into a similar rage during the trial. He is trying to avoid pouring fuel on the fire and says, "I only know the forensics director completed the work late yesterday afternoon."

"So, what could be in the report that makes you so worried?"

"Not knowing what is in the report bothers me."

They leave the issue at that point and walk together to the courthouse.

––––––––––

On the morning of the day on which the newly discovered evidence will be presented, Dr. Ross makes a long-distance call to the Hilton Garden Inn in the Mexican border town of Nuevo Laredo, just across the Rio Grande, and reserves a suite for two nights. He chooses this convenient, safe, and relatively luxurious hotel in a city known for its drug-related violence, hoping to find a secure haven at the hotel. The friendly reservation clerk advises Dr. Ross to obtain a pre-paid reservation for a safe parking spot inside the hotel and to be sure to reach the hotel before dark.

"We recommend a room on one of the upper floors, for they are quiet and comfortable. The room comes with complimentary breakfast," the hotel staffer says. "We even have an omelet bar and a spicy menudo stew available every morning." Dr. Ross has never had menudo soup before. "It's spicy and delicious," the clerk says. "Squeeze two slices of lime over it, and you will enjoy a truly traditional treat."

"I may bring a guest along, too." Dr. Ross says.

"Be sure your guest carries a passport," the employee says. "Well, unless she is local."

XIV
Trial Lawyers and the Doctors

It is a fact that physicians in the United States carry malpractice insurance to protect themselves from lawsuits by patients who may experience adverse results from medical treatments, encounter side effects from prescribed drugs, or sustain undesirable complications during surgeries. The annual premium for this insurance takes a good chunk of their income. The cost of that coverage is much higher for surgeons than for pediatricians or internists. The plaintiff's lawyers regularly sue doctors for malpractice in civil court, hoping they will get a desirable judgment. To protect physicians who have been sued, insurance companies hire experienced lawyers to defend the doctors. Each team, both the plaintiff and defendant, will line up expert witnesses to get the desired testimony to strengthen their position.

Naturally, those doctors hired by the trial lawyers to testify as expert witnesses against their colleagues are incredibly unpopular in the medical community. The usual snide comment about them is, "They are physicians who failed in regular practice and therefore are tempted to appear as expert witnesses by the substantial fees paid by trial lawyers. They are traitors."

On the other hand, the doctors who defend their colleagues in such cases carry the status of heroes among practicing physicians. Dr. Hartman seldom testifies for or against a doctor. "A physician should focus on practicing medicine!" he tells the other faculty members in the department. In a case involving the Dean's brother, a neurosurgeon, he is obliged to appear for the defense and decides upfront that his fee will be donated to the University's Research Fund. The plaintiff, a pregnant woman, involved in a car accident where she sustained a concussion and had a subdural hematoma, underwent surgery by the Dean's brother. The plaintiff's lawyer claims that the subsequent loss of her pregnancy was caused by the surgeon's hasty intervention. Against the testimony of the plaintiff who limps into the witness stand assisted by a nurse, and makes a scene, sobbing and pleading for justice, the formidable testimony by Dr. Hartman changes the direction of the trial in favor of the defense.

"The doctor saved the life of the patient by performing a timely procedure without which she would not have recovered from her deep coma," Dr. Hartman states calmly. "Miscarriage after a serious accident with a head injury, such as the one the plaintiff sustained, is extremely probable."

When the trial resumes after Barrera has had a day to consider his strategy in light of the new evidence, the judge calls both prosecutor and the defense to the bench to verify that neither of the attorneys plans to call more witnesses except for the appearance of the director of the forensic laboratory to present his analysis of the newly discovered bullet. The judge instructs the parties to prepare for their closing statements promptly after the forensics director's testimony.

The judge calls the trial to order, and when the jurors are in their seats, the prosecutor presents the new evidence. He calls the forensics expert to the witness stand. The director of the forensic laboratory is a short man with a goatee, more like a professor than a DA staffer. His voice is scratchy, and he wears a thick pair of glasses. Barrera and the defendant are silently watching the prosecutor's actions. After the seating of the forensics expert and formal procedures, the prosecutor begins questioning the expert.

He holds two boxes containing one bullet apiece, walks to the witness stand, and asks the forensics expert, "Earlier in the trial, you testified about these two bullets. To remind the jury, have you thoroughly examined these bullets?"

The expert says, "Yes, sir. I have. The first is the bullet that lodged in the leg of the defendant. It was fired from Marcel's handgun. The second is the bullet that killed Marcel. It was fired from the handgun of the accused."

The prosecutor retrieves a third box containing a bullet. "And what about this bullet?"

"It is the bullet that killed Saul, the defendant's son. It was too badly damaged to determine which handgun it was fired from."

"Were you able to determine from your examination how many bullets were fired in total, and from which handgun?" the prosecutor asks.

"Yes. The defendant's handgun fired three bullets, and Marcel's handgun fired two, for a total of five bullets," the forensic expert testifies.

"So, would you agree," continues the prosecutor, "that since one of the bullets from Marcel's handgun was recovered from the leg of the defendant, if we were able to find another bullet fired from his handgun, it would necessarily imply that any other bullets that might be recovered would have to have come from the defendant's handgun?"

"Yes, I would agree with that," says the forensic expert.

The prosecutor then moves to his table and retrieves another box. "Have you also examined this bullet in this small box?"

"Yes, sir. This bullet was found in the neighbor's yard two days ago and was submitted to our lab for examination," the expert says. "We concluded this bullet was discharged from Marcel's handgun, hit and injured Saul's arm, went through it, and ended up in the neighbor's front yard. The striations on the bullet prove that it came from Marcel's handgun, and the DNA on the bullet matched that of the victim, Saul. Furthermore, the position of Marcel at the time of the shooting supports that this bullet hit Saul in the arm."

The prosecutor smiles and looks at the members of the jury, some of whom look stunned at this revelation. He turns back to his witness. "To be clear, how many bullets did Marcel's handgun fire that day?"

"Two," answers the expert.

"And where were the two bullets fired from his handgun recovered?"

"One in the defendant's leg, and the other in the neighbor's flower bed."

"So, how many bullets did the defendant fire?" the prosecutor asks.

"Three," says the expert.

"Where did the defendant's bullets end up?"

"One killed the intruder, Marcel. A second bullet has not been recovered. The third bullet must be the dented bullet that was recovered at the scene, the one that killed the defendant's son, Saul."

It has been several weeks since Dr. Hartman has felt any pain in his right breast. Now, on the last day of the trial, during the forensics expert's testimony, he suddenly feels a sharp pain in his right breast around the nipple. When he touches the breast, he feels a lump underneath the nipple. He mumbles, "It could only be a spasm from the scar tissue."

He knows that sometimes it takes several weeks for scar tissues to form and cause symptoms of pain or produce even a hard swelling like a lump. Esther notices his glum face, but she relates it to the expert's shocking revelation.

XV
The Bullet That Killed the Son

"Ladies and gentlemen of the jury, the gun that fired the bullet and killed the professor's son has been identified," the prosecutor announces triumphantly. "Permit me to draw a picture of what happened on that dreadful day. After Dr. Hartman arrives at the scene, he arms himself with a semi-automatic handgun, faces Marcel, waves his handgun toward the young man, and threatens to kill him. Marcel also pulls a handgun from his pocket and fires his handgun. Marcel shot two bullets, as he was being shot and severely wounded by the defendant," explains the prosecutor during final arguments. He pulls up the exhibits showing the bullets and the DNA tests one after another, walks toward the jury, and speaks in measured tones. He announces that based on the facts, and based on the evidence presented by the director of the forensic laboratory, the second bullet is the one that killed Saul, the son of Dr. Jordan Hartman, who is the defendant in the case.

"Ladies and gentlemen of the jury," the prosecutor elaborates. "Allow me to explain to you that altogether a total of five bullets were shot in the exchange of gunfire between Dr. Hartman and Marcel, who, like Saul, the defendant's son, dies as a result of the gunshot wound. The first bullet hits Dr. Hartman's leg. The second bullet hits Saul's chest and passes through, and eventually kills him. This bullet smashes against the sidewall of the house. The third lodges in Marcel's abdomen and fells him to the ground and eventually kills him from internal bleeding. The fourth, which is discharged from Marcel's handgun as he was collapsing, hits Saul's arm and produces only a limited injury; this is the bullet discovered in the garden of the neighbor's yard. And the fifth bullet is a stray bullet, which is discharged from the defendant, Dr. Hartman's handgun, as he was falling to the ground. This one has not been found."

After a pause, he resumes the argument: "As I mentioned, the second bullet, the one that killed Saul, was fired by his father, Dr. Jordan Hartman. Yes, I am confident that we have a case of filicide on our hands. And filicide is a crime which must be punished severely."

Esther listens to the prosecutor's argument in horror. Shaken, she pulls out a pen and writes a note for Barrera. It begins with, "Please consider this note when presenting your final argument." In the short break, she passes the note to Barrera. Surrounded by the glum atmosphere of the situation and after writing the note to Barrera, Esther succumbs to profound melancholy. She no longer listens to the last sentences of the prosecutor's final argument. Suddenly, she recalls the poem "Daddy" by Sylvia Plath, and she sobs quietly. A moment later, she regains her composure. She pulls a pen from her handbag, jots down a few lines, a confessional verse to soothe her wounded spirit. She writes:

O, pensive heart
The sun unleashes its fury
Disperses the tempestuous clouds
The world spins, moon with her brooding face
Crawls the dark sky; alas, I see
The emaciated son on the cross
Blood flowing from the wounded chest
Father's ladder scorched
The nails pierced the flesh
A dagger searches for a heart.

With a booming voice, the prosecutor addresses the jury, "Honorable members of the jury, the defendant is not only guilty of fatally wounding Marcel, his neighbor, but he has also committed the heinous crime of killing his son. This defendant hides a criminal mind behind his impressive academic résumé. He is capable of shooting and killing anybody, even his son, in a burst of anger. Be forewarned, the defendant, Dr. Jordan Hartman, is a danger to society. Yes, do declare him guilty as charged. Send him to a correctional facility to serve his sentence."

Listening to the prosecutor's final arguments accusing him of killing his son makes Dr. Hartman deeply despondent. The combination of shame and guilt overwhelms his state of mind. He turns away from the jury's pathetic faces, does not look at his lawyer, and even more so loathes the face of the prosecutor. He wishes he could become invisible and disappear from the court. The weight of having caused two fatalities becomes unbearable for him. The image of a cold dungeon, a cubicle where the air is thick, cloying with the smell of urine completely unravels him.

Dr. Hartman is in a bleak mood. So, when Barrera rises and begins the closing argument on behalf of the defendant, Dr. Hartman is as deaf as a stone, like Beethoven in his last years of life.

Barrera faces an uphill battle. He realizes the challenging situation he has to overcome to win the case. He begins calmly, "The defendant has not only saved countless lives and healed many patients, but he has also helped numerous couples who could not have children overcome their infertility problems and have children stemming from their own body. This most loyal husband has dedicated his life to his wife, patients, staff, and the faculty of the university. A genius, as many of his peers have acknowledged, he has made the university a star in the Texas healthcare system." Barrera pauses for a moment to drink water. Then he goes on, "As has been mentioned during earlier trial testimony, on the day of the shooting, the doctor reluctantly responded to his wife's urgent call for help. He was lecturing, teaching medical

196

students, and was reluctant to leave the University. He thought his wife was capable of dealing with a simple quarrel between two teenagers. However, he responds to her second, hysterical call and hurries home to defend his family from a violent drug dealer who has invaded their property. He tries to dislodge the intruder by yelling at him, in vain. When he sees the handgun in the pocket of the intruder, his concern increases radically. And then, Dr. Hartman hears the threat against his son and his wife. When the defendant hears the intruder threatening to kill Saul if he does not get the money, Dr. Hartman jumps toward Marcel and tries to push him away from Saul, but he gets a severe blow to his stomach and falls flat on the driveway. Dr. Hartman pulls himself up, hurriedly leaves the scene, goes inside, retrieves a handgun from his house, runs out to the driveway of his home, and waves the gun toward Marcel and orders him loudly to leave the driveway. As stated by the forensics director, what happens next is the shooting by Marcel, which hits the defendant's leg. In a frenzy, Dr. Hartman acts swiftly to disable Marcel by shooting at him while he is in pain and bleeding. Bullets fly through the air, and unfortunately, two of his shots hit the teenagers. Dr. Hartman acts in self-defense. He had no intention to kill anybody, but he's forced to act to defend himself and save his family.

"Ladies and gentlemen of the jury," Barrera walks closer to the jury, looks at them, and says, "I trust you understand the precarious situation that Dr. Jordan Hartman faces at that very moment when Marcel pulls out his handgun and aims it at him. What happens next is the natural reaction of a physician who is in the business of saving lives, who has saved so many lives over the years. Now he must act to save the lives of his son, his wife, and his own life when the drug dealer is shooting at them, a drug dealer whose mind is poisoned by illicit drugs, out of control, about to shoot and kill Dr. Hartman and his family members because they would not pay him ten thousand dollars.

"Ladies and gentlemen of the jury, our defendant is a remarkable man, a loyal husband, a caring physician, extremely busy at his important job of advancing medicine, so intent on finding new techniques to save other lives that he and his wife agreed to leave the caring of his son in the capable hands of his wife. Yes, what happened in that dreadful moment was totally out of control of the defendant. Dr. Hartman had no intention of killing anyone, neither the intruder nor, of course, his son. However, during the mayhem of shots flying every which way, the intruder was shot and fatally wounded. Let us remember that the intruder actually caused his death by shooting at the doctor and his family and that Dr. Hartman only acted in self-defense when he shot and fatally wounded the man who attacked his family.

"Sadly, his self-defense, although with the best of intentions, caused the loss of two lives. When it comes to the loss of Saul, the defendant's son, the pain and suffering of the family are unimaginable," Barrera looks up at the bright window shimmering with the bright San Antonio sun and says, "No *father* wants to see a son killed at such a young age."

The prosecutor is taken aback by the comparison. He shakes his head in disdain. A few jury members understand the resemblance between Saul's death and that of the Lord.

After a short pause, Barrera completes his presentation. "The defendant was a wounded man bleeding from his leg, barely holding himself upright. In the heat of the dangerous situation, the only option for the defendant was to disable the killer. Saving his wife and his own life is an instinct for anyone of us, and this is precisely what the defendant did. He never intended to shoot and kill anybody. He was defending his family inside the boundary of his property. He never wanted to witness his offspring being shot accidentally and dying in front of his house. Unfortunately, Saul, the defendant's teenage son, was shot and fatally wounded because of bad luck. Yes, bad luck brought Dr. Hartman to the scene, and it was bad luck for Saul to be hit by a stray bullet.

"Ladies and gentlemen of the jury, I implore you to understand a father's pain and suffering and accept his plea to declare Dr. Hartman not guilty and send him back to his lovely wife. Let him resume his medical research at the University. Please, support the University's life-saving endeavors."

Both Dr. Hartman and Esther are furious at the prosecutor's closing argument and stunned by the revelation that Dr. Hartman's bullet killed Saul. The devastated couple can take in only parts of Barrera's final argument. Their minds are filled with shocking grief, bitter anguish, embarrassment, and a strict sense of revulsion. Esther can no longer bear to hear any more words about the case. She cannot even glance at her husband, and he, in turn, looks down, his head still, brooding. He is overtaken by shame and cannot stand to look at anybody in the courtroom.

XVI
Excruciating Pain

During Barrera's closing argument, while Dr. Hartman is drawn into his disconcerting thoughts about the possibilities, an intense pain coming from the right breast, shooting into the shoulder, arm, and radiating to the hand, the hand that once held the handgun, jolts Dr. Hartman's mind. He touches his right breast and feels a sore spot under the nipple. He mumbles, "It's only the scar of the biopsy." Shortly after the sharp pain subsides, Dr. Hartman touches his breast once more. This time, he feels a hard lump in the area underneath the scar the size of a quarter. "It is a real lump. I am not imagining," he whispers, "It got to be malignant."

When Barrera finishes the closing argument and sits next to Dr. Hartman, he is startled to discover his client holding his hand over his right breast, his face pale, pearls of sweat covering the forehead. "Are you alright, Doctor?" Barrera asks.

Dr. Hartman turns his head and says, "I'll check it out."

"What are you talking about?" Barrera asks Dr. Hartman.

"Don't worry. I'll visit Dr. Key."

Confused, Barrera reckons that Dr. Hartman is probably talking about the case. "What did you think about my presentation?"

"I did not follow all of it," Dr. Hartman admits.

Barrera is surprised. "The jury listened to every word I said. I'm optimistic."

"I hope your impression is correct," Dr. Hartman says. "I believe they were more impressed by the prosecutor's argument."

Finding Dr. Hartman in such a gloomy mood, Barrera turns his attention to the judge, who is now calling the lawyers and the foreman to come to the bench.

Esther is not pleased with the course of the trial. The words of the prosecutor are still resonating in her head, deepening her despair. The disclosure that the second bullet had killed Saul rolls through her thoughts like a haunting *idée fixe*. The walls of the court look gray, the sun is no longer piercing through the windows, and the air is thick and suffocating. She wishes she could turn into a ghost, fly away into the dark sky and disappear from the scene, from the miserable day that has brought the horrific revelation. She mumbles, "History has witnessed the father who murdered the son."

After conferring with the lawyers, the judge declares that the pleadings are finished and announces a fifteen-minute recess. After the recess, the bailiff calls on the audience to rise. The judge enters the court and settles into his large leather chair. "You may be seated now," the bailiff announces. The judge

199

re-opens the session by informing the jury that they are now facing the serious task of deliberating the case. He reads a series of instructions to the jury, "These are called the judge's charge to you. You must pay full attention to them." He states the issues in the case, defines several terms, and emphasizes the critical importance of the phrase "beyond a reasonable doubt." He says, "This is a criminal trial, and as such, you must only consider the credible evidence, not every claim and statement that has been presented to you by the two parties, not even every testimony that you have heard during the trial. You must consider only those pieces of evidence that, in your judgment, are credible." He nods at the members of the jury and continues, "Base your conclusions on the evidence presented in the trial, and please remember that the opening and closing arguments presented by the prosecutor and the defense lawyer are not evidence." In the end, the judge explains that the jury must find the defendant either guilty or not guilty as charged—nothing else.

The judge orders the court clerk to deliver copies of the said instructions to the jurors and take them to the jury chamber to begin deliberating. It is late in the afternoon when the exhausted jurors follow the foreman to their chamber.

During the ride home, Esther is sitting in the back seat, aimlessly staring at the sidewalks and shops that are passing by. Shaken by the prosecutor's terrifying revelation about the bullet that killed Saul, her state of mind is in a barely contained frenzy. She cannot utter a word and avoids eye contact with her husband. For his part, Dr. Hartman is spinning into an abyss of humiliation. He stares down at his shoes and avoids looking at his wife. In the silence of the car, sitting in the back seat, the spouses are avoiding each other, oblivious to each other's abysmal state of mind, each wrapped into their suffocating and isolated world, unable to offer any comfort to each other. In the front, Barrera is sitting in the passenger's seat perplexed by the dizzying development of the last day of the trial. Dr. Ross does not say much either, focusing on driving the Hartmans back to their home.

———

On the morning of the second day of jury deliberation, Barrera calls Dr. Hartman and informs him that the foreman has asked the bailiff to submit three questions to the judge and requested clarification. The most important one is that the jury is concerned about the difference between manslaughter, which is defined as a reckless but unintentional act, and homicide involving an intentional killing that may be mitigated but not excused because of the provocation of the victim.

"So, they are focusing on these two evils," Dr. Hartman says. Now, he is worried that the jury will declare him guilty of one or the other option. It is at this very moment when, against his defense attorney's advice, Dr. Hartman decides to flee the city that night.

"The jury has only two choices, either to declare you *guilty as charged* by the prosecutor or *not guilty*," Barrera says.

Dr. Hartman shakes his head in disagreement and says, "They are not considering declaring me *not guilty*." He mumbles, "I simply need to get out of here."

"Where will you go? The judge has forbidden you to leave the county," Barrera stresses to Dr. Hartman.

Dr. Hartman is quiet. He does not want to tell his defense attorney that he plans on fleeing to Mexico.

"You must be present when the jury delivers the decision. When the defendant is absent, the judge usually postpones the hearing of the jury's verdict until the defendant returns to court," Barrera says. "Otherwise, the judge may declare you a fugitive and order your arrest."

As if Dr. Hartman did not hear Barrera's warning, he says, "I can't stand the court."

Barrera insists. "Doc, I don't want to hear another word."

After Barrera leaves the house, Dr. Hartman asks his devoted junior faculty member, Dr. Ross, to drive to the university, pack up essential files from his office, and prepare for a drive to the Mexican border. Esther vehemently disagrees with the decision, but she cannot change her husband's mind. She calls Ruth and asks for help, and when the Dean comes to the phone, she tells him, "My husband does not want to answer any calls. He is busy packing his luggage and preparing for the trip."

A few hours later, the trio of the Dean, Dr. Ross, and Dr. Hartman confer in Dr. Hartman's home about the move. Disgusted with her husband's decision, Esther has gone to the library to converse with the Dean's wife, Ruth, who is her trusted friend. The two women walk to the kitchen and quietly drink some water, and Esther turns her mobile phone off.

She asks Ruth, "Is there a Jewish convent nearby?"

"My dear Esther, you are losing your sanity," Ruth smiles at her. "I'm not sure there is such a thing as a Jewish convent to purify one's spirit."

"Isn't there a place to go and hide from the world, some retreat?" she asks.

"Yes, there are retreats for Jews who wish to separate themselves from a dire condition, but not from the world," Ruth says. "Although at most retreat centers you are encouraged to limit the use of computers and phones, still, you do have access to modern technology, even a mobile phone."

"I wish I could go to a monastery, a tomb, or hide in a catacomb."

"My dear friend, do yourself a favor. Go see a psychiatrist before it is too late."

"I am not crazy, Ruth," without waiting for a reaction from Ruth, Esther continues, earnestly looking at her friend. "I want you to know that I have registered with Vantage Adventure Tours to travel to the Middle East and visit

Esther's Tomb. And I am glad I made the decision, even before my husband's fate is decided."

Ruth says, "Yes! That sounds like a real escape. Do go visit the tomb."

The question of who should give Dr. Hartman a ride to Laredo is a serious topic of discussion among the triumvirate.

"We need Dr. Ross to stay in the department," the Dean decides. "Let us give Dr. Parsi a few days off so that he can drive you to Laredo."

"Is he agreeable to the task?" Dr. Hartman says. "Does he know if I'm convicted, he could be indicted for helping me escape to Mexico?"

"I'm not sure, but I'm confident Dr. Parsi will do it. I understand you have offered him a junior faculty position in the department," the Dean says. Dr. Hartman nods in agreement. The Dean turns to Dr. Ross. "Get Dr. Parsi on the phone."

Dr. Parsi confirms that he is willing to drive Dr. Hartman to the border. Dr. Ross calls in an order for a large pizza while Dr. Hartman takes a long warm shower, and the Dean calls his wife Ruth, who is with Esther and tells her not to prepare dinner for him.

While the triumvirate of Dr. Hartman, the Dean, and Dr. Ross are eating pizza, Esther, who is with Ruth, declares that she is determined more than ever to leave the country and visit the tomb of Esther in Hamadan, Iran. "I can't take it anymore," she tells Ruth. "I will travel as soon as possible and go to the Middle East." She contemplates a possible life as a volunteer at the tomb, guiding tourists, and instructing them on the history of the ancient Jewish Diaspora in Persia. It is going to be a retreat for me also to do some writing."

"It is not as easy as you think. Have you heard the news?" Ruth asks Esther.

"What do you mean?" Esther snaps out of her dreams.

Ruth explains the news about recent developments surrounding the tomb of Esther. She says, "I'm not sure you will want to hear this: the mullahs in Tehran who are sworn enemies of the state of Israel have found a new outlet for their hatred toward Jews. They have recently instructed the authorities in Hamadan Province to downgrade the status of the tomb of Esther and Mordechai to an ordinary 'tourist attraction' instead of a sacred Jewish place. That means it is no longer on every tour of Hamadan unless specifically requested by travelers. They have gone even further and removed the sign that identified the mausoleum of the biblical figures as an official pilgrimage site in Hamadan. The official Iranian news agency upended the ancient allegory about Esther, and, instead of highlighting the grave danger of extinction of Jews in the Persian Empire, the officials are publicizing the Islamic tourist agency's version that the Purim story was a Jewish plot to massacre 75,000 Iranians."

Ruth hands over a printed copy of the article from the internet that states that the official policy toward the Tomb of Esther was changed after a throng of 250 militant members of a rogue Islamic student organization surrounded the tomb and threatened to destroy it. It is retaliation against Israel and Jewish people for the Israeli excavations under the Temple Mount in Jerusalem, which is a sacred place for Muslims.

"There is another controversy surrounding the location of the tomb," Ruth says. "The city of Shushan in Israel holds a burial place and claims that the Jews brought the bodies of Esther and Mordechai to Eretz Israel, and buried them in the Holy Land. They have posted the written accounts from the Middle Ages that indicate the burial place of these two ancient Jews is actually in the Galilean village of Bar'am along Israel's northern border with Lebanon."

XVII
Guilty Beyond Reasonable Doubt

Late in the afternoon on the second day of jury deliberations, Barrera receives a call from the judge's office that the jury has sent out a new question about the exact meaning of the term "presumption of innocence." To elucidate the issue for the jury, the judge chooses a chapter of a folio from his alma mater, Harvard University Law School, and adds the definition of "Proof Beyond a Reasonable Doubt," from Chapter 2, "The Burden of Proof in the Texas Penal Code."

His staff makes 12 copies and gives them to the foreman. The caller tells Barrera that reading and discussing the code is likely to keep the jurors busy for the next several hours.

Barrera is elated, as it is the first time since the introduction of the evidence about the newly discovered bullet that he feels a glimmer of hope, the possibility that the jury is debating whether his client could be considered "not guilty." Excited, he calls the Hartmans' home phone but reaches only their voicemail. He tries to contact Esther, but again he is transferred to voicemail. He calls his client's mobile phone, but the phone keeps ringing for a long time before it finally disconnects. Barrera calls Dr. Ross to get help locating Dr. Hartman, but that mobile phone is off, too, for Dr. Ross is in the operating room performing surgery. His next call to the Dean also goes to voicemail. Perhaps the Dean is packing for his trip to Italy. He muses, "Apparently, the jury is moving towards either declaring him not guilty or convicting him of involuntary manslaughter due to self-defense or accident." He postulates that the prosecutor's emphasis on filicide might have backfired. "It is extremely improbable for a father to kill his son intentionally. Even if it does happen occasionally, it usually happens accidentally." Barrera ponders the case. "The prosecutor took a risky gamble that may produce an adverse result for him and a favorite outcome for us."

Indeed, the prosecutor's accusation that Dr. Hartman deliberately killed his son has become a complicated theory for the jury to accept. Barrera muses that it is the prosecution's burden to prove the charge. The law's basic guarantee is that no guilt can be presumed until the allegation has been proven beyond a reasonable doubt. Even though the grand jury gave the green light to a charge of manslaughter based on probable cause, the judge's instructions to the jury emphasize that the prosecutor must present evidence to convince the jurors beyond a reasonable doubt that Dr. Hartman committed a felony, else he must be presumed not guilty. Barrera murmurs that the principle of *Ei incumbit probatio qui dicit, non qui negat* places the burden of proof on the one who declares, not on the one who denies. It is the principle that the defendant is considered innocent unless proven guilty. After defending a large number of criminal cases in San Antonio and repeatedly researching this issue, he knows that in many countries the presumption of innocence is a legal right of the accused to a criminal trial, and it is regarded as an international human right under the UN's Universal Declaration of Human Rights. In the case of Dr. Hartman, the burden of proof is thus squarely placed on the prosecution's shoulders—as was demanded by the grand jury when they produced their opinion. The jury, on its part, is constrained and obligated by law to consider only actual evidence and testimony that is legally admissible and lawfully obtained.

When the next day, around eight in the morning, Barrera receives a return call from Dr. Ross, he quickly asks him, "Tell me, where is Dr. Hartman?"

"I'm not sure of his whereabouts," Dr. Ross responds.

"Is he in Mexico?"

"I don't know."

Barrera says, "Perhaps it is best for me not to know his whereabouts, so whatever he has done remains unknown to me." Barrera ends the conversation and turns off his mobile phone.

When the judge arrives at his office shortly before nine, the foreman is waiting for him. "Your Honor, the jury has reached its decision," the foreman says.

The judge looks at the foreman's face and detects a sign of relief. The judge nods as he speculates on the jury's decision. The foreman says, "Your Honor, after you produced the information regarding the issue of presumption of innocence, it didn't take much longer for the jury to reach the decision,"

"I'm glad it helped," the judge says.

"Indeed, it did. Two of the jurors were ignorant of the issue and kept arguing with the rest of us."

"That's good enough. I'll call the parties to come to court soon."

In the late afternoon of the last day of the jury's deliberation, and before leaving town, Dr. Hartman pays a visit to Dr. Key and discloses his decision to drive to Laredo and flee to Mexico.

"You are going to be fine anywhere you go," Dr. Key assures him. "Being the genius that you are, the outside world will receive you with open arms."

They both are unaware of the latest inquiry by the jury regarding the definition of "presumption of innocence" and the repeated calls from Barrera to Dr. Hartman's house and his mobile phone.

Now, Dr. Hartman unbuttons his shirt and exposes the area of his breast, which is slightly red and swollen. He touches the spot that feels tender and hard. His face tightens when he presses on the lump. He looks at Dr. Key.

"I feel there is something new here, a tender lump under the scar in my right breast," he tells Dr. Key. "I have been up all night more because of this lump than the impending jury's verdict."

Dr. Key realizes the main reason for the visit by Dr. Hartman is the breast problem. Otherwise, he would have left town without bidding him farewell. He examines the breast and agrees there is a new lesion, which requires a biopsy as soon as possible.

"How about a quick needle aspiration, as if you were doing a Pap smear?" Dr. Hartman says. "From the needle aspiration, just do a slide, place it in the solution and send it to our friend, the great cytopathologist, to scan it."

"An excellent idea. Let's do it now," Dr. Key says.

After the completion of the needle aspiration and preparation of the cytology smear, Dr. Key says, "Call me tomorrow. Hopefully, I'll have the result by noon."

"Call my home phone and leave a message," Dr. Hartman says. "My mobile phone may be off for a while."

"Okay," Dr. Key says. "Where are you going to be after crossing the border?"

"Probably Mexico City," Dr. Hartman replies. "However, I'd prefer to contact my colleagues at London University to find out whether they might have a place for me there."

Dr. Key says, "My friend, that is the same path that was chosen by another genius, Roman Polansky. Go to London and see Professor Clark, the chairman of the Surgery Department at the Imperial College. When you are there, ask for Dr. Hamilton. He is the chief of the surgical oncology division. He is the inventor of the intelligent knife that produces no scar."

Dr. Hartman's face suddenly cringes with a stabbing pain in the right breast at the area of the biopsy. He touches the dressing gauzes over the site and says, "I told you from the onset that the lump is not a canard. It's something more serious than an inflammatory reaction."

"Stop imagining cancer. It was inflammatory tissue then, and it could still be the same now." Dr. Key waves him off. "I will presume it is as simple as scar tissue unless the cytology reveals something else."

"It feels like breast cancer," insists Dr. Hartman.

"Baloney! You know better than that. Go and drive to the border, my friend."

———————

After another long day while the jury is deliberating his case, Dr. Hartman arrives at home, he notices a metallic silver-color Prius parked in the street. Both Dr. Parsi and Dr. Baldwin are standing near the front door, waiting for him. He shakes hands with both of them, unlocks the front door, and waves them into the house.

"Is there anybody home?" Dr. Hartman shouts. The silence of the house disappoints him. "Esther must not be here," he says. "I don't know where she is now. Unfortunately, I cannot contact her. She must have turned off her mobile phone."

"Dr. Hartman, we are here to take you to Laredo. Are you ready?" Dr. Parsi asks.

"I've almost packed. I did it earlier, but I need about fifteen more minutes. Please help yourself in the kitchen," Dr. Hartman says.

The sun has set, and the house is dark when they unceremoniously leave the neighborhood. Dr. Parsi is driving while Dr. Hartman is in the backseat and Dr. Baldwin in the passenger's seat. They are quiet for a long time.

Dr. Parsi finally breaks the silence. "I hope the jury comes out with a favorable decision."

Feeling gloomy about the trial, his health, and his family, Dr. Hartman says, "Judging from the jury's initial questions, I'm afraid they will render a guilty verdict."

Dr. Hartman looks outside, and in the darkness of the night, the lights of distant homes glow nakedly. The passing SUVs in the left lane and 18 wheeler trucks on the right shake the small Prius. The Sirius XM classical music station plays Schumann's Cello Concerto at a low volume. Dr. Hartman would prefer a violin piece by Mendelssohn or one of Mozart's last symphonies to help soothe his agitated mind. He pulls out his mobile phone and clicks Esther's number on his favorites list. However, the phone shows there is no signal in the area. He turns the phone off and drops it into a small carry on, and again looks out the window. Dr. Baldwin and Dr. Parsi are whispering about a recent movie they have seen together. The car swallows the road and encounters fewer and fewer cars passing or coming at them.

XVIII
Crossing the Border

It's late at night when Dr. Parsi stops the car at the Marriott Courtyard Hotel in Laredo. His two passengers are Dr. Hartman and Dr. Baldwin. They all get out of the car and enter the hotel. At the registration desk, Dr. Parsi asks and receives a suite with two queen beds. After Dr. Parsi receives his digital keys, Dr. Hartman turns to Dr. Baldwin, "I'd like to move on and cross the border before midnight." His weary face shows the long stressful days of the jury deliberation.

"You look exhausted, Dr. Hartman," Dr. Baldwin says. "Don't you want to take a break?"

"I prefer to move on," Dr. Hartman says. Feeling as if the guilty verdict were chasing him, he wants to flee the United States as soon as possible.

Dr. Baldwin says, "Okay, I'll drive you to your hotel in Nuevo Laredo, Dr. Hartman."

"What about Dr. Parsi?" Dr. Hartman says. "Isn't he coming along?"

"It's too risky for Dr. Parsi to cross the border," Dr. Baldwin says. "Regardless of how innocent he is, being born in Iran is enough to cause him some trouble at the entry point."

Dr. Hartman, who is drawn into his precarious situation, only nods and says, "Okay. I need a cup of coffee in the reception area. Then, I'm ready to move on."

While Dr. Hartman and Dr. Baldwin are sitting in the reception area, Dr. Parsi pulls his carry-on luggage to his suite on the second floor, washes his hands, and looks at his tired face in the mirror. He contemplates, "What a mess we are in! What happens if Dr. Hartman is convicted and declared a fugitive? Are they going to come after us because we assisted in his escape to Mexico? What about Dr. Baldwin, who is crossing the border into Mexico? Is she at a greater risk of losing her freedom and her career?" Dr. Parsi washes his face with warm water and pushes these disturbing thoughts aside and whispers, "Dr. Hartman has a thick skin like a crocodile. He is sure to weather this storm, but not us. Win or lose; we are at the mercy of his situation." He leaves the room and returns to the reception area.

The receptionist brings three bottles of water and says, "Our compliments to y'all."

Dr. Hartman nods to the receptionist and says curtly, "What about some coffee?"

"It's coming, sir," the receptionist says.

Dr. Hartman turns to Dr. Parsi, "So, you are staying on this side of the border, aren't you?"

"Yes," Dr. Parsi agrees, "Dr. Baldwin will take you to your hotel south of the border. I'll stay in Laredo until she returns from Mexico." Dr. Parsi does not need to explain further to Dr. Hartman that it's safer for him to remain on the U.S. side of the border.

"It is shameful what the new government in Washington is doing to millions of contributing, hardworking immigrants in the United States," Dr. Baldwin says.

Dr. Hartman looks at Dr. Parsi, "I'm deeply grateful to you two for your help in this terrible ordeal."

Dr. Parsi nods.

After drinking the water and a few sips of black coffee, Dr. Hartman gets up and says, "Let's get a move on, Dr. Baldwin. The sooner I cross the border, the safer it is for me."

Dr. Parsi says, "Dr. Hartman, please check your mobile phone connection, for we need to get in touch with you as soon as we hear the news about the jury's decision."

"Well, Dr. Ross has my number, I'm sure he will call you too," Dr. Hartman says. "Anyway, I don't expect any call for a day or two. The jury is taking its time."

Dr. Hartman turns away and walks to the parked car in front of the office. He takes the seat on the passenger side while Dr. Baldwin, who has followed him, occupies the driver's seat. She adjusts the mirrors and the seat to suit her smaller stature. She asks Dr. Hartman, "Are you ready to cross the Mexican border?"

"Yes. Let's go," Dr. Hartman says. He rolls down the window and looks at Dr. Parsi, who has come outside to say goodbye to Dr. Hartman. "Dr. Parsi, look, I'm sorry for all the pain that I have caused you." Now, Dr. Hartman's eyes are glossy with a few drops of tears and his voice trembling. "I have been an asshole in the way I have treated you. Please forgive me."

Dr. Parsi is surprised. He could have never imagined seeing Dr. Hartman cry and apologize to him. "I'm sincere. Please, forgive me."

Surprised, Dr. Parsi nods, and turns around, and walks into the hotel.

———————

Even very late at night, the traffic is inching slowly forward when Dr. Baldwin and Dr. Hartman's car approaches the border crossing. Traffic moves even slower through the U.S. exit and continues to the other side of the river. Dr. Hartman is slumped in the passenger seat, idly observing the Mexican border patrol officer in his shaggy uniform, a machine gun hanging from his shoulder, who asks Dr. Baldwin for their passports. Dr. Baldwin hands over the two passports and waits for further instructions.

In broken English, the officer says, "Going for a short visit, yeah?"

"Yes," Dr. Baldwin says.

The border guard looks at them with curiosity, returns the passports, and says mischievously, "Have a fantastic time," and waves them to proceed.

In the wee hours of the morning, the streets are quiet, the stores with their colorful signs, their walls with peeling, old paint, are closed. Dr. Baldwin follows the map through Sector Centro onto Ave. César López de Lara, which they follow for a while.

Reflecting on their border crossing, Dr. Hartman observes, "It is easier to leave the United States and enter Mexico than to return to our country."

Dr. Baldwin agrees, "Yes, especially these days with all the adverse publicity coming from the U.S. government against innocent immigrants, such as Mexicans and Middle Easterners."

"Well, it is wise for Dr. Parsi not to cross the border. Our border agents would have probably detained him for a while," Dr. Hartman says. "Well, read the news. You see the reports about Muslim suicide bombers attacking innocent bystanders in European cities. I wonder when these terrorists will show up in America."

Dr. Baldwin loses patience with Dr. Hartman. "Come on, Dr. Hartman. In this country, we have had far more terrorist attacks by homegrown radicals of the Christian faith than by Muslim immigrants. Read the FBI reports; since 9/11, the real terror threat in America has been homegrown. Not a single act of terror in the U.S. was committed by people from those seven countries that the government has targeted."

"But, let's agree that most of these terrorists were Muslim," Dr. Hartman insists.

"Dr. Hartman, except for 9/11, the majority of the recent killers have come from inside the country. They were American-born people, and most of them non-Muslim," Dr. Baldwin insists. "Don't you remember the Sandy Hook massacre and Adam Lanza, who killed 26 pupils and teachers plus his mother? Not a single Iranian-American was among these homegrown terrorists!"

"Okay, Dr. Parsi is not a terrorist," Dr. Hartman concedes.

Dr. Baldwin bites her lips and hides her anger. She wishes somebody else had volunteered to drive Dr. Hartman to Mexico.

Dr. Hartman cannot stop ranting. "Okay, I agree. Let's not mix up our good Iranian-American citizens with these crazy mullahs who are sponsoring terrorists all over the world. Just read about Hezbollah in Lebanon and Hamas gangs in the Gaza Strip. These mullahs provide them with a lot of arms and money."

Dr. Baldwin takes a deep breath. She has to remind her colleague of the facts. "We are talking about Iranian-American immigrants, not about the mullahs. Do you know that there is not a single Iranian person among the hundreds of suicide bombers and terrorists who have caused havoc in Europe, in the Middle East, and here in the United States? And surely you remember that none of the 19 terrorists who attacked the Twin Towers was Iranian."

In bitter silence, she continues driving along, block after block of empty and quiet streets in downtown Nuevo Laredo until she turns into Ave. Reforma. She stops the car in front of the Nuevo Laredo Hilton Garden Inn.

The doors are locked, and she waits in the car until an armed security guard shows up and waves for her to lower the window. After checking their passports and finding Dr. Hartman's name on the guest list, he unlocks the heavy steel gate and allows the car to enter the hotel courtyard. They stop near the locked entrance door. A sleepy receptionist shows up after a few rings on the brass bell and apologizes for the delay. He pages through Dr. Hartman's passport and compares the information with the hotel guest list.

"You are late!" she admonishes Dr. Hartman, "We expected you last evening. Please come in."

Dr. Hartman nods and follows the receptionist to his counter and waits for his room assignment. Dr. Baldwin locks the car and follows them.

The receptionist looks at the reservation date and says, "Sir, because we already charged your card for last night, I'm upgrading your room to a one-bedroom suite without an extra charge." Then, she programs two room keys and says, "Here are your keys. I hope the young madam will enjoy her stay."

"She is not staying. I need only one key," Dr. Hartman says.

She looks at Dr. Baldwin and says, "Madam, please enjoy our spicy breakfast before you leave. We serve delicious menudo on Fridays and every morning on the weekends."

Dr. Baldwin smirks, for she despises menudo and says, "Thanks. But I'll be gone before you start serving breakfast."

When the porter is about to carry Dr. Hartman's two large suitcases and a knapsack to the room, Dr. Baldwin says farewell to Dr. Hartman, assuming she won't see him again for a long while.

Dr. Hartman follows the porter to a spacious one-bedroom suite with a separate workstation, two phones, a queen bed, and a large, clean bathroom. "Your internet connection is free. Just sign in with your last name and the room number," the porter says, pocketing the tip, leaving, and softly closing the heavy wooden door behind him.

Dr. Baldwin has already left when Dr. Hartman returns to the lobby. He shakes his head and murmurs, "Well, she is in a great hurry to join that Iranian-American fellow."

———————

It is around ten in the morning when the jury members enter the court and settle into their seats in the jury box. The foreman is sitting in the corner seat next to a plump female member, who looks disheveled and exhausted.

The judge calls the court to order and announces that the jury has reviewed the case, deliberated earnestly and thoroughly, and evaluated the evidence presented during the trial. He turns to the jury bench and asks the foreman, "Have you reached a verdict?"

The foreman stands up and says, "Yes, Your Honor, we have!" The judge is about to instruct the foreman to read the jury's decision when he notices the empty seat next to Barrera and realizes that the defendant is absent. He asks the foreman to wait and turns to the two attorneys. "Before we hear the jury's decision, I need both the prosecutor and defense attorney to approach the bench and clarify some issues before we proceed."

The two lawyers approach the judge. The judge asks Barrera, "Where is the defendant?"

"Your Honor, I am not certain about his present whereabouts. I'm aware that he mentioned a severe pain in his right chest late yesterday afternoon when I saw him last," Barrera says.

"Could he be in the hospital?" the prosecutor asks Barrera.

"He could be there," Barrera says. "He mentioned he would be visiting his surgeon last evening."

The judge says, "The defendant should have notified you of his condition."

"Your honor, he did before being seen by the surgeon," Barrera says. "In any case, your honor, my client waives his right to be present at the reading of the verdict."

The judge who was contemplating postponing the session, remembers the foreman's last comment: "Your honor, it didn't take much time for the jury to decide after you gave us the information regarding the issue of presumption of innocence." The judge recalls the foreman's facial impressions, which indicated that the jury's verdict could be in Dr. Hartman's favor.

The prosecutor raises a question regarding the procedure, "Your Honor, are you going to go ahead with the session without the defendant?"

After a short hesitation, the judge says, "Yes, I'll go ahead with the conclusion of the case."

"Your Honor, wouldn't it be more appropriate to postpone the reading of the verdict until we have the defendant present in the court?" the prosecutor asks.

Because the judge has already made his decision, he ignores the prosecutor's plea and announces firmly, "No, there will be no more delay. We shall proceed."

When the judge calls the court to order, he looks at the spectator section. He recognizes representatives of the media, which include *The San Antonio Express-News*, *The Current*, and the Spanish TV stations. The press members quickly notice the absence of the defendant as well as his wife, Esther Hartman. The Spanish TV correspondent tells the *San Antonio Express-News* reporter, "Well, the judge has his options. He could have postponed the session instead of going ahead and asking the foreman to present the jury's verdict."

At this point, the attorneys have taken their respective seats, the bailiff is following the judge's order and calls out: "All rise!"

The members of the jury are also standing up as the foreman unfolds a piece of paper with the names of the jurors and their decision handwritten at the bottom of the page. In reply to the judge's question regarding the jury's verdict, the foreman is ready to announce the jury's decision. Both the audience and the jurors are standing and looking at the foreman.

"Please read the jury's decision," the judge says.

The foreman clears his throat. "Your Honor, in the case of the government against Jordan Hartman, the jurors have reached a unanimous decision. We, the jury, declare Dr. Jordan Hartman *not guilty* of all charges."

There is deep silence in the court. The astounded prosecutor rises and requests the foreman to read the jury's verdict once more. The judge nods and orders the foreman to do so. Then, the prosecutor asks the judge for permission to call each jury member to rise and verify their vote. One after the other, the members of the jury rise and confirm that the foreman has read the correct verdict. After a frustrated glance around the court, the prosecutor sits back, props his head on his hands, and stares in disgust at his feet. On the other side of the courtroom, Barrera keeps his delight to himself and calmly stacks his papers. The judge announces the jury's decision one more time and expresses his gratitude for the jurors' careful deliberations. He releases them from their assignment and orders them to leave the court.

After crossing the Mexican border back into the U.S., it is past four in the morning when exhausted Dr. Baldwin reaches the Marriott Courtyard Hotel in Laredo. She finds Dr. Parsi deeply asleep in one of the queen beds. She quietly changes and takes a long shower. She puts on a nightgown, drinks a glass of cool water, and settles in the other bed. Her mind wonders awhile, thinking about Dr. Hartman, his racist comments in the car, and his condescending attitude toward Dr. Parsi. She decides that it would be hard, if not impossible, to work on a team with Dr. Hartman even if he is cleared from the charge of murdering the two teenagers. She is livid. "The jury is surely not going to let him off the hook." To clear her mind of Dr. Hartman's disturbing comments, she connects the earphones to her mobile phone, plugs them into her ears, clicks on the Amazon Music app, and listens to classical music from the Romantic era. Chopin's preludes soothe her frustrated mind, and before the timer stops the music, she has fallen into a deep slumber.

When the morning sun appears in the room and wakes Dr. Baldwin, a breakfast tray with fresh coffee, orange juice, and almond pastries are waiting for her in the sitting area of the suite. Dr. Parsi is reading *USA Today* when she joins him. Well-rested and her face adorned with a charming smile, she greets Dr. Parsi, who gets up and opens his arms to embrace her. A kiss follows the hug, but then he steps back.

"Wow, you are brave to drive around Nuevo Laredo alone and in the middle of the night. I'm sorry I did not manage to stay awake till your return, but I'm delighted you came back safely."

"Me, too, Bahman," Dr. Baldwin says.

"Driving to the hotel in Mexico, I suffered through a disgusting conversation with Dr. Hartman." Dr. Baldwin grimaces, "I prefer not to repeat his words, but now I'm thoroughly convinced we will be better off finding other employment in San Antonio for next year. I agree with you that no matter what happens to Dr. Hartman, I am all for leaving the university and going into private practice with you."

"I love what you just said," Dr. Parsi says. "Yes, we are going to be better off in private practice. You and me in the same group. That'll be wonderful."

Dr. Baldwin looks him straight in the eye and says, "Yes, we will be happier together in private practice."

Dr. Parsi takes her hand and steps close to her, and he embraces her and whispers into her ears, "Linda, I love you." Encouraged by her glowing face, her broad smile, he takes the big step, "Linda, will you marry me today?"

Dr. Baldwin had made up her mind some time ago. "Oh, my dearest. Let's get married right away."

They embrace, kiss, and move to one of the beds. Their breaths warm and salty, they make passionate love for the first time.

XIX
Unexpected News

Early in the afternoon, Dr. Ross succeeds in reaching the desk of the Hilton Garden Inn in Nuevo Laredo and asks to be connected to Dr. Hartman's room.

The operator greets Dr. Ross in Spanish. When Dr. Ross apologizes that his Spanish is insufficient, the operator immediately switches to English, "Sir, nobody is answering the phone in Dr. Hartman's room."

"Please try and locate him," Dr. Ross implores the operator. "I have an urgent message for him."

"Okay, sir. Please hold the line. Let me connect you to the room." When the call goes unanswered, she transfers to the manager.

"Who is this?" the manager asks in fluent English. After listening to Dr. Ross, he asks, "Sir, please hold on for a minute. I will locate your friend in no time."

The manager finds Dr. Hartman near the pool reading *One Hundred Years of Solitude*. "Sir, you have an urgent call from San Antonio."

Dr. Hartman marks the page, closes the book, and follows the manager. He carefully picks up the phone and hears Dr. Ross's booming voice, "Great news, Boss! The jury has declared you 'Not Guilty.'"

Dr. Hartman is stunned, speechless, his hands tremble. He holds onto the corner of a table to keep his balance, and stammers, "What did you say?"

"Dr. Hartman, the jury's verdict is 'Not Guilty,'" Dr. Ross repeats. "Please, pack your bags and hurry back. Dr. Baldwin will pick you up as soon as she can get across the border."

———————

A few minutes later, Dr. Parsi's phone rings. It is Dr. Ross. "Listen, can you believe it? The jury has issued a 'Not Guilty' verdict."

"No way, are you sure?"

"Absolutely. I just called Dr. Hartman. He'll be waiting for you to pick him up from the hotel in Mexico," Dr. Ross says.

"Hold on. Here is Dr. Baldwin," Dr. Parsi says. "Please, talk to her."

"Why don't you both go together?"

"You seem to forget where I was born. With these new regulations regarding people born in Muslim countries, I may not be able to re-enter the country."

"Yes, yes. I completely forgot," Dr. Ross says. "Okay, let me talk to Dr. Baldwin."

———————

In mid-afternoon, Dr. Baldwin leaves the Marriott Courtyard in Laredo and approaches the border. The road is packed with cars, most of them with

American license plates, barely moving and creeping along in tight queues toward the American border checkpoint. The border guard waves her on. She joins the line of cars crossing the bridge to the Mexican side of the border. As she is inching ahead, she glances at the continuous chain of people in the fenced-in walkways on the far side of the road, most of them lugging large shopping bags home to Mexico. It takes Dr. Baldwin more than an hour to reach Mexico's inspection barrier.

At the Mexican border, a patrol officer in a green uniform, sweating in the afternoon heat with a machine gun hanging from his shoulder, stares at Dr. Baldwin. He takes her passport and warns her, "Lady, our region is a dangerous place. An unaccompanied lady should not drive around on her own. You can shop much more safely in your own country."

Dr. Baldwin smiles, "I'm just picking up a professor from the Hilton Hotel across the border, that's all. Then I'll come right back."

"Okay, then. Go ahead," and the agent waves her across the border.

When Dr. Baldwin enters the courtyard through the wide-open gates of the hotel, she finds Dr. Hartman sitting on the shady patio lounge-chair outside the big glass doors to the reception hall, his luggage nearby. She stops the car a few yards away and unlatches the trunk. Dr. Hartman waves at her and calls a porter to pull the suitcases to the car and deposit them in the trunk. The porter does the same thing with the knapsack, opens the passenger door and waits for the tip. Without paying attention to the porter, Dr. Hartman slides into the passenger seat and shuts the door.

"Wow. What a night, what a day I had. I will never forget these 24 hours for the rest of my life. Thank you, Dr. Baldwin, for coming to get me." For once, Dr. Hartman seems to be grateful to Dr. Baldwin for her assistance.

"You're welcome. I'm happy for you about the trial," Dr. Baldwin says. "However," she pauses and hesitates to say how sad she is about the loss of his son. Instead, she says, "It has been a wrenching time for all of us."

Dr. Hartman nods, "Have you heard anything from my wife?"

She says, "Neither Dr. Parsi nor I have received a call from her."

Dr. Hartman becomes quiet and sighs deeply. He worries about how he can face Esther. "It will be challenging," he murmurs. "What am I going to say to her. How can I possibly justify my reckless action?" Suddenly the words of the prosecutor ring in his ears, those heartbreaking words. The horrific revelation by the forensics director on the last day of the trial that he, Dr. Hartman, is the one who shot and killed his son.

"I wish I had been involved in a car accident when I hurried home from the university to our house."

Dr. Hartman looks out at the dusty buildings, shabbily painted columns, and crowds of people walking in and out of handicraft and souvenir shops. He turns his face away and wonders quietly, "How can I look at the faces of my students and not see the image of Saul. We loved him so much. Why could he

216

not grow up to be an ordinary boy graduating from a good school, have an ordinary life?"

When Dr. Baldwin looks at Dr. Hartman's disconsolate face, she sees a man who is legally free yet entangled in a complex mix of the bittersweet realms of ambiguity. She contemplates, "How could I work with the man, a mad professor who inadvertently killed his son in a fit of rage during a shootout?" She shakes her head and wonders whether Dr. Hartman reads her mind.

They pass through the security post on the Mexican side of the border, and after a cursory wave of the guard, move on toward the U.S. entry and stop before the barrier. Responding to the instructions from an American customs agent, Dr. Baldwin turns into the designated parking space, stops the car, and clicks at the button to pop the trunk open. The agent walks a leashed dog around the vehicle and lets it sniff inside the trunk. Dr. Hartman's knapsack draws the dog's attention. The agent motions for them to get out of the car and unzip the knapsack. The agent discovers two full bottles of medicines, one with OxyContin capsules and the second one with benzodiazepine tablets, both purchased in Texas. Dr. Hartman explains that an American surgeon had ordered the medication. He shows his valid Texas medical license and also copies of the prescriptions written by Dr. Key. "They are for a nagging backache and chest pain that keeps me awake most nights," Dr. Hartman explains. Dr. Baldwin, however, wonders what drove Dr. Hartman to bring such a large supply of the medications to Mexico. A thought in her mind warns what he might do with them when he gets home.

Eventually, the inquiry ends well, and the agent lets them leave the American border station. They drive toward the Marriott hotel and soon join Dr. Parsi for early dinner at the Marriott Hotel. Now, the trio is eager to finish the dinner, check out, and take I-35 North back towards San Antonio. Dr. Hartman sits in the back seat, deeply immersed in gloomy thoughts; Dr. Baldwin is dozing quietly in the passenger seat; and Dr. Parsi is driving, following the caravan of cars ahead of him. None of them talks. The romantic piano music from Sirius classical music station breaks the silence in the car. Dr. Hartman recognizes Chopin's Piano Prelude in A minor as it evokes different emotions in the anxious minds of these three physicians. Dr. Hartman feels a strange dark space in his world wherein the feelings of guilt and shame now fill his soul. He thinks about Esther and how he could ever dare to look in her eyes again. The face of Saul, pale and frightened, squeezed by Marcel's hands, helplessly looking at him, seeking to be rescued, march in his mind, and the unexpected jury decision that has caught him off guard.

Dr. Hartman tries to make sense of this unexpected situation: his freedom after many stressful months, the weight of the indictment for murder, the trial, and the suspense of waiting for the jury to determine his fate. He pictures his office, the Dean's face, the curious gaze of students in the lecture halls, and Esther, his wife, who may avoid him altogether. And what should he decide about Dr. Parsi and his future employment in the department? And what will happen to his status at the medical school? Could he stand the prying gaze of the students?

Dr. Baldwin breaks the long silence in the car, turns back and looks at Dr. Hartman, who is holding his Kindle Fire. She smiles at him, holds up Dr. Parsi's hand, and says, "Dr. Hartman, we would like to share something exciting with you." When Dr. Hartman turns his gaze to her, Dr. Baldwin says, "Well, this morning, Dr. Parsi proposed to me, and I have delightfully accepted. We have decided to get married soon."

Dr. Hartman pulls himself together and said, "Congratulations! I am not surprised. I figured you two would get married soon. I wish you well." Then he promptly returns to reading from his Kindle.

Dr. Baldwin is also not surprised by Dr. Hartman's terse response, for he could be preoccupied with thoughts of the challenges facing him in the department, in his life, and the difficulties of repairing the damages to his personal and medical reputation from the trial. She looks at Dr. Hartman's face with a sweet smile and says, "We are thrilled with our decision." However, she is not sure whether Dr. Hartman has absorbed the news or appreciates their joy.

Esther leaves San Antonio International Airport on a flight to Europe that stops at DFW Airport. Her flight to Frankfurt will take about ten hours. Esther settles into her comfortable seat in business class. She opens the brochure of her tour, "Treasures of Persia," provided by Pioneer American Travel. Despite frequent headlines about visa restrictions for visitors coming to the United States from seven Muslim countries, including Iran, Esther's travel agency had no difficulty obtaining her tourist visa, which is valid for three months. She has customized her trip, so after visiting Tehran, Tabriz, Yazd, and a few other ancient archeological sites like Persepolis near Shiraz, the tombs of Hafiz and Saadi, the ancient site of *Bisotun* boasting an inscription by Darius the Great, and also the city of Kermanshah, she will end the tour in Hamadan to visit the Tomb of Esther, the Queen of Persia. She hopes that when she is in Hamadan, she will be able to join the local Jewish volunteers and become a tour guide at the Tomb.

During the four-hour stopover in Frankfurt, where Esther joins the group that is enrolled in the tour of the "Treasures of Persia," she is pleased to realize that the majority of tour members are highly educated and know as much or more about Persian history than she does. The tour director is quick to let everyone know that he has a master's degree in the ancient history of the Middle East from Harvard University.

"We are going to meet our local tour director at Tehran International Airport," he announces. "We will have breakfast in the VIP lounge, while airport employees will be collecting our luggage, checking our passports, and getting entry permits. You are going to enjoy the incredible generosity of Iranian hospitality immediately upon your arrival in Tehran."

XX
The Dark and Dreary House

When Dr. Hartman gets out of Dr. Parsi's car, he pulls his luggage to the front door and knocks on the door several times. When he doesn't hear a response, he presses the doorbell several times and waits awhile. Surprised, he unlocks the door and enters the hall. The house is dark and laden with a dreary muteness. He pulls the luggage to the bedroom and walks around.

After looking into the deserted library, Dr. Hartman notices a gap in one of the stacks where Esther's collection of books about the Middle East Jewish diaspora was located. He's disappointed when he searches his wife's desk and finds no note from her. Dr. Hartman is alarmed. He feels as if he were abandoned by Esther. He dials Esther's mobile phone number but hears a busy signal. He dials again. This time he is directed to her voicemail. Dr. Hartman leaves a short message asking Esther to return his call. He walks to the dark kitchen, turns on the lights. He recognizes no change from the time when he left the house as if no one has entered the kitchen in the last few days. He walks back to the bedroom and occupies himself with unpacking his belongings. When Dr. Hartman calls Esther for the third time, the call is again directed to her voicemail. He collapses on a chair in the library and tries to comprehend his situation. He feels an unbearable lightness floating in the library, and the house is filled with the air of a place abandoned after a passing storm.

Perturbed, Dr. Hartman goes to the bar and pours a generous serving of Scotch whiskey and opens the door to the backyard. He walks over the scattered fallen leaves on the patio, wipes off a chair, and sits down. A light wind rolls the leaves around the gray garden. He returns to the library and notes the blinking of the phone, indicating recorded messages. He gulps down the whiskey and pushes the button and listens, hoping to hear Esther's voice.

The first message is from Dr. Key. He says, "Hey, this is Dr. Key. Congratulations on your victory. Let's celebrate it very soon. I also want you to know the result of the breast aspiration cytology smear. Unfortunately, it is positive for cancer. The cells are called highly atypical malignant cells, indicating a high-grade of invasive cancer. I'm astonished. I have already set up an appointment for you to see Dr. Becker, the head of the San Antonio Cancer Therapy and Research Center. He is a great surgeon specializing in breast cancer treatment. As you may know, the center is now affiliated with the MD Anderson Cancer Institute in Houston. I'm confident you will come out of this problem victorious, too."

"I knew it. It felt like it was cancer from the very onset," Dr. Hartman murmurs. He listens to the message again and angrily pushes the delete button. "It's so embarrassing to die of breast cancer." As he is absorbing Dr. Key's news of breast cancer, he hears the doorbell. When he opens the door, he finds a FedEx agent standing there with a thick, certified parcel.

The agent says, "Sir, are you Dr. Jordan Hartman?"

"Yes. I am. May I help you?" Dr. Hartman says.

"Please, may I see your driver's license?" the agent says.

After inspecting the driver's license, the agent asks for his signature and then hands the parcel to Dr. Hartman. He looks at the name and address of the sender and recognizes the name of Marcel's family's lawyer. He shakes his head and murmurs, "Those sons of bitches. Why don't they wait for a while before filing a civil lawsuit?" Disgusted, he walks to the bar and pours another serving of single malt Scotch. He does not add water to it and takes a large sip. He goes to the bedroom and pulls the bottle of benzodiazepine tablets and takes two tables and swallows them with another sip of whiskey.

It's late in the evening when the phone rings. Dr. Ross is the first person who calls Dr. Hartman after his return. He opens his eyes and turns over and picks up the phone. "Welcome back to your kingdom," Dr. Ross says. Thinking about the thick legal-size parcel from Marcel's family's lawyer and Dr. Key's message, Dr. Hartman dismisses any notion of kingdom and replies, "Look, I never had a kingdom."

"Do you need anything, some food, groceries?" Dr. Ross asks.

"I need to be left alone for a day or two to recoup." Dr. Hartman says. "I'm exhausted." He hangs up the phone and pulls the blanket over his head.

Dr. Hartman sleeps poorly during the first night after his return from Mexico. His shallow sleep is interrupted by pain from the cancerous lump in his breast, which is now firm and stretches the skin, producing a tender bulge. Because of the pain, the lump seemed to be larger than a week ago. He is disgusted by Esther's disappearance and by the prospect of returning to work and having to encounter the curious eyes of faculty members, staff, residents, and students.

The students, regardless of the jury's verdict, will see him as the one who had killed his son, the one who got away with murder. He compares himself to O. J. Simpson, who was declared not guilty in the gruesome death of his ex-wife and her friend by the jury in Los Angeles but still lost the related civil lawsuit. Dr. Hartman contemplates, "How dreadful it is. I'm following the footsteps of an infamous murderer." The persistent image of Saul's body lying in a pool of blood in front of the garage keeps running through his mind. Saul's face now flashes on the dark screen of his mind. He opens his eyes and gazes at the ceiling fan that is noiselessly spinning above his head. As soon as he closes his eyes, Saul's helpless face comes back and keeps staring at him.

Dr. Hartman stays in the house the next day. He walks around the living room and avoids going into the backyard or anywhere outside, fearing the neighbors might see him. He goes and sits in one of the chairs in the library. Oddly, Dr. Hartman wonders whether it might have been better if the jury had not declared him "Not Guilty." Bewildered, he murmurs to himself, "Instead, I could have gone to a place far away from the United States, where I would not face the people in this town." Dr. Hartman has never felt this lonely, disconcerted, and hopeless in his life. He contemplates, "How can I interact with the neighbors, the one who testified against me, and Marcel's father, who like me is lamenting the loss of his son and is now suing me for the wrongful death of his son?"

He walks to the bed, tries to read but cannot follow the narrative. He listens to an audiobook novel by Tolstoy but fails to fall asleep. He goes to the drug cabinet and takes two tablets of benzodiazepine and two capsules of OxyContin and walks to the bar. He swallows the four pills with a large sip of whiskey and returns to the bed. He sinks the Bluetooth earbuds with the Kindle Fire and turns on the audiobook and listens to *Crime and Punishment*. It doesn't take him long to fall asleep.

It's late in the morning when the doorbell rings repeatedly and awakes Dr. Hartman. He throws on a robe and walks to the door. It's a FedEx employee who has a yellow legal-size envelope for him. He signs the receipt, takes the parcel, and walks to the library. He stares at it, surprised by the sender's name and specialty. It's from the law offices of Stuart and Kline. Like any physician, his first reaction about the nature of the package from a law office to a physician is not encouraging, for it often portends an impending malpractice lawsuit. However, this law firm is known for its extensive practice in family law and newsworthy divorces. He remembers these same lawyers represented a former mayor of San Antonio in a dispute with his wife's family and also were involved in an oil tycoon's highly publicized divorce. Disgusted, Dr. Hartman drops the envelope on the dusty glass table and moves off. Dr. Hartman surmises he should get away from whatever trouble this legal document is bringing to him. Not hearing from Esther, he suspects these lawyers are representing her. He murmurs, "I'm not going to call anybody. I'm sick of lawyers. I have had enough of them."

During the day, he, like an inmate who has escaped prison and is now hiding in a dark place, isolates himself and doesn't answer any calls. In the afternoon, he goes to the library and glances at the stacks of books. His eyes stop at one of his favorites, a collection of plays by Arthur Miller. He pulls the book from the shelf and thumbs through and stops at the play "Death of a Salesman." Flipping through the pages, his eyes focus on the section where Willy Loman is found dead by his wife Linda in the backyard.

Dr. Hartman picks up a pen and scribbles a note on the title page of the book. Caught between a glorious academic career and an abject failure to raise his son, he reaches his fateful decision to leave the world. He writes that he cannot bear to face medical students anymore. He writes an apology to his wife and blames himself for the tragic death of Saul. Now he gets up and walks to the medicine cabinet and takes the bottles of OxyContin capsules and benzodiazepine tablets and lines them up next to each other on the table in the library. He then goes to the bar and opens a new bottle of his favorite single malt whiskey and brings it with a tumbler to the table and settles himself in front of it. He begins sipping the whiskey and swallowing the medicines, several pills at a time until he has completely emptied the two bottles of pills and the bottle of whiskey. He scratches a few more lines on the page and puts his initials at the bottom of the page. Gradually he feels dizzy and finds it difficult to keep his eyes open. He drags himself to the bedroom and climbs into the bed. Within several minutes, he becomds unconscious and sinks into a deep sleep.

The morning after their return from the Mexican border, when Dr. Parsi is doing the round of the patients with residents and students, Dr. Ross abruptly enters the ward and interrupts him. "I have something important to tell you. Please follow me to the nursing station for a minute." At the nursing station, Dr. Ross tells Dr. Parsi, "The Dean's office has received a copy of the NIH letter to Dr. Hartman regarding your application announcing the approval of your grant." Dr. Ross adds, "Congratulations. Now, your job in the department is secure."

"I'm not staying," Dr. Parsi says. "We have decided to enter private practice."

Dr. Ross is stunned. "What do you mean, by '*we*' have decided? Who is '*we*'?"

"Dr. Baldwin and I are the 'we.' We are getting married, and she is not staying here either," Dr. Parsi says.

"What?" Dr. Ross says in disbelief.

"She was begging for the job, and so were you! You need to explain the situation to the Dean."

Later that night, when Dr. Baldwin tells her mother that she has accepted Dr. Parsi's proposal of marriage, she is surprised at her mother's lukewarm reaction.

"Are you sure you want to marry him?" her mother wonders.

"Mother! I love him. He is a great doctor, also a wonderful man. He will make me happy," Dr. Baldwin says.

"I've had an inkling for some time that you two might get married," her mother says. "I just hope he will not convince you to convert to his religion."

"Don't you want me to be happy?" Dr. Baldwin says. "He loves me a lot, and religion is not going to come between us, ever."

"Well, all right then. Your father and I want you to be happy."

"Thanks, Mom, but there is more. Dr. Parsi and I have decided to enter private practice after we finish our programs at the medical school." She knows that her parents will support her in every professional decision that she makes, but they are eager to get into a discussion about the wedding arrangements.

The next day Dr. Baldwin's mother and father call her to discuss their biggest concern, which is whether they will have a secular or a religious wedding ceremony. Luckily, Drs. Baldwin and Parsi have already made up their minds and decided against trying to design a combined Jewish and Zoroastrian wedding. Instead, the two doctors have agreed on a civil ceremony followed by a wedding celebration to which parents, relatives, and mutual friends will be invited.

"We plan to have the wedding ceremony in San Antonio at the country club to which the members of our future medical group belong," Dr. Baldwin tells her parents. "And don't you worry, we promise to choose a date that will suit you."

"Who is going to preside over your marriage ritual?" her mother asks.

"Oh Mother, we will have a judge marry us, while three San Antonio Symphony musicians play Mendelssohn's 'Wedding March.'"

"Darling, it seems that you have already arranged everything. Times have changed. In our day, a civil ceremony was frowned upon. But we want your happiness," her father concedes. "As you know, I like classical music and approve of your choice. But promise us that you'll let us know what we can do to make this an exceptional event for you, our only daughter!"

Earlier, the two physicians had informed Dr. Brannan, the vice-chairman of the surgical department that they plan to join a private practice and leave academia once they complete their programs at the department. The next day they are both sitting in the office of Dr. Bruce Aflack, president of San Antonio Surgical Associates, perusing their employment contracts.

"You are welcome to take the contracts home and have a lawyer review them," Dr. Aflack tells them, "But I can assure you that your contracts are, word for word, the same contracts that all the other partners in the group have signed."

They are left alone for a while as they scrutinize the contracts. They also look at the copy of an agreement that had been signed earlier by the last surgeon who had joined the group before them. They decide to avoid a delay and pass up a review by a lawyer and announce that they are ready to sign the contracts. Once they have signed the contracts, Dr. Aflack presents each of them with an envelope. "This is your signing bonus," he explains. "We welcome you aboard and wish you a successful practice with us. And we hope the money will be useful for your wedding expenses," Dr. Aflack says. "Each envelope holds a check for $10,000."

XXI
Elegy for a Genius

A large audience attends the memorial service for Dr. Hartman in the main amphitheater of the medical school. The highlight of the solemn gathering of senior faculty, surgical residents, and medical students, with the Dean presiding, is an elegy read by the vice-chairman, who is now serving as acting chairman of the department. He begins with a quotation: "A heap of dust alone remains of thee; / 'Tis all thou art, and all the proud shall be!" Then he continues, "Let's remember Dr. Jordan Hartman, the Genius, who masterfully organized this department and brought us respect and fame by recruiting top-notch researchers and educators to this medical school. And let's remember how dedicated Dr. Hartman was to science and medicine, so much so, that he sacrificed his health, losing his son, his welfare, and in the end, even losing the love of his precious wife, and worst of all eventually his own life." Dr. Brannan, who has been assigned as the acting chairman, also refers to the dark side of Dr. Hartman's character. "The great man was undoubtedly fallible. The surgical residents gave him the nickname Volcano because of his furious and unpredictable temperament. His fiery outbursts, unfortunately, culminated in the bloody tragedy in front of his own house and ultimately destroyed his family and his life.

"What happened to Dr. Hartman must be a lesson to all of us. We need to create balance in our lives and avoid single-mindedness, focusing only on our endeavors, as he did. If we don't, we will sacrifice family and friends. For the sake of achieving his goal of a better department, he neglected the well-being of his son. It was not easy to be around him, to work with him, even more so to be his vice-chair. Within the relatively short period of three years in my position, he summoned me six times to inform me that I had been fired, only to change his mind within a few days." An appreciative chuckle runs through the audience. "Yet, the loss of Dr. Hartman will be felt by all of us. Let's remember his achievements and forgive and forget his shortcomings."

At the end of the event, the Dean of the medical school comes to the podium and says with teary eyes, "What forced our Genius to commit suicide was not only the stressful trial. Deep shame had filled his heart because he felt he was responsible for the fatal tragedy that caused the death of two teenagers and the emotional disaster of a divorce from his beloved wife. Most strikingly, however, what he ultimately regretted was his failure to stand by his son and save him from falling into the trap of drug abuse."

The Dean concludes the memorial service by reading from Dr. Hartman's suicide note, which includes a quotation from a verse by John Dryden:

All human things are subject to decay,
And, when Fate summons, Monarchs must obey.

I die to be punished
To be forgiven for the sin
The son I took to tend and care for
Killed in the fire.

XXII
Esther Hartman Seeks the True Story of Esther

Esther has made up her mind: she will write a novel once she is settled in Hamadan. Through her friendship with Dr. Parsi, she has concluded that she will be able to employ her sense of imagination with the knowledge that she has amassed through her research of both Jewish and international sources and write a historical novel dedicated to Esther, the Queen of Persia. When she arrives at the tomb of Esther in Hamadan, she is greeted by a group of Jewish-Persians who were informed of her arrival by the travel agency, and they welcome her with a bouquet of fresh flowers. The rabbi of the nearby synagogue introduces the director of the tomb and the three volunteers who serve as guides in different shifts. He says to the director, "You will be pleased to know that this lovely lady has traveled from the U.S. to visit the tomb and requests to be part of your team." The rabbi also introduces his wife to Esther, who carries a basket of fruit and Persian pastries as a welcome gift. One of the volunteers has another bouquet for Esther, too. "These tuberoses will add a delightful fragrance to your hotel room. It is the perfume of Hamadan," the volunteer explains.

The tomb's director leads Esther on a private tour and translates some of the inscriptions on the walls of the tomb as they pass along. Esther tells the director that she wishes to reside in the city for a while. She is surprised when the director tells her some facts about the situation concerning becoming an official guide, and also about the Jewish people in Hamadan. "For you to officially become a guide, you are required to complete several forms and submit them to the Islamic Government officials. But regarding the Jewish diaspora in Hamadan, the situation has changed drastically. In the Middle Ages, over 30,000 Jews were residing in this city, and probably that many or more during the time of Xerxes the Great, some 2,700 years ago. Unfortunately, we are now reduced to less than thirty Jewish families in town. Most of our visitors to the tomb are international tourists or Jewish people visiting from other Iranian cities."

The rabbi rejoins Esther and the tomb's director when they end the tour. The rabbi, with a gloomy face, translates a Farsi language poster, which is affixed to the entrance wall of the tomb along with an official note from the Iranian government. "This is the Tomb where Jewish people from around the world come to pray and pay respect to the rescue of the Jewish people during Xerxes the Great's kingdom. The original building was constructed in the seventh century. It has repeatedly been destroyed, rebuilt, and renovated over the ages. According to various notes from visitors during the Middle Ages, under the brick dome rest the bodies of Esther, the wife of Xerxes the Great, and her uncle Mordechai who served the king as an aide."

In answer to the rabbi's question about the duration of her visit, Esther says that she would like to reside somewhere in town for at least a few months, while she serves as a volunteer and completes the novel she envisions. "I have researched and read a great deal about the various tales of Esther and the Feast of Purim," Esther says. "I believe I could be a well-informed volunteer at the tomb."

The rabbi shakes his head. "My dear, I'm moved by your enthusiasm, but the situation is quite difficult for us here. Most of our ancestors chose to come to this land after Cyrus the Great freed them in Babylon because they preferred the comfortable life in the Persian Empire to an arduous existence rebuilding their devastated homeland around Jerusalem. Our ancestors were respected and occupied important positions at the court of the Achaemenid kings. Nowadays, though, the situation is entirely different. Our people are emigrating in droves. Please, enjoy your stay here with us, but go back to your home in America." The rabbi smiles. "My dear, we don't have that many visitors to the Tomb anymore. So, what are you going to do in your free time?"

"I'll read and write while I am here," Esther says. "I'm determined to follow a plan: using the information I have collected about the Jewish Diaspora in Ancient Persia, I have begun writing a novel. I may use the title 'Esther: A Novel' for the book.

"My dear, I wish you well. I'm certain the project will keep you busy for a long while."

To say Esther is disappointed by the rabbi's lackluster reception of her plans is an understatement. She has traveled thousands of miles to reach the tomb and has prepared herself to stay in Hamadan for months. "I have no reason to return home," Esther demurs.

Though the rabbi is surprised at Esther's words, he decides not to inquire any further. "Well, as you wish. I'll walk you to your hotel, but my wife and I would like to invite you to dinner at our house. Even though your hotel offers much better Persian food, if you care to come, you will see our dishes are kosher."

When Esther returns to the Azadi Hotel, the receptionist gives her the key to the assigned luxury suite on the third floor with a private balcony overlooking the garden and a view of Alvand Mountain. "Your luggage is already in the room," the receptionist says. "I apologize, but we must keep your passport in the office during your stay."

She accepts the key and walks to the concierge who speaks adequate English, although with a thick accent. Esther picks up an English-language brochure with information about the tourist attractions in the area. The concierge embarks on her rehearsed speech. "Welcome to the Azadi Hotel. We are a four-star hotel surrounded by greenery in the foothills of Alvand. Our hotel is small but elegant and has only 55 rooms, but we are located in a quiet area of town and within walking distance of the Tomb of Esther."

Esther takes the brochure and reads that the hotel is fully air-conditioned and offers free wi-fi to its guests. "My dear, you need no password. Just type your room number and your last name, and you will promptly get connected," the concierge explains.

Esther enters a luxurious suite with a sitting area and a desk. She opens one of her two suitcases, pulls out the charger, connects it to an adapter, plugs it in, and begins charging her mobile phone. She takes a quick shower in the spacious bathroom, and when she glances at the fully charged mobile phone, she sees several notifications on the small screen. There are two messages from Ruth with the subject "Very Urgent," two from Dr. Parsi, and one from Dr. Ross.

She reads Ruth's text. The same text is repeated in the other one: "Dear Esther: I must share terrible news. When your husband did not show up at the medical school for several days, we went to the house, and with the help of the police, we forced the front door open. Unfortunately, we found your husband dead in the bedroom. He had swallowed two bottles of sedatives and opioids after writing his valedictory statements on the first page of a book. Poor man, he must have emptied the bottle of Scotch to enable him to swallow all those pills. Because the body had been deceased for several days, the sight and the smell in the bedroom were sickening."

Stunned, Esther wishes the rabbi were in the hotel so that she could converse with him. She has a hard time comprehending that her husband could even conceive of taking his own life. "It is simply beyond my imagination," she murmurs. She was so sure that Dr. Hartman was too proud of himself, so self-absorbed, that he would have never killed or even hurt himself.

Pondering ancient Greek tragedies, she contemplates, "It should have been me who commits suicide, while he should have blinded himself so he wouldn't be able to see the light of day."

She texts Ruth and expresses her sadness at her husband's suicide. "I'm stunned. Confused. Hope he has now found peace." She changes the subject adds a few words about the Tomb of Esther. "It is a well-kept secret place with a large yard and two burial tombs under a newly renovated blue dome. There is a gap between the two graves, into which pilgrims drop their contributions and pledges." She attaches two JPEG photographs from the site, and a third of herself surrounded by a group of Jewish-Persian well-wishers presenting welcome pastries and flowers to her.

After a while, she absorbs and accepts the news of her husband's suicide and sends another text to Ruth. "My dear friend. I have made up my mind. There is nothing for me in San Antonio. I will stay here, research the ancient Persian documents in the museums and wherever they could be, and write the true story of Esther, the Queen of Persia."

Now, she anticipates visiting the rabbi's family and sharing the tragic news of her husband's suicide with them. She pulls out a black scarf and tightly wraps it around her head, concealing every strand of hair.

www.ingramcontent.com/pod-product-compliance
Lightning Source LLC
Chambersburg PA
CBHW030539030726

47495CB00004B/1053